# THE SOLAR WAR

*Other Novels and Novellas*

*Many of these titles are also available as abridged and unabridged audiobooks.
Order the full range of Horus Heresy novels and audiobooks from
blacklibrary.com*

*Download the full range of Horus Heresy audio dramas from*
blacklibrary.com

THE HORUS HERESY®
SIEGE OF TERRA

# THE SOLAR WAR

*John French*

BLACK LIBRARY

## A BLACK LIBRARY PUBLICATION

First published in 2019.
This edition published in 2022 by
Black Library, Games Workshop Ltd.,
Willow Road, Nottingham, NG7 2WS, UK.

Represented by: Games Workshop Limited – Irish branch,
Unit 3, Lower Liffey Street, Dublin 1,
D01 K199, Ireland.

10 9 8

Produced by Games Workshop in Nottingham.
Cover illustration by Neil Roberts.

The Solar War © Copyright Games Workshop Limited 2022. The
Solar War, The Siege of Terra, GW, Games Workshop, Black Library,
The Horus Heresy, The Horus Heresy Eye logo, Space Marine, 40K,
Warhammer, Warhammer 40,000, the 'Aquila' Double-headed Eagle
logo, and all associated logos, illustrations, images, names, creatures,
races, vehicles, locations, weapons, characters, and the distinctive
likenesses thereof, are either ® or TM, and/or © Games Workshop
Limited, variably registered around the world.
All Rights Reserved.

A CIP record for this book is available from the British Library.

ISBN 13: 978-1-78999-290-8

No part of this publication may be reproduced, stored in a retrieval
system, or transmitted in any form or by any means, electronic,
mechanical, photocopying, recording or otherwise, without the prior
permission of the publishers.

This is a work of fiction. All the characters and events portrayed
in this book are fictional, and any resemblance to real people or
incidents is purely coincidental.

See Black Library on the internet at

# blacklibrary.com

Find out more about Games Workshop
and the worlds of Warhammer at

# games-workshop.com

Printed and bound by CPI Group (UK) Ltd, Croydon, CR0 4YY

---

*To all who have reached the end with us, readers, writers, artists and
creators. And to all those we wish were still here to see it.*

# —THE HORUS HERESY®—
# SIEGE OF TERRA

### It is a time of legend.

The galaxy is in flames. The Emperor's glorious vision for humanity is in ruins. His favoured son, Horus, has turned from his father's light and embraced Chaos.

His armies, the mighty and redoubtable Space Marines, are locked in a brutal civil war. Once, these ultimate warriors fought side by side as brothers, protecting the galaxy and bringing mankind back into the Emperor's light. Now they are divided.

Some remain loyal to the Emperor, whilst others have sided with the Warmaster. Pre-eminent amongst them, the leaders of their thousands-strong Legions, are the primarchs. Magnificent, superhuman beings, they are the crowning achievement of the Emperor's genetic science. Thrust into battle against one another, victory is uncertain for either side.

Worlds are burning. At Isstvan V, Horus dealt a vicious blow and three loyal Legions were all but destroyed. War was begun, a conflict that will engulf all mankind in fire. Treachery and betrayal have usurped honour and nobility. Assassins lurk in every shadow. Armies are gathering. All must choose a side or die.

Horus musters his armada, Terra itself the object of his wrath. Seated upon the Golden Throne, the Emperor waits for his wayward son to return. But his true enemy is Chaos, a primordial force that seeks to enslave mankind to its capricious whims.

The screams of the innocent, the pleas of the righteous resound to the cruel laughter of Dark Gods. Suffering and damnation await all should the Emperor fail and the war be lost.

The end is here. The skies darken, colossal armies gather. For the fate of the Throneworld, for the fate of mankind itself...
The Siege of Terra has begun.

# DRAMATIS PERSONAE

| | |
|---|---|
| THE EMPEROR | Master of Mankind, Last and First Lord of the Imperium |
| HORUS | Warmaster, Primarch of the XVI Legion, Ascendant Vessel of Chaos |

### The Primarchs

| | |
|---|---|
| PERTURABO | 'The Lord of Iron', Primarch of the IV Legion |
| JAGHATAI KHAN | 'The Warhawk', Primarch of the V Legion |
| ROGAL DORN | Praetorian of Terra, Primarch of the VII Legion |
| SANGUINIUS | Archangel of Baal, Primarch of the IX Legion |

### The IV Legion 'Iron Warriors'

| | |
|---|---|
| FORRIX | 'The Breaker', First Captain, Triarch |
| VULL BRONN | 'The Stonewrought', 45th Grand Battalion |

### The V Legion 'White Scars'

| | |
|---|---|
| JUBAL KHAN | 'Lord of Summer Lightning', Master of the Hunt |
| CHANGSHI | Bladeward to Jubal Khan |

### The VII Legion 'Imperial Fists'

| | |
|---|---|
| SIGISMUND | Lord Castellan of the First Sphere, First Captain, Marshal of the Templars |
| HALBRACT | Lord Castellan of the Second Sphere, Fleet Master |

| EFFRIED | Lord Castellan of the Third Sphere, Seneschal |
| CAMBA DIAZ | Lord Castellan of the Fourth Sphere, Siege Master |
| FAFNIR RANN | Lord Seneschal, Captain of the First Assault Cadre |
| BOREAS | First Lieutenant of the Templars, First Company |
| MASSAK | Librarian |
| ARCHAMUS | Master of the Huscarls |

## The XVI Legion 'Sons of Horus'

| EZEKYLE ABADDON | First Captain |
| HORUS AXIMAND | 'Little Horus', Captain, Fifth Company |
| FALKUS KIBRE | 'Widowmaker', Captain, Justaerin Cohort |
| SADURAN | Warrior of the 201st Assault Battalion |
| IKREK | Warrior of the 201st Assault Battalion |
| THONAS | Justaerin |
| GEDEPHRON | Justaerin |
| TYBAR | Justaerin |
| RALKOR | Justaerin |
| SYCAR | Justaerin |
| URSKAR | Justaerin |

## The XV Legion 'Thousand Sons'

| AIIRIMAN | Chief Librarian |
| IGNIS | Master of the Order of Ruin |
| MENKAURA | Blind Prophet of the Corvidae |

## The XVII Legion 'Word Bearers'

| ZARDU LAYAK | 'The Crimson Apostle', Master of the Unspeaking |
|---|---|
| KULNAR | Slave of the Anakatis Blade |
| HEBEK | Slave of the Anakatis Blade |
| THE APOSTLE | |

## The Chosen of Malcador

| LOKEN | Knight Errant |
|---|---|

## The Mechanicum

| KAZZIM-ALEPH-I | Magos-Emissary |
|---|---|
| CHI-32-BETA | Enginseer |

## The Dark Mechanicum

| SOTA-NUL | Emissary of Kelbor-Hal |
|---|---|

## The Neverborn

| SAMUS | The End and the Death |
|---|---|

## Imperial Army

| NIORA SU-KASSEN | Solar Command Staff, former Admiral of the Jovian Fleets |
|---|---|

## Imperial Personae

| MALCADOR | Regent of the Imperium |
|---|---|
| ARMINA FEL | Senior Astropath |
| HELIOSA-78 | Cult Matriarch of the Selenar |
| ANDROMEDA-17 | Personified-scion of the Selenar |
| MERSADIE OLITON | Prisoner of the Unnamed Fortress, former Remembrancer |

*'That is my home of love: if I have ranged,*
*Like him that travels I return again,*
*Just to the time, not with the time exchanged.'*

— attributed to the dramaturge Shakespire (fl. M2)

# PART ONE

# FROM THE NIGHT RETURNED

# THE WARP

∞

'Father…'

He is waiting. He has always been waiting. In this place there is no time, not truly, not unless the forces within its tides dream it into being. Here, eternity is truth.

'Father…'

Slowly, with weariness and reluctance, He forms the idea of eyes, of a mouth, of limbs, of the chair beneath Him. Far off, there is another chair, and a thread of thought and will that tether Him back to a place of metal, and stone, and time.

'Father…'

He opens His eyes.

Darkness lies before Him, extending through every dimension. Darkness, and Him alone. In that moment He feels the echo of every man or woman who has ever woken beside a guttering fire to see the night creeping closer as the flame-light fades.

The darkness becomes a black mirror. He looks into His

reflection: a man on a stone chair, old, dark skin clinging to the hollows of His cheeks. Iron and snow streak His beard. The shoulders and limbs beneath His plain, black robes are thin. Dust marks the bare soles of His feet. His eyes are clear, and there is neither kindness nor pity in them.

The chair and the man sit on a narrow stone platform. Behind Him burns a wall of fire that curves up and away, blazing and flaring like the surface of a star.

The reflection changes. For an instant, a figure of iron and blades with coal-furnace eyes is looking back at Him from a throne of chrome. Then it is gone, and the reflection is a blur of images falling one atop another: a golden warrior standing with drawn sword before the gates of a towering fortress, a figure before the mouth of a mountain cave, a boy with a stick and fear in his eyes, a queen with a spear atop a cliff, an eagle with ten wings beating against a thunder-threaded sky – on and on, images tumbling over each other like the faces of cards tossed through the air.

'Is there any truth in you?' asks the voice that comes from the dark.

The images vanish and the darkness hangs before Him. It falls into the abyss beneath like a cascade of obsidian sand.

'At the root of your lies, is there any truth, father?'

The darkness becomes a forest, dark trunks reaching to an untouchable sky, roots crawling out and down into the abyss beneath. The man on the chair is sitting on the snow-covered ground, a fire burning before Him. A shadow moves out of the dark between the trees. It is huge, sable-furred and silver-eyed. It drags its shadow with it as it comes forwards. It pauses on the edge of the light.

'You claim to be a man,' says the wolf, 'but that is a lie revealed to any that can see you here. You deny you wish godhood, but you raise up an empire to praise you. You call yourself the Master of Mankind, and perhaps that is the only truth you ever spoke – that you wish to make your children slaves.'

The wolf tilts its head, and for a second it is not a wolf, but a bloated shadow, veined with lightning, its eyes holes punched into a red furnace.

'But this son…' growls the wolf, muscles coiling under black fur, lips peeling back over teeth, '…this son has returned to your cradle of lies.'

The wolf leaps. The forest blinks to a sheet of curdled black and migraine colour. The shadow of a man reaches across the dark with hands that are claws. The fire flares, roaring up to become a burning wall and the claws rake the blaze. Shadow burns to ash and cinders. The wolf recoils, howling. Lightning laces the dark of the forest. The wolf pads along the boundary of the firelight. Behind it, other eyes shine in the deeper shadows between the trees, bright and cold as the light of cruel stars.

The man turns His head. He is not looking at the wolf, but to the blackness beyond.

'I deny you,' He says, and in this place that is more real than life, yet as unreal as a dream, His words shake the dark like thunder.

'Will you not even talk to me, father? Now, as your empire of lies ends, will you not tell me the truth?'

'You are shadows,' says the man, 'nothing more. You offer nothing. You *are* nothing. You come with a puppet child, but you did not tell him why you need him. You need him because you have nothing that is true, no sword that is not a falsehood, no strength that is not a lie. You need him because you are weak. You need him. You fear him. And he will fail.'

Laughter fills the night, beating like wings, rattling with

the sound of the dying trying to breathe, coiling over and over in chuckling loops. The darkness billows forwards stretching, coiling, squeezing. The man on the stone chair flinches. The fire bends and shrinks. The image of the man flickers too, and for a second He looks like a corpse sitting on a throne, the bones of His hands gripping its arms in pain.

He closes His eyes.

The image begins to blur, as though seen through a dusty wind. The laughter rises higher and higher.

It has always been this way: again and again, in countless forms and metaphors, death and darkness wearing countless faces. On and on the cycle, repeating and growing in strength as the Night crowds hungrily in. And just as then, so now; there is only one answer to it.

Murder.

Blood and endings.

Sacrifice and death.

'I am returned,' comes the voice of the wolf in the dark.

'I deny you,' says the man, as the image fades to the echo of a dream and laughter that does not end.

# ONE

---

Zero hour
Remembrance of wolves
Onslaught

*Terra*

On the first of Primus the sirens rang across Terra.

On the myriad worlds conquered and ruled by the Imperium of Man, they talked of year divisions, of time sliced into a thousand equal slivers. First division, second division, third, and so on, without variation or character, until the weight of counting reached a thousand, and one year tipped over into the next. On worlds of endless night or blinding days, a year was the same. In an empire spanning a galaxy, anything else would have been meaningless.

0000014.M31 was how surviving records would mark the first moment of that day, stamped and corrected for temporal accuracy, standardised and stripped of any meaning. But, here, on the world whose night and day and seasons had given mankind its concept of time, the old counting still meant something and so did the moment that one year died and another was born: the Feast of Two Faces, the Day

19

of New Light, the Renewal – on and on went its names. But for longer than memory it had been the first of Primus, first-born of the three hundred and sixty-five days that would follow, a day of hope and new beginnings.

The turning of that year began with snow on the northern battlements of the Imperial Palace, where three brother demigods watched the night skies above. It began with the dawn light and icy chill reaching into a tower-top chamber and stirring the painted cards dealt by a man who was older than any knew. It began with the sirens calling out, one at first, high on the Palace spires, before the cry was picked up by others, on and on across the turning globe. The sound echoed through the mountain-sized space ports and rasped from vox-horns in the deep strata of the Atlantean Hives.

On and on it went, stilling the hands of people as they ate and worked. They looked up. In caves beneath the earth, and hive vaults, and under the smog drifts, they looked up. Of those that could see the sky, a few thought they could make out new stars amongst the firmament and froze at the promise of each pinprick of light: a promise of fire and ash and an age of loss. And with the sound of sirens, fear spread, unnamed but still spoken.

'He is here,' they said.

*Prison ship* Aeacus, *Uranus high orbit*

*'I understand you have a story…' she said. The wolf stood before her, the fur of its back silver beneath the moonlight. 'A particularly entertaining one. I'd like to remember it, for posterity.'*

*The wolf turned, its teeth a smile of sorrow.*

*'Which story?'*

*'Horus killing the Emperor.'*

Mersadie Oliton woke from the memory-dream with sweat

on her face. She breathed, and pulled the blanket over her from where it had slipped onto the floor. The air was cool and dank in the cell, scented with the tang of air that had been exhaled too much. She blinked for a second. Something was different. She reached out a hand and touched the metal wall. Moisture clung to the rivets and rust scabs. The thrum of the ship's engines had gone. Wherever they were, they were stationary in the void.

She let her hand drop and let out a breath. The tatters of the memory-dream still clung to her eyelids. She focused, trying to pull back the threads of the dream even as they slid into darkness.

'I must remember…' she said to herself.

'The prisoner will stand and face the wall.' The voice boomed out of the speaker set above the cell door.

She stood instinctively. She wore a grey jumpsuit, worn and faded. She put her hands on the wall, fingers splayed. The door unlocked with a clang, and footsteps sounded on the grated floor. The guard would be one just like the rest: crimson-clad and silver-masked, the humanity in its voice concealed by vox distortion. All the gaolers were the same, as constant as the ticking of a clock that never struck the hour.

Small spaces, locked doors, questions and suspicions – such had been her world for the seven years since she had come back to the Solar System. That was the price for what she had seen, for what she remembered. She had been a remembrancer, one of the thousands of artists, writers and scholars sent out to witness the Great Crusade as it brought the light of reason to a reunited humanity. That had been her purpose: to see, to remember. Like many clear purposes and shining futures, it had not worked out that way.

She heard the footsteps stop behind her, and knew the

guard would be placing a bowl of water and a fresh jumpsuit on the floor.

'Where are we?' she asked, hearing the question come from her mouth before she could stop it.

Silence.

She waited. There would not be a punishment for her asking, no beatings, no withdrawal of food or humiliation – that was not how this imprisonment worked. The punishment was silence. She had no doubt that other, more visceral methods were used on other prisoners – she had heard the screams. But for her there had only been silence. Seven years of silence. They did not need to ask her questions, after all. They had taken the memory spools out of her skull, and those recordings would have told them everything they wanted and more.

'We are still in the void, aren't we,' she said, still facing the wall. 'The engine vibrations have stopped, you see. No way of missing it if you have spent any time on ships... I spent time on a warship once. You never lose the sense of it.' She paused, waiting for a response, even if it was just the sound of retreating footsteps and the door shutting.

Silence again.

That was strange. She had tried talking to guards in the early years, and their response had been to leave her without reply. After a while, that had felt worse than if they had struck a whip across her back. They had never beaten her, though, or even touched her. Even when they opened her skull to remove the memory spools, they had sedated her, as though that made the violation that followed more acceptable.

She supposed that such small mercies had to do with Qruze or Loken. The former Luna Wolves had watched over her as much as they could. But that had still left her a prisoner of the greatest and darkest prison in the Imperium.

Loken had said that he would free her, but she had refused. Even while it pained her, she understood why she had to remain locked up. How could she not? After all, had she not seen the true face of the enemy? Four years of life on the *Vengeful Spirit* amongst the Sons of Horus, in the shadow of their father, who now had set the galaxy alight with civil war. What other reward could there be for remembering those days? A galaxy shrunk to silence and plasteel walls, with only dreams and memories to speak to her.

She had begun to dream memories after a few months, dreams of her home on Terra, of the sunlight shattering across the edge of the Arcus orbital plate, her mother laughing and calling after her as she ran through the hydro-gardens. And she had dreamed of her time amongst the Luna Wolves, and the Sons of Horus, of people now long dead. She had asked for parchment and pen, but none had been given to her. She had gone back to the old games her mind-nurse had taught her, ways of tucking memories away when she woke from sleep, ways of remembering the past even as it fled into the distance. In the silence, she had found that memories and dreams were all she had, all she was.

'Are we still somewhere in the Solar System?' she asked, and twitched her neck to look behind her. Why was she still talking? But then why had the guard not left? 'The ship doesn't feel like it's preparing for translation. Where are we?'

They had come for her in her cell on the Nameless Fortress three nights ago. They had loaded her into a box barely big enough to stand upright in. She had felt the box judder and sway as machines had lifted it and her. They had let her out into this cell, and she had recognised the vibration of a void-ship under power. It had been comforting at first, but her dreams had not been, and now the silence of this moment was feeling stranger with each elongating second.

'Why was I taken away from the fortress?' she asked. 'Where am I going?'

'Where we all wish we could go, Mistress Oliton,' said Garviel Loken. She whirled, and the end of her cell was gone and a wolf was rising from a pool of dark water beneath the moon. Its eyes were black spheres, and its bared-teeth grin was wide as it spoke. 'You are going home.'

In the dark of her cell, Mersadie Oliton woke to silence and lay still, waiting for the dream to fade or for herself to wake again.

*Strike Frigate* Lachrymae, *Trans-Plutonian Gulf*

The first ship of the onslaught died as it breached the veil of reality. Streams of plasma reached out from gun platforms. White fire smashed into the ship's prow. Lightning and glowing ectoplasm streamed behind its hull. Macro shells detonated amongst the molten wounds already cut into its skin. Turrets and spires sheared from its bulk. Towers broke from its spine. It kept coming even as its bows were torn apart. The burning wreck struck the first of the mines scattered across the dark. Explosions burst around it. The front portion of the ship sheared from the back. Prow and gun decks hinged down. Atmosphere vented from the exposed interior. Debris scattered, burning for an eye-blink before the flames ate the air trapped in the wreckage.

'Ship kill,' called a sensor adept from across the bridge of the *Lachrymae*.

Sigismund watched the intruder's death as it spread across the pict screens above the command dais. He was armoured, his sword chained to his wrist and resting point down on the deck at his feet. He did not blink or move as the dying ship tumbled across his sight. In the still depths of his mind he heard the words that had brought him to this place and time.

*'You must choose where to stand. By the words of your duty, or by your father's side at the end.'*

Around him the command crew was silent. Eyes fixed on instruments and screens. This was the beginning of the moment they had all known would end the years of waiting. Some, perhaps, had thought or hoped that it would never come. But here it was, marked with fire.

*I chose, Keeler,* he thought, and in his mind, he heard again the words that Dorn had spoken in judgement of that choice.

*'You will continue in rank and position as you have, and you will never speak to any other of this. The Legion and the Imperium will not know of my judgement. Your duty will be to never let your weakness taint those who have more strength and honour than you.'*

*'As you will, father.'*

*'I am not your father!'* roared Dorn, his anger suddenly filling the air, his face swallowed by dusk shadows. *'You are not my son,'* he said quietly. *'And no matter what your future holds, you never will be.'*

'I chose,' he whispered to himself, 'and here I stand at the end.'

The fire from the dead warship spread across the displays.

*'If they come at us like this, the slaughter will barely be worth the sweat,'* growled Fafnir Rann.

*'They will not give us that luxury,'* replied Boreas from further back on the platform. Sigismund did not look around at where the holo-projections of the Assault captain or his lieutenant hovered at his shoulders. Each of them stood on the command deck of one of the *Lachrymae*'s sister ships.

Rann wore void-hardened Mark III armour, with reinforcing studs bonded to his shins and left shoulder. The scars of battles fought here, at the edge of the system, ran beneath the fresh yellow lacquer. His tall boarding shield hung in his right hand, the twin axes mag-locked to its back echoed in the heraldry painted on the shield's face. Sigismund imagined he could see the warped smile on Rann's face as he turned to Boreas and shrugged.

The holo-image of the First Lieutenant of the Templars did not move. Unhelmed, his face was a single twisted scar, and if there was any emotion beyond cold fury behind his eyes, Sigismund could not see it. Boreas' sword of office stood almost as tall as he did, its guard the cross of the Templars, its blade etched with the names of the dead.

'All ships, stand by,' said Sigismund softly, and heard the orders ripple out.

The vibration in the deck rose in pitch. The dull ache that had been building in his skull for the last hours was sharpening. He noticed one of the human deck crew shiver and wipe a hand across a bead of blood forming in her nose.

'Hold to our oaths and the strength of our purpose,' he called.

Whispers buzzed at the edge of his thoughts, razor tips scratching over metal. They had needed to sedate every astropath in the fleet two hours before, as a wave of psychic pressure had sent them babbling and screaming. It had become more intense with every passing moment, and it presaged one thing: it was the bow wave of a truly vast armada coming through the warp, bearing down on the Solar System like a storm front. Horus and the traitors were coming.

'Etheric surge detected!' shouted a sensor officer.

'Here it comes,' said Rann, and brought his fist to his chest. 'Honour and death.'

'*For the primarch and Terra,*' said Boreas.

'For our oaths,' said Sigismund. The images of his two brothers blinked out.

He reached down and pulled his own helm from his belt and locked it in place over his head. 'May my strength be equal to this moment,' he said to himself as the helm display lit in his eyes. The data of the battle sphere overlaid his sight.

The Plutonian Gulf glittered with weapon platforms, torpedo shoals and mine drifts. Together they formed a great web, tens of thousands of kilometres deep, stretching from the very edge of night to the orbits of Pluto itself. Ships glinted amongst the defences: fast gun-sloops and monitor ships that were little more than engines and weaponry. They had been built in the orbital forges of Luna, Jupiter and Uranus and dragged to the edge of the sun's light. Alongside them lay the fleet of the First Sphere: hundreds of warships, all in motion. And beyond the warships, the moons of Pluto waited. Studded with weapons and hollow with tunnels, each was a fortress that could have stood against a fleet.

The sheet of stars erupted with lightning. Rents opened in the vacuum. Nauseating colours and dazzling light poured out as ship after ship surged from nothing into being. Tens, and then hundreds. The sensor servitors in the *Lachrymae* twitched and gabbled as targets multiplied faster than they could vocalise updates.

Mines detonated, explosions leaping from one to another in chains that stretched across the dark. Gun platforms opened up. Macro shells, rockets and plasma struck metal and stone, bored in and exploded. Ships died even as they tasted reality, armour stripped by fire, guts spilled into the dark. In the first ten seconds, over a hundred vessels burned to wreckage. Most had been former warships of the Imperial

Army, crewed by humans who had given their oath to Horus and been rewarded with the honour of being the first to draw their blades in this battle. They died for that honour, burning too in the ruin of their ships, hulls shredded around them.

But they kept coming.

Ship after ship, tearing reality like flags waving in front of a gun-line. The first Legiones Astartes warship surfaced from the warp. It was named the *Erinyes*, and it was a bombardment galleon of the IV Legion: a five-kilometre-long hull wrapped around a trio of nova cannon barrels. She loosed all three shots as the void kissed her skin. Each nova cannon shell was the size of a Battle Titan, its core filled with unstable plasma. They had no target, but they needed none. They ran straight into the heart of the defences and exploded with the force and light of a star's birth. Gun platforms vanished. Mines lit off in spheres of red flame. Fire poured from the defences as more ships rammed past the debris of their dead kin.

The light of the blaze flooded through the *Lachrymae*'s screens and viewports. Sigismund's helm display dimmed.

'Engage,' he said, and the *Lachrymae* leapt forwards. Twenty strike cruisers and fast destroyers followed in tight formation. Lance fire speared out from them, slicing into ships as they cut across the front of the enemy fleet. Plumes of ghost-light and ectoplasm stretched like arms through the dark as more ships punched through from the warp.

A backwash of etheric lightning struck the Imperial Fists cruiser *Solar Son*. It spun, its hull cracking and crumpling as the laws of reality went into flux. The *Lachrymae* and its sisters did not pause but plunged on. They had one purpose in this moment: to kill as many of the enemy as possible while they clawed from the warp onto the shore of reality.

For the moment, the Imperial Fists' prey was vulnerable, and the First Sphere fleet were predators.

The *Lachrymae*'s guns found the skin of the gun-barge *Fire Oath* before it could light its void shields. Macro shells punched through gun decks and exploded. Munitions cooked off in loading hoists. The *Fire Oath*'s hull bulged, then burst. Building-sized pieces of hull scythed out, caught the flank of a battle cruiser as it emerged from the warp and tore its command castle from its back. The warp breach it had emerged from pulsed and swallowed the wreckage.

'Hold,' called Sigismund, his voice passing through the ships of his command via crackling vox-link. 'For our oaths, we hold true.'

The *Lachrymae* sliced on while its mortal crew screamed as ghosts and nightmares flooded their sight. Reality in the battle sphere was now little more than tattered scraps blowing in the night. The *Lachrymae* rolled, her guns finding enemy after enemy. But for each one that died, another three came from the warp.

Deadfall torpedoes set in the void triggered and speared forwards. Carcasses of ships split and burned. Pluto's fortress-moons found their range to the first of the invaders and spoke. Newly lit void shields flashed as they collapsed. Volleys answered. The reserve fleets holding close to the moons powered forwards and began to kill and die. The light of battle swelled, blurring with the glow of thousands of warp transitions, until which side was firing and which was burning was lost in a rippling blaze tens of thousands of kilometres across. Hours later, the light of that fire would glimmer in the night above the battlements of the Imperial Palace as the sirens called and alarums rang to tell that Horus had, at last, brought his war to the birth system of humanity.

# TWO

Silence's shadow
Ash and iron
Daggers drawn

*Bhab Bastion, The Imperial Palace, Terra*

Silence flowed across Terra under the sound of sirens. It fell in the water markets of Albia as the shouting of buyer and seller faded and became looks held between strangers. It crept into the room where the cries of an hours-old child echoed as words of comfort died in a father's mouth. It followed the smoke carrying the smell of the burning refuse from the spoil ranges. On the towers watching the highways that ran to the feet of the Damocles Space Port, the soldiers ceased their pacing and looked up at the night sky. In cave shelters, billions of conscripts glanced at the roofs of rock before looking back down to the guns in their hands. They sat in loose groups – families, hab-block neighbours, manufactory shifts – saying nothing.

Waiting.

In the administrative strata of the record-hives, scribes moved between parchment spools and auto-quills, following

31

routine as though it would make a lie of the warning alarms. On the walls of the Imperial Palace, warriors watched the sun rise over the teeth of the eastern wall and heard only the sound of the wind and the shrill of warning. Terra was a world waiting for the first blow to fall. And in the last inch of waiting, panic had found stillness.

In the heart of the Grand Borealis Strategium in the Bhab Bastion within the Imperial Palace, Admiral Su-Kassen felt the silence crawl into the moments as she watched holo-projections of scrolling data. This was the primary command for the entire system, its view like that of a god looking down on a realm held in the light of the glowing displays. Primary fleet concentrations stood out as green runes, each a war command of tens of thousands of warships, monitor craft and others that had been pressed into service.

'Update display – primary fleet force readiness,' she said. She had repeated the command every fifteen minutes for the last six hours.

'Compliance,' droned a servitor, and the display stripped itself down to a few markers haloed with green data. The largest fleets held station beside Pluto, Uranus, Jupiter, Mars and Terra. These were the five Sphere commands. Signals took hours to pass from the Throneworld to the system edge, too long for the second-by-second control of battle. A lord castellan of the Imperial Fists commanded each layer of defence: Sigismund, Halbract, Effried, Camba Diaz. Rogal Dorn commanded the fifth, final sphere around Terra. Other commands deferred to the lord of the closest Sphere. Troop concentrations were marked with coloured dots. The size of a force and its strength flickered around them in abbreviated code. The few Legion units beyond the bounds of Terra glowed like hot coals, the other forces cold motes of fire. Amber specks marked fixed defences around planets or hanging in the gulfs between them. These were everything from void-fortresses to shoals of gun platforms and space stations. Clouds of tiny blue spots folded through the spaces between the larger defences, indicating the vast clouds of mines, deadfall torpedoes and proximity drones that had been cast amongst the dark like dust from a hand. Once the battle was done, the approaches to the inner system would be laced with death until the star itself died.

*Once the battle was done…* If there was anything left besides ashes.

Su-Kassen shook herself. The first wall of any fortress was the mind, and doubt could burn it from within before the enemy had even raised a blade.

She scanned the data again. It had not changed, of course. Out there in the heavens above, the fires of battle were already burning, but here the reality of that truth had yet to arrive.

'Report update,' called a signal officer, from behind a bank of machines.

'Show me,' she said.

'By your will,' said the officer, and she could hear the forced control in the man's voice.

Machines clattered and whirred, stitching the silence as it stretched. The holo-display fuzzed, flickered and then came into focus. She looked at the image and blinked. Crimson flecked the edge of the turning display. Her mind began to parse the marker runes and data abstractions. Strategic logic-conditioning shunted aside thoughts as she absorbed the updated defence data. It was an odd sensation, one that she had never got used to in all the decades of her life and service. Every now and again her thoughts and understanding would jump, like a needle on a data cylinder, and she would find herself understanding something she had not an instant before.

Bit by bit the mass of runes and symbols resolved into meaning.

*The Khthonic Gate…* she thought. *So, it begins, just as we predicted and feared.*

Starships had to translate from the warp at the edge of a system, beyond the Mandeville point, that arcane and invisible line that marked the boundary between safety and suicide. Arrive inside that point, and the competing forces of reality and paradox would rip a vessel apart. 'Rebirth death' the Navigators called it, when they talked of such things. Most established systems had navigation buoys and well-trodden points where it was safest to drop from the warp back into reality. Once back in the cold embrace of the void, ships then had to move in-system under the power of their real space engines. The journey from system edge to the planets of the core took even the fastest ships days.

The Solar System, though, was older than any colonised by humanity. Star travel and warp navigation had been birthed here, and over tens of thousands of years more secrets, wonders and terrors had been raised and lost within its bounds than existed in all the galaxy beyond. Two such relics of the past were the Twin Gates: stable points in space and the warp where ships could translate safely. Both tracked the orbits of planets as they orbited Sol. The Khthonic Gate lay off Pluto, and the Elysian Gate lay close to Uranus. The latter offered a further layer of paradox, as it gave ships a way to re-enter deeper in the system far beyond the point where they would be wrecked if they chanced it normally.

Anyone who planned to attack Terra in force would want to secure the Twin Gates to move their forces into the Solar System quickly. That Horus would pour everything he could into taking them was a certainty.

'That cannot be correct…' croaked Kazzim-Aleph-1 from

where he hovered at her shoulder. The magos-emissary had only been attached to the command cadre for a week, and Su-Kassen was still trying to understand him. He seemed logical and emphatic but also hesitant, a combination she had never thought to see in someone who was so much more machine than flesh. His cranium whirred, cogs flipping around in slots that ran the length of his skull as the projection and screens updated. 'There is an error. This data indicates a warp-reality translation via the Khthonic Path of over a thousand ships...'

'More,' she said quietly. 'A lot more.'

'That cannot be. It is an error. There is a Falcon fleet that can reach Pluto in five hours. They can–'

'No,' she said, dropping her voice under the buzz of the machines. 'All other forces are to hold position, magos-emissary.'

Even as she spoke she felt the words pull against her instincts.

'Admiral,' said the magos, 'my calculations show that the Plutonic defences can hold if reinforced. If the enemy has committed its main force strength to take Pluto as a bridge-head and then can be held there–'

'They cannot be held,' said a voice from across the chamber. 'Not at a cost we can afford to pay.'

Blast doors withdrew into the walls. Warriors in yellow armour and black cloaks poured in. Light caught the edges of ready weapons and sheened from armour plates. Threat radiated from them, sharper than their blades, roaring from their silence.

And with them came the one who had spoken. Cold illumination struck the burnished gold of Rogal Dorn's armour and lit fire in jewels clasped in the claws of eagles. Control radiated from him, vibrating through air and through light, the lightning promise at the edge of a storm. To the billions that lived on Terra, he was the wall against which the coming enemy would break, defiance and strength embodied. But in person he was not the idea that the desperate clung to as they thought of what was to come; he was a force of nature that moved and spoke, a lightning bolt pulled from the sky and chained to flesh to fight until the universe broke him.

The Imperial Fists standing vigil at the chamber edges brought their clenched fists to their chests, but only Su-Kassen bowed to the Praetorian as he advanced. The officers and adepts who served in the Bhab Bastion were human for the most part. They were the finest war staff Su-Kassen had ever seen, drawn from the old Solar military elite. War-savants of the Saturnine Ordos, warriors of the Jovian Void Clans like her, tacticians from the Terran war-courts: every man and woman in the chamber knew their craft well enough to rival even the command skill of the Legions, and all of them knew that when Rogal Dorn, primarch of the VII Legion and Praetorian of Terra, entered they had a duty to continue in their tasks, rather than to bow. It had been Dorn's first order when he had created this command cadre. Su-Kassen saluted for all of them.

But as the blast doors sealed again, she knew the presence of the three who walked with Dorn would test their obedience.

Jaghatai, Great Khan of the White Scars, walked on Dorn's left, his eyes dancing with the turning light of the holo-displays. On Dorn's other side came an angel armoured in gold, white wings furled at his back. Sanguinius, primarch of the IX Legion, looked across the humans at their stations and then at Su-Kassen. He smiled. Last of all came an old man in the grey robes of the Administratum, leaning on an eagle-topped staff. Wrinkled skin hung from his

face, but his eyes were cold and bright. Malcador the Sigillite seemed older and weaker than Su-Kassen had ever
seen him, but it was he as much as the three primarchs that
made her hold her head bowed. The silence in the chamber
deepened, seeming to press closer as the three loyal sons
of the Emperor and His Regent halted beneath the turning holo-display.

'The First Sphere forces cannot hold,' said Dorn, his dark
eyes fixed on Kazzim-Aleph-1. 'And it will not be reinforced.'

The magos-emissary was still, the cogs protruding from
his skull rotating slowly. For a second Su-Kassen thought he
was going to argue. For a second, she hoped that he would.

'Lord Dorn, there are options–' began Su-Kassen, before
she could stop herself.

'No,' said Dorn, and the word and his glance fell on her
like a blow.

'As is your will, Lord Praetorian,' said Kazzim-Aleph-1
at last.

Out of the corner of her eye, Su-Kassen saw the Khan flick
a look at Sanguinius. The Angel's face remained impassive.

Rogal Dorn came forwards, eyes moving from the magos
to Su-Kassen.

'The initial battle data indicates that your projections were
incorrect, admiral.'

She nodded and opened her mouth to reply.

'They were inaccurate by a factor of at least thirty per cent,'
cut in Kazzim-Aleph-1, 'maybe more. We cannot yet be precise, of course, but if the core data is correct, the enemy has
brought a force numbering many thousands of vessels from
the immaterium.'

'Thank you for your clarification, magos-emissary,' said
Dorn. Su-Kassen almost flinched at the ice in the words.
Kazzim-Aleph-1 seemed oblivious to it.

'I am charged by the Fabricator General to aid your command in addition to representing the positions of Mars. I am...' he paused, as cogs turned and buzzed, '...pleased that my function is of utility to you, Lord Praetorian.'

Su-Kassen thought she heard Malcador stifle a cough that might have been a laugh. For a giddy moment she found herself almost wanting to smile herself, and then clamped down on the feeling. It was tension and the truth of what was happening finding a way of bleeding out, of breaking the silence. She wondered for a second if somewhere out there, under the blanket drone of alert sirens, there were people laughing as they felt the seconds tick by and future come closer.

It was Sanguinius who broke the silence, walking forwards and raising a hand to dip his fingers into a turning sphere of light.

'It will be Uranus next,' he said. 'And if the attack is not already under way, it will be soon.'

Su-Kassen let out a breath she had not realised she was holding. Around her she felt the command staff relax and refocus. That had been deliberate, she thought. With but a few words the Angel had bent them all in a direction of his choosing.

'Signal relay to the outer spheres is still clear, lord,' said Su-Kassen, 'but there has been no word from Lord Halbract at Uranus yet.'

'You are still sure this is the path?' asked the Khan. He had held back, close to the doors and, apart from his glance at Sanguinius, he had remained utterly still. There was something in that stillness that was like the flash of lightning frozen in the eye. 'There are other ways – Horus could be scattering his might out in the depths beyond, and then circle them in, closing from all sides, strangling us as he cuts us.'

Dorn looked at the Khan.

'This is Horus. Do you still think he will be anything but himself?'

'He is not himself,' said Sanguinius without turning from where the holo-light played over his hand. Su-Kassen felt the tension snap back into place in the room. She felt as though she and the rest of her staff had intruded on a conversation that these demigods had brought with them. 'You have not seen him, Rogal,' continued Sanguinius. 'You have not seen the face of what has taken our brother.'

'He may have changed,' growled Dorn, now as still as the Khan, the low light of the displays setting his face in cold lines and hollows of night. 'But the constraints he faces have not. Time. He does not have time. Guilliman breathes at his back. Horus has to come for us with everything he has as quickly as he can, or he will have nothing.' Dorn shook his head, a smile that was a ghost passing across his face. 'Besides, it is not his way.'

The silence flowed back in.

'So, we let him take the gates?' said the Khan, his voice soft but edged. 'We wall ourselves up and wait, and hope that those walls will prove strong enough?'

Dorn did not answer, his gaze locked with his brothers.

'We hold every wall and we make them pay in time and blood for every step forwards.'

'Just so,' said Sanguinius, lowering his hand and gaze from the holo-display, and turning to look at his siblings. 'And a price in blood it shall be.'

Malcador's staff struck the floor. The blow was not powerful, but Su-Kassen felt the air leave her lungs.

'There,' he said, looking around, his eyes bright and hard. Everyone in the chamber, primarch and human alike, was looking at him. Su-Kassen watched a sad smile form on his face. 'You see? Peace is possible, if only for a moment and amongst ourselves.'

The Khan laughed, and the frozen tension in the chamber vanished.

'Quite so, quite so. We forget our place and company.' The primarch of the V Legion unfolded from his stillness and came forwards, his movements fluid and relaxed. He circled the display, glancing up at it and around. 'This is fine work.' He looked at Su-Kassen and nodded. 'Your cadre is to be commended, admiral.' She bowed her head. For a second, she had felt as though the Khan had looked right through her.

Beside her, apparently oblivious to what had been occurring, Kazzim-Aleph-1 glanced up from where he had been fidgeting through the raw data-screed.

'The customary astropathic communications from across the system are absent,' he said. His eye-lenses rotated in a way that created the distinct impression of a frown. 'At this time, and given the delay in other signals, delays inherent in the distances involved, it would be most advisable to make use of telepathic methods of communication. Also, the astropaths' ability to sense warp displacement would be a significant advantage.' He paused, looking up at the primarchs and command staff as though just seeing them. 'Do you not concur?'

'There will be no astrotelepathic messages from inside or outside the system, magos-emissary,' said Malcador, his voice low and edged by a weariness. 'Nor any warning of more ships or fleets exiting the immaterium.'

'Why is that?' asked the magos.

Malcador closed his eyes, and Su-Kassen saw him shift his weight to his staff. 'Because all around us, the warp is howling.'

\* \* \*

*Battle-barge Monarch of Fire, Trans-Uranic Gulf*

Clouds of dust filled the Elysian Gate. An open volume of space three thousand kilometres across, it glittered with folds of fine particles. Hundreds, perhaps thousands of years of void-ships translating to the warp at this point had seeded it with drifts of the soft, grey matter that formed in the wake of a closing breach. The Jovian clans and the Navigator houses had a name for it. Siren Ash, they called it. There were tales, they said, of prospectors who had tried to harvest the dust and could desire nothing else once they'd touched it. True or not, the dust remained, slowly coiling through the volume of the Elysian Gate, like smoke caught in a glass orb.

The gate had always been guarded. Things had come out of it during Old Night, things that the Uranus Habitats remembered in tales of star-vampires and iron men. They had built the first fortresses around the gate, watching it with guns and warriors. These stations were called the Eyes of the Old God, and they had kept their vigil as the rest of the Solar System slid into the depths of the Age of Strife.

Then the Great Crusade had risen from Old Earth and brought the Uranus Habitats and moons into the nascent Imperium. The watchful stations had grown, their hereditary warrior clans augmented by Martian weaponry. Ships had begun to pass through the gate into the immaterium, and others had returned. The Navigator houses re-established their fiefs amongst Uranus' twenty-seven moons, and the volume of space between the gas giant and the Elysian Gate had become an ever-glittering stream of light as ships looped from the warp to the profusion of orbiting habitats and void-stations.

Horus' war had changed that. The flow of ships had become a sullen trickle, and the stations keeping the long watch had bloated with fresh armour and weaponry. Every foothold of humanity that could mount a macro cannon or host a fighter squadron had found itself made a fortress. Amongst this, facing the dark of the Elysian Gate, the ships of the Second Sphere hung motionless, crenellated and beweaponed, in the glittering abyss.

In the gate, the dust moved. A slow swirl gathered and coiled in on itself. Clouds hundreds of kilometres across flowed and folded. The dust began to spark. Tiny worms of lightning flicked between grey motes. The clouds began to glow, now green, now bruised violet, now bloodied ivory.

The waiting fleets of warships lit their drives. In their sanctums, astropaths began to weep. In the habitats and stations, the low howl of warning sirens woke millions from dreams of shadows swallowing the sun. On the bridge of the *Monarch of Fire*, Lord Castellan Halbract, commander of the Second Sphere of Sol's defences, watched the reports blur across his sight as the helm of his Terminator armour locked in place.

'Fleet- and defence-wide transmission,' he said, the rich accent of the Nordafrik Conclaves weighting his words. He saw the thousands of units under his command come to readiness in his helm-display. The echoes of a hundred warships' acknowledgements and salutes whispered across the vox. He breathed out and spoke.

'For the light of Sol and the earth of Terra, we stand. For the oaths we made, we stand. For the blood in our veins, we stand.'

He heard it then, growing in the air outside his armour as the hundreds of crew on the *Monarch of Fire*'s bridge took up the words.

'For the stones laid by our ancestors, we stand.'

And now the words were echoing across the vox, overlapping from thousands of mouths.

'For the days that have passed and the days that shall come, we stand.'

The swirl of dust in the sphere of the gate was moving faster, the light growing brighter.

'For the living and the honour of the dead, we stand.'

Shapes formed in the glare, blinking into sight like shadows cast by the flash of lightning. The inner ring of gun platforms around the gate began to fire. Hundreds of shells blazed into the flashing dust. Some exploded, some vanished. The multicoloured swirl contracted. The gun platforms kept firing. Then the dust and light burst outwards.

A split opened at the gate's centre, black beyond night. Across the gulf of the vacuum, the humans on the nearest gun platforms flinched as a ululating scream filled their ears. The dark hole flexed, its edges growing like a tear pulled wide in ragged fabric.

The fire from the gun platforms was a deluge now. Shells tumbled into the spreading breach. Those that exploded burst like water as they touched the warp. A trio of shapes appeared in the dark. Bloated and monstrous, they pushed into reality.

They had been macro-transporters once, made to shift the output of worlds across the galaxy. Each was bigger than even the largest warships. Slabs of raw iron had been welded to their flanks, and clusters of void shield generators blistered their skin like boils. They had borne other names in their former, ponderous lives, but the will of Perturabo had remade them, and had given them new titles to bear. *Alekto*, *Megaera* and *Tilphousia* were their names, and they had been reborn to die in the first moments of this assault.

The second cordon of defences opened fire. Long-range

turbo lasers burned hundred-metre-wide channels through the blazing dust in the gate. The *Alekto*, *Megaera* and *Tilphousia* pushed onwards, molten metal weeping from their prows. Their void shields lit. Fresh storms of lightning blazed through the dust clouds, as ether-charged Siren Dust kissed the forming skins of energy. The deluge of fire began to find its mark as the three huge ships shot forwards.

The plasma reactors from hundreds of half-dead machines filled the trio's decks and holds. They lit one after another. Power poured into engines and shields. Volleys of macro shells slammed into them as they shot out in different directions. Plasma conduits inside their guts began to rupture. Reactor containment began to fail, and thousands of the servitor crew died as their flesh cooked. Shells and las-fire crumpled shields and bit into iron skin. Fire chewed at them like rain into blocks of salt.

It did not matter, though. They had not been made to live. In another age, back when Terra had oceans, such vessels were called fire ships: crude mechanisms of horror and destruction in a time of primitive explosives and wooden vessels.

On the defence platforms, the gunnery officers saw what was about to happen as the three ships hurtled closer towards the first line of defences. They did everything that they could to prevent it.

Macro cannon fire tore savagely into the prow plating of the *Tilphousia* as her shields collapsed. A chunk of smelted iron the size of a hab-block peeled back, tumbling away as lance fire reached inside the first wound and burned into the huge ship's bones.

The *Tilphousia* erupted in flame and light. The blast wave reached back to the warp gate, staining the dust cloud orange. Twenty gun platforms vanished, their deaths marked by blinks of light within the blaze as their magazines cooked off.

It was only as the defenders' auspex and targeting systems went dark that the true spite of the ironclad vessels' makers became clear. Laced into the heart of the *Tilphousia* and her sisters were machines looted from dead forge worlds. Half-wreckage, their spirits violated and rebound by the priests of the New Mechanicum, these engines had once been wonders of lost arts of communication. Now they were instruments of cacophony. Waves of wild electromagnetic distortion, scrap code and haywire radiation ripped out with the *Tilphousia*'s death fire. The distortion wave scratched its way into systems, darkened signal receivers and sent gunnery servitors into feedback convulsions.

The void-fortresses and weapon platforms fired with everything they had. Half-blinded they clawed burning holes in the hulls of the remaining sisters.

It was not enough.

The *Alekto* detonated as she breached the inner lines of defences around the gate. The *Megaera* exploded minutes later. Weapon platforms the size of manufactoria became shrapnel sprayed out into the dark. A blinding fog of fire and exotic radiation swallowed the gate, cloaking it in brightness.

Halbract had held his ships back, but loosed his first battle groups now. These were monitor ships, blunt craft of raw firepower and armour. Crewed by humans pressed from the Solar privateer clans, they knew the business of killing. They cut down channels between the fortresses and platforms. Gun batteries had fallen silent as their auspexes fogged. Torpedoes were shot blind into the fire-cloaked heart of the gate. For a moment, thousands of strands of light streaked the dark.

Within the cloak of fire and radiation surrounding the

gate, eight main force class battleships translated into reality, guns primed. Each had been selected for their mass, armour and the discipline of their crews. They were all ships bound to the Iron Warriors and crewed by officers who had failed the IV Legion before. That failure had earned them the honour of crossing this breach first. Forgiveness awaited those that survived, and the release of death those that proved weak.

The guns of the eight were discharging even as they arrived. Nova cannons ran down the spines of four, and they began to fire blind. The squadrons of monitor craft responded with every weapon that could find a target.

The nova shells hit first. Each one was over fifty metres in diameter and longer than some of the smaller warships in the battle sphere. Accelerated to within a breath of the speed of light, each carried a ship-killing payload. Spheres of exotic energy and primal destruction burst into being.

Some caught gun platforms and void-stations and tore their shields and armour from them. Graviton and haywire torpedoes struck the defences next, seeking out mass and reactor signatures. Sensor arrays shorted. Crushing gravity fields yanked void bastions out of alignment and cracked the shells of the monitor ships.

The torpedoes fired by the defenders cut into the battle sphere. A cluster of twenty slammed into one of the eight vanguard ships and swallowed its flank and spine in a stuttering blaze. The ship listed, plunging downwards as it died. Burning atmosphere vented from its wounds in vast streams.

On the bridge of the *Monarch of Fire*, Halbract watched the first minutes unfold. This would not be a swift battle, but these moments would be crucial. The enemy had to race to establish a foothold in reality, a tipping point where the number of their ships outstripped the rate at which the defenders could kill them. So far, the odds of them succeeding were finely balanced.

'Lord Halbract, something larger is coming through,' called one of the sensor officers. 'It casts a shadow even through the distortion.'

A shape pushed through the firelit dust and haze. At first it looked like a pitted asteroid or a wreck. Then the bulk behind its prow burst through the swirl. The dead of millennia of war amongst the stars were its mass – mangled carcasses of starships, asteroids, towers and broken star fortresses, all crushed together by the immaterium. It was a macro-agglomeration of debris and dead things secreted by storm tides, a pearl of sorrow, a space hulk. The New Mechanicum had dragged it from the tides of the warp and remade it. Launch bays had been cut into its mass, reactors lit in its heart and shield generators bound to its surface. Pushing and hauling it through the warp had cost a dozen ships, and once pushed back into reality, it would never move again. That, though, was not its purpose. The size of one of Uranus' moons, it was made to be a besieger's redoubt at the gate of a greater fortress. *Daughter of Woe*, it had been named.

The ships that had already exited the immaterium slewed aside as the hulk grew and grew. Its bulk was breaking through the cloud on all sides of the gate, now. Hundred-kilometre arcs of warp lightning writhed from the tearing edge of the vast hole it was boring in space.

The dust of the Elysian Gate streamed down its face like water falling from a leviathan breaking from the depths of a dark sea. The wreckage of already-dead ships impacted on its surface. Torpedoes and battery fire slammed into it. Chunks of rock and metal tore from it. And it kept coming. Assault craft began to launch from it in clouds. Small frigates that had made the journey bound to its skin broke their tethers and slid into the void.

Lord Castellan Halbract watched as the *Daughter of Woe* lit with fire from the rings of defences. This had not been anticipated, but it changed little. His orders and oaths still stood. The only question was how much they could make the enemy pay, and the price his forces paid in turn.

'Light our guns,' he said, and the *Monarch of Fire* shook to his order.

### Battle-barge War Oath, *Supra-Solar Gulf*

The herald ship surfaced from the night. Bit by bit her shape grew, spear-blade prow and gun-serrated flanks emerging from a lightless ocean. Shadows fumed from her substance like black ink dropped into water. The sun shone beyond her armoured bows. She had been birthed in the light of that sun but had not seen its light in over a century. The Emperor Himself had named her *War Oath*, and she still bore that name, but like the Legion that commanded her now, time had remade her. Ghost-light clung to her turrets and pooled in the scars that marked her flanks. The marks of the Imperial Fists had long been removed, and the wounds done to her at the Battle of Phall were now repaired, but signs of her one-time masters still lived in her bones.

Ezekyle Abaddon looked out at the void light through the armourglass dome of the *War Oath*'s observatory. Perched atop a slender tower on the ship's command castle, its purpose had been to watch and chart the stars. A great stack of brass machinery hung from the dome's apex, its lenses, dials and mirrors filmed with dust. Abaddon doubted that anyone had ever used the instruments; what need was there for such poetic flourishes on a warship equipped with sensors and long-range auspex? A neverborn hissed in his ears as it dissolved from the bones of the ship. A spectre with orb-eyes and a smile of needle teeth ran the tip of its claw down the observatory's dome. It grinned. Abaddon met its gaze as it faded to nothing. The bright, distant jewel of Sol glowed through the fading shadow of its mouth. He caught a glimmer at the edge of his eyes, glanced around and saw the image of the sun shining from an octagonal silver mirror set at the centre of the chamber's floor. He froze, eyes fixed on the circle of light floating beneath the surface of the dusty silver.

'The gods bless us, and bring us to the light of truth,' said Zardu Layak from where he knelt on the stone floor. Candles of human tallow burned with rainbow-streaked flames around him. Eight heaps of ash and blackened bone lay around the Word Bearer. They had been chosen from amongst Layak's mortal flock and had burned where they knelt as the *War Oath* translated from the warp into reality. None of them had made a sound as they were engulfed. That silence had clenched the muscles along Abaddon's jaw. Part of him had thought of ordering the Justaerin Terminators standing at the edge of the room to open fire and reduce the Word Bearers and their foul sacrifice to pulped meat and shredded armour.

Witch-frost cracked from Layak's armour as he rose. The two red-armoured warriors that had stood guard over his vigil bowed their heads. Layak extended his hand and his staff coalesced into being in his grasp.

Abaddon looked into the rows of glowing eyes running down the cheeks of Layak's horned mask.

'It is done?' he asked. Layak nodded.

'By the will of the Four and the Eightfold star.'

Abaddon felt his lips pull back from his teeth.

'You do not have faith in the gods?'

'I have faith in our Warmaster,' growled Abaddon, and opened a vox-link to the ship's command echelon. 'Report readiness condition.' Static chopped through the replies. He listened, his mind folding each report into a precise map of the ship's current strength and capability. Satisfactory. If needed, they could fight and kill now. The need was unlikely, if all had gone as it should, but you always drew a blade before stepping into the dark. The fingers of his right hand twitched, curling for an instant before he stilled them. For a second, he had felt the ghost of his false-father's knife bite into his forearm as he squeezed.

*You are a fool, boy!* He could see the eyes above the blood-stained teeth, could feel his fingers digging into the neck beneath them. *'It will… slip through… your fingers…'*

'You were not born under that light, were you?' asked Layak. Abaddon blinked. The Word Bearer had come to stand next to him in front of the view of the sun. 'But in a sense, I suppose we all were. This is our cradle, is it not, brother?'

*The Luna gene-wright rose, chromed and cold, its six bladed limbs opening above his naked flesh in a spider embrace.*

*'You will be born anew…'* it had whispered as it began to cut. *'Moon-wrought and blooded.'*

'You are not my brother, priest,' said Abaddon, and the threat in the words was enough to bring Layak's bodyguards forwards, their blades drawing, cracks of fire spreading over their armour.

Abaddon looked at them, his eyes glittering above a cold smile.

Layak stilled them with a twitch of his head. The pair paused and nodded once before stepping back.

A blurt of data filled the vox for a second. Abaddon listened, and then cut the link.

'The Thousand Sons ship translated successfully.'

+It did, and we are here,+ said a voice that rolled in Abaddon's skull. His teeth clamped shut as he shrugged the telepathic communication away.

An image unfolded in the air, translucent and shimmering: crimson armour, edged in ivory. The eyes set in the smooth face shone with a cold, blue light. Ahzek Ahriman nodded once to Abaddon and walked closer, his ghost image trailing light and frost in the air. Layak's bodyguards had begun to draw their blades once more. Ahriman's image turned to look at them. They met his gaze. The light of their eye-lenses had begun to burn red, and yellow embers were trickling from the splits that had opened in their armour. Ahriman tilted his head. Ice ran across the floor.

+Tell the warlock to muzzle his dogs,+ he sent, without moving his lips.

The eyes in Layak's mask were glowing, and blood was seeping from between its metal fangs. A smell of sulphur and burnt sugar mingled with ozone. Abaddon glanced at where the four Justaerin stood at the edge of the chamber. The glance held them in place.

'Cease,' growled Abaddon. Layak looked at the image of Ahriman for a second, and then turned away. His two bodyguards slid their blades back into their sheaths. The splits closed in their armour. The light in their eyes dimmed.

Ahriman turned and glided towards the viewport. An instinct to flinch away from the ghost-figure tugged at Abaddon's muscles. He held still, eyes following the Thousand Sons Librarian as he looked out at the view of Terra beyond the dagger point of the ship's prow.

+Home.+ Ahriman's mouth did not move, but the shadows of his brow furrowed. +What creatures are we that come from the night, to hearth and home, and find only strangers on the threshold?+

Layak made a sound that might have been a hiss of laughter.

'Kaelic of Noropolis,' said Abaddon. 'From the *Songs of Passing*. "And what stranger beasts do the eyes of fathers see who after long years stand by open doors and wait…"'

Ahriman turned to look at him. The light of the stars glimmered through the gauzy image of his frown. He raised an eyebrow. 'We are warriors, not barbarians,' said Abaddon. Then he nodded at the distant sun. 'Where is the rest of the armada?'

+Watch,+ sent Ahriman.

Sheets of aurora light formed in the night beyond, flowing and curling across the dark. The light of the sun and the stars blurred as it fell through the curtains of colour, sliding out of place until it seemed that the heavens had been twisted into a new position. Shadows formed in the folds of light, jagged silhouettes like the shards of broken spears.

Millions had died to make this possible. Tens of thousands had been bled into offering vats or been jettisoned from hangar bays into the warp. Most had died with pleas for mercy on their lips. Some had spoken prayers of thanks to the gods. Slaves taken from conquered worlds, helots from the deep decks of the ships, even some chosen from amongst the soldiery that had sworn loyalty to Horus, all had died, their blood and souls poured into nothing to make this possible. The powers that Horus had bound to his cause had seen his ships through the warp, and now they had slid them back into being well past the Mandeville point of the Solar System – that invisible barrier created by a star's gravity past which it was unsafe to translate ships to and from the warp. There had been a price, of course, a price and a limit. The price had been paid in blood, and the limit was that for all the neverborn could bend the rules to place these ships deep within in the Solar sphere, they could not violate them utterly. They had not been able to return the Warmaster's ships directly into Terran orbit. Not yet. But what the blood and death had bought was what some would have called a miracle, even so.

The jagged shadows in the coiling light faded momentarily. A fork of green lightning whipped across the void, branching across thousands of kilometres. The light froze for an instant. A shiver ran across Abaddon's skin under his armour. His gaze was locked on the scene beyond the glass. He felt his twin hearts each beat once.

The frozen flash of lightning exploded. He blinked. Ships filled the void around the *War Oath*, tens of thousands of vast, dark metal shapes fuming pale smoke. The stars swirled, and the aurora light folded over and over, caressing their hulls as thousands of vessels shivered into full reality. Sons of Horus, Word Bearers and the New Mechanicum, enough to conquer star clusters, all hanging above the sun like daggers.

Abaddon watched the ships settle and the ghost-light fade from their hulls. Behind him, the image of Ahriman faded too. A moment later he heard the door release, and Layak and his bodyguards withdraw. Abaddon turned when he heard the doors reseal. He inhaled, bringing emotion to a point of focus. He loathed how they had come here. He loathed more the weakness of his own Legion, implied by the aid given by the Thousand Sons and Word Bearers to make this impossibility a reality. But here and now, his loathing did not matter. All that mattered was the weapon that his father, his Warmaster, had placed in his hand. He heard his oath then – not the oath he had knelt and given at the foot of Horus' throne, but one given long ago beneath the light of the sun that waited for him at the end of this path.

'Will you serve me, Abaddon?' Horus had asked, the coin held out in his open palm.

'I will,' he had replied, and taken the coin.

'All ships,' he said, hearing his voice echo as it reached across the void through the vox. 'By my word, and the word of the Warmaster. The blade falls.'

One by one, the ships lit their engines and slid down towards the waiting sun.

# THREE

Wake and remember
Son of Horus
Blood and luck

*Prison ship* Aeacus, *Uranus high orbit*

Sleep came for Mersadie like a thief stealing the light, closing her eyelids and pulling her down into the dark. She had tried to stay awake. Even though she knew that she would never be able to outrun it, she had stared at the caged lamp in the ceiling of her cell, stood up and paced a tiny circle between the walls when she felt her eyes fluttering shut.

She wanted very much not to sleep. The dream of the night before had left a shiver of fear in her. Loken, the *Vengeful Spirit*... It had seemed so... vital, and she knew that you could not dismiss what happened in dreams as insignificant simply because they were not real. She had spent years living her memories again and again, trying to recall and hold on to every detail she could. Now it was all she could do not to smell the blood and hear the screams. So, she had fought back sleep, and tried to think through what was happening as she walked the scant metres of her cell and stared at the light.

She tried to keep her mind filled with questions about the present: why had she been moved from the prison around Titan to a ship? Was that Loken's doing? Or was there another reason?

She shook her head as she felt herself contemplate stopping for a moment and sitting down. There was no night in this box of metal, but it must have been almost a day's worth of hours since she had slept. She had to stay awake.

She was on a ship and guarded. Was she alone or were there others with her? An instinct told her that there would be more prisoners on the ship, but she could not be certain. If there *were* others, where were they going? It would not make sense to move prisoners that were a threat to the Imperium. Unless…

She blinked up at the caged lamp, swaying. She had to stay awake. She had to…

*Unless…*

She raised her head from the pillow and looked up at the ceiling. Painted birds soared through a painted sky of clouds and sunlight. She sat up. The window was open, and the wind was blowing warm from outside. She could smell citrus blossom. The trees under the hydro-dome enclosure were in late flower, heavy with scent and pollen and the promise of fruit. She stared around her for a moment, taking in the nightstand, the bookshelves of catula wood and the half-drunk glass of water left on the windowsill.

'No,' she said out loud, testing to see if she had a voice. 'This is a dream.'

The breeze coming through the window slackened, and in the quiet she heard a distant, soft clacking, as though someone were placing pebbles on a sheet of plasteel.

She rose and went to the door. The corridors of the manse opened in front of her as she followed the noise. She did not look around her as she went. She was sure that in this dream every detail would be as perfect as her memory.

At last she stepped from a wide spiral of stairs into the Sunrise Gallery. It was set at the highest point of the manse; from here you could look all the way across the Aska mountain range and see the distant towers of Terra's equatorial hives. High, peaked windows were open to the air outside, and translucent curtains stirred in a wind that carried the smell of rain drying in the first heat of a new day. She could see the sunlight glinting off the great chrome-and-glass dome that enclosed the gardens beyond. Held back beyond it, the upper strata of Terra's blanket of pollution tinted the air a vivid mauve. A woman sat on the floor at the centre of the room, her back to Mersadie.

'Hello,' said the woman, half turning her head. A rush of fleeting recognition passed through Mersadie, but she could not grasp it. 'Where is this place, if you don't mind me asking?'

'Home…' said Mersadie, pausing to touch a leather-bound volume sitting on a shelf. 'My home on Terra, before I left.' She opened the book. *The Edge of Illumination, from the hand of Solomon Voss* ran across the title page in hand-brushed script.

'You have not dreamed of it in a long time, have you?' said the woman sitting at the centre of the room.

'It was not a place that made happy memories,' said Mersadie, and closed the book.

'You never went back.'

'No,' said Mersadie. 'Home was not somewhere I ever wanted to return to.'

'So, you followed your talent, and it led you out to the stars and into the company of wolves.'

'Yes, it did,' said Mersadie. She turned towards the centre of the room. The other woman still had her back to her, but Mersadie could see that she was busy with something that sat on the low table in front of her. 'Who are you?' Mersadie asked. 'I don't remember you. So why am I dreaming you?'

The woman laughed, the sound brief and clear.

'Don't you recognise me?'

Mersadie blinked, then started forwards.

'*Euphrati?*'

The woman on the floor turned to look at her and smiled. 'It is good to see you.'

Mersadie stopped. Even in this dream, Euphrati Keeler looked different to how she remembered. The smile on her face was sad, her features lean and drawn, her hair cut short and streaked with grey and white. The beautiful remembrancer who had shared Mersadie's time amongst the Luna Wolves, and their fall to darkness, was gone, replaced by something harder, something defined by purpose.

Mersadie looked around again, then back to Keeler.

'This is not a dream, is it? This is like before, when you spoke to me about Loken.' That dream had come years before, but Mersadie had been able to remember it without effort. It had been more real than real, a moment of connection made possible by means that Mersadie could not explain without reaching for words like 'miracle'. 'You are really here, aren't you, in my dream?'

Keeler was still for a second, then nodded. 'I need to tell you something, and then I am afraid I need to ask something of you.'

'What?'

'First you must understand,' said Keeler, looking back to what was on the floor in front of her. Mersadie moved around until she could see. She stopped and frowned. A disc of brass sat on the top of the polished wood. It was as wide as a dinner plate and divided into rings. Circles of polished stone and metal had been slotted into depressions in the wood, and Mersadie could see more discs cupped in Keeler's left hand.

'Those are the signs of the planets and moons from–'

'From the time before Old Night, yes,' said Keeler, slotting more of the discs into place in each of the rings. 'The Planet of War, the Maiden of Dreams, the Bringer of Joy. And these beside them are the phases of the heavens, the symbols used by the scryers of the Suund – the Burning Tiger, the Bloody Sagittar, the Weigher of Souls, the Crown of Oceans, and so on.'

'I know them,' said Mersadie. 'I read the Chaldeantis scripts while I was in the Conservatory towers of Europa.'

'Strange to think that part of humanity held on to such things even after we had gone to the heavens they were meant to represent, don't you think?' asked Keeler with a humourless smile. 'Relics of misguided philosophy, but like all of the things that humanity clung to as it aged, there is more truth in them than most would care to admit. It is crude, a lie of sorts, but to describe what is happening it will serve.'

Mersadie frowned. There was something in Keeler's words that sent a prickle of ice over her skin. Behind her, the curtains stirred as a gust of wind blew in through the open windows.

'Euphrati, what's wrong? You never talked like–'

'You need to understand, Mersadie.' Keeler looked up and her eyes were hard, her voice like the falling of an iron blade. 'You must understand, or all is lost.' And her hand spun the disc. The symbols of stone and metal blurred as each ring of the disc began to spin at different speeds – blurred, yet somehow Mersadie could still see each symbol as it flicked around.

'As above, so below. As in the heavens, so on Earth. As in the immaterium, so in the material.'

Mersadie found that she could not look away from the blur of symbols.

'Horus is coming to take the throne of humanity and slay the Emperor. The forces of the warp ride with him. Never has such power been turned to a single goal. In the material, in the world of flesh, the battle is one of blood and fire, but as that battle rages so another battle is being fought beyond. Just as Terra sits at the centre of the cosmos in the beliefs of dead stargazers and fortune tellers, so the Emperor and Terra sit at the centre of the forces aligning in the immaterium.'

The spinning rings of symbols were slowing now. At her back, Mersadie felt a cold blast of air. She almost turned, but Keeler was speaking again, her voice louder than the rising wind.

'The Emperor is holding them back by force of will and by art. He is holding them back and they cannot break Him in the realm beyond. So, they have sent their champion, Horus, to do with bloody hand what they cannot do in spirit. If the defences in the physical world can stand, He can keep the forces of the warp at bay. But if they fail...' The last ring of the disc was slowing. The wind was billowing through the chamber now. A book tumbled off a table, pages flicking over. 'The defences are strong and Rogal Dorn is ready, but he does not see the whole scope of the battle. This is not a battle of three dimensions or even four. It is a war split between realms, in which the actions taken in one world affect the other, in which acts done with mortal hands can echo beyond.'

Mersadie was looking at the arrangement of symbols on the brass disc. She read the alignments, and memory unfolded the meanings in her mind from old parchments that she had thought mere curiosities when she'd read them. She read the position of the planets and the meanings of each of the symbols brought into concordance with them. She looked up at Keeler.

'This is not just a metaphor, is it? These symbols are not based *on* the planets, they *are* the planets. This is a design. A ritual alignment.' She stopped. The glass was shaking in the window frames. The warm dawn light had darkened.

'Marked by blood and slaughter. As above, so below,' said Keeler. 'This is the dimension that Rogal Dorn does not see. If Horus can bring this into being, then the Praetorian's defences will mean nothing. You must reach him. You must tell him before it is too late.

'Remember!' Suddenly she was shouting. 'Remember what you have seen!'

And the circles of symbols rose before Mersadie, no longer stone and metal but burning in the air. She felt them press against her mind, unfolding into inference and meaning that she could not comprehend even as they poured into her.

'Why me?' called Mersadie over the howl that no longer sounded like wind. Light was draining from the dream. 'Why have you asked me to do this?'

'Because I cannot,' said Keeler. 'And because Rogal Dorn believed you before and will again. You showed him the truth of Horus turning on the Emperor. He will believe you.'

'I am in a cell – how can I reach him?'

'A way will open,' said Keeler, her voice lifting over the howl of the rising wind. 'But you will have to walk it.' The floor of the room was shaking. The sky outside was bruised purple and iron. 'They will try to stop you,' said Keeler's face in the dream. 'Old friends and enemies alike. They will come for you.'

A vase toppled off a side table. White flowers and water scattered onto the floor.

'How long until Horus comes?' she shouted.

'He is already here.'

The glass in the window shattered. The storm wind billowed in. Mersadie could smell ash and fire.

And her eyes opened to a world filled with the scream of sirens.

*Void Fortress 693, Trans-Plutonian Gulf*

'Three minutes to impact.'

The voice blared in the dark. Saduran kept his eyes closed, his thoughts still, his heartbeats rising. The double rhythm was still an alien surge through his blood.

'Blood on the stars,' came the call from Ikrek, and the echo roared back from the mouths of the twenty warriors in the assault ram. Saduran shouted the words, but behind his eyes his soul was silent. He heard the clink of mirror-coins and kill talismans against armour and weapon cases.

'Down to the dark, we hold the coins of their lives,' growled Targo, the Cthonian rough-edged as it came from his mouth. Others barked malformed replies. The words, like the clan runes scored into their armour and the gang talismans rattling against their battleplate, were mass-wrought. None of these warriors had even seen Cthonia, much less earned scars in its warrens. They were a mongrel brood pulled from the dark corners of a dozen worlds: Norane, Vortis, Manhansu, Cylor, Neo-geddon and other places forgotten before they were ever known. Gang killers, clan warriors, murder-cult dross. They were alike in

only one way – they all had the capacity to survive what
had been done to them.

The Apothecaries and bio-adepts had begun their produc-
tion in batches of tens of thousands. Drugs and gene-activators
had been dumped into the prospects. Thousands had died
in those first minutes, their bodies pulled from the racks
and dragged to the render vats. The process had continued
without pause. Cutting, implanting, injecting, information
deluged into their brains by hypno-rigs. And as they left each
step, another batch of meat took their place. More died. The
remainder survived, grew, were hacked into the shape of Space
Marines.

When it was over, when they were bonded with armour
and oathed to the Legion, they found themselves Sons of
Horus, warriors in a war that they had not seen the beginning of and which would likely end long after their death.

Many of the new Sons of Horus took the traditions of the
warriors who had been made before the Emperor's betrayal,
and wrapped those trappings around themselves, children
aping adults in the hope of finding a way to belong. Cthonian was the language of that belonging, the emblems of
its gangs the signs of status. Warrior cults proliferated in the
ranks of the newborn: the Sons of the Eye, the Corpse Makers, the Brothers of the Seventh Crow, and more, all threaded
with ritual and the mangled cultures of the worlds that had
given the Legion its fresh blood.

Saduran spoke the words and wore the marks like the
rest, but he had no need of the comfort of belonging. He
could see this universe and this time for what it was – an
age of cruelty and killers, and he needed no mark to know
his place in it.

'Thirty seconds, stand ready,' came the pilot's voice.

Saduran opened his eyes. The red and blue of his helm

display flooded his vision. Ikrek sat opposite, bolter clamped to his harness, a red plume topping his studded helm. The sergeant slammed his closed fist into his chest as the assault ram's booster fired.

'For the Warmaster!'

A scream vibrated through the fuselage as the magna-melta engaged.

The ram's impact snapped through Saduran with bone-breaking force. For a second, he was blind as G-force drained the blood from his eyes. Then the mag-harness snapped free and he was running forwards, the deck ringing under his feet.

His vision cleared in time for him to see Ikrek's head vanish. Ceramite and bone shards rang on Saduran's armour.

The chug-boom of heavy cannons. The double thud of his heartbeats rising.

A round hit Ikrek's corpse as it fell.

Saduran ducked left. His bolter was in his hand.

A round hit the legionary behind him. The warrior gasped as he crumpled.

Target runes flashed red across Saduran's sight. He fired.

They were in a vaulted junction between three wide corridors. Air was rushing out of the edges of the breach punched by the assault ram through the exterior wall. Blast doors were already dropping across the mouths of the corridors. The automated cannon had dropped from a hatch in the roof. Machine-slaved and shielded with ceramite plates, it was pouring shells down onto Saduran and his squad without pause.

'Breach the doors!' shouted Saduran as he fired up at the cannon again. Explosions flashed off its armour plates. Shrapnel scattered from it. Micro-shards pinged from Saduran's helmet like hail. The cannon barrel twitched around to track him.

Four of his squad mates ran towards the closing doors. The cannon barrel swung away from Saduran and put wide holes through two of them. Saduran saw the gleam of a targeting lens nestled next to the cannon's barrel. He put a burst of three rounds into it. The cannon spun, firing blind, shells punching into the deck and walls.

There were no troops yet, but they would come. This was one of the star forts that guarded the approaches to Pluto and the volumes around the Khthonic Gate. Like all the rest it was the size of a battle cruiser, a behemoth of stone and metal three kilometres across, studded with batteries and void shield generators. It took a battle group to kill each one, and ships would be lost doing it. There were ships to spare, though, hundreds of them, and if taken, this star fort could protect a corridor towards Pluto's fortress-moons. Ships could pour through that opening. So, a battalion of newborn Sons of Horus had been unleashed to take the star fort by blade and blood. It was like driving a wedge into a stone sphere – drive deep enough and the sphere would crack, then shatter.

Two of Saduran's squad-brothers reached one of the closing blast doors. They pulled melta charges from their backs, swung them into the ever-narrowing opening at the bottom of the doorway and leapt aside. The charges armed an instant before the descending door met them. Spheres of blinding light screamed into being. The lower section of the door collapsed in a wash of molten metal. Saduran was already running at the breach.

A pressure wave almost knocked him off his feet as a second assault ram punched through the fortress' skin. He kept moving forwards.

Las-fire whipped down the corridor towards him. He could see a barricade slung across the passage, gun barrels jutting from above a slab of plasteel. A cluster of shots hit his left pauldron and forearm. Chunks of ceramite cracked and blew off. He heard shouts as his squad came through the breach behind him. Bolts flew past him and struck the barricade. Mangled Cthonian war cries rose above the sound of gunfire.

There was no point in pausing to fire back; that would get him killed. He needed to be close enough that they would not be able to bring their guns to bear, close enough that the barricade did not protect them. The spear-strike doctrine, many of the other newborn would have called it, perhaps with a touch of reverence and pride in their words. Saduran could see the similarity, but for him it was nothing to do with the old Legion or aping its traditions. It was simply the best way to win.

A las-bolt burned through exposed cable on his left thigh. A warning rune pinged in his sight. He felt the servos in his left leg stutter. He was ten paces from the barricade. There were more of his squad behind him. He exploded into the last few strides and leapt. He saw a trooper in a void-sealed dome helm jerk back, gun rising. The eyes behind the view slit were wide.

Saduran felt time fill the instant, become liquid, become a promise of what was to come. His mind reached back across the short years to running across the chem-crags on the world of his birth, the howls of hunters behind him, the hunger in his stomach and the fear in his chest. That was what the rest of his siblings did not understand. The gang crests and kill marks, the Cthonian war words and titles – all of it was just a false skin over the true gift they had been given.

He hit the top of the barrier and vaulted down into the space beyond. The nearest trooper turned to fire at him.

Saduran fired first. The bolter kicked in his hand. The trooper exploded in a spray of blood and disintegrating armour. Saduran charged down the line of the barricade, bolt-rounds spearing ahead of him. A trooper, braver than the rest, stabbed at him with a chain bayonet. Saduran caught the rifle's barrel behind the spinning blade and yanked it downwards. The trooper's arms snapped, and his shriek rose and cut off as Saduran slammed the human into the barricade wall. Blood slicked the floor, gunfire pulsed in the smoke. Saduran felt his beating hearts and the roar of his blood in his ears, a roll of thunder rising from within.

This was where they were truly reborn, where the skin of their pasts fell away. Not beneath the chirurgeon's blades or in the gene-changes wrought on their flesh, but here in the heat and stink of battle. Here they were remade.

An officer came at him out of the smoke, a glowing power sword in her hand. Saduran felt himself smile as lightning sheathed the human's blade. This was joy, and glory, and life balanced on a razor edge. The officer lunged. He pivoted to the side, switching grip on his gun to fire point-blank into her gut. The bolter clacked empty. The blade stabbed into the air where he had been. She was fast – very fast – and dazzlingly fluid.

Saduran punched forwards, but the officer's sword flicked aside. The blade whipped across his forearm. Ceramite parted. Blood poured out, flashing to smoke as it met the blue haze around the cutting edge. Saduran felt the stimms thump into his blood as his physiology cut the pain away. He rammed his weight forwards. The officer moved aside, and her sword slashed across the plate under his arm…

Fresh pain and the reek of burnt meat inside his armour.

This was the gap between the old and the new. He had been a killer for most of his life, but a warrior of the Legion for only months. He was transhumanly strong and had all the skills that six months of battle hypnosis could give. But he, like his newborn kin, lacked finesse, the honed skill to match their ferocity and strength. This human was just a human, and legionaries should not bleed to the cuts of mortals. He was faster and stronger, but at some level he was still just a youth with the desire to kill, hot-housed into something more than human, but far less than a god.

He dropped his bolter and pulled the combat blade from his belt. The human officer was coiling back, spinning her blade to cut at the vulnerable join at the back of his leg. He reached for her, the fingers of his left hand open to grasp a limb, his knife coming up in his right hand to slam into her gut. Not fast, and not as elegant, but it would still spill her entrails onto the deck.

He did not see the warrior in yellow come for him until it was almost too late.

He caught a blurred reflection in the burnished dome of the officer's helm and leapt back. That one moment saved his life. A chainsword churned sparks from his pauldron. He turned, catching a glimpse of a warrior in yellow battleplate with a plough-fronted helm. He did not have a chance to react other than to bring the combat knife up to jam the cutting teeth of the chainsword as it ripped up towards his gut. With a scream of shearing metal, the blade ripped from his hand. Adamantine teeth sprayed out as the chain track unwound. The warrior in yellow did not even pause but punched the guard into Saduran's faceplate. Saduran staggered, hit the barricade wall behind him and cannoned forwards, dipping his shoulder to hit the yellow warrior – but his foe was no new breed. This was a veteran son of Dorn, seasoned both in war and in killing former brothers. The warrior stepped back, lightning-flash fast, brought a pistol up, and fired.

Saduran fell backwards, pain exploding through him. A second shell exploded in the crater ripped by the first. Blood, black bone and shattered armour sprayed out. He fell, gasping, pain flooding his nerves and blood drowning his breath. The warrior in yellow had shifted his aim to pump shells into Saduran's brothers as they came at the barricade. The human officer was moving towards Saduran, blade still ready. A ragged clutch of soldiers were at her back, firing. None of them were looking at Saduran. He was dead, a bag of meat in the shape of a legionary thrown aside by the tide of war. His world was a red-smeared blur.

The officer stepped close to him, put a foot on his ruined chest and brought the point of her sword to his neck. He drew a bloody breath as she tensed to ram the blade tip up under his chin. His hand flashed out. She tried to stab, but his hand was already around her wrist, gripping and crushing. Bones shattered, and he yanked her off her feet. He turned the blade in her hand, breaking fingers like twigs and sawed it into her neck.

He rose, roaring as the pain tried to pull him down. Blood and fragments of his blasted armour fell from him. The Imperial Fist turned, but too slow and too late. Saduran rammed the human officer's powerblade up into the legionary's gut.

He heard shouts and the shrieking boom of a melta charge blowing a hole in the barricade, but his world was red, and smelled of iron, and the sound of his hearts beating in his chest drowned out the rest.

*Prison ship* Aeacus, *Uranus high orbit*

Mersadie awoke and came to her feet as the cell flooded with red light. Sirens howled. The floor was shaking. Everything was shaking. Gunfire and ricochets echoed through the cell door. She took a step back.

The door slammed inwards. She had a second to see a guard in red armour and a silver mask, a gun rising in his hands. The holes in its black barrel loomed wide in her eyes. The deck pitched. Mersadie slammed into a wall as the room turned over. The guard's gun fired. Shot and sound filled the air. She struck a wall, and felt the air rush from her lungs. The guard tumbled from the door, arms and gun flailing. The room spun over again. Mersadie rose from the wall, floating, scrabbling at air. The guard hit a wall and rebounded. Red pearls of blood sprayed out from the bottom edge of his mask. She crashed into him. The gun went off again, and the guard's gun arm yanked him up with a crack of shattering bone. Shot ricocheted off the floor and walls. Mersadie screamed as she felt something punch into her back. The guard was spinning back, limbs slack, blood seeping from him in spheres. Mersadie was turning over and over, the open door, ceiling and walls flicking past.

Gravity snapped back into force, and hauled her to the ground. The guard landed on top of her in a tangle of limbs. She gasped. The sirens screamed on, the world red. She tried to shove the guard off her. Muscles wasted by seven years of confinement in small spaces screamed. The guard spasmed. A wet gurgle came from his cracked chrome mask. Mersadie shoved up with all her strength and pitched him onto the floor. She scrabbled to the side. The guard was twitching, retching. She looked at the door, red light flashing beyond. She could hear shouts and screams over the alarms.

'*You must reach him,*' Keeler's voice hissed in her thoughts. She pushed herself up and took a step towards the door.

'Pl…' the guard wheezed. Mersadie hesitated, then turned. 'Please…' he said. She could hear the pain in his voice.

She could see a sliver of his face through his broken mask: young, blood running from lips and grey eyes looking back at her. She took a step back towards him. His eye was steady on hers. The gun came up. It was a pistol, the barrel a black circle looking up at her. She had a frozen second to realise that he must have been working it free as she pushed him off. She saw the effort twist his face as he began to pull the trigger. She dived back at the door. A bullet struck the frame. She twisted and scrambled back as another bullet slammed into the wall just above her. She gripped the cell door by its locking handle and yanked it shut. Then she was up and running, bare feet thumping into the grated floor as bullets struck the plasteel behind her.

She ran past more cells. Some were open. Bodies, red and wet, lay on the floor inside. She heard hands hammering and muffled shouting from others. The floor lurched again. She could see a sealed door across the corridor ahead, yellow and black chevrons painted across it. She was thirty paces from it. Her run faltered.

The yellow-and-black door slammed open. Mersadie froze. Guards in red-and-black armour with silver masks came through, alarm lights flashing from their visors. Shouts filled the air. She could see a wider space beyond the door, metal, blinking light filling a wide, vaulted junction.

'Help!' The shout came from beside her. The first guard through the door had a quad-barrelled cannon braced in his arms. Mersadie had a second to see her reflection in the guard's mask. There was nowhere to go, nowhere to run.

The space beyond the yellow-and-black door vanished. The shriek of shearing metal tore through the air. The guard with the quad-cannon flew back through the doorway as though yanked by a rope. Mersadie lunged for an open cell to her left. A howling wind poured down the corridor. Her hand caught the edge of a door as the deck pitched down. She cried out as her full body weight wrenched her arm. Debris streamed past her. Where the end of the corridor had been, there was now starlight and flame. For a second she stared down at it, unable to look away.

She could see the pale blue orb of a planet hanging against a field of stars. Shapes glimmered in the dark, light catching on the hulls and prows of ships, and the towers of void-stations. It was beautiful, a serene and terrifying image. Fire streaked across the view. Explosions burst into being. Lines of flame and energy latticed the void. A piece of debris spun across the view, blocking out the sight of the planet and stars. Dust scattered into the vacuum from the chewed metal.

*No*, the thought flashed through Mersadie's mind. *Not dust. Those are people.*

An emergency blast door slammed shut over the breach. The howl of evacuating air stopped. The red alarm lights still flashed, their rhythm stuttering. The sirens had silenced. Ash drifted past Mersadie as she hung, panting, blood draining from the open cell doors in the corridor above to patter on the wall below like rain. Mersadie could suddenly hear her own heaving breaths. Gravity lurched again, and the corridor pitched back to near-true. She half fell to the floor and then pulled herself upright.

The sudden quiet was somehow worse than the noise it had replaced – as if she had been plunged into water and was waiting for the air in her lungs to run out.

'Help!' The shout came again, louder now, echoing off the metal surfaces. She looked around. 'Here! Over here!'

She saw it then – an eye pressed against an open view hole in a sealed cell door.

'Get me out!' called the voice.

She looked away, up at the other end of the locked corridor. Her mind was racing.

'Listen, you have to get me out,' said the voice, high with panic. 'This ship is coming apart. Whatever air we have is not going to last.'

Mersadie looked at the cell door. It was a rust-edged slab of metal. The lock control beside it was a cog-ringed set of slots.

'Find one of the guards,' called the voice, as though reading her hesitation. 'There will be the corpse of one of those bastards somewhere. They had key medallions around their necks.'

Mersadie did not move.

'Who are you?' she asked, meeting the gaze of the eye looking through the view hole.

'Who am I?' said the voice. 'I am like you – someone who has spent a long time locked up and doesn't want to die.'

Mersadie held the gaze. No matter where she was now, the Nameless Fortress that had been her prison had held people who for one reason or another were too dangerous to set free.

A shiver ran through the deck. Metal creaked. Mersadie looked up as the sound ran up and down the passage.

'This ship won't last long,' called the voice. 'That explosive decompression meant that it's already taken a heavy hit or been ripped in two. What's left of it is going to shear apart.' Mersadie took a step away from the cell door. 'I can help get us both out.'

'How?'

'I know ships. This is a Promitor-class transport. We are in a sub-level two decks down from a hangar bay. I can get us there.' Another creaking shiver echoed down the passage. 'Do you want to live or not?' Mersadie held still for a second, and then she was moving along the tilted corridor, looking in the open cells.

'Quickly, quickly!' called the voice from behind her.

There were corpses and bits of corpses in every cell: limbs and bodies piled at the lower edges of the sloping floor. She found the body of a guard wedged in a cell doorway. The heavy hatch had clanged shut like a mouth when the gravity had pitched, mashing the guard against the door frame. She pushed the door wide, and began to feel for the lock medallion around the corpse's neck. A raw-meat reek was rising in the remaining air. Mersadie tasted bile as her mouth ran with saliva, and fought to keep herself from vomiting. The scars of point-blank shotcannon blasts marked the cell walls, and the body of another prisoner lay sprawled close by.

She stopped, the facts piling up to conclusions in her mind. The guards had been going down the cells, executing the prisoners when the ship was hit. They had been making sure that no one got out, that no one fell into... enemy hands.

*'How long until Horus comes?'*

*'He is already here.'*

'Faster, faster!' came the voice down the corridor. The walls were creaking. A pipe burst beneath the floor grating. Steam billowed into the corridor. Her hand found the medallion on a plasteel chain, wrenched it free and ran back to the closed cell door. The medallion was slick with blood, the edges toothed like a cog. 'Come on, come on!' She slotted the medallion into the lock. It turned. The door released with a thump of bolts and pistons. 'Yes-yes-yes!'

A figure came through the door as it hinged wide. He was tall, very tall, and rake-thin, grey-white skin pulled taut across his bones, jumpsuit hanging like a sack from his frame. Mersadie looked up at his face, and froze. A band of metal circled his skull, riveted in place, holding a thick disc of iron across his forehead.

'You are a Navigator...' she breathed.

'Well observed,' he said, glancing around as a fresh tremor shook the deck. The Navigator hissed an expletive and began to run with long, loping strides. Mersadie followed.

The corridor pitched and twisted, throwing them into a wall as they reached a sealed hatchway barring their path.

'Gravity systems are failing,' said the Navigator. Mersadie pushed herself up and tugged him back onto his feet. His arm felt almost fragile in her grasp. 'Structural collapse won't be far behind.'

'How far to the hangar?' asked Mersadie. Her head was spinning.

'Ten minutes, maybe,' said the Navigator, starting off again. 'If it is there at all.'

'You said–'

'I said that I knew ships. If this death-hulk has a standard layout, and *if* the decks beneath this one have not been flooded with fire or reduced to slag, then there should be a hoist shaft a few turns beyond this door.'

Mersadie slotted the key medallion into the hatch lock, and hoped that whatever luck had smiled on her so far would do so again.

Lights flashed a dim green on the lock console, and the hatch opened a crack, then the green lights faded. Mersadie shoved and felt the power-drained servo hinges give. A narrow gap opened. She squeezed through, the Navigator following.

Fading yellow emergency lights filled the wide passage beyond. Mersadie could smell smoke and burnt plastek. She moved forwards, matching the Navigator's loping strides. 'Of course, I'm presuming that there is nothing that's going to try to kill us between here and there,' he said.

Gunfire laced from the dark. Mersadie ducked against a wall, bracing as a shape scuttled into view, hugging the ground on chromed spider legs, a gun mount on its back. Blasts of las-fire burned from the thing as it came forwards. The Navigator was curled against the passage wall, hands pressed against his ears.

'Is that the hoist?' shouted Mersadie. She could see a chevron-marked recess set in a wide opening fifteen paces down the passage between them and the spider-machine.

'It is in the right place, but–'

She ran, ducking low and aiming for the door to the hoist platform. Las-blasts scattered across the deck behind her. She reached the opening and darted inside. The hoist platform swayed under her.

'Come on!' she shouted back at the Navigator. The spider machine had paused, its gun tracking to get a clean shot at her. The Navigator glanced up and sprinted towards her, hands still held to his ears. The spider-machine pivoted its gun and fired. Las-blasts left glowing splashes on the walls. Mersadie jammed the key medallion into the hoist door controls, hoping that they still had enough power to function. The floor under her feet lurched and began to slide downwards. The Navigator gave a cry, rose and sprinted towards the hoist opening. Las fizzed in his wake as the spider-machine scuttled after him, firing wildly. He dropped onto the descending platform beside her, yelping with pain as he landed.

The spider-machine reached the lip of the opening as the roof of the hoist came down. Its gun rotated down to fire an instant before the edge of the roof crushed it into the floor. Something in its body exploded. Bits of metal and rubber showered down onto Mersadie.

'Whatever luck you bring seems to be holding,' laughed the Navigator.

'If the shuttle is there, can you pilot it?' asked Mersadie as she gasped for air.

'Yes,' said the Navigator, 'I can.'

Mersadie coughed, and gulped breaths as the hoist juddered down through the dark. Every now and then she felt the shaft shake and the groan as the metal of the ship strained.

The shuttle was there when they reached the bottom. Three shuttles, in fact, red and black, their wings swept forward, held silent in the cradles above the hangar deck. Everything else was carnage. Mangled servitors lay on the deck, crushed by machinery that had tumbled through the space and now lay in smashed heaps. The reek of fuel hid the smell of blood, and her feet splashed in puddles of promethium as they ran to the remaining craft.

'No…' hissed the Navigator, glancing at the first shuttle, and then moving on. 'No…'

He reached the last, gave a snort, keyed a rune on the cradle and pulled himself up onto the ramp of the machine. Mersadie followed. He was already strapping himself into the pilot cradle, muttering and keying controls.

'I am going to need your help,' he said, eyes moving over the console, as Mersadie strapped herself into the second cradle.

'What do you need me to do?'

'Hand on the controls and hold her steady,' he said, his fingers moving over buttons and dials like a clavier player's.

The shuttle lurched, and then began to hum. Engine noise rose.

'I don't know how far this will get us,' he said, 'but so far our luck is holding… Now, hold steady.'

She did not answer. Exhaustion had begun to fall on her like the blow of a hammer. Her head was throbbing with pain.

'Nilus,' he said.

She raised her head.

'My name is Nilus,' he repeated and gave a smile. 'Nilus of House Yeshar.'

He keyed a control. The blast doors to the external void shook, trembling as power-starved systems fought to obey. A crack opened, grew wider and stopped. The air in the hangar drained out, rocking the shuttle in its cradle.

'Mersadie,' she said, eyes fixed on the doors. 'I am Mersadie Oliton.'

Nilus grinned. 'Well, Mersadie Oliton, I am not sure this thing will fit through that gap, so I may have begun introductions prematurely.' As the shuttle's engines roared to life, the spilled fuel soaking the hangar deck ignited in the last of the air. Flames streamed past the shuttle through the open doors. Mersadie found her hands were gripping the controls hard.

The docking cradle released, and the shuttle shot forwards, through the gap, fins almost catching the doors. Behind them, the chewed stern of the ship that had been their prison tumbled on through a cloud of its own debris.

G-force punched through her, draining blood from her sight, forcing the breath from her lungs in a gasp. She had a brief image of smeared stars and flashes of white fire. Nilus had gone still, his long-fingered hands locked on the controls.

'Sweet blood of the ancestors...' he breathed. Then the world went black and she could feel the burning void reaching out to greet them.

# FOUR

---

Burning heaven
Prisoners
The Falcon and the cage

*Cordelia Void Habitat, Uranus high orbit*

The stream of plasma flicked across the domed viewport, touched the next dock spar along from the *Antius*, and cut it from the habitat in a silent burst of fire. A kilometre-long arm of stone and metal hinged free of the station, then began to tumble away, scattering molten debris. The ships locked into the docks on the severed spar fell with it. One ship fired its engines to try to get free and ripped the skin from its hull. It flew into the void, spinning, scattering its guts to glitter against the light of the planet. A blast wave of micro debris hit the *Antius* a second later. The hauler's hull rang as though it were a tin roof in a hail storm.

Cadmus Vek saw cracks spread across the dome as pieces of shrapnel struck it. The ship was shaking in its dock clamps.

'Get us loose!' he shouted.

'We have to wait for the captain,' called Sub-mistress Koln. 'She was on the main dock limb.'

'You are the captain now – get us free!' he shouted.

'But–'

'Now!'

Koln hesitated. Her lined face was pale, eyes wide with growing panic. Some of the crew around her had stopped; some even looked like they were about to make for the bridge doors.

'No, I can't,' began Koln. 'The captain–'

Vek pulled the pistol from his gown. It was small, but it felt heavy and strange in his hand. Koln looked at the pistol as he levelled it at her. Shock pulled her mouth wide.

'Cast off,' he said. He saw anger flush red into her face.

Something huge exploded in a starburst of blue and white beyond the dome above. Koln flinched, and nodded.

'All stations, make ready to cast off. Begin the count.'

'There are still people crossing in the dock limbs,' called one of the junior officers.

'Sound the disconnection alarms,' said Koln, 'they will run if they want to live.'

Vek could see anger hardening in Koln as she gave the orders. She would never forgive him for what she was having to do. If she found the courage, she might one day try to kill him for it. If they survived the next five minutes, he could live with that.

'Reactor output rising to sixty per cent,' called Chi-32-Beta. Out of all the crew, the enginseer seemed the least concerned about the events unfolding around them. Hunched and swathed in her robes of patchwork red and dirty-white, she moved between the bridge systems as though there was no hurry in the world. The rest of the crew were scrambling to get wired into their posts, shouting orders or questions.

'All systems confirm ready to cast off,' called Koln. The

replies came, rattling off loud, tension finding an outlet in noise.

'Engines, aye!'

'Helm, aye!'

'Auspex, aye!'

On and on. The hull was vibrating now as cold machines woke in its guts. The *Antius* was a small ship, barely a third of a kilometre from stern to prow. Most of its bones and skin had been hauled from a wreck-drift and remade by skilled hands now long dead and forgotten. It was neither fast or slow, but it had reliably moved indentured labour and ore between Uranus' moons and asteroid belts for centuries. It had stood up to pirates and survived a conquest that had been renamed 'compliance'. Now Vek hoped she would prove to be the survivor again.

Koln turned.

'There are still people running along the dock limbs towards the ship. We can't cast off.'

'Give the order,' snapped Vek. *And if you truly listen, Lord and Master of Mankind,* he said in his thoughts, *have mercy on me for this.*

Sweat beaded on Koln's sagging cheeks and hung from her chin.

'Seal all doors and hatches,' she said. Lights flashed on consoles. Quiet had fallen across the bridge as suddenly as the falling of an axe. A junior officer looked up at Koln and nodded. 'Release anchor cradle, release docking limbs.'

Koln looked back at Vek, fire in her eyes again, lips pulling back from teeth to spit whatever she was about to say.

A glint caught Vek's eye. He began to look up at the dome in the roof of the bridge. Something huge was moving across the pale circle of Uranus' light.

A flash.

He opened his mouth to shout...

White light...

So bright it swallowed sense and sound...

Blindness...

Gasping...

The metal deck beneath his hands and knees.

Then a roaring, shouts filling his ears as he rose, neon scars swimming in front of his eyes.

'Full power to engines!' shouted Koln. She was clinging on to her command console, her face drained of colour. Something struck the ship and the deck pitched. Beyond the viewport, the void was on fire.

Cordelia Habitat was gone. Chunks of debris rode a silent wave of destruction, spinning like pieces of shattered rock. He could see the shapes of habitation clusters, and the long tines of a dock spur with ships still locked in place, their hulls holed, fuel and air trailing after them. The *Antius* lurched and the view slid, and he saw streaks of light slicing across the stars, flashing the colours of jewels – burning topaz, ruby fire, cold sapphire. Ships moved across his vision then, either so vast or so close that he could see their jagged outlines with his naked eyes...

Hundreds of them...

*Thousands* of them.

It was almost beautiful...

The ship bucked forwards. Pitted metal plates began to slam shut over the view. Koln was shouting orders.

'Drop us down fast, then cut power.'

'If we do that we'll lose manoeuvrability,' called one of the other officers. 'We won't be able to get–'

'You want to look like a threat to whatever just cooked the whole habitat?' Koln yelled. 'Follow your orders or you can go and join those we just left behind.'

*Those we left behind…*

Vek found that he still had the dead weight of the pistol in his hand. He looked down at it. He was shaking.

'Sir.' The voice was low, pitched to draw attention from him but no one else. He looked up. Aksinya stood just by his shoulder. He felt a wave of relief at the sight of the lifeward.

She had served his mother before him and his grandmother before that. Tall, with the willowy thinness of the void-born, she looked as though she would break at a touch, an impression enhanced by the signs of her age. Ash-white skin clung to skeletal limbs, dotted with dark liver spots. A crest of false, carbon-thread hair sat atop her head, and she held herself straight and stiff. The grey-and-black mesh-woven fabric of her long coat, and the white lace at her cuffs and throat completed the impression of a noble's tutor, or widow-matriarch, an impression that was utterly false. She was old, that much was true, but he had seen her move so fast you could blink and miss it, and break plasteel with a blow from her open hand.

He caught a reflection of himself in her implanted optic lenses: a man running to fat, swathed in a heavy silk and brocade gown, dark skin sheened with sweat, a gun that he was not sure how to use hanging in his hand. The contrast with the woman who guarded his family was so stark in that moment that it might have made him laugh.

'Are they safe?' he asked.

'In the captain's quarters with Nikal and Coba standing guard. It might be too much to hope that they sleep, but they are quiet at least.' Aksinya gave a small smile and the wrinkled skin of her face creased beneath the black lenses of her eyes. 'Oh, if we all had the strength of the young.'

'Thank you, Aksinya,' he said, and heard the crack reach into his voice. 'For everything.'

Aksinya gave a small shake of her head, still smiling.

'It is my life and my service, sir.'

He nodded, not sure what else to say. She was the reason he, his daughter and his son were alive. It had been her who had picked up the threat alert on the habitat's command comms channels before the alert sirens were triggered. That had given them enough time to alert the *Antius* and reach the dock. Barely...

'How many...' he began, his eyes pulled back to the gun in his hand.

'About a thousand made it onto the ship,' said Aksinya, replying to the question as it caught on his tongue. 'Most of them are in the cargo holds. I took the liberty of ensuring that the bulkheads to the rest of the ship were sealed. They are in shock for now, but that won't last, and shock and grief can change to anger as reality sinks in.'

He nodded. People had swarmed towards the docks as the sirens had wailed, driven by raw terror. He could remember, years ago, when the news of the Warmaster's rebellion against the Emperor had arrived. There had been riots. Peace enforcers had been brought in. There had been deaths, arrests. After that, the hand of the Praetorian had fallen firmly on everything and had not let go. Harsh order and unforgiving rule had settled on them – uncomfortable at first, but then familiar. Vek had seen some of his assets seized, stores of metal ore requisitioned under edict and two of his family's hauler-ships pressed into service as troop transports. Others had suffered worse, too, but discomfort was not loss.

Time had passed, and the fear that war would come to the Solar System had become a promise that would never be fulfilled. There had been incidents – the Ariel mining operation shutting down, the alert and lockdown, a wave of detentions – but the lies put out to explain them had been enough to return people to the comforting sense that the conflict was a long way away. That state, like the warships passing through orbit, the checks on movement and the ever-watching eye of authority, had just become the way things were. Life had gone on.

When Aksinya had woken him a few hours ago and said that he and his family needed to get to a ship *now*, he had wanted it to be a lie.

'And how many... how many were in the dock when we cast off?' he said.

Aksinya shook her head. 'I don't... Sir...' She paused. 'That is not a wise question to ask.'

He looked at her and was about to reply.

The ship pitched.

Lights flashed across consoles on the bridge. Warning chimes sounded.

Vek looked around.

'Blast wave,' said Koln, without looking around. 'Calis Station just detonated.' Her voice was cold, shuttered with control. 'There are a lot of big energy and mass signatures out there. A lot...'

'Warships?' Vek asked.

Koln shrugged but still did not turn to him. 'We only have basic navigation sensors – how am I supposed to know?'

'Signal incoming!' shouted one of the deck officers.

'Source?' called Koln.

'Small craft. It's close. Maybe a shuttle. The message is in clear,' said the signal officer. 'It's a distress call using Solar void-cant.'

'Cut it,' said Koln. 'We can't–'

'No,' said Vek. The sound of his own voice surprising him. Koln looked at him, and he could see the anger rising up her neck, flushing colour into her face.

'They could be anyone,' said Koln. 'It's a military craft. Picking it up makes us a target.'

'Everything out here is a target,' snapped Vek.

'You order us to leave thousands of people behind and now you want us to–'

'We would have died with them,' shouted Vek, his own anger rising. 'This is someone we can save.' He shook his head, exhaustion quenching the rage as quickly as it had ignited. Koln was looking at him, confusion plain on her face. 'This is someone we can save...' he repeated, turning and dropping into an empty seat beside a console.

Koln looked at him for a long moment and nodded.

'Answer the distress call,' she said.

The shuttle's rear hatch released with a hiss. Mersadie unfastened her harness, and then paused. Nilus was already up out of his seat and moving towards the opening hatch. He looked back at her.

'Come on,' he said. She did not move. 'What in the name of the stars could be keeping you there?'

Mersadie shook her head. A sudden feeling had flooded her, drowning the relief she had felt when the ship had answered their distress call. She had come to as the shuttle spun through a void filled with the flash of explosions, racing towards the promise of a sanctuary. Now the sudden quiet of the hangar after the outer doors had closed on the fire-touched void somehow felt more threatening than the light of battle and the flare of dying ships.

Nilus frowned, the expression creasing around the metal plate riveted to his forehead.

'What?' he asked.

The hatch touched the deck outside.

'Out!' came the hard command. 'If you have weapons in

your hands, we will shoot. If you do not comply, we will shoot.'

Mersadie took a deep breath, raised her hands and walked out into the light.

The hangar outside was small, a box of weathered metal just large enough to take the shuttle and leave space for the group of figures that waited for them. There were five: two nervous-looking troopers in blue-and-silver uniforms, which were too clean for them to have seen much use; a very tall woman in black and grey; another woman in a blue and gold-braid uniform Mersadie could not place; and lastly a heavy-framed man with polished-walnut skin. Bonded opals dotted his forehead, and his eyes were cautious. One of the troopers shifted his grip on his shotgun.

'Who are you?' snapped the woman in the blue and gold-braid uniform.

'You're the captain of this ship?' asked Mersadie.

'This is smelling more wrong by the second,' snarled the uniformed woman at the heavyset man.

'Please,' said Mersadie. 'I need to speak to your captain.'

The very tall woman raised a hand. She had barely moved since Mersadie had exited the shuttle. The woman's face was old, but there was a strength to it and a sharpness to her gaze that reminded Mersadie of a sword's edge.

'That shuttle is a Corona-class lander,' said the tall woman, carefully, without looking away from them. 'Well-maintained and armed, but with no markings. Military or paramilitary, but look at her clothing.' The woman pointed a long finger at Mersadie. 'Worn, utilitarian, nothing metallic even on the fastenings, alphanumerics stitched into collar and cuffs – prison garb.' The tall woman turned and looked at the man with the opal studded brow. 'Sir, you own this ship, what do you wish done?'

The man stepped forwards. He looked exhausted, thought Mersadie, as though the universe had already piled more onto his shoulders than he ever thought he would be able to bear.

'Who are you?' he asked, looking just at Mersadie.

'My name is Mersadie Oliton,' she said.

'Why were you a prisoner, Mersadie Oliton?'

She looked at him, thinking of what the truth would do in this moment, and then gave the only answer that came to mind.

'I can't say.'

'Then you must remain a prisoner on this ship,' he said, and nodded to the tall woman. The troopers moved forwards.

'Please,' said Mersadie, sudden panic rising as they gripped her arms. 'I need to reach Terra, I need to reach the Praetorian.'

The officer in blue and gold-braid laughed, and then turned away as the troopers shoved Mersadie down to her knees and bound her hands behind her back.

*Bhab Bastion, The Imperial Palace, Terra*

Su-Kassen heard the door lock behind her, and closed her eyes. The smell of her chambers grew as she drew her breath. Relief crept into her for a moment as the quiet inside replaced the pulse of the sirens outside the Palace. She remained still, letting the moment stretch as she held the familiar scents in her nose: the tinge of hulkar smoke, cold stone and old fabric.

As senior officer of the Solar Defence command, she rated a mansion complex amongst the Imperial Palace's tangle of towers and halls. She had avoided having to refuse such an offer by requesting a billet in the Bhab Bastion itself. Rogal Dorn himself had asked her why.

'*I learnt my craft on warships,*' she had replied. '*I rest where I fight.*'

He had nodded but not smiled, but an hour later she had been granted her request.

The Bhab Bastion stuck up from the mass of the Imperial Palace like the stump of a felled tree. Half a kilometre wide at its base, it was a cliff-sided block of undressed stone. It had been built when the land around it was a wasteland. For decades it had sat inviolate as the Palace had grown around it, replacing the desolation it had guarded with colonnades, domes and statue-capped spires. There had been rumours that it had defied multiple attempts to level it with increasingly apocalyptic quantities of explosives, until the Sigillite himself had ordered the mason-armies to leave it standing. Now, with gun nests crowding the Palace roofs, and void shields sparking above the armour-coated towers, the Bhab Bastion's defiance seemed less of an ugly reminder of the past and more a warning of the future. When Rogal Dorn had begun to fortify the Palace in the wake of Horus' treachery, he had made the Bhab Bastion the seat of his command. And for half a decade, a cluster of three small rooms set one-third of the way up its northern face had been Su-Kassen's home.

Sleep. By all of Jupiter's storms, she needed sleep.

A static crackle ran over her skin, and a smell of burnt dust and storm-charge replaced the taste of smoke. They were test-firing the bastion's tertiary void shields again.

She opened her eyes, and was met by the gloom of the main chamber. She blinked and hung her uniform jacket from the iron hook on the wall without needing to look. A pair of round eyes lit at the other end of the room as Kelik woke. A clicking caw disturbed the quiet. She smiled and went forwards, picking up the falconer's gauntlet from a low table.

'Hush,' she said. 'It's still day, not time for you to hunt yet.' The gyre-hawk gave another unimpressed call as Su-Kassen released the catch on the cage. Kelik eyed her for a moment and then hopped onto her arm, ignored the gauntlet and climbed up to her shoulder. His claws dug into the ballistic weave and she winced. He blinked once, slowly, giving the distinct air of contempt. Su-Kassen laughed and moved to light the water pipe. It began to bubble as she moved around the room.

A low table of ancient cedar sat at the centre of the room between two worn floor cushions. A Saturnian power sabre hung on the wall above a brass-framed box that held one of the twin shot-pistols she had taken from a drift pirate captain in her first ship action – long ago now.

She should sleep. She only had two hours before she was back on station, but she knew she would not be able to, and besides, she found more rest in these few moments of mundane reality than in the dreams that would come to her if she slept.

She was drawing a cup of spice tea when Kelik flinched on her shoulder, head suddenly raised, eyes open and fixed on the door. The knock came a second later. She froze for a second.

Who would come to find her here? If it was an alert or crisis there were procedures, signals, but the vox set into the chamber wall remained silent. She lifted the shot-pistol out of its box, loading and cocking it with practised smoothness. There were guards throughout the bastion, security screens, and warriors of Dorn's Huscarl retinue. But something had sent ice prickling her skin, and she had nearly died enough times not to ignore that warning.

'Identify yourself,' she ordered, levelling the pistol at the closed door.

'One who would have your counsel,' came the reply. Su-Kassen felt the breath hiss from her lungs with surprise. Then she shook herself and released the door lock.

'My apologies for disturbing your rest, admiral,' said Jaghatai Khan.

'My lord...' she began, bowing her head.

'Please,' he said, smiling and bowing his own head. 'The impoliteness of an unexpected visitor negates all need for formality.'

'What has happened?' she asked, mind still whirling.

'Nothing,' said the Khan. 'At least nothing that requires you for the moment.' His eyes were like shards of ice catching sunlight. His presence was like the touch of the wind blowing across a mountain. On her shoulder, Kelik gave a soft call, and shifted his perch. She shook herself and stepped aside.

'Please,' she said, pulling the Chogorian words of hospitality from memory, suddenly aware of the shot-pistol still in her hand. 'Enter as a friend.'

The Khan's smile broadened.

'I am humbled. May fortune flow from your generosity.'

He bowed his head before stepping forwards to pass through the door. The movement was slow, she noticed, unhurried, like the padding of a snow leopard across a glacier. All of that inhuman, dazzling speed was absent, replaced by poise. He did not wear his armour, but a coat of soft, black leather, lined and edged with white fur over layers of silk. The jewelled pommels of knives gleamed at his waist, and silver rings circled his fingers with falcons and snakes. His hair gleamed with oil and clinked with beads of copper, lapis and moonstone. He looked, she thought, just what he was: a warlord untamed by time or place.

She motioned to the cushions on the floor, tapping more

glow-globes to life. The Khan's gaze moved across the room with a fleeting glance that she was sure had taken in every detail. His eyes paused as she unloaded the shot-pistol and replaced it in its box beside the empty space left by the other half of the paired weapons.

'A spoil of battle without its twin,' he said, sitting on one of the cushions. Arrayed in half-plate and silks, he somehow looked utterly at ease in the small space despite his size.

'I gave the other away,' she said, offering him a glass of spice tea.

'To another warrior?' he said, accepting the glass and taking a sip.

'To my daughter.'

'Of course… Where does she serve?'

'I think you know that, my lord.'

She held his gaze for a second. His smile dimmed, and he nodded.

'Captain Khalia Su-Kassen Hon II, last recorded deployment as officer commanding the *Thunder Break*, attached to the Sixty-Third Expeditionary Fleet under the command of the Sixteenth Legion… the Sons of Horus.'

She nodded and held his gaze. Her thoughts had gone very still.

'Yes, my lord.'

'Prior to the betrayal, of course,' he added.

'How may I serve, lord?' she said, taking a seat opposite him.

He looked at her and then around the small room.

'You have doubts about my brother's method of fighting this war.'

'I helped devise the battle plans, lord. I have no doubts.' She paused.

The Khan smiled, but his eyes had moved to where Kelik

still perched on her shoulder. The gyre-hawk gave a soft caw, unfolded his wings and glided to the Khan's wrist. He grinned, eyes flashing as they met the bird's gaze.

'A Jovian void officer who speaks Chogorian, keeps a gyre-hawk and serves Terran spice tea on a table of cedar wood. You are a strange example of your kind, admiral.'

'Perhaps, but are those things truly strange, my lord? I grew up in ships, in orbital shoal habitats, in corridors and spaces of metal where there was no sky, and trees lived only in tales.'

'A cage,' said the Khan, raising a finger and stroking Kelik's crest. 'You lived in a cage of ideas. You broke its bars and now find more comfort in reminders that life is more than iron and stone, and death in darkness.'

'I like things that are different from what I knew.' She shrugged.

'But after this time is past, after your rest is done, you return them to their cage. You put back the ideas and oaths and become the warrior that you were made into. You go back to the small spaces you ran from.'

Su-Kassen felt herself frown. The thread of this conversation had flowed and turned in just a few moments in ways that made it difficult to follow. It was as though there were something that the Khan's words were circling but not touching, some end which she could not see.

'The first reports from Uranus arrived just after you left the command chamber,' he said, and glanced at her, then looked back at the gyre-hawk. Kelik flicked his wings and opened his beak wide. Su-Kassen had the sudden impression that the bird was smiling.

'A beautiful creature. Too beautiful to be in a cage. Keep one like this from the sky and it will go mad. You let him hunt, though, I can tell.'

'When I can, I take him up to the parapets, and let him fly.'

'And he always returns?'

'Yes.'

The Khan smiled, then his face darkened, the expression like cloud passing over the sun.

'The sirens sound outside, on and on. At Actinus Hive, an hour ago, ten thousand people took their own lives by sealing a zone of the hive and cutting off the air that kept them alive. The last message from inside the zone said that they could hear the howling of wolves when they dreamed and when they woke. There are others, too, smaller in scale but multiplying by the hour. Mars has fallen silent. Fire and fear spreads and spreads. Just before I knocked at your door, I was told that there have been pleas from Triton and the moon colonies of Neptune. They can see the battle-light from Pluto. They are asking for the ships taken from their orbits to be returned. They want help. They want the Praetorian of Terra to save them.'

Silence filled the moment.

'Uranus holds?' she asked at last. She thought of the ships, the hundreds of ships that had been redeployed from other planets to bolster the defence of the Elysian Gate. She thought of the resources pulled from Neptune to bolster Uranus' defences. She thought of the cost paid by every enclave left undefended so that the traitors would have to fight and bleed to control Uranus and the gate it guarded.

'I am called the Warhawk,' said the Khan, 'but maybe only because I was given a sky to fly in. My brother, Dorn, has only ever known cages – duty, honour, strength. And for every bar of every cage that has been placed around him by someone else he has made those bars stronger. He has made his cages smaller and stronger until to spread his wings would rip him apart.'

The Khan raised his arm and Kelik spread its wings and glided back to Su-Kassen's shoulder.

'You are right to question the way that this battle is being fought, admiral,' he said. 'You are right to allow your heart to doubt, and you are right to speak those doubts to my brother. He listens to you. He trusts you. And the way that he is choosing to fight this battle is maybe the last cage that he has made for himself.'

'You think he is wrong?'

'No, I think he is right, but that what he is having to do is breaking him. But he needs to hear the voice that tells him the price and lets him choose to do as he must. He needs to be allowed the moment of flight before he returns to the cage of necessity.'

The Khan stood and bowed. Su-Kassen rose to her feet, but he raised a hand to still her.

'My thanks, admiral, for your hospitality, and for letting me speak as I will.'

She bowed her head, unsure what to say.

The Khan walked to the door, opened it, and then turned, looking back at her.

'The enemy have come through the Elysian Path off Uranus in great force. The orbits of its moons are aflame. But Uranus holds.' He gave a sad smile. 'It holds.'

PART TWO

# THROUGH THE
# ECHOING DARK

# FIVE

Lord of Summer Lightning
Inferno at the edge of light
Brotherhood

*Battleship* Lance of Heaven, *Supra-Solar Gulf*

The Falcon fleets turned in the abyss at the edge of the light. Quartets and trios of grey-white ships, they sailed alone in the dark, the orbital plain of the Solar System beneath them, the light of the sun a burning dot. They were ships of the V Legion, sleek and swift killers all. Having come to Terra, the Khan had broken his fleets into shards and cast them above and below the Solar System's plane of orbit. There they circled the light of the sun like hawks around a falconer.

Some amongst the command hierarchy had wondered if the ships of the V should not have been added to the fleet strength around Luna and Terra, or sent to reinforce the Martian blockade, as had been done with the warships brought by Sanguinius. The Khan had said no. His warriors would stand on the soil of Terra, but his ships were not dogs to be chained to watch a hearth. Their strength was in movement, in swiftness and flight. Rogal Dorn agreed and that put an end to the dispute. The ships of the White Scars were scattered high and low above the circle of the planets, soaring free to watch the dark.

The inner limit at which ships could translate from the warp was, fundamentally, a sphere centred on the sun. Ships not using the navigational gates at Uranus or Pluto could translate at any point on the invisible skin of that sphere. And just because the Elysian and Khthonic Gates were primary beachheads that did not mean the traitors would not come from the plane above or below the system's orbital disc. In fact, in some form, that seemed a certainty. So, the falcons of the V soared far from the sun's light and watched and waited.

On the bridge of the *Lance of Heaven*, Jubal Khan knelt in armour, and let his thoughts circle. His guandao sat on the deck before him. Incense smoke rose from twin bowls set to either side of him. The *Lance of Heaven* had no command throne, just a raised platform of ebony and yellowed bone. Around it the crew moved, near silent except for when an order was barked.

Through his slowed breathing, Jubal listened to the rise and fall of movements and the hum of machines. Always this moment before battle was the true storm, the building of silence and pressure before the flash and thunder. It was coming. Reports of death in the void had come from Pluto and Uranus, and the ship's sensors had seen the light of battles burning. Here, looking down on the disc of the system, those lights might seem distant, remote, but Jubal knew that was a false perception. This would be a battle to end all battles, a cyclone that would envelop all and leave nothing untouched by its passing. He could hear the storm's approach in the quiet.

Memories of the past fell into his thoughts like raindrops.

He remembered duels fought for pride, and wars fought for ideals that now seemed like lies told to children. He remembered the faces of all those he had been close to: Sigismund, his soul chained to his oath and his sword; Boethius, frowning as he worked to master the guandao as the White Scars watched and laughed with derision and joy; Abaddon, bending to close the eyes of a dead brother in the red dust. He found himself unable to smile at the fragments of the past.

What would become of them?

What would become of them all in this storm that sought to wipe the truths of the past clean?

He heard the rhythm of the command deck change and opened his eyes.

'What is seen?' he asked.

The *Lance of Heaven*'s sensors saw one ship, then a second and then more, ship after ship descending like a sheaf of arrows. Auspex readers hit paradox as they tried to identify individual vessels. Data drowned the minds of sensor servitors. Enemy strength values became approximations within seconds: ten, twenty-five, one hundred and six, hundreds, thousands...

Out in the dark, at a distance so vast that the fires of their engines were lost against the arc of stars, an armada bore down on the *Lance of Heaven* and its three companion warships. The ships of the armada had begun their acceleration soon after they had materialised in the void and flew now in a dense mass.

'They have seen us,' called an officer.

Jubal Khan read the shock in the humans before he saw the data. The orders that came from his lips did so without hesitation.

'To the wind,' he said.

The *Lance of Heaven*'s engines flared to blue heat and the

great ship shot upwards towards the descending armada. The three ships riding with it kicked forwards at its side. Thrusters fired down each of the four ships' lengths, punching them into spiral paths.

Signals reached back towards their kindred fleets circling the sun and rippled towards Terra.

'Enemy sensors have multiple firing solutions,' came the call across the *Lance of Heaven*'s bridge. 'Approaching estimated maximum weapon range.'

'Choose the mark, and send the call,' said Jubal, his voice level and calm. A second later the image of a single ship at the front of the armada flickered to being in a cone of holo-light. It was a cruiser, large but not one of the monstrous vessels that rode at its side.

This was how they lived as warriors, how their primarch and their forebears had fought on Chogoris – the marking of an enemy warrior in the first rank as battle was joined. Not a general, for a strong enemy would never let the arrows hit home, but not a soul without consequence either. The first kill had to be noted by the great, and awe those that followed.

Jubal watched the marked and chosen ship grow as auspex and cogitators parsed its identity. It was the *Fourfold Wolf*, a Legion vessel taken as a prize by the XVI when they were but the Luna Wolves. A good mark. A worthy kill.

Jubal rose, his guandao in his hand. He felt the judder of his ship beneath him as the spirit of its engines called out in fire. On the command screens he saw the enemy horde draw closer, reaching out and out to the edge of sight. A cloud. A storm come from beyond a dark horizon. He realised he was smiling.

'Loose,' he said.

Torpedoes burned free of each of the White Scars ships, running straight and true towards the *Fourfold Wolf*.

'They have range to us!' called an officer.

'Wheel,' said Jubal. The *Lance of Heaven* and its escorts cut their engines for an instant, fired thrusters and flipped over. Their engines ignited again, blazing as they drained power from every other system.

The lights on the bridge of the *Lance of Heaven* dimmed. Jubal listened to the rhythm of voice and machine as the *Fourfold Wolf* realised what was about to happen and tried to turn aside from the torpedoes converging on it. It fired its thrusters, but it was going too fast. The torpedoes slid through its shields like iron arrows through cloth. Red fire blossomed, then grew. It pushed forwards for a moment, its momentum carrying it on even as the explosions sent it tumbling. The ships riding close to it tried to pull clear. Then its guts opened to the void, a red-and-orange flower of light.

'The first cut,' said Jubal to himself, still smiling.

*Strike Frigate* Lachrymae, *Trans-Plutonian Gulf*

Fire wrapped Pluto. When the enemy had come to the gates of Terra before, they had come hidden under a cloak of lies. The Alpha Legion had bloodied the orbits of Pluto through deception before they were turned black. This time the defences stood ready, and those that wanted to pull them down had come openly, and with overwhelming might.

Thousands of warships spun through the void around Pluto. Engagements of hundreds of vessels formed, coagulating in fire and then dissolving back into the dark. The Khthonic Gate itself had been lost to the invaders days before. In the end it had simply been a question of numbers. The attackers lost ships, but for every hull left as molten debris, many more came to replace it.

The waves of enemy vessels increasingly bore the mark

of the warp and the wounds of old battles. Great troop carriers and gun-galleys, their hulls bleeding from the touch of daemons, their vox-transmitters droning unwords. Bit by bit they had enveloped the planet's orbits. Sigismund's First Sphere defences were now surrounded, the void on every side swimming with enemies. But the defences held. The Imperial Fists ships that remained moved and fought without cease as the space they cut through grew smaller and smaller.

The enemy had taken Nix and Charon, and since then the fortress-moons had been firing at each other as they turned around their parent. Battles both small and large had burned hot, lighting the defences with fire. Even as Horus' forces overran the moons, they found their warrens of passages laced with traps. Key systems failed. On Nix, the plasma conduits running to a quarter of the surface batteries fused and ruptured. On Charon, a cohort of murder-servitors poured into the corridors from oubliettes in the walls and floors.

But the traitors too had sown seeds of treachery before them. And on the moons and stations still held by the defenders, those seeds blossomed. On gun-studded Kerberos, a senior officer of the Solar Auxilia walked into a communications control room and fired a digital plasma weapon into the primary targeting cogitation cluster before turning the weapon on himself. On Hydra, viral and nerve agent reservoirs, planted in atmosphere scrubbers during the Alpha Legion attack months before, laced the air in the lower vaults with death.

And on the dance of fire went in the dark without, ever changing, never ceasing. Lance beams tens of thousands of kilometres long flicked between the ships and the fortified moons of Pluto. Millions of tons of munitions poured out of the guns of Kerberos. Explosions blossomed in the dark, growing, fading and lighting again.

The ships of the First Sphere moved amongst the fortress-moons and Pluto. They powered from engagement to engagement, doing enough to hold the enemy back for a few more hours and then moving on. They had another purpose, too. Bit by bit they were stripping the defences of munitions and troops. It had been long-planned, and the details kept secret, but there were eyes amongst the defenders of Pluto who watched for the Warmaster, and soon the enemy would know that every Space Marine and primary line unit was gone from the fortresses.

The only hope was that they would not know what it meant.

On the bridge of the *Lachrymae*, Sigismund's hands were tight on the hilt of his drawn sword. Soot, blood and the scars of battle marked his armour. Dozens of oath papers hung from his pauldrons. Some had been half burned away, others were new, the words on the parchment freshly inked.

*In the duty I do, I will be unflinching.*

*In the deeds I must do, I will be resolved.*

*Though I walk in darkness, I will not falter nor turn aside...*

On the words marched. He had written them himself in the years before this moment, had mixed the ink with the grave-ash of the dead that had fallen. They were the oaths already made, carried with him to this moment and all the moments that would come after.

Before his eyes, a cluster of nova shells struck Kerberos, stuttered and howled as they burst void shields and tore the skin from half a kilometre of the fortress-moon's face.

*'Fleet strength at sixty-five per cent, and holding,'* said Boreas. The hololith of the First Lieutenant had remained silent at Sigismund's side for the last few hours as the *Lachrymae*

had manoeuvred into place. Every part of the fleet needed
to be at a precise location and on a precise vector, and the
purpose behind all of it needed to remain hidden from the
enemy. It was an act of will as much as skill at arms. Under
the hand of any other Legion besides the VII it would have
been all but impossible.

'The moment is coming,' said Boreas.

Sigismund shook his head after a long pause.

'It is here,' he said. 'This is the tipping point. Any more,
and there will be nothing left.'

Sigismund closed his eyes for a moment, his gauntlet
tightening on his sword.

'There is time to signal Terra to confirm the order, my lord.'

'This is the will of the Praetorian, of our...' He paused,
hearing again the wind blow across the Investiary as Rogal
Dorn looked down at him.

'I am not your father!' the primarch had roared. 'You are not
my son,' he said quietly. 'And no matter what your future holds,
you never will be.'

'... of our father,' Sigismund continued. 'It will be done.'

Boreas bowed his head.

'Of course. But there are other ways. We could–'

'We are not made to question, brother,' said Sigismund,
and heard the edge in his voice, the echo of words that
had cut him from everything he had ever valued and ever
known. He breathed out, and his voice when he spoke again
was lower. 'Our duty now is to obey, to be loyal to the last.
No matter the cost, no matter the deeds to which we must
turn our hands.'

'I understand,' said Boreas.

Sigismund nodded. He looked back to where a spear-
head of enemy ships thrust towards Kerberos. The moon's
surface was still writhing with the light of the nova strikes.

Beyond the curve of Pluto, Nix was coming into alignment. Flashes pinpricked the fallen moon's face as it began to fire on its sibling.

Sigismund turned from the view. 'As soon as Kerberos falls, send the signal. Full withdrawal, all ships to burn towards the system core.' He felt the words form bitterly on his tongue. 'Signal Terra. Pluto has fallen.'

*Battle-barge* War Oath, *Supra-Solar Gulf*

*'Take it, boy.'*

*The man's face crawled with flame-light and shadows. Scar tissue had swallowed his left eye, and his breath reeked of meat and still-liquor as he leant in.*

*'Take it,' he hissed again, holding out the bone-handled knife. The light of the fires burning in the beaten bowls around the cave stained the polished blade orange and red. The old man moved even closer. His hair was crimson and bound high into a top-knot that fell between his shoulders. Muscle covered his shoulders, less than it had in his youth, but still enough to fill his frame. Fire-charred armour covered his chest, iron kill-rings darkened his fingers and mirror-coins clinked on long strings as he moved. Further back, against the cave wall, the throng of warriors that called this man lord stood, silent and watching.*

*The boy looked past the old man at the four figures kneeling on the floor. A warrior stood behind each of them holding the chains wound around their necks. There was Gul, her shoulders heaving as she fought to keep herself controlled. Her hands were shaking, and the blackened mirror-coins braided into her hair clinked. Anyone who did not know her might have said it was fear. It was not. It was her trying to contain her rage. Kars was unmoving beside her, long limbs drawn up close, his ragged blond hair hanging over his face. He glanced up, bright blue eyes flashing for an instant before the guard shoved his head back down. Dask looked asleep, his boulder head sunk low on his chest. Graidon was twitching, his fingers flexing as they felt for his knives.*

*'Take it, Abaddon,' said the old man who was his sire, then leaned in again to whisper. 'Do not fail me, boy. You are to be a king. This is the price of crowns and thrones.' He gripped Abaddon's hand, placed the blade. 'Learn to pay it now.'*

*His father stepped back. Abaddon looked down at the four who had run with him in the years of his childhood. They had saved his life, he theirs. He knew their laughter and their voices as well as he knew his own. Gul had taught him to trust, and Graidon to lie. Bonded companions, kin by blood oaths, they had grown with him, made him; they were a part of him as much as the hand that now held the knife.*

*'Now hear, now see,' called Sekridalla the crone from where she stood behind his father. Soot covered her bald head and arms. Rust powder rimmed her eyes. White ash marked the palms she held up to the shadowed ceiling. 'At this time, at this place, under the eyes of all, by blood and by right does this son of the Iron Cord come of age. He returns from the time before birth, from the lightless pools and by bloody hand takes his place amongst us. See him as he approaches. Watch his red hand rise.'*

*Abaddon looked at the four kneeling on the cave floor. His hand flexed on the bone hilt of the knife. He took a step forwards, level with his father. The old man's eyes were dark, their edges arcs of reflected firelight. Abaddon could feel the instant grow taut. He turned his head slowly and looked at his father.*

*'I do not want to be a king,' he said, and rammed the knife up into the old man's gut.*

He opened his eyes.

'Fire,' he said.

The *War Oath* roared as the ash-white ships came to meet it. Prow batteries fired. A pulsing spear of plasma caught a frigate and exploded its hull an instant after its shields collapsed. Blasts of energy chased the other White Scars ships even as they turned and burned back into the night.

'Why do they do it?' said Zardu Layak. 'They are insects trying to eat a leviathan. What foolish hope burns in their hearts that they come again and again?'

Abaddon did not answer, but turned to the tech-adept who governed the ship's communications. The creature was wired into a column of oil-slicked metal. Cables swathed what remained of its features, and a vox plugged the area of its mouth. It reeked of static and spoiled meat.

'Signal to the rest of the fleet to maintain course and speed.'

The cable-wrapped creature began a clicking acknowledgement, but Abaddon was already moving towards the doors off the bridge. Behind him, the ship's guns still chased the White Scars craft across the holo-displays and targeting screens.

He heard the steps of Layak and his bodyguards follow him, and felt anger rise. He stepped from the buzz of the bridge into the gloom and silence of the adjoining atrium. A dome of armourglass and iron capped the open space above – a typical mark of its Imperial Fists makers. The flare of the *War Oath*'s guns glinted across the starscape beyond.

'You do not watch the engagement,' stated Layak, still following. Abaddon did not reply, but strode on. There would be a council before the armada divided, and he would need to be ready for that. Every detail of each ship that was going into each fleet lived in his head. It would be simple to trust that all would happen as it must, but that was not how one made war. For as much as victory lived in the sword swing and the death of enemies, it lived too in the preparation of forces, the harnessing of leaders and the measuring of plans. Chosen from amongst his brothers for this task, Abaddon was neither a butcher nor driven by melancholic fatalism. He was a supreme warlord amongst warlords, and that reputation rested as much on his skill as a general as it did the edge of his sword.

He heard Layak and his two bodyguards halt behind him. He did not pause in his stride towards the door at the far end of the atrium.

'You are never guarded,' called Layak.

The words made Abaddon frown, and he slowed and then stopped, turning to look slowly from Layak to the two Word Bearers that followed him everywhere. They never removed their helms, nor spoke. Both wore sheathed swords at their waists. Blade slaves, that was what some called them. Like everything about the Word Bearers, the reek of the warp hung over them like foetor over rotten meat. Layak tilted his head. The red eyes running down the cheeks of his mask were glowing coals under the starlight.

'You have no personal guard,' said Layak, as though resuming a conversation that had merely been interrupted rather than never having started. 'Even the Warmaster has his Justaerin, but you, who are his sword hand, walk alone.'

Abaddon returned Layak's stare for a long moment, then looked slowly between each of the blade slaves. One of them tilted its head slowly in echo of his master.

'I am not alone,' said Abaddon, and turned to walk away again. 'I am never alone.'

'You dislike my presence and my questions,' said Layak.

'You have found a truth, priest,' growled Abaddon.

'You dislike me very much, do you not?' he said at last.

Abaddon smiled coldly.

'On that we agree.'

'I am a servant of the same ends and masters that we all serve. In that we are brothers.'

Abaddon held his gaze steady, his body utterly still.

'No,' he said. 'You are a dog that smells the meat of a kill made by its betters. The carrion eater does not call the wolf brother.'

'Who is the wolf and who is the carrion eater?' asked Layak. Abaddon thought he saw the iron fangs of Layak's mask flex, as though the metal itself were breathing. He felt the anger rise then, felt it wash against the ice of his will. One of the blade slaves shifted forwards.

*No*, he thought. *This shall not pass.*

He made as if to turn away, but then snapped back, closing the distance to the three Word Bearers in an eye-blink of surging muscle and armour. He was wearing standard battleplate rather than the jet-black Terminator armour of the Justaerin elite. His only weapon was a short-bladed gladius hung at his waist. He drew the blade as he charged. The power field lit with a snap of lightning. Layak was moving back, staff spinning to a guard in his hands.

The blade slaves were faster. Much faster. Both drew their swords. Cracks ran up their arms. Fire and ashes poured from the splits in their armour, as their forms bloated. The swords stretched in their grasps, fusing with the hands that drew them, dragging light and shadow to them as they sliced out.

Abaddon saw the first blow come, ducked under it and lashed his blade into the base of the sword where it melded with the arm. Blood scattered, blackening to ash as it fell. The sword screamed, and twisted to strike like a snake, but Abaddon was already pivoting to meet the cut of its twin as it lashed towards his head.

Others that had fought him would have said that he was

fast, beyond even the speed common to one of his trans-
human breed. That missed the real truth, though. There were
others amongst the great warriors who were faster: Jubal
Khan, Sigismund, Lucius, Sevatar – even the fool Loken. It
was not that Abaddon was fast; it was that he did not think
of speed, of parry and riposte, of attack and defence. Living or dying did not matter. Bloodshed did not matter. His
life did not matter. All that mattered was victory. That made
him more than fast, more than skilled. It made him death.

He slammed forwards into the second blade slave before
its sword could find its mark. A reek of burning flesh and
hot iron filled his mouth. He gripped the neck beneath the
jaw of the blade slave's helm. He felt his fingers burn as
they dug into the warp-filled flesh. He lifted and twisted,
momentum and strength flowing through him and sending
the blade slave tumbling through the air towards its twin.
Ash and orange fire scattered from it. The other blade slave
dodged aside and lunged forwards, but Abaddon was already
on Layak. He read the warding blow of the Word Bearer's
staff and took its force on his shoulder guard. Layak staggered. Ghost-light crawled over the staff. The priest's mask
was snarling, iron fangs chewing air. Abaddon looped his
arms around Layak, reversed his grip on the gladius, and
brought the point of his blade to the priest's side.

Layak went very still. Both blade slaves froze where they
were.

From a distance it would have looked almost like an
embrace, but it was nothing so kind. Any movement and
Abaddon would pull the blade into Layak's chest, punctur-
ing each and every rib, heart and lung with a single trust.
On Cthonia they called it the murderer's greeting. The two
were so close now that Abaddon could smell the incense
reek of the Word Bearers priest.

'Brotherhood is not about what misguided craft went into both our making,' hissed Abaddon. 'It is about the choices we make.' He turned his head slowly to look at the two statue-still blade slaves. 'I look at you and see a thing that has made those who were his brothers his creatures. And in that I see all I need to know of you.'

Abaddon tensed for a second and let the power-sheathed tip of the gladius burn the side of Layak's chest-plate. Then he let go, and stepped back. The blade slaves snapped forwards, but Layak raised a hand as he straightened.

'And I see in you all that the gods have spoken of,' said Layak. 'My thanks.'

'For what?' growled Abaddon.

'For illumination, and for giving me my life, Ezekyle Abaddon. Such an act creates a bond between souls, and a bond is a gift.' He bowed his head briefly, turned and began to walk away, staff tapping. The two blade slaves shrank to their normal size and sheathed their weapons. Abaddon watched them as they walked to one of the doors out of the atrium.

'The gods see you, Abaddon. They see you walk alone even amongst those you choose to call brothers.'

# SIX

Incremented destruction
Cascade
Send this word

*Battleship* Iron Blood, *Trans-Uranic Gulf*

The flames of battle stretched from the Elysian Gate towards the orbits of Uranus like the arm of a jewelled god. The *Daughter of Woe* hung over the gate itself, a new and ugly false moon amongst the planet's true children. Uranus' defences fired on it without cease. Explosions burst on the space hulk's surface. Shreds of its substance puffed into the void like dust exploding from raindrops. It had no guns to fire back on its tormentors, but the ships that orbited it spoke in its stead. Rolling barrages of missiles and macro shells streamed from them. And behind it, shielded by its bulk, more and more ships dropped through the hole in reality.

In the three days since the first ship had breached the Elysian Gate, the battle for Uranus had spread across its orbit. The outer circles of the planet's defences had fallen within eighteen hours of the first shots being fired, but since then the assault had slowed. Now the fight was for the hundreds of stations, moons and habitats – from the Mechanicum outpost Tau-16-1, which hung like a black needle in low orbit, to the ancient Cadum Station, its geodesic sphere pitted by millennia of dust impacts. Each of the planet's seven moons held small clouds of their own void-stations, and untold billions of humans lived in these scattered islands of life and air.

Assault groups waded through fire to hack and burn their way into stations and habitats. Torpedoes and munitions shot into orbit to plough hours-long paths into their targets. So far, the defenders had retained their dominance, but day by day the attacking forces grew. Stations died or fell, and the sphere of Uranus bled flames without cease. Defence forces counter-attacked, taking back stations while they were still burning with the fires of their first defeat. The vast bronze-and-plasteel star of the Sinderfell dynastic enclave had changed hands three times in as many days.

The moon of Umbriel swung across the sunward edge of Uranus as the fourth day of battle began. Armoured hab-domes dotted its craters, and tethered gun bastions hung in its airless skies. A quartet of assault carriers detached from the *Daughter of Woe* and boosted towards the emerging moon. Layered in armour and void shields, their hulls groaned with troops suckled from the guts of the hulk. A pair of battle cruisers fell in beside the quartet of carriers and the IV Legion strike cruiser *Aesculus* dropped into the lead of the formation.

A group of six warships lay across their path. Smaller than the traitor cruisers and assault carriers, they were Legion ships, four of the Imperial Fists and two of the Blood Angels. Their troop complements had been stripped to garrison Terra, but their commanders were still some of the finest

void warriors in the Imperium, their crews trained and
drilled to Legion standards.

They began to fire, moving and rolling in the void as they
closed with the oncoming enemy. Torpedoes surged from
the prows of the attackers. Squadrons launched from the
defenders' ships to tear the warheads from the void. Lance
beams danced over the assault group's shields.

The six loyalist craft accelerated, their guns singling out
an assault barque. The ship listed, its belly crawling with
flame, skeins of oily energy stuttering around its hull as its
shields failed to light. In its holds, a hundred thousand soldiers taken from the Grey Worlds of the Kayuas Belt became
ash as plasma vented from cracked conduits.

Fire criss-crossed the void as Umbriel's defence turrets
targeted the oncoming torpedoes. Explosions ringed the
small moon. Then the nova shell struck it. Fired from a
bombardment cruiser far out of the battle sphere, it had
been timed to strike just at this moment. Primed with a
haywire generator and thousands of scrap-signal initiators,
it burst on Umbriel's surface. Clouds of distorting energy
and ghost auspex signals fogged the defence sensors just as
they locked on to incoming torpedoes. Graviton and haywire
warheads struck Umbriel moments later. Crushing gravity
fields yanked the moon's tethered bastions out of alignment
and cracked the shells of surface habitats.

The strike was not decisive, but it made Umbriel's defences
blink – and that was enough. A stutter in the deluge of fire
from the guns, a split-second's pause, and the assault carriers began to shed breaching pods like seeds from ripe
corn-heads. Their warship escorts came about to meet the
six defenders head-on.

Gunships cut through the void around growing thunder-
heads of burning gas. Their targets were the gun platforms

tethered to the moon. Those craft that struck true poured troops into the guts of the moon's bastions. Corridors lit with gunfire. One bastion detonated its magazines, and the fire-scattered night was dotted with a brief new star.

Forrix watched the data strand from the Umbriel assault for a single second more, then let it dissolve back into the tide of symbols and numerals that cascaded before his sight. Across the entire sphere of the battle, Umbriel was but one amongst dozens of assaults, amongst hundreds of engagements, where counting losses on either side in anything less than thousands was meaningless. As First Captain and chief logistician of the Iron Warriors, he had lived every second of this operation as simulations spooled through the *Iron Blood*'s cogitators. The reality, even seen in the cold flow of symbols and numerals, was breath-taking.

Nearly four thousand primary-grade warships had already exited the warp from the Elysian Gate, pouring into the Trans-Uranic Gulf. They had paid for every kilometre advanced, but they had the coin in ships and firepower. They had pushed and pushed forwards, spreading out and advancing on the defenders not at a burning charge, but slowly, inexorably, like the erosion of mountains by ice. And just as mountains inevitably became dust, so this victory was assured. That was one of the things that made it beautiful.

Forrix's current role was to control and marshal the forces still exiting the warp. That alone was a monumental task. For all the power they had brought to this battle already, there were still twice as many ships waiting in the immaterium. Normally, many of them would have been carried away in an etheric riptide or assaulted by neverborn creatures by now. But while storms were churning the warp, they had not touched the ships that came to make war under the light of the sun. The gods and their daemons – for even

Forrix had begun to call them that – held back their hunger and spite from the warriors of the Warmaster.

Forrix heard the low click of pneumatics and looked to where Perturabo, primarch of the Iron Warriors, stood at the centre of the strategium. Pistons and layers of armour whirred as his gaze moved to a different cascade of holo-lithic symbols.

'The condition update from the assault on Pluto is over-due,' said the primarch.

'Analysis of the battle-light from its orbits indicates an engagement on a larger scale than we predicted,' said Forrix.

'Than Aximand predicted,' said Perturabo.

'He still has enough main force to deploy that he should achieve domination within the required time.' When Per-turabo did not respond, Forrix said, 'Something troubles you, my lord?'

The primarch turned his gaze on Forrix.

'So far each of the strategic projections has held true. The intelligence from the Twentieth Legion has proven accurate, and where tactical reality is different, it is predictably so – the moving of main fleet forces from Neptune to Uranus, the lacing of the Plutonic Gulf with additional munitions. All of it is within a narrow band of cautiousness. We progress as we intended, and they respond as predicted. Everything is as predicted.'

'You mean that there is something wrong with a plan that is executed as intended?'

Perturabo was silent for a long moment. The plan for the assault of the Solar System was many things, but chiefly it was the creation of Horus and Perturabo, bound with Mag-nus the Red's semi-corporeal ghost of insight. It was a work of inhuman genius, a battle plan that existed not only in the four dimensions of time and space, but also in the realm of the warp. And Perturabo had been the architect of the opening moves. Even in abstract, to wield forces on the scale involved had taxed Forrix's abilities, but the Lord of Iron had alloyed force and time and space into a strategy that would take the Khthonic and Elysian Gates in days. It was direct, incremental and irresistible: war as bloody art. But now, looking at the smooth fit between reality and theory, Forrix saw the flaw.

'It should not be so clean,' he said. 'The defenders fight hard, and make us pay, but they do nothing that we have not anticipated.'

'My brother,' said Perturabo softly, his eyes still on the flow of data, 'is many things, and his flaws were always hidden by the praise heaped on him. Call him steadfast, and that is merely a lacquer given to blunt unreason. Loyalty in him is merely a need to belong. Nobility is the gilding to base pride...'

Forrix held himself still. He had not heard Perturabo talk of Rogal Dorn directly in years.

'But the one thing my brother is not, is a fool.'

Perturabo lapsed into silence. Forrix did not know what to say.

The Lord of Iron remained silent as the data of the battle danced on the black orbs of his eyes.

'Continue as planned,' he said at last. 'Bring the lost sons through the gate.'

*Freighter ship* Antius, *Uranus high orbit*

'Transmit again,' said Vek. 'Make it clear it is for the primary overseer.'

'There is no response, sir,' replied the signal officer. The woman glanced up at Vek and then down at her instruments.

'Try again!' snapped Vek, then caught himself and raised a placating hand. 'Try again,' he said, and turned away, running a hand over his face. He closed his eyes for a second, saw the bubbles of colour blossom briefly behind his eyelids. His hand was shaking. He should sleep, but for the love of all that was precious how would he be able to...?

His hand strayed to where the small pendant had hung around his neck for these last few years, hidden from other eyes. It stopped and dropped to his side. The pendant was not there. Somehow, in the panic to get off Cordelia, it must have broken and fallen to the floor. This was what? The tenth time in as many days that he had reached for the small golden aquila. He found himself trying to remember the words of the prayers that his wife had taught him. She had been the reason he had kept the pendant, just as she was the reason he had joined the quiet faith of the *Lectitio Divinitatus*. She had been the reason he had done a lot of things.

'Transmitting on all available frequencies,' said the signal officer. Vek nodded but did not look around. He should go and sleep... How long had it been? A day? Two? More? It had taken that long to drop over the arc of Uranus to its sunward side. Koln had danced them on a jinking path while the battle spread in silent flashes behind them. The destruction had yet to reach this hemisphere of the planet's orbits. But chaos had run ahead of the fighting. Ships crowded towards every moon and habitat, clamouring for shelter, for help – for anything that they thought would shield them from harm.

The *Antius* had made for Oberon and its girdle of refinery and ore-processing plants. Fewer ships had fled here; it was further out, and its pipes and industrial platforms offered less obvious sanctuary, compared with Titania's city-warrens and belts of defence stations. But its approaches still swarmed with craft trying to get close, trying to dock, trying to get the attention of the moon's rulers. The *Antius* had to correct its course minute by minute just to keep from colliding with other craft. Vek had connections on Oberon, good connections that had proved true even when things went wrong. It seemed now that those past alliances counted for little when the heavens were ablaze.

'Still no response, sir,' said the signal officer. 'I can't even tell if they are–'

The signal officer broke off. Lights had sparked across her consoles, and parchment had begun to spool from a data transcriber.

'What is it?' asked Vek.

'Officer of the watch!' she called. The alternate sub-master that Koln had left in charge started forwards, but Vek snapped out his question again.

'What is it?'

The officer looked around at him, blinking. There was a fog in her half-focused eyes. *Terra's pact, but she is exhausted*, realised Vek.

'We are being hailed, Master Vek,' said the officer. Her hands were shaking as she peered down into the flickering green screens in front of her.

'By Oberon governance?' asked Vek.

'No, it's a military transmission, from a warship…' Her voice trailed off.

Vek went still.

'What does–' he began.

'They are requesting confirmation of our report that we picked up a prisoner adrift in the void… They want us to confirm that she is alive.'

'Where is the ship?' asked Vek, before the duty officer could ask.

'I don't know. Close, I'd guess, to have picked us out.'

Vek rubbed his hands over his forehead. This could be a chance… They needed to dock at Oberon, unload the hundreds of souls in their holds. Maybe he could even use this to barter transport for him and the children to Saturn or the inner system.

'Confirm and respond that we will hand the prisoner over in dock at Oberon. Ask them to follow us in.'

The signal officer blinked at him, then at the watch officer, who looked relieved that someone other than him had decided. The signaller began to key controls.

'Stop!' The call came from the doors to the bridge. Vek turned as Aksinya vaulted up the stairs onto the helm platform. His lifeward's face was flushed, her eyes wide. 'Do not transmit!'

'What–' began Vek.

'Don't transmit that signal,' called Aksinya, striding forwards, but the signal officer was keying her controls with fatigue-narrowed focus. Aksinya leapt towards the officer, but the distance was a fraction too far and the officer's hand pulled the transmission lever a fraction of a second before Aksinya yanked the woman's hand back. The officer let out a yelp of pain. Aksinya looked down at her for a moment, breathing hard, then she turned to Vek and grabbed his arm. 'Sir, you have to come with me now,' she hissed, just below the hearing of everyone but him. The bridge crew were looking around, puzzlement blending with the exhaustion on their faces.

'Why?' he said, trying to pull his arm free as Aksinya shoved him towards the bridge's main exit.

'Why would they want to confirm whether the prisoner is alive? Why in all that is happening would they seek us out to make sure?'

Vek felt the blood in his limbs become ice.

He could see the great bulk of another freighter through the pitted armourglass of the viewport, so close it appeared you could have jumped from one to the other.

He opened his mouth.

Macro shells struck the freighter beyond the viewport and tore it into shreds of metal and tatters of flame.

'Listen to me!' Mersadie shouted at the door. 'I need to speak to your master. He needs to speak to me!' The door remained shut.

'They won't listen,' said Nilus. 'Think about it. They have no reason to, and every reason to think that talking to an escaped prisoner might be a very bad idea.'

She did not reply but looked at the door. Nilus shifted from where he sat in the corner of the chamber and poked at the single bowl of broth the guard had brought.

'There has to be a way to make them listen.'

'To what?' asked Nilus, looking up from the bowl. 'What are you going to tell them? You haven't even told me why you need to get Rogal Dorn, and we have the bond of mutual suffering, and now this rather inadequate cell, to share.'

She glanced at the Navigator, but he had gone back to stirring the broth suspiciously. She had woken to find Nilus curled up in the corner of the cell. It wasn't a proper brig, just a small storage space by the look of it. The crew of the freighter had ripped out the inner locking mechanism, and sealed them in with a bowl of broth, and a plastek jug of water that tasted like metal and dust. She had slept in spite of herself, exhaustion overriding fear and uncertainty. Mercifully, she had not dreamed. This had been the first time she and Nilus had spoken to each other since they had

reached the *Antius*. Given the breathless scramble to escape
the prison ship, it was also, she realised, the first time they
had ever really talked at all.

'It's all right,' he said. 'You can keep your secrets. I am
sure you have more than a few.' He paused, then glanced
up at her, eyes sharp and wary. 'You were the remembrancer,
weren't you?'

Mersadie stiffened, cautious.

'I was *a* remembrancer,' she replied after a moment, then
folded her legs to sit on the floor. 'There were a lot of us.'

'But I recognised your name. You were well known, a bit
famous even, yes? You and… What was her name? The imagist.'

'Keeler,' she said, the name heavy in her mouth. 'Euphrati
Keeler.'

'That was it. You were both quite the thing, weren't you?'

'That was our job,' she said, and shrugged. 'To see the
Great Crusade for people who would never be able to see it.'

He smiled, the expression a crooked twist to his mouth.

'But, I remember the talk – you got close to the heart of
things. Very close. Practically a step away from the Warmaster.'

She blinked, and…

*…a door slamming open, followed by heavy metal-on-metal
footsteps. Mersadie knew it was a Space Marine even before the
impossibly huge shadow fell over her. She turned to see a shad-
owy form behind her, robed in a cream tunic edged with sea-green
trim. The Warmaster's equerry, Maloghurst, was known as 'the
Twisted', as much for his labyrinthine mind as the horrible injuries that had broken his body and left him grotesquely malformed.*

*'Loken,' he said, 'these are civilians.'*

*'I can vouch for them,' said Loken.*

*Maloghurst turned his eyes to her…*

She shivered. Nilus was watching her, the oily black of his
whiteless eyes glittering above his crooked smile.

'Why were you in the Nameless Fortress?' she asked him.

'Was that what they called it?' He snorted. 'How very predictable the methods of oppression become.' He shook his head and took another spoon of broth. 'Where was it?'

'Titan, I think,' she replied.

'But here we are somewhere off Uranus, hoping somehow that this bucket of rust doesn't catch a shell in one of the biggest void engagements in history.'

'They were taking us somewhere,' said Mersadie. 'For whatever reason, they decided to move us. When the invasion started they must have decided–'

'To kill us all rather than let such a dangerous set of prisoners fall back into the hands of the enemy.' He laughed. 'They thought very highly of us all.'

He shook his head and stabbed his spoon at the surface of the grey broth.

'Why were you a prisoner, Nilus?' asked Mersadie again, after a moment.

'Why were any of us? Why are we alive, here and now? Wrong place, wrong time.' He laughed again, the sound hollow and high. 'You actually want to know?'

She nodded.

'I was a Navigator on board a warship,' he said, and shrugged. 'Not even the prime Navigator, but that ship was called the *Akontia*, and it was–'

'Part of the Sixty-Third Expeditionary Fleet,' she finished. He nodded.

'Indeed. One of the Imperial Army vessels honoured by the Warmaster to accompany him to war… An honour that does not bring kindness to its crew or Navigators when they fall into the hands of the Emperor's *loyal servants*.' He spoke the last words through bared teeth.

'You… The ship fled to the Solar System?'

'Hardly,' he said. 'The officers mutinied after Isstvan. Half of the military commanders and units on board were die-hard Horus loyalists. But the captain and the other half wanted nothing to do with it. They came to us, to the Nav-igators, saying that they needed our help to get out... and we agreed. My house does not like this war, not any part of it or any side of it. So, when we can remove ourselves from it, we do.'

He paused and shivered. Mersadie found herself won-dering what could make a creature that looked out on the immaterium afraid.

'The next time we translated into the warp we took the ship off course,' said Nilus eventually. The diehards were sup-posed to be dealt with then, but... they lived up to that title. It became a battleground inside the ship. Storms came, and... something else, too. By that point we were lost on the tides, rolled by the storm. So, we... I... dumped us back out into reality. And here we were, within touching distance of the light that shines on Terra. They, the ones that found us, killed the rest of the crew I think. Clean sweep, fire and screams...'

'But they kept you alive,' said Mersadie.

'Yes,' he said, looking at her with his midnight eyes. 'Don't ask me why.' The side of his mouth twitched up in a smile. The expression somehow made her feel colder.

'And you, Mersadie Oliton, remembrancer and friend to the Sons of Horus, what happened to you, and why do you think you need to speak to the Praetorian of Terra?'

She shivered. Behind her eyes she saw a wolf rising from black water under a sickle moon.

'I–' she began.

'You said to the masters of this ship that you needed to reach Terra. Forgive me if I am curious as to why you want to speak to Rogal–'

Nilus broke off and his head twitched around, his gaze flicking between the corners of the room. The broth tumbled to the floor as he came to his feet.

'Something is happening,' he said, breathing hard. 'Something is–'

And the lights blinked out as the world began to shake.

Vek opened his eyes. Light and sound filled the bridge. Explosions lit in the view beyond the viewports. Pieces of metal blasted outwards from the first ship struck and caught another ship's engine cowlings as it passed close by. They tore like parchment in a shotcannon blast. The ship began to skid across the void. The *Antius* rocked. Cracks pinged across the viewports as a wave of micro-debris broke over them.

'Damage!' someone was shouting.

'Where?' Vek shouted back.

'I… I don't know. Port…'

'Find out.'

Vek began to push himself up. The deck pitched and he slammed back down onto the metal. He could taste blood in his mouth. A thin hand with a grip like a machine closed on his arm and hoisted him up. He looked up at Aksinya.

'Sir, you need to come with me.'

'What is happening?' Koln shouted as she pulled herself up the stairs onto the helm platform. The brevet captain was pale, eyes wide, bordering on panic.

'I…' stammered the watch officer. Beyond the viewports, the ship with the shredded engines hit a smaller ship prow-on. A new blaze of light blanked the night.

'Full astern!' shouted Koln. 'Thirty degrees down angle! Do it now.'

The *Antius* began to judder as its engines and thrusters

pushed it back and down, away from the expanding cloud of destruction.

Vek shook his head. His thoughts were racing, putting together the pieces that he hadn't seen at first. 'They fired on us, didn't they? Those shells were meant for us.'

'They missed,' said Aksinya, trying to pull him away. 'But the warship that fired is still out there, and the odds are low that it will make the same mistake twice.'

'The prisoner...' he said. 'They checked that the prisoner was still alive before they fired...'

He shook himself free of Aksinya's grasp.

'Get the children to a shuttle,' he said. 'Be ready to launch if we get hit.'

'Sir, you need to–'

'I am going to speak to her, now. If we are going to be killed by our own side I want to know why.'


Mersadie was banging on the cell door again. There was blood on her knuckles.

'Listen to me!' she shouted. 'You need to listen to me!'

She roared; a pit of anger was opening in her now. She had accepted her fate long ago. She saw the consequences of her years spent with the XVI Legion and could not fault the judgement of the Imperium. It was the price for the truth of what had happened to Horus, what had happened to everything. Except now there was something more important, just as there had been all those years ago when she and the other survivors of the *Eisenstein* had brought Dorn the news of the Warmaster's treachery. It felt so much the same. But this time, she was the only messenger.

'That's a blast wave vibration,' said Nilus. He was crouched in the corner of the room, legs drawn up. His head was raised, eyes darting around the walls as sounds clanged from spot to spot. He was breathing hard, sweating. 'Ships like this have no shields. If someone tries to shoot a hole in it, we are not going to last long.'

Mersadie raised her hand to strike the door again.

The locks disengaged with a clang, and the door swung outwards. The rotund man with the polished skin and opal-dotted forehead stood in the space beyond. A guard stood with him, hands twitching on a lasgun.

'What have you brought down on us?' said the man. There was fear in his eyes but anger in his voice. A booming shudder ran through the metal walls and floor. The guard flinched.

'What is happening?' asked Mersadie.

'Someone is trying to kill us to get to you.'

Mersadie stared at a him.

'I was a prisoner,' she began.

'People don't kill ships to execute one prisoner,' he growled, biting off the next words. 'What have you done?'

'I…' she said, and then stopped, calm replacing confusion. She looked at him levelly. 'It's not what I did, it's who I was, who I knew.'

'Your name…' he murmered, stepping back, looking at her with the light of realisation in his eyes. 'Oliton. In the Great Crusade, before the war… I heard your name. Reports from the front. You… were a remembrancer.'

'A remembrancer to the Sons of Horus,' she said, simply. 'To the armies of Horus.'

'By the Throne's grace…' hissed the man, stepping back, eyes wide. Another rumble shook the hull. 'They aren't just trying to kill you. They *are* trying to kill us. They are trying to kill us because we have talked to you.'

The guard, who had been listening, raised his gun, finger fumbling at the trigger. The big man slammed the barrel down just before the guard fired. The guard struggled, but the big man pulled the gun out of his hand and shoved the guard back.

'She is death,' gasped the guard. 'She has killed us all.'

'I can help,' said Mersadie, as the man turned back to her. 'I think I can save you, save us. But I need to get away from here. I need to–'

'Reach the Praetorian,' said the man. 'How do you even begin to have a reason for that?'

'Because I need to tell him something that may save everything that he is fighting for.'

The man looked at her; the guard had hauled himself to his feet.

*He does not have any reason to believe me*, she thought, and then a phrase he had used rose in her mind, clear and bright. *'Throne's grace…'*

'How could–'

'Because I am carrying a message from a saint,' she said. 'From a friend. From someone called Euphrati Keeler.'

The man looked at her, mouth half-open, not blinking.

'And you can help?' he said, and she could see the hope rising behind the fear. 'You can protect us?'

'Maybe,' she said. 'But not if we die now.'


In the dry poetry of the void-born, this manner of disaster was called a fire cascade. One ship exploded, and the debris was catapulted out as shrapnel. The debris struck another ship in close proximity, which exploded in turn, and then its debris destroyed another, and another, the disaster leaping from one victim, to many, to countless multitudes in a few bounds. It was a rare event, the vast distances involved in void manoeuvres saw to that. But the ships navigating the approach channels around Uranus' moon Oberon were very close to each other. So close that several catastrophes had already been avoided by the narrowest margins. When the first ship exploded, the fire cascade followed within moments.

Wreckage flew out on silent waves of flaming gas. Pieces of torn metal the size of tanks struck unshielded hulls and punched through. Fuel lines ruptured. Promethium met plasma and roared out, ripping and burning.

Hundreds died – gasping for breath as billows of fire stole the air from where they slept, or stood, or crouched in the arms of those they loved, seared to dust and ash in super-heated infernos, tumbled into the vacuum. On and on the cascade ran, seeded from one explosion into another.

Thousands died – cut apart by shearing metal, shot through by grains of debris flung through hulls in hundred-metre-wide shot blasts.

Hundreds of thousands died – spinning over and over in the torn chunks of their ships.

Shock waves spun the *Antius* as it turned and tried to run to the edge of the spreading cloud of death. Its engines fired, cut out and then slammed it forwards as a piece of hull the size of a Titan blasted through the space it had just vacated.

Sound roared through the *Antius'* bridge. Crew shouted, some asking for orders, others just screaming. The hull groaned. Alert gongs boomed in spaces beneath the deck plates. Lights blinked constellations of crimson and amber across every machine.

Vek caught the edge of the stairs to the helm platform as he hauled himself up. Mersadie was in front of him. Somehow, she was calm, almost serene, as though she had seen this face of existence before and looked on it with famili-arity. Vek turned as they reached the top. Sub-mistress Koln saw Mersadie and lunged for a sidearm clamped to the side of the helm console.

'No!' snapped Vek, moving between Koln and Mersadie.

'We should shoot her and dump her into the void,' snarled Koln. Her eyes were bloodshot, the gun barrel shaking in her hand.

Mersadie had stopped, her eyes wide as they took in the strobing fire beyond the viewports.

'She can help us live,' said Vek. Another blossom of flame opened in the near void.

'She caused this!' roared Koln.

'If there is a chance that she can help us survive then I am going to take it.'

'They want her dead, so we give them what they want.'

'They will kill us anyway,' said Vek.

'I am captain of this ship. I will not–'

'My ship,' said Vek, his voice suddenly low and dangerous. He saw Koln's eyes flick to the guard's gun, which he still had in his hands. 'My ship,' he said again. The pistol in her hand shook more. He could see the anger and fear moving beneath the skin of her face. He realised that the cacophony of the bridge had dimmed, that most of the crew were watching what was happening.

Koln lowered the gun.

'Whatever you can do, do it now,' he said to Mersadie.

She shook her head.

'I can't stop this,' she said, still staring out of the viewport. 'We must run. Get us out of this and into the sunward gulf.'

'You said you could help,' snarled Vek.

'You think they are going to stop?' said Mersadie, looking at him, and something in her voice held him silent. 'If we can get away from this, they will come after us, after you. They just fired into a mass of civilian ships to try to kill us. They will hunt us down even in the middle of this war.'

'That is insane.'

'Not in the minds of the people who held me prisoner. To them, this is the battle and they have the will to see it through. To them, innocence proves nothing.'

'Then we are dead,' breathed Vek.

'No,' said Mersadie. 'That is not certain.'

Vek looked at her and blinked, and an image rose from memory into his mind's eye: an old boat of wood tossed on a high sea beneath a sky of black clouds and forked lightning. It had been an illustration in a book that he had read when he was small – a real book of paper that smelled of strange earthy scents, a doorway into alien realms for a boy born into the void habitats of Uranus. It had come from a distant world with his mother, and the pictures on its pages had shown him things that he still thought of as truer than the picts and holos he had seen of other places: forests of trees with orange leaves, the sun rising behind snow-capped mountains, and the boat on a sea in a storm…

He had come back to that picture of the boat again and again, staring at it, until at last he asked his mother what it meant.

She had smiled.

'That is us,' his mother had said. 'Our lives and all we do are the boat, and the sea is the universe. Sometimes it is calm, and seems our friend, there to give us delight or comfort. And sometimes… sometimes it is a storm that can flip the boat of our lives over, break us and swallow us down. It means that sometimes we are small, and the tides we travel cannot be bargained with or bent to our will. Sometimes we can only hold on and hope that the storm is kind.'

'What do you need?' he asked Mersadie.

'I need to send a signal,' she said. 'You said that you sent a signal about me before, on military channels?'

'Yes,' said Vek, frowning.

'Send another signal now. Send it on the same channel you sent the last transmission.'

The ship bucked beneath them as its engines pushed against the fire-soaked void. A chunk of debris struck their spine, and the deck pitched.

'What should this signal say?' asked Vek as he pulled himself back to his feet.

'Just my name, and one other word.'

'What?' asked Vek, glancing at the prow viewports as the ship dived into a cloud of gas lit by the flare of more explosions.

'Loken,' said Mersadie. 'It should just say "Loken".'

# SEVEN

The wall within
Kerberos
Spaces

*Battle-barge* Throne of the Underworld,
*Trans-Plutonian Gulf*

The wolves closed their jaws on Pluto as the sons of Dorn
fled. The Imperial Fists had prepared for flight, that much
was clear. One moment there were hundreds of ships spinning in the dance of weapon exchanges. Then, every weapon
station and fortress-moon still in the defenders' hands fired.
Rolling volleys of shells, and short-fused torpedoes shook
the void and lit the dark with bubbling shoals of fire. The
attacking ships' sensor systems chattered in distress as they
filtered the sudden squall of energy spikes.

And the volleys kept coming, rolling over the top of each
other like the rising beat of drums. The loyalist ships wheeled
as one and turned, thousands of vessels coming together and
diving for the inner system.

The engine light of his fleeing enemies gleamed in the
eyes of Horus Aximand as the *Throne of the Underworld* cut

through Pluto's orbit. It was a battle-barge, not the equal of the great Gloriana-class ships, but still a monarch of destruction. Two companies of Sons of Horus stood ready in its holds, a thousand of the Legion's best killers, and it mounted cannons that could hammer targets to ruin. The spear-tip force it led had been aimed at Kerberos, a primary strike to take the fortress-moon's main batteries. That blow would now be left to others. The newborn and the IV Legion could take their objectives and bear the cost. And there would be a cost. Even with the cover of their fleet gone, the fortress-moons were still ship-killers. Tens of thousands would die to take them. That did not matter. All that mattered was that this gate to the Solar System was in their hands.

Aximand could see each of the next moves he had to make, all the gradations of victory and how to reach them. It was as simple as breathing. He understood it in his mind, but also with his soul. That was what had seen him rise in the Legion – his sheer tactical genius. There had been others who were better at the point and edge of killing – though they were few – but Aximand was able to measure war, and to weigh possibility, and then make decisions that won battles. He was 'Little Horus' because his face had resembled that of the primarch, but the deeper resemblance lay here, in his ease in the crucible of war. The face that had given him his half-mocking title had been flayed away, but the commander's soul beneath remained. Seeing the battle sphere of Pluto change, he already knew why and what to do.

'Battlefleets Ullanor and Shardspear, engage the fleeing enemy ships. Run them down. Fourth Legion battle groups, divert and begin assault on Kerberos, Charon and Hydra.'

Beside Aximand, Vull Bronn sucked in a breath to speak. The veteran warsmith had survived the Iron Warriors' withdrawal from Krade, but a strike on the last transport had left him with a bloody cave in his side.

'They are not breaking,' he rasped. Compression pistons in his rebuilt torso hissed and released. 'The key values of their force and strength have not fallen to collapse. We should hold to our current deployment.'

'No,' said Aximand. 'They are withdrawing. This is a battle they knew they would lose. They held for as long as they could, slowed us and bled us as much as they could, and now they will run to Terra.'

'The dog-sons of Dorn do not run,' said Vull Bronn. 'They hold past the point of sense. This is something else.'

'They have other lines and defences to use,' replied Aximand, 'and billions of people who can die on their walls.' He turned his flayed grin to Vull Bronn. 'What they don't have is ships. They cannot lose more. Their strength is their fortifications and the number of mortals who will fight for them. But fortresses cannot be moved. Their ships are the only way for them to redistribute their strength. They lose those ships and all their strength is trapped.' He turned and began to walk towards the doors that led from the bridge to the hoist down to the launch decks. 'So, they are running because they must, to keep their ships alive. And we will not let them escape.'

'Where are you going?' asked Vull Bronn.

'To draw my sword and bury it in their back,' said Aximand. 'One-third of your ships may join the pursuit, but the rest of the fortress-moons are yours. Live up to your reputation – take them now.' He could see his words light a fire in the cold eyes of the Iron Warriors commander. Vull Bronn understood what Aximand had explained – of that there was no doubt – but the Iron Warriors' way of war moved like a glacier over stone. They had no time for such caution. The

Ultramarines were coming, and with them all the enemies they had left undefeated in these years of war.

'As soon as the main defences fall, we should bring the reserves through,' said Vull Bronn, and Aximand could see that it was an act of will for the other warrior to not bite back. Good. The two chains that formed the Iron Warriors' bridle were loyalty and pride. Now pride would work to overcome caution. 'We should bring all the rest of our forces through the gate on an accelerated timetable.'

'Agreed,' said Aximand. 'So ordered.'

*The Imperial Palace, Terra*

'Admiral.'

Su-Kassen looked up into the face of the Huscarl. A black cloak hung from his shoulders and snow leopard fur covered his shoulders. He held his brush-crested helm in his left hand, and his right rested on the pommel of a sheathed sword. His face was clean-shaven, his eyes hard but bright.

'Yes, Captain Archamus?' she said. The name still felt strange to say to this young warrior, and for a moment she saw the face of the man who had borne the name before, her friend: bearded, unreadable, as immovable and eternal as a granite cliff. Then she blinked and the new face nodded, as though seeing the memory in her eyes.

'Come with me please, admiral,' he said. She frowned and glanced around at the Grand Borealis Strategium. The circles of officers and tech-priests did not look up. The shimmer of holo-projections and the buzz of machines flowed on unceasing.

'General Kaze,' she said to a lean-faced officer standing one step down from her station. 'You have the watch.'

She stood and followed Archamus as he walked from the

chamber. She did not ask where she was going or why; that it was Archamus meant that this was the Praetorian's will, and she would discover the reason soon enough.

Two figures in massive amber-yellow Terminator plate flanked the door they eventually reached. Archamus paused for a second in front of them, and then the door to the chamber beyond opened. He stepped aside and motioned for her to enter.

The room was circular, and wide enough that it would have taken her twenty strides to reach the opposite wall. Thick, embroidered curtains hung over tall windows. Dusty glow-globes sent shadows across the domed ceiling above and the carpeted floor below. It smelled of pipe smoke and time soaked into rich fabric. Four figures looked up from the circular table as she entered. She knelt instantly.

'Stand, admiral,' said Rogal Dorn. She obeyed. Behind her, the door closed behind Archamus and she heard the brief buzz of servos as he too began to kneel, and then stopped himself. There was a clack of ceramite as he saluted, fist to chest. She smiled inwardly. As one of the Huscarls, Archamus did not kneel unless his lord did; it was a rule that he was still getting used to. But well he might have knelt.

Beside Rogal Dorn stood Sanguinius, face grave beneath his golden locks, and with them the gilded presence of Constantin Valdor. The Chief Custodian looked up from the parchment-strewn table, and gave Su-Kassen a short nod.

'Admiral,' he said, his voice an echo of the gravity in Sanguinius' expression.

Malcador, alone of the four, was seated. The Regent of Terra had never looked older to Su-Kassen's eyes. The hood of his robe was lowered, and she could see the skin of his scalp through the white strands of his hair. The lines of his face looked to be cut deeper into his brow and cheeks, and the skin had drawn tighter over the bones of his skull. A jolt of shock ran through her as he looked up. There was pain in his eyes, and a distance that reminded her of the eyes of her father in the last days of life.

'Thank you for attending us here, admiral,' said Malcador, his voice was as clear and steady as ever. A small smile twitched the edges of his mouth. 'Excuse my remaining seated.'

'Of course, Lord Regent,' she said.

'Oh, please can we move past the tortuous formalities?'

Su-Kassen looked around at the sound of the voice. A woman in grey robes, with chromed hair, sat cross-legged on the top of a polished wooden cabinet. She was resting her chin on her hands. Her posture looked bored, but her eyes were alight and glittering. Su-Kassen knew who she was instantly, even though they had not met in person before. The woman was called Andromeda-17, and she was one of the last of the Selenar, a scion of the near-extinct Luna gene-cults that had helped the Emperor raise the Space Marines from armies to Legions. She was a specialist in empathic and non-linear reasoning, and was part of a hazy grouping of servants that existed between Dorn and Malcador. Su-Kassen knew Andromeda-17 by rising reputation, and disliked most of what she heard. Nothing that she saw of the woman in the flesh undid that impression.

'It's all right, admiral,' said Andromeda. 'Despising me at first sight is what most people do.'

Archamus shifted, and if Su-Kassen had not known better, she would have thought that the Huscarl was trying to suppress a smile.

'Thank you for the attempt to leaven the mood, Mistress Andromeda,' said Malcador, looking directly at Su-Kassen. 'This is a council, admiral, after a fashion, but not one that can involve the wider staff, you understand?'

'In all honesty, I don't, my lord. I believe I am aware of all the dimensions of the defence, and the senior staff also knows all of those details. If it is a matter of trust...'

'It is not,' said Rogal Dorn. 'It is a matter of perspective, of judgement.'

Sanguinius looked at his brother primarch for a second, and the gravity in his expression became a brief flash of raw emotion.

'It is not weakness, brother. Our limits are what make us.'

Su-Kassen thought she saw something within Dorn's gaze then, like the flare of lightning hidden by a far horizon.

'What they are trying to say,' said Andromeda 'is that they are struggling with some things that don't fit in the normal patterns of war.'

'Specifically?' asked Su-Kassen.

'Things unseen and incomplete,' said Malcador, sounding very tired suddenly. 'Shadows on the wall...'

'If you would indulge us by summarising the position, admiral,' said Valdor, activating a micro holo-projector that spun a display of the Solar System into the air.

'The enemy progresses through the gates off Pluto and Uranus as planned for,' said Su-Kassen. 'They have also, by other means–'

'By sorcery,' injected Andromeda.

'–inserted a large force above the plane of the Solar System. That fleet has divided into two, with both elements making speed for the inner system, for us and for Mars.'

'Why?' asked Dorn.

She looked at him. 'To divide our efforts. To put direct pressure on the inner-system defences while they take the gates off Pluto and Uranus. They pin us in place around the Throneworld and pour forces in from the outer system and overwhelm us.'

'Will it work?' asked Sanguinius, lightly.

Su-Kassen paused.

'It can work. In the end, my lord, they have numbers and mobility. It is just a question of time.' She paused, then decided to give voice to her suspicion. 'But you all know this just as well as I do. The enemy know that others are at their heels, that they do not have time. This battle for them must be swift, and our greatest defence is to slow them, to make them have to grind through every step they take forwards. This... manoeuvre is much further in-system than we would expect. It is extraordinary, but it is not enough. It will not work quickly enough.' She looked up and met Rogal Dorn's gaze. 'And they will know that. They will know that we can defeat them with time even if we lose these battles. So the question is – what are they doing that we cannot see?'

Dorn nodded.

'They are either blind or desperate, or there is another dimension that we do not see,' said the Praetorian. 'That *I* do not see.'

'The warp,' said Malcador simply, and Su-Kassen could not miss the weariness in the word. They all looked at the Regent. 'This has always been a war fought on two fronts. One in the physical world, the world of guns and bullets and flesh. The other a war in the realm beyond the physical, a world of things that dream they were gods, and where power has different dimensions.'

'The wall without,' said Dorn, 'and the wall within.'

'Indeed,' said Malcador, 'and you have always known that, Rogal. But now Horus comes here not just in the physical realm, but in the warp...' He broke off, and closed his eyes for a moment. 'I can feel it, and see it. Just as you all can, just as every soul in the circle of the sun can. Fear and despair grow stronger, and feed the storm that rides at Horus' back.

This is just the prelude, the beginning. The storm builds still and has yet to break…'

Sanguinius moved next to the old man, and placed a hand on his thin shoulder. Malcador let out a breath and closed his eyes again as something spasmed across his cheeks.

'And everything that happens here,' said the Angel, 'has an echo in the warp, in the beyond. In war, one might unleash terror to break the will of the enemy, or sow confusion. In this war that terror is the end in itself. Everything they do must be seen as having two purposes, one we can see and one we cannot.'

'Can you not look?' Su-Kassen asked, looking at Malcador. 'Forgive me, but like the beloved Emperor you are–'

'I cannot see. There is a… a darkness in the warp, screaming, blinding and growing deeper. It is a constant pressure and with every moment the pressure becomes greater… I cannot see.'

'The Emperor–' began Su-Kassen,

'The Emperor is our wall within now. He and He alone,' said Sanguinius. 'He is… He is holding it back alone.'

'And He can hold,' said Valdor. The Chief Custodian seemed to shiver. 'At great cost, but He holds and protects.'

'Holds?' said Su-Kassen. 'Not triumphs?'

'That is triumphing. As things stand, Horus cannot win the battle within,' said Malcador, 'and so his hope must be to break us without.'

'Then they will fail,' said Su-Kassen. 'The enemy do not have time. We will move primary fleet forces to intercept them, and even at great loss, they will not be able to have victory before Lord Guilliman arrives at their back.' She looked at Dorn. 'I was preparing the fleet redeployment orders. I assume you are ready to order the *Phalanx* into the line?'

Dorn's face showed no expression.

'Not yet,' he said quietly.

'My lord...'

'He knows,' said Dorn, and Su-Kassen could see in the stillness around the table that they had arrived at the point they had been unable to resolve. 'Horus knows all that we have said and seen already. He knows what we know of this battle so far, and he knows what we cannot see. And he is Horus.' Dorn looked at Sanguinius, and the two primarchs' gazes met. A small, sad smile formed and faded on Dorn's lips. 'Was he ever less than brilliant? Can we assume he is less than that now?'

'This is the question,' said Valdor. 'For my judgement, we must proceed against what we can see, not what we can't.'

'Agreed,' said Su-Kassen. Dorn looked at her sharply, but she held his gaze. 'We have planned for this battle, my lord. We have laid the ground. You know better than I that the unexpected is inevitable. We must not let it lead us. We must be firm in purpose.'

From behind her she heard Andromeda-17 give a snort of approval.

'And if that is what Horus wishes us to do – for me to follow my nature, which he knows so well?'

'I don't see that we have a choice,' said Su-Kassen.

'And that is one of the things that worries me more than anything,' said Dorn, softly. He looked up and away, his gaze focused somewhere far beyond the tapestry-hung walls. Su-Kassen felt a shiver run down her back at the implication in the words. In all her years at his side she had never seen a crack of doubt in the stone of his being.

'*He needs to be allowed the moment of flight before he returns to the cage of necessity,*' said the memory of the Khan's voice.

'With all respect, my lords,' she said. 'There is no choice

to make. We can only fight the war we can see, and so that is what we must do.'

'See?' said Andromeda-17 from the side of the room. 'I told you she would set you true.'

'What else worries you, brother?' asked Sanguinius, frowning.

Dorn looked around the table and then at the Angel.

'The same question that all of us have asked, but not spoken yet,' said Dorn. He looked at the holo-projection and gestured so that it shrank to a sphere that he could rotate with his fingers. 'Where is Horus?'

Silence answered. Dorn turned his gaze around the circle, slowly, meeting and holding each of their gazes.

'Just so,' said Dorn at last. 'And there is no answer we can give, and no guesses that would give comfort.' He looked back at the holo-sphere hanging between them, and keyed a control on the projector. The image folded into an image of Terra turning to show its face through day and night. Locations marked in a rainbow of colour spread across its surface. 'There are other matters to be discussed,' he said.

The conference ended an hour later, the gathered masters of the Imperium leaving without formality.

'Admiral,' said Malcador, as Su-Kassen made to go, 'a moment of your time.'

Behind her, Andromeda-17 was just leaving. Su-Kassen caught the gene-witch's eye, and saw that there was sorrow in her look – sorrow, or perhaps pity.

Then the door to the chamber closed, and it was just her and the old man who was the Regent of the Imperium, alone in a long moment of silence. A thin sheet of parchment sat on the table in front of him, she noticed. It was a spool from an auto-scribe, one of the types used for archive reports. A section of the words on its face had been underlined in red.

'There is something that you should know,' he said. 'Please, sit down, admiral.'

### Fortress Moon Kerberos, Pluto

'Breaching charge,' called Saduran, and one of his brothers charged forwards. Saduran came around the corner and fired up into the cluster of rotor cannons set in the ceiling above the blast doors. Target runes went red in his helm. His brother with the breaching charge was past him. Saduran fired. Bolt shells breathed from the barrel of his gun. Explosions burst amongst the rotor cannons.

The rest of his squad was with him now, firing up at the defence weapons. The cannons fired back. A deluge of hard rounds hit the warrior to Saduran's right and punched him back off his feet. Ceramite splintered. The warrior with the breaching charge was halfway to the door. Ten paces, a second's sprint. One of the rotor cannons spun around. Targeting beams reached through the smoke. The cowled statue beside the blast doors trembled. Hidden seams in the bronze split wide with a boom of pistons.

The ground shook again as a battle-automaton stepped out from where it had stood behind the shell of the statues. Fuel cables snapped free of gun pods and limbs. Weapons rose with a melody of gears and a chuckle of building energy.

Saduran felt the moment blur as his hearts kicked, and stimulants flooded his veins.

It had taken them hours to reach this point. They were deep in the core of the Kerberos fortress-moon. The unbreakable heart of Pluto's defences had proved to be quite breakable in reality. It was just a question of the cost. With the Imperial Fists in flight towards the inner system, it had only been a matter of time before Kerberos' surface defences had failed. Then Iron Warriors bombardment barques had torn a kilometre-wide chunk from its face with mass drivers, and waves of assault craft had poured into the breach even as debris was still spinning outwards from the wound. Half of the first wave had died in seconds. Those that did reach the crater ripped in the moon's flesh found the guns of battle-servitors waiting for them.

Half a million dead.

That was the cost of the first wave. Half a million human soldiers pressed from mongrel clans of void pirates and ship wreckers. They served their purpose, though.

A cohort of Iron Warriors Terminators had teleported into the main battery still functioning close to the breach. It had cost two strike cruisers, but the Iron Warriors had paid without hesitation. The crews manning the mountain-sized guns were still loading and firing as the Terminators cut them down. The fire from the wounded side of the moon dwindled, and fell silent. Ships slipped forwards, landing craft buzzing from their flight decks.

Companies of Sons of Horus and battalions of Iron Warriors entered the battle as the first wave foundered. Masters of signal had analysed the casualty and engagement data and chose targets as the gunships and torpedoes were in flight. Where the defenders were weak, where they had retreated, where their guns were stammering, there the Legions struck like knives plunged into already-open wounds. Saduran and his brothers had been in that second wave. Almost all were newborn, Legion warriors of years or months. These last days of battle, though, had made veterans of them all. Those that had survived.

It was murder in the tunnels of the moon. Most of the defending troops that had not fled with the Imperial Fists

were of Mechanicum stock, weapon servitors and modified machine helots. Individually they were no match for a
legionary, but they had numbers and time to prepare. Endless gun nests and traps met the assaulting troops, and the
resistance increased the deeper they went. There was no
retreat amongst the defenders. Either through programmed
control, or desperation, or hate, they fought to the last.

The floor and walls of the fortress-moon shook and shook
without cease. Its remaining gun batteries were still firing
even as the attackers bored into its heart. Across the orbits of
Pluto, Kerberos' siblings were already falling, aflame, ringed
by ships, their innards burning as the IV and XVI Legions
cored them out, passage by passage. Pluto belonged to the
Warmaster. It was just a matter of crushing the last fingers
of resistance that still clung on in the face of the inevitable.

Looking up at the automaton striding out to defend Kerberos' heart, Saduran realised that he would not see that
victory.

He dived aside as the weapon on its shoulder fired. Blue
light scored a line across the decking. He rolled. The beam
struck two of his squad brothers. They vanished into dust
and ash. Saduran came up firing.

'Use the charge,' he shouted into the vox as he fired. He
could see his squad mate with the breaching charge running for the automaton's right leg.

Bolt-rounds splashed across the automaton's chest. Its gun
mount rotated towards Saduran. Energies lit within the barrel.
An explosion enveloped the automaton's side. Saduran staggered as the blast wave rolled through the air and floor. The
automaton listed like a punch-drunk brawler. Smoke and flame
snaked up its side. Pipes vented burning oil from beneath torn
armour. Sparks crawled across its body. But it did not fall.

It straightened, gun mount swivelling to aim. Saduran felt

a snarl of laughter and rage come to his lips. He raised his bolter to fire a last shot of defiance.

The automaton froze.

Saduran's last bolts smacked into its torso. For a heartbeat it did not move. Then it folded to the ground with a sound of releasing pistons and unwinding gears. Saduran stared at the machine as it settled onto the ground, still burning.

On the ceiling, the rotor cannons stopped firing, their barrels spinning on momentum in the sudden silence.

'What…' began one of the other survivors from the squad, but the question vanished behind a rolling chorus of clanks and thuds. Every door leading off the chamber thumped open. The air began to stir and billow as wind blew through the space. The vox began to chatter with voices. Every system across the fortress-moon had just shut down, every door had unlocked, and all the batteries had fallen silent at once.

A clanking boom trembled the deck as the blast doors to Kerberos' core started to open. Metre-thick layers of metal peeled back one after another. Saduran found himself rising, stepping forwards.

'Brother?' called one of his squad mates, but he ignored the word. Silent dark filled the space beyond. He stopped on the threshold, paused and removed his helm. The air smelled of burnt plastek and hot wiring. He could see small lights winking on banks of machines now, blue, red and green, stuttering in time with the pulse of the machines. The chamber was vast. He could feel it in the air even though his eyes could not reach to the edge of the shadows. He took another step, gun low but ready. Nothing moved.

A stutter of lightning split the dark, rolling up the side of a vast metal sphere at the heart of the chamber.

Saduran paused again. There was another note in the air, a high vibration that ached in his teeth. The vox chopped between the voices of Iron Warriors and Sons of Horus legionaries. The moon had gone dead, as though something vital had been cut...

Another arc of lightning flashed up the side of the metal sphere ahead. The ache in his teeth was a shrill call in his ears now.

He took another step.

Another flash, and he saw the servitors hanging from their cable links. He nudged one with the barrel of his bolter. It swung slackly. Its weapons clinked. As though something vital had been cut...

Three flashes of lightning, and in the white glare he could see the tech-priests lying on control gantries high up on the sides of a forest of smaller metal spheres. Red lights were winking on control consoles.

Something cut... or something drawn back, like the back-draught of a fire, or the inhalation of a beast...

Cold lanced into his core. He turned and began to run for the doors that were open to the rest of the moon, the moon they had spent blood and time taking, the moon that now was ringed with warships and filled with troops. His squad mates shouted at him, but he was calling into the vox, shouting through the chop and hiss that was rising in time with the buzzing in his ears.

Behind him, lightning bolts flashed and flashed, bleaching the reactor chamber blinding white. And he knew it was too late, that these were the last stretched moments of his life, and that this war that had remade him had now come to claim him.

A flash...

Brighter than lightning, and a sound beyond hearing that filled him for the endless instant before there was nothing.

* * *

*Strike Frigate* Lachrymae, *Pluto*

Sigismund opened his eyes. The blade of his sword was cool against his forehead. He had waited in silence, his thoughts turned inwards. But now he needed to return to his purpose. The murmur of oath-words filled the bridge of the *Lachrymae*. He lowered the sword, but did not sheathe it. Boreas and Rann's holo-projections met his gaze.

'The moment is here, brother,' said Rann.

Sigismund nodded, feeling the words he was about to speak gain weight on his tongue.

'Turn the fleet,' said Sigismund. 'Cut them down.'

Kerberos detonated.

It was no small thing to destroy a moon. The agents of the Fabricator General had resisted. To them, such an act was a violation, the killing of machines – a tragic loss of function and knowledge. Rogal Dorn had not relented, and so it was done. Munitions had arrived on Pluto's moons in vast numbers. Their magazines swelled with macro plasma cores, blocks of explosive and cylinders of accelerant. All of it had been done so that it would seem part of preparations for the coming war. The eyes of Horus amongst the defenders saw only stores arriving for a siege, and did not ask or think any more of it.

The tech-priests had done their work, layering in time-delayed overload routines into primary, secondary and tertiary reactor controls. Charges were set in the bloated munition stores, all synchronised to a single command that would make them all parts of a single, great act of destruction. The data-jinn that the tech-priests created to enact the design had needed to gestate for months in the data-looms of deep-void facilities, and when it was complete all those involved had the memories of what they had done removed. It was a thing of artistry and genius, a hymn to the limits of knowledge and machine-craft, but none of those who wrought it would ever wish to claim their due for their work. They gave it a name, though, a designation that wove its purpose with a whisper of forgotten dread.

They had named it *Vanth-Primus-Nul*.

As the Imperial Fists retreated, the data-jinn had begun its work. Incubated in the core data-reservoirs of each fortress-moon, it uncoiled into full being. Tentacles of code in a dozen machine languages reached through data-cables and photon lines and noospheric connections. From system to system it spread. It overwrote command codes and retasked servitors. Data altered, and cycles of unmaking began in the spirit of each machine it passed through. Even on the moons already in the attackers' hands, Vanth-Primus-Nul carried on doing its work, increment by increment, silent and unseen. By the time the Iron Warriors and Sons of Horus had begun their assault on Kerberos in earnest, the process was already past the point where it could be undone.

The blast wave of Kerberos' death killed two hundred and five ships. Void shields vanished. Armour melted. Chunks of wreckage the size of mountains tore through hulls. Static rolled through the vox-channels. Seconds later, Hydra and Charon followed their brother. The magazines and fuel of hundreds of warships added their fire to the inferno. Detonations leapt between the vessels manoeuvring too close to the moons. Explosions chained all the way back to the Khthonic Gate. Ships at the edge of the blast scrambled to get clear. Order vanished. Mayhem and death ringed the last planet of the Solar System, and Pluto shook in its orbit.

Out in the reach, towards the sun, the ships of the Imperial Fists turned. Thrusters flipped them back over in mid-flight.

The Sons of Horus vessels pursuing them ploughed onwards even as the realisation of what had happened rippled through them. On the bridge of his ship, Horus Aximand saw the fleet that had been fleeing but a moment before turn and roar back directly towards him. At his back, the shouts of officers and servitors filled his ears. Behind his mask of flayed skin, understanding slid into him, cold and sharp.

The guns of his ships roared as the fleet of the First Sphere met them head-on.

*Bhab Bastion, The Imperial Palace, Terra*

'Admiral…'

'Yes?' Su-Kassen blinked, not looking at where Archamus stood just inside the closed door out of her quarters. She could almost feel the Space Marine's discomfort.

'There is a signal,' he said.

'Of course there is.' She was still staring into the open pistol case on the stone mantle. The weapon's pepper-pot barrel gleamed blue-black in the low light of the single glow-globe she had lit.

Why had she come back here? She was needed in the command bastion. There were things that needed to be done. Time would not stop or slow for this instant. Why would it? Death was history, its tread and pulse. No one death would shake it from that course.

But here she was.

Archamus had gone with her when she left Malcador's chamber. She had begun to walk, and the Imperial Fist had silently followed. She had not questioned why, but a part of her mind that felt like it belonged to someone else wondered if Dorn had asked him to go with her, to watch over her in this moment. She did not consider it for long – there

was no space in her for thoughts, just the words of the recent
past ringing in her ears. So she had let the Huscarl walk with
her and did not think about why.

It was quiet. The last weeks had stripped the continent-city
of its crowds and bustle. Nothing moved in its halls except
the twitching guns of the weapon servitors that watched
everything with crystal eyes. Stab-lights washed across the
high windows of the Silesian Cloister as they crossed into
the Northern Circuits.

It was night outside, she realised. The time had been
drained of meaning over the last days. What did it matter
if the sun was rising when your mind was focused on planets halfway across the system?

On she walked, not minding her path or steps. The places
she passed through were empty. When she did see other
humans they moved in clusters, flanked by soldiers. She
recognised the green-and-silver cloaks of the Qui-Helic
Guard, the crimson armour of the Inferalti Hussars, and
the grey-and-ochre fatigues of the Cordesh Cavalry – the
regiments of the Old Hundred deployed within the walls
in what might be the last days of the Imperium they helped
found. Nothing and no one moved unescorted within
the Palace, except the Tenebrae. Malcador's eyes and ears
watched and listened from the shadows and passed like
breaths of chilly wind as they hunted whispers.

Hundreds of millions lived in the Palace tending its func-
tions, from those holding high bureaucratic office to the
serfs performing the lowest menial tasks. Most remained,
attending to the crucial duties that kept the Emperor's seat
of power working, but whatever solace their positions had
given them before offered little comfort now. Every district
and enclave had been locked down. Food, water and information had become rationed as the intra-system convoys

halted, and the reality of war, often distant, had made its presence known. A black market had sprung up within days. Su-Kassen had read the reports: a senior supervisor of records caught crossing security lines with the water he had bought with the jewelled rings from his fingers; the high matriarch of a noble scribe-clan who had refused to turn back from a containment line, striding past with a laugh, only to be gunned down; the northern records district that was still burning after a chemical stove had exploded. It would only get worse with time, and then...

'Are you all right, admiral?'

She had blinked and looked up at Archamus.

The Huscarl had glanced down at her. 'It is just that I am not certain as to your purpose in walking the Palace.'

They were crossing a stone bridge that spanned a ravine between two internal Palace walls. A chilly wind blew across her face. She blinked at the strangeness of the question and the double strangeness of who was asking it. She frowned, not certain how, or whether, to answer.

'I apologise,' said Archamus after a moment. 'I should not have intruded.'

They lapsed back into silence.

They walked on, through passages narrow enough to brush Archamus' shoulder guards, and others wide enough that a platoon of soldiers could have marched down them line abreast. Most were dark, lit by a scattering of lamps or not at all; fuel and power, like everything else, was a resource that now had to be hoarded and spent with care. All corridors and spaces were empty, echoing.

After half an hour, Su-Kassen realised that they had recrossed their path several times. A while after that she finally had to admit to herself that she had no idea where they were. As if in answer to that fact, they joined a spiral stair of brass and began to climb. Archamus had not tried to guide her, but just followed. At last she realised that her steps had taken them back to the Bhab Bastion – and so she had found herself staring down at the shot-pistol.

'We always return to our cages...' she said to herself. Across the room, Kelik stirred his feathers in reply.

'Do you wish something?' asked Archamus.

'Nothing,' she said, still not turning. 'I will just be a moment.'

There were scratch marks on the pistol's trigger guard, she noticed, silver metal showing through blue-black. Hundreds of gauntleted hands holding the bone grip had made those scratches as their fingers curled around the trigger. The trigger guard itself was big too, enlarged to fit a digit wrapped in void-armour. She wondered how many people had called the gun their own? How many had died with it in their grasp?

She looked at the empty space in the velvet beside the gun, the empty outline of its twin. She reached out, as though her fingers would find something in the space that her eyes could not see.

*'I am sorry,' Malcador had said. 'We must have had this information for a while. For years, but the connection was never made.'*

*She had not looked up from the scroll of parchment in her hands. It was thin enough to be translucent, she realised, the black machine-scribed letters seeming almost to float. So insubstantial, so... unreal.*

*'Why now?' she had heard herself ask. Then looked up at Malcador. The Regent's eyes were steady on hers.*

*'The Khan made a specific request, a demand actually, that we find anything and everything we could. He seemed to think it important that if there were answers to be had, you had them. I agree. Now of all times we must be certain of ourselves.'*

*She had looked back at the parchment, at the words that had been highlighted with a neat line of red ink.*

'...wreckage assay confirm warship Thunder Break destroyed with all hands while trying to flee from the Isstvan System. Indications of command mutiny by traitor elements in crew leading to ship's loss of power and destruction by main gun force of traitor vessels. Peripheral indications that captain had ordered ship to break from Horus' force.'

'I...' she had begun to say and felt a numbness soak in from her skin. 'I need to get back to my command.'

'Of course,' said the Regent, and was standing before she could protest. The effort sent a twinge of pain across his face. He walked with her to the door, leaning on his staff for each step.

'It is wrong,' she said as they reached the door and it hinged open. He stopped and looked at her. 'This is one of thousands, of tens of thousands of front-line loss reports. There will be others, Lord Regent. Who knows how many millions waiting for news that has already become lost in history. That is wrong.'

He nodded.

'War makes the simplest failings cruelty, admiral.'

'Yes,' she said. 'It does.'

She lifted the pistol out. Its weight, once so familiar, now felt different. She looked at it, sitting on her palms.

Captain Khalia Su-Kassen Hon II; killed in action, Isstvan. That is what the updated record would read. An end of sorts, she supposed.

'Admiral, the rating of the signals has increased to Vermillion-Aleph-four,' said Archamus. 'Your presence and response are required.'

She took the ammunition cylinder from the case, opened the breech and snapped it into the pistol. A single smooth movement readied it and pulled the safety off. One squeeze of the trigger and a blizzard of metal shards would rip anything closer than twenty strides into tatters. Not a clean way to die. She hefted it. In her mind she saw Khalia accept its twin from her hand, and felt the awkward silence deepen as she tried to find something to say and her daughter tried to find a way of responding.

'Admiral…'

She looked around the shadow-filled room, released the safety catch and unreadied the weapon.

'That belt and holster, there on the door. Hand it to me.'

Archamus blinked once and then did as she asked. The weight of the pistol settled on her thigh as she walked from the room and mounted the stairs back up to the Bhab Bastion's command chamber.

*'I am proud of you,' she had said, at last. Khalia had looked at the weapon, a thing that had spent more time in her mother's company than she ever had. Su-Kassen had thought her daughter was about to say something. Then Captain Khalia Su-Kassen Hon II had come to attention and bowed her head.*

*'I am honoured, admiral,' she had said, her voice perfect in its formality.*

She reactivated her direct vox- and data-link. Messages and command-grade transmissions began to ping in her ears. She cut them off and looked around at Archamus. The Space Marine would have been monitoring the communication flow and parsing the situation while he waited.

'Situation precise,' she said.

'The First Sphere fleet has begun the counter-attack at the Khthonic Gate,' he said. 'The crown of Pluto's moons is burning.'

# EIGHT

Rule of slaughter
An end to duty
Oathed to this moment

*Strike Frigate* Lachrymae, *Pluto*

The Imperial Fists fleet plunged back into the orbits of Pluto while they were still aflame. Drifts of cooling debris spread from the death points of the planet's five moons. Ships still coming from the warp at the Khthonic Gate ploughed into a wall of wreckage travelling fast enough to shred their hulls. Brief stars flashed as ship reactors overloaded. Of the thousands that had come to take the outermost planet and its gate, hundreds remained, clawing for space in the burning dark.

Into this crucible the ships of Sigismund's fleet cut and began to kill. They came in a long diamond. The fastest ships led at the fore, their heavier sisters following. It was a formation that would have led to their destruction in most battles, but now they came to a battle sphere of scattered and wounded prey. The Three Sisters of Spite were the first to engage. They each carried a commander of the First Sphere:

the *Persephone* was Fafnir Rann's, and carried his Assault
Cadre, while the *Ophelia* was the ship of Boreas, First Templar and Sigismund's lieutenant. The *Lachrymae* remained
Sigismund's steed of war, as it had been since he had taken
command of the outer system defences. Faster than all their
kin, the three ships took the wounded battle cruiser *Fire
Gorgon* first. Its engines damaged, its failing shields broken
under the guns of the *Ophelia* and *Persephone*, it tried to bring
its batteries to bear on its killers. The *Lachrymae* loosed its
payload of torpedoes at point-blank range. The *Fire Gorgon*
became a blink of light. The Three Sisters burned past the
debris of their kill, already firing at their next victim.

Behind them the Imperial Fists fleet followed, every gun
firing without cease. There were targets enough and they
were there not for battle, but for reaping.

On the *Lachrymae*, Sigismund felt the rolling beat of the
guns and his hearts rising in concert. He was not a creature of emotion. There were many who looked upon him
with fear and awe, and some who thought him bellicose,
driven by zeal: a warrior-fanatic of the Great Crusade. He
was all those things in other eyes. But he was just a function, a necessity of time and need. He had been made one
way by chance and time – the boy in the drift camps who
was quick and fast, and took the beatings given by the other
children but never let them break him, who survived for
years after his father was lost to the dust-lung fever. He had
been remade again, given strength and purpose, and an
ideal to follow to the end of his life. And what he had been
remade into was a weapon, a tool that shaped the world
with its edge. That was his purpose, and he would follow it
to the end of all things, until his edge was blunted and the
strength in his arm unequal to his will. And that purpose
did not require him to feel, only to go forwards. It was will,

not fire, that moved his world: cold fire bound by chains. Even in shame, he had held to that. But this moment sung a chord in his soul that had been waiting within through every bitter defence and sacrifice.

Vengeance, righteous and pure, filled Sigismund as he watched ships become fire and atoms. It felt cold, burning like the touch of ice. He opened a vox-channel with a glance at an officer.

'Burn them from the stars,' he said.

And the blade of ships followed his command. Torpedoes were loosed almost blind into the traitor ships drifting amongst the debris. Bombers sped into the dark from battle-barges, spinning amongst the clouds of shredded metal and rock. They found the fleet carrier *Synobarb* tumbling through the wreckage of its escorts. Its prow ripped from its body, it was still trying to relight its engines. The bombers bored into it, flying into the exposed ribs of its superstructure to loose their payloads deep in its core. Melta bombs ripped the shielding from its reactors. Wild plasma poured out, burning through the carcass and sending tongues of flame breathing through the holes in its skin.

Some of the traitor craft still had the wit or the power to resist. Five swift-strike vessels in the black and yellow of the Templar elite penetrated the debris sphere left by Kerberos as they hunted a pair of Iron Warriors frigates. The grand cruiser *Barb of Nostramo* was waiting for them. It had fought its own war in the years since the first treachery, and its crew and masters had loyalty only to their own spite.

Its reactor signature masked by the death-echo of the moon, the *Barb of Nostramo* had slid into the shroud of asteroids and waited. It met the five Imperial Fists strike vessels with a cloud of assault craft. Warriors in midnight armour poured into the Imperial Fists ships. Two escaped. The remainder died by inches, their decks flooded with the screams of those who had already fallen, their chambers and passages darkening one by one as power was cut. The few Imperial Fists on each fought to the last as the screams became silence, and the night surrounding them lit with red eyes and laughing voices.

The two dozen frigates of the Saturnine Void Cohort curved deep into the space between Pluto and the Khthonic gate. They began to unleash barrages of torpedoes, some blind, others aimed.

And amongst the slaughter, the Three Sisters moved and killed, splitting to thread the battle sphere in search of prey. They could not linger, but for this moment this was their kingdom, and its rule was slaughter.

Horus Aximand heard the hull of the *Throne of the Underworld* groan as it made its turn. Steam and fluid vented from the pipes above as forces sheared and tugged at rivets and welds. The void shields were collapsing and sparking back to life as the outwash of debris from the moons' detonations struck them.

'Select and coordinate targets,' he growled into the vox as he crossed the threshold into the teleportation chamber. 'We will tear them from the dark.'

The *Throne of the Underworld* and its fleet had been burning hard in pursuit of the fleeing Imperial Fists ships when the moons had detonated. The loyalist ships had turned about and arced back to the sphere of the outermost planet. Some had turned to meet Aximand's vessels, but their only purpose was to delay, to allow Sigismund's force to strike into the chaos around Pluto. It had worked. It had cost the Imperial Fists those ships they had sent as a distraction, but it had worked. Pluto was a death ground, the ruin of Aximand's assault ash and wreckage in its orbits.

But it would end now. He would take a blood price from the sons of Dorn, and he would do it with his own hand.

'Find their command ship,' he ordered over the vox. Around him, a cohort of his company veterans stood ready as the machines set into the teleportation chamber's ceiling and floor began to sweat arcs of light. 'Find Sigismund.'

A rolling storm of fire struck the *Lachrymae* as she curved past a near-crippled warship. Her auspex did not have time to detect the source of the volley before her shields collapsed. Gravitic shells hammered into her flanks, crumpling and twisting armour with waves of shearing force. A pulse of plasma a hundred metres in diameter hit her engines and reduced half of them to gas and slag. She began to spin, the flame- and iron-filled void a blur around her. On her bridge, Sigismund felt explosions shake the deck. Red light pulsed through the air. The crew were shouting now, orders screamed as the hull shrieked.

'Batteries nine through fifteen lost…'

'Motive power at thirty-five per cent…'

'Course stabilisation lost…'

'Void generator power shunts offline!'

'We are unshielded!'

'Lord,' called a signal officer. The man was gripping the edge of a console, the alarm lights staining his face red. 'Lord, there is an enemy ship closing, fast. Class unknown but it's big. They are launching assault craft.'

'Sound a primary alert throughout the ship,' said Sigismund. 'Prepare to repel boarders.'

'Etheric spike!'

The cry rose a second before a thread of light coiled in the air above the command platform. The squad of Templars scattered through the bridge began to run towards the platform. Sigismund had time to raise his sword as light and shadow reversed and time stuttered. A pillar of lightning flashed into being, slamming into the deck and ceiling. It pulsed. Shapes stood within the light, vast shapes of metal and death. Then the light vanished, and gunfire roared through the sudden dark as the Sons of Horus opened up.

Sigismund was already moving forwards, sword lit, the words of an old oath on his lips. The edge of his blade took the first of the Sons of Horus in the throat even before the flare of teleportation had faded. He was amongst them, cutting and cutting, killing with single blows as gunfire and blades reached for him.

And on the *Lachrymae* fell, bleeding into the void as swarms of assault rams and claws punched into its flanks.

Fire and the clamour of killing filled the bridge of the *Lachrymae*. Warriors in sea-green armour spread out, shooting as they moved. Pulped flesh and blood puffed into the air as bolt-rounds exploded amongst the crew and servitors. Sigismund saw the handful of Templars that had been on the bridge with him go down, singled out for overwhelming bursts of fire and then dragged down by blades. That fate would have been his too if he had submitted to it.

The seconds faded. The world was running to the beat of his twin hearts, reduced to the edge and point and turn of his sword. They were all around him now, sea-green armour, descending blades, gun barrels turning to look at him with the empty eyes of a lost stranger. Too many. Too close. Too swift.

He saw Aximand then, standing back from the killing whirl of his warriors, a snarling bronze-fronted helm beneath a red crest, a great sword sheathed at his back. A half-moon of jet and silver sat on his shoulder beneath the red eye of Horus.

The weight of the sword in Sigismund's hand seemed to vanish. The chains were gone. It would end here. All the years of war would end here.

*Death... alone and unremembered.*

He could see it all. The arc of a chainaxe sweeping down to cut his sword arm, the blow of a sword, the path of the rounds that would chew his legs from beneath him, on and on – the spinning truth of blades writing the words of death. He could read it all and see that there was no unravelling it.

Death...

Alone in the stars, not at his father's side.

Keeler had been wrong.

Death and failure...

He would die here.

The realisation sank through him, and for the first time in perhaps all his life, he felt peace.

*But I will not die alone...*

His sword met the chainaxe blade edge to blade edge. Sparks and lightning shrieked through the air. He cut through the axe head, sword juddering in his grip as chain teeth sprayed into the air. He pushed the cut on and down into the chest of the warrior that had swung the axe. The traitor did not have time to fall. Sigismund rammed his weight forwards, pushing the blade down and out of the bottom of the warrior's torso.

A power sword thrust into the space Sigismund had just left. Its power field split the armour over his ribs. He slammed an elbow into the new attacker's face. Bolts exploded on the deck and in the air around him, but he was already moving forwards, pulling his sword around to take the legs from under the warrior with the power sword, even as his comrade collapsed to the deck in a wash of gut-fluid and blood.

This was not the swordplay of the duelling cages. It was what Khârn of the XII would have called 'the truth of battle'. Stabbing, hacking, breaking. Killing without pause or cease as blood painted the world. It had a rhythm, though – a terrible and pure beat drummed out in the clash of blades and the roar of guns and the surge of muscle and blood. It was all around him, and within him, the last refuge of his soul, the home he had carved himself cut by cut.

The Sons of Horus were good, battle-hardened and chosen for skill and ferocity. They were killers all. But they went backwards, formations and fire lines distorting as they tried to bring their guns and blades to bear on the Lord of Templars. Sigismund drove into them, every movement of his sword a strike. He barely registered the mass of them, his eyes fixed on Horus Aximand amongst the throng of his warriors. The jolt of blade parting armour, the steps that pushed him forwards past the cuts of his enemies – all fell away leaving only the path to this one enemy. He was going to die here. Sigismund knew that. The only choice left to be made was how.

'Alone and unremembered…' came the ghost-voice of Euphrati Keeler.

He shrugged aside a blow from a hooked axe, felt its force crack his right pauldron and cut down. A gasp of fresh blood into the air, another body falling, another step forwards. Aximand was moving towards him now, his own blade unsheathed and lit. A shell exploded on his damaged shoulder. The ceramite shattered. Pain exploded through him and his next cut twitched aside from its mark. He caught the failed cut and raised his sword in time to meet a maul swung from just out of sight. Then another blow swinging in, hacking at his midriff, the attacker one amongst a crowd. A chainsword spun sparks as it raked down his arm, shredding armour from wrist to forearm.

Blood. He could taste blood now.

Aximand was coming close, unhurried. The sword in his hand was as broad as a mortal's shoulders, a slaughterman's blade.

Sigismund turned another strike and sliced his own sword across a throat under a bronze faceplate. A concussive boom, and an explosion in his side. Pain. A world shattering into white slivers. He was not going forwards now, and the crowd of green armour was all around, striking, roaring.

Aximand was almost there, a red cloak spilling from his shoulders, eye-lenses red in the tusked grotesque of his faceplate, a devil-king come to deliver the last gift to a crippled foe.

'Come to me!' breathed Sigismund.

Pillars of light unfolded in mid-air across the deck. Blast waves tore out. The Sons of Horus caught in the glare blurred to shadows before they came apart. Figures in yellow armour stood in their place. Sigismund saw the shapes of boarding shields locked in defensive circles. Bolters fired, and the sound of explosions chased the fading thunder of teleportation. Traitor legionaries fell, punched off their feet by impacts. The circles of Imperial Fists broke apart and flowed back together, shields locking into a single wall. Sigismund saw the twin axe emblem burned into the pitted yellow, and Rann's black shield at the centre of the line as it charged. They fired as they came, shooting from the loopholes in their high shields. It was brutal perfection, like a perfect axe blow to shatter a skull. And as Sigismund rose, his own blade cutting into the enemies surrounding him, he heard the shield-wall crash into the Sons of Horus.

The mass of sea-green warriors reeled back, but they were neither humans nor newborn Space Marines. They were the XVI Legion as they had once been, warriors who had earned in blood and death the high place from which they had fallen. They reformed to meet the Imperial Fists shield-wall. Gunfire punched out. Streams of plasma and melta-beams struck a single shield and vaporised both shield and warrior. The scattered Sons of Horus came together in a narrow wedge to force open the break in the shield-wall before the gap closed. A command roared out above the heads of the Imperial Fists, echoing across the vox.

'Open!' shouted Rann.

The wall pulled apart, wide spaces appearing between the shields. Warriors in yellow and black charged through the openings. Enamelled laurels crowned their helms, and the swords in their hands lit with blue fire. At their head ran Boreas, his white tabard of office flecked with blood and burned by flame. The Templars struck the Sons of Horus as the shield-wall closed behind them.

It was as though a thunderbolt had reached ahead of the closing storm front. The bridge was suddenly a press of bodies and weapons grinding together like bloody teeth. Power weapons split flesh and armour, and now the deck was a swirl of hacking, slicing and battering. Sigismund saw Boreas put his sword through a warrior in sea-green, and fire half a clip of bolt-rounds into the face of another before kicking the corpse off his blade in time to meet the downward cut of a chainglaive. Another slice of time, and the jaws of battle closed over Boreas.

Sigismund was cutting forwards against the tide; he could feel his wounds clotting inside his armour. There were warriors in green and bronze all around him. Another line of pain across his ribs as a blow from behind lashed into his side. He reversed his sword and stabbed it up under his arm. He felt it punch home and ripped it back, spinning the blade in his hands and bringing it down and up to cut the warrior in front of him from groin to shoulder. He stepped forwards and paused.

The fingers of his left hand would not close on the grip of his sword.

There was something in his side, something embedded in his ribs, something scattering pain into his nerves.

'Lord!' He heard the shout, close by but dim against the din of clashing blades and gunfire.

He could taste iron in his mouth.

The battle parted in front of him.

His left arm was numb, his strength draining red onto the deck.

Horus Aximand came for him. Little Horus did not offer words or posture for the kill. Those were the mistakes of lesser warriors, of those who believed that contempt led to victory. Aximand simply charged and swept his great, broad-bladed sword up in a killing blow.

Sigismund stepped back, but Aximand's first cut became the second and the third. Sigismund parried the last one-handed and felt the force of the impact tear the muscles in his right shoulder. Little Horus kept coming, swinging faster and faster. Sigismund cut back but found only air; Aximand was fresh and Sigismund could feel his world contracting away from the battle around him. This was a moment that the Sons of Horus had left for their lord, weakened prey for the teeth of the alpha wolf.

Sigismund read Aximand's next cut and hammered a back-handed counter at his head. Aximand met the blow and the two swords ground against each other. Sparks arced out from the competing power fields. Little Horus forced his blade forwards. Sigismund jerked back, releasing his locked blade, but Aximand had felt the pressure give and was lunging forwards. Sigismund raised his sword. But the parry never met.

A long blade slammed Little Horus' sword down.

Boreas rammed his weight forwards into Aximand as the lord of the Sons of Horus dragged his blade back up and turned to meet this new opponent. Boreas punched the pommel of his sword into Aximand's right eye-lens. Red crystal shattered. Boreas struck again and again, giving Aximand no space to cut. Armour crumpled. Blood spattered from torn ceramite.

Boreas stepped back, raising his sword to cut down and in. It was perfectly timed, the product of experience and training and the lessons of ten thousand battlefields. It was also a mistake. The blow would not land. Not because Boreas had made an error in technique, but because the opponent he was facing was a lord of traitors, a son of Horus schooled by the Warmaster both before and after his fall. Aximand twisted and rammed his faceplate into Boreas before the Templar could strike. Sigismund saw Boreas stagger, then the press of battle closed over his view.

Sigismund shoved forwards but a warrior with a crested helm barred his path and swung a two-handed mace. A shield caught the blow. Light and lightning exploded off the black-faced shield. The warrior with the mace staggered. Rann rammed his shield forwards and buried his axe in the warrior's neck.

'They have teeth after all,' growled Rann, pulling his shield close as a squall of bolt-rounds exploded off it. Sigismund was at Rann's side, the old patterns of war slotting back into place without question. There were Imperial Fists all around them now, forming a triangle of overlapping shields.

'Low!' shouted Rann as a beaked hammer's head hooked over the top of his shield to pull it down. Sigismund braced, holding his sword low in his one good hand. Rann gave for an instant and then surged forwards, muscle and armour and decades of sharpened skill flowing into the movement. The shield went high, yanking up the hammer hooked over its edge. Sigismund stabbed his sword up and under the bottom of the shield. He felt it ram home through armour and into meat, and pulled it back before the dead weight could pull it down.

In the brief opening he glimpsed Boreas and Aximand. There were Sons of Horus all around Boreas now, and blood lacquered the First Lieutenant's armour.

'The teleport sequence is initiated,' called Rann. 'The *Persephone* will be in range in four minutes. Think we can live until then?'

Sigismund shook his head.

'We advance to Boreas' side,' he shouted to Rann. The Assault captain's laugh boomed out.

'You really do want to die, don't you? Boreas was right. We came for you and you want to die to these dogs? The ship is crawling with the bastards.'

'Our oath was to this moment,' shouted Sigismund.

'And our duty is to the war,' roared Rann.

'We will not abandon him.'

Rann glanced around at him, green eye-lenses unreadable in his helmed face.

'All right. As you will it.' He braced into the shield. 'Forwards on my lead!' The shield-wall surged ahead, battering into a gale of gunfire and blades.

One pace, two paces, muscle and servos screaming as they absorbed blows, bolters firing into their path.

'Opening!' shouted Rann and a second gap opened in front of the shield-wall. Sigismund saw Boreas again. He was on the deck, his armour and body a bloody ruin. Aximand stood above him in triumph, sword reversed and descending for the final blow.

Sigismund's sword met the down-thrust. Light sheared from its edges. Aximand jerked back from the contact. Sigismund stood above Boreas, beyond the wall of shields.

'Brace for teleport extraction!' shouted Rann into the vox, but Sigismund was not listening. He was taking another step, his eyes reading the arc of Aximand's rising sword, his own muscles and blade aligning. Nothing else was real. Nothing else mattered. His truth was and always had been an echo of this moment, the descent of the sword like breathing out, like life.

His first blow struck Aximand's sword arm and took hand and blade off at the wrist. A second cut followed the first. No pause. No breath drawn. Blood falling as the tip and edge of Sigismund's sword passed through chest-plate. Blood flared bright on green armour, the colour of a sea in storm.

Aximand staggering, bleeding.

The air around them screaming.

Light expanding to drown sight.

Sigismund raised his sword for the killing blow.

And the world vanished in blinding light.

The Imperial Fists left the *Lachrymae* to the blades of their enemies. The surviving ships dived for the void and the distant mote that was the sun. Most were wounded, many were burning, and some would die before they reached the battles that waited for them.

On the teleportation deck of the *Persephone*, Sigismund lowered the sword that he had raised on another ship. The dissipating thunder of teleport discharge faded from the air. Around him, streaked in blood and soot, stood the brothers that had come for him. Behind him, unmoving on the deck, lay Boreas. Blood was seeping from him, pooling on the floor.

'Apothecaries!' shouted Rann from nearby.

Sigismund did not speak. The numbness in his left arm had become fire in his flesh. He looked down at his sword, still chained to his other wrist, and then raised it and touched the flat of its blade to his forehead.

# NINE

Slayers of kings
Spear of many blades
The truth of knives

*Battle-barge* War Oath, *Supra-Solar Gulf*

The holo-images of Kibre and Sota-Nul collapsed into static and then darkness. The psychic projection of Ahriman lingered. The Chief Librarian of the Thousand Sons looked at Abaddon for a moment, then spoke in thought.

+Farewell,+ he said, and then his image was gone, leaving a ghost of psychic frost on the air. +May all be done as it is willed.+

Abaddon looked unblinking into the space vacated by the two sub-fleet commanders. Above and behind him the council chamber rose and spread out, the empty air silent to its shadow-draped walls.

'May all be done,' said Abaddon into the empty dark.

Such was the intent of what they did that the ultimate ends of each part of the attack were known only to the most senior commanders. Of that cadre, only some were aware of the interlocking purposes of their actions. And even then, only a few, a very few, knew the inner knots of the War-master's design. No one else could know, even amongst the highest ranks of the Legion or its closest allies. So, the last gathering of those commanders, before they took to their own paths, had taken place in the empty dark, without aides or companions.

Abaddon stood still at the centre of the room for a moment, his eyes reaching into the dark but not seeing it.

Torchlight danced in the distance.

*Blood hazed his sight.*

*'This is him?' came a voice, low but clear and strong. Abaddon looked up and felt the chains tighten around his neck. Two shadows loomed above him. Both held torches of bright flame. 'He looks barely alive.'*

*'We would not have got him if he hadn't been that way. He went through thirty of the deep-warren gangs before we found him. That was after the rest of his followers had fallen. He was making for a tunnel when we reached him.'*

*'He will survive those wounds?'*

*'If he doesn't, then do we want him?'*

*A low grunt of acknowledgement and then one of the loom-ing shadows came forwards and squatted down. The light of the torch it carried pulled streaks of orange and red across grey-white armour. Dark eyes looked at Abaddon from a face of scar tissue and jagged tattoos.*

*'You see us, don't you, boy?' said the face.*

*Abaddon did not reply.*

*He had been in the deeps leading a raid against the warren holdings of the Headtakers. There had been an ambush. They had been waiting, three clans' worth at least, come to take the head of the exiled prince. Hundreds of gang killers pouring from tunnels, the boom of frag mines detonating, hard rounds buzz-ing through the air... They had killed half of his oath siblings* with the first blasts. It was butchery and cowardice, but he had come out of the smoke and dust and hit the first ambusher he had seen with a backhanded blow that had split the man's head along the hinge of his jaw to the back of his skull.

'You know who we are?' asked the face, its gaze unflinching. Abaddon met it and nodded.

'You are the takers of the dead,' he said.

The face laughed.

'That we are, boy, that we are.' The figure held up a coin in armoured fingers. The silver disc's face was mirror-polished. 'I have a coin for your life.'

Abaddon did not move but held his face and gaze still. There was pain in his side. He could taste blood. He was going to die, but he was not going to give these creatures that looked like men the trophy of victory. If they had come for his life and soul, then they would have to rip it out of him. The takers of the dead had always been there. They lived in the night and stars that circled through Cthonia's skies. They watched, judged and took the worthy up to the dark to become like them. Some thought them just a story, but whole clans had vanished during the gang wars of recent years and were never seen again. The takers were real.

'We have been looking for you,' said the face, 'for the exiled prince who killed his father rather than murder his oath-companions and become a man.'

Abaddon remained silent. The other figure, still half out of sight, shifted and gave a bark of laughter.

'You won't get anything from him, Syrakul. Look at him. He is not a talker. There's too much anger looking for a way out. That's why he is here. That's why he nearly died in those tunnels and got everyone who believed in him killed. He may be a killer, but he is filled with so much fire that he will burn everything he touches.'

The second figure stepped into Abaddon's blurred sight. This one wore the same grey-white armour as the first and held a comb-topped helm under his left arm. Abaddon's eye caught the sign of a crescent moon marked on the helm above the right eye. The man's skin was the black of polished cinder-wood. A close-cropped mohawk of hair ran across his scalp. Wide, silver-grey eyes glittered above a smile. 'That's right, isn't it? You will look upon us and not say a word, even if we reach into you with knives and cut out your soul.'

The first figure, the one called Syrakul, stood.

'Is my brother right, boy?' asked Syrakul. 'Or do you have more than anger flowing in your veins, Abaddon?'

He felt his face twitch at the sound of his name, and his eyes flicked between the pair looking down at him.

'Yes. We know your name,' said the figure with grey eyes. 'We know who you are, and what you have done. We know that you killed almost all the clan of your birth, and that those that remain have hunted you ever since. We know that you killed everyone sent against you, and then found who sent them and did to them what they failed to have done to you. We know all this. We know you are a killer, and a survivor, Abaddon, son of Tarkerradon. What we don't know is if you have the strength to be more.'

'I don't...' Abaddon forced the words out through broken teeth and pain. At some point in the fight after the ambush, something had shattered half the bones of his face. 'I don't want to be a king.'

Laughter boomed out again.

'That is something you will never be, Abaddon,' said the warrior with grey eyes. 'Either you will die here, or you will become one of us. We are the slayers of kings and the killers of tyrants. We are brothers in war, and blood. We live for each other and die for the future we make, and that is all we will ever be. Can you be that, Abaddon?'

He looked up at them. The pain was trying to pull him down

into its grasp. He sucked a breath, heard the chains clink. In his mind he saw the cave of becoming again, his father falling from his bloody hand, him turning fast but too slow as one of the guards yanked back Kars' head and sawed a knife across his blood-sibling's throat.

'Is what you say true?' Abaddon asked, pulling the words from the pit of his pain. 'Do you swear that it is true?'

Syrakul glanced at his companion, and then nodded.

'It is true, boy. By the oath I took on this moment, it is true.'

Abaddon tried to rise but the chains held him.

'I am...' he said, hearing his voice rasp. 'Then I am yours.'

They did not move. He could feel them watching him, weighing him in their eyes.

'Break the chains,' said the grey-eyed warrior.

Syrakul stepped forwards and took hold of the links of Abaddon's bonds and broke them as though they were rotten rope.

Syrakul and the grey-eyed warrior watched him. Abaddon drew a breath and then pushed himself upright, inch by agonised inch until he stood, bloody, his face a broken mass. His left arm hung by his side, broken, the hand hanging by a strand of skin and sinew. Pain shook through him.

The grey-eyed warrior exchanged a look with Syrakul, and then nodded.

'I am Hastur Sejanus. There is a long road ahead of you, Abaddon, and much of it will be marked with greater pain and loss than you have known. There is no reward at the end except to be one of us, to be a brother of warriors and wolves. If that is not enough, then it is better to never begin.'

Abaddon swayed, refusing to let himself prove weaker than his wounds in front of these warriors.

'It will not be enough,' he said. 'It will be everything.'

Syrakul laughed.

'I like him. He is going to be trouble.'

Abaddon watched the dark replace the past, then turned
and walked away.

*Freighter ship* Antius, *Trans-Saturnian Gulf*

Mersadie awoke with a start.

'No...' she gasped with a breath that had been drawn in
a dream of a wolf turning to smile at her with bloody teeth.

The staterooms were quiet around her, the thrum of the
ship a low murmur swallowed by tapestries and cushions.
She breathed hard for a moment, looking around at the
shadows folded over the furniture by the single glow-globe
mounted on a turned bronze stand. The cushions of the
couch beneath her were damp, and her clothes clung to
her skin.

'Bad dreams?' asked Nilus. The Navigator sat in an uphol-
stered chair across the room, his long legs drawn up under
him onto the seat, so that he looked like an old statue of a
mystic that she had once seen in a Conservatory collection.
He had found some clothes to replace his prison overalls:
loose black-and-red fabric now hung from his spider-thin
frame. He had a blanket half wrapped around him but he
did not look like he had been sleeping.

'The merchant's sour-faced bodyguard left you some
clothes,' he said, nodding to a neat pile of fabric on a small
table. 'I don't think she likes you much.'

Mersadie pushed herself up, scratching sleep from her
eyes. There was a metallic taste in her mouth, like copper
or iron.

'Where are we?' she asked.

'Somewhere in the gulf between Uranus and the orbit of
Saturn,' he said, and shrugged. 'At least that is what I would
guess. You have been asleep for a while, but this is going to

take days, even if this bucket of bolts and rust can make it. It's really just an orbital hauler. I doubt it's ever even done a full run from core to system edge.' He smiled, and shook his head. 'We may all die yet.'

Mersadie did not answer, but stood up and went to the pile of clothes.

The *Antius* had broken free of the cascade around Oberon and powered outwards towards Uranus' outer orbits, and the gulf beyond. No one had challenged or tried to intercept them, but they were just another panicked small ship amongst many more. No reply had come from the signal they had sent, either, but she had expected none. For all her confidence in front of Vek, it was an act of desperation not certainty, a stone thrown into a pool in the hope that someone would see the ripples.

She lifted the folded clothes – loose, grey and red.

'She said she would be back for you,' said Nilus. 'The bodyguard that is. I think she wants to talk.'

He stood, unwinding his limbs from the blanket, rolling his head on his neck and then moving towards one of the hatches that led to a different part of the staterooms.

'I will leave you to your privacy,' he said, and went out of sight.

She put the clothes on, the soft, clean fabric strange on her skin.

The main doors to the staterooms opened. The tall silhouette of Aksinya, the bodyguard, stood framed by the amber glow of lumen-strips. Pale eyes met Mersadie's gaze for a second. Something in the cold intensity of that stare reminded her of something, a fragment of an image lost in the cracks of the past. Aksinya jerked her head, and turned back to the corridor.

'Follow,' she said. Mersadie complied.

They walked in silence for long minutes, descending ladders and stairs into spaces that smelled of raw oil and hot metal.

'Where are we going?' asked Mersadie. Aksinya did not answer, but keyed a control on a heavy door crossed with chevrons. The door released with a hiss and thump of pneumatics. The smell of human sweat and breath washed out. Aksinya moved aside and gestured for Mersadie to go through.

The light beyond was a different hue, dim but cold, like a stab-light running on low power. They were standing in the corner of a cargo hold. Its roof arched up to a flattened apex some ten metres above her head. It was small compared to the vast holds on a macro-transporter or warship, but somehow it felt even smaller to Mersadie as she looked at those who waited there. A loose wall of people faced her, staring eyes set in exhausted faces. She saw every age amongst the faces, children peeking out at her from between parents' legs, the old, the young, all staring with a little curiosity and a lot of fear. They wore fabric of every kind and quality: the vulcanised rubber and oil-smeared suits of void dock-luggers, jackets of velvet dotted with brass buttons, smocks of service-stencilled drab, all grubby and stained with days of wear. None of the faces moved, most eyes barely seemed to blink. She heard sounds coming from the other side of the crowd, and realised that there must be people that she could not see, filling the hold space. Ribbons of cooking smoke coiled into the air. She coughed as the smell of excrement and urine touched the back of her throat.

'Who are you?' asked a clear voice from down near the floor. Mersadie looked down, and saw two brown eyes looking up at her from beneath a matted mass of ash-white curls. Mersadie glanced up at the adults standing next to the child, but they did not move or speak. They and all those others that she could see were looking at Aksinya, who had come to stand just behind her. She looked back at the child and bent down, so that she was level with that big, brown gaze.

'I...' began Mersadie and stopped, not sure what to say. 'I am called Mersadie. I used to tell stories.'

'What kind of stories?' asked the child.

'True ones.'

'I like the stories that my grandfather tells. They aren't true, though. They have ghosts and ships of treasure in them, and the kings and queens of the sun, and the knight of the moon. The ones about the knight are the best. She rides across the stars, you know, and she can never speak, not ever, and she has a sword that you can't see, and she doesn't dream because she had to give her dreams to the sun to keep while she went to find the creatures that live in the night.'

Mersadie found herself smiling.

'I like stories like that, too.'

The child nodded, face serious.

'My grandfather will tell me a story when we get back to Cordelia. That's our home. We had to leave, but we will go back, but I have to tell the stories to myself until then.'

A hand reached down and took the child by the shoulder and tugged her back. Mersadie looked up into the face of a hard-eyed man with a Uranus indentured service tattoo circling his cheek.

'Come on, Sibi,' he said, then looked at Mersadie. 'You bring any food down here with your nice words and clean clothes?'

Mersadie straightened, suddenly aware that the line of people had moved almost imperceptibly forwards. There was anger in their eyes now.

'No...' she began. 'No, I am sorry. I didn't know I was–'

'What's happening?' came a call from further back.

'I...' Mersadie began.

'Where are we going?'

The line was a crowd now, sliding closer, so that she could smell the sweat and breath and feel the static charge of fear.

'Why are you here?' came a growl, and a hand reached for her. Aksinya stepped forwards and batted the hand down. The crowd shrank back from the bodyguard.

'Go,' said Aksinya, pushing Mersadie towards the door they had entered through. The crowd did not follow them, but Mersadie thought she could feel their stares even after the chevron-crossed metal closed. She stood for a second in the passage. Aksinya moved to walk past her.

'I understand,' she said to the bodyguard.

'Do you?' said Aksinya, stopping and looking at Mersadie. 'There are six holds on board. All of them just like that. How much food do you think a ship like this has in its stores? How long do you think it will last when split between hundreds of mouths? How long, do you think, until they are not happy to stay where they are? How long until they try to get out? What does your understanding say about what happens then?'

'I am sorry, but I didn't cause this.'

'No, you didn't, but you stopped it getting any better. If we could have docked, we could have got some of those people off, and we could have got supplies. There are people hunting us now, people looking for you – people who will shell fleeing ships on their own side to get to you. So now we all have to run. That little one you were talking to, what do you think happens to her if the people hunting you find us? Have you ever seen what that kind of violence is like?'

'Yes,' said Mersadie, holding the bodyguard's cold gaze.

After a long moment, Aksinya nodded.

'Perhaps you really have, but it makes no difference. I am bound to protect my master and his family. That's it. This ship and the people on it are not mine to shield. That can be no other way.' She took a step closer, and now she was so close that Mersadie could feel the thread of the other woman's breath. It smelled like metal. 'But you… you have pulled the fates of everyone on this ship, and made them yours. I do not know, and I don't care, why the master believes you, but I want you to know that whatever happens to him and these people won't be his fault. It will be yours, teller of stories. It will be yours.'

Aksinya turned and walked away down the dim passage.

'Go back to your quarters,' she called back at Mersadie without looking around. 'He will want to talk to you soon.'

Mersadie Oliton stood still for a second and then followed.

*Battle-barge* War Oath, *Supra-Solar Gulf*

The armada split as it plunged towards the sun. Battle groups began to pull onto separate paths, first the smallest, which rode at the edge, then the larger ships, one layer of formation at a time peeling apart like a knot of rope unwinding into threads.

Far out, circling the dividing fleet, the White Scars saw the formation of enemy ships begin to change. They made kills then, driving in to pick off smaller frigates and gunboats as they broke from the safety of the herd. But the reformation of the armada went on, recasting the single fleet as many without it slowing down.

The White Scars plunged back in, but as they struck, a flock of hundreds of smaller ships broke from the divided armada. They were the fastest of the invaders' ships, crewed by rogue traders and renegade privateers. They had flocked to Horus' call and been given this task in exchange for promises of wealth and power. They were the crows of war that had followed the Great Crusade out to the edge of the dark, and now came back to feast on the corpses of their masters. They scattered outwards from the armada, spiralling out to meet the Falcon fleets. Hundreds of small battles spread across the dark, tumbling in the wake of the main mass of the armada.

And the shape of the armada continued to change. With the skin of smaller craft gone, the main force was revealed. Many vessels bore the livery of the Sons of Horus, blooded war crones like the *Last Light*, the *Oath of Moment* and the *Spear Wolf*. The legionaries on board were veterans, born in the time before the betrayal, breakers of their oaths to the Emperor and keepers of their bonds to their primarch. Beside them rode vessels of such different lines that they seemed less a fleet and more a collection of creations formed of mankind's ingenuity in ship-craft fused with insanity. Galleons of black metal, their skins dotted with chrome pyramids; sleek needles of serrated bronze five kilometres long; slabs of red stone the size of mountain ranges hoisted into space and made into city-ships, their insides filled with ever-turning machines – these were the craft of the disciples of Kelbor-Hal and his New Mechanicum. No two were alike, their size and shape reflections of the magi who commanded them.

One by one the Legion and Mechanicum ships began to separate, pulling into twin spear blades. For a few hours the two formations continued to descend towards the disc of the Solar System together, leaving the Falcon fleets and the privateer carrion feeders behind to spin in battle. Hour by hour, the two fleets moved further and further apart, until each of them could see the light of the other's engines only as a single dot of starlight.

Abaddon watched it all on a display enhanced by scan data, not moving from his place as the hours passed. Around him the business of the *War Oath*'s bridge went on in near silence. It was an act of will for him to remain still, his mind following all the details while the sound of his heartbeats filled his ears, restless and unsettled. But there he remained, watching time and distance pass. There would be battle and bloodshed before victory, but that all rested on these moments. From here, each part of the armada would follow its own path to its own target and its own battles. The White Scars would have seen this first division, and they would track both blades of the divided spear. But not yet. That could not happen yet. There was one more moment of vulnerability and secrecy still to come, one more sliver to be broken off this spear blade.

Abaddon felt the prickle across the skin of his back. His muscles twitched, his armour amplifying the tiny movement with a buzz of servos. He kept his eyes on the display, but bared his teeth.

'I did not call you to my presence, priest,' he said, 'and I have no use for your counsel.'

Zardu Layak halted at his side. The incense reek of the daemon priest filled the air.

'I go where I am needed, not where I am called.'

'You are part of the comet strike force. That is where you *need* to be. The ships of the Fifteenth and your Legion are ready to depart.'

'But *I* am not to depart,' said Layak. Abaddon looked back at him, but the priest was already stepping close, his eyes on the display, his staff tapping the stone floor. 'I remain here, with you.'

'You will go to join the spear thrust to the comet,' said Abaddon. 'That is my will.'

'But it is not the will of the gods.'

'I do not care.'

Layak was silent for a moment.

'These hands were once those of an iconoclast,' he said at last, holding up a fist. 'Did you know that? The warrior who became me burned gods and lived to send the devout and the deluded to the flames.'

'Your conversion is of no interest to me,' said Abaddon.

'I was not a convert,' said Layak. 'The man whose face lies beneath this mask was taken, broken and remade. My faith is sacred because it is a lie, and all lies are music to the ears of the Pantheon. Piety like that is false, a creation, but it is pure. You live for Horus, for your Legion, for your brothers. That is your truth. Mine is that I am nothing. I am a son who left his father. I am a brother who made those brothers his slaves.' Layak nodded to the still and silent figures of the blade slaves standing eight paces away. 'I am like you, Ezekyle Abaddon.'

The choler beating in Abaddon's blood lit to rage.

'I am–'

'On Isstvan, were the warriors that you slew not of your blood? Had they not bled with you? Had they not shared bread and oaths and deeds at your side, and you at theirs?'

*Abaddon saw the ruins again, the smoke coiling into the sky, the ash blowing on the dead wind.*

'*Betrayer,*' *Loken had said. Abaddon tasted the words of his reply, still bitter even in memory.*

'*There was nothing to betray.*'

Layak inclined his head towards the blade slaves. 'I put swords into my brothers' hands. You sheathed your sword in the hearts of those who had trusted you and thought the bonds between you unbreakable.'

Abaddon could not move. In his mind the images of the

past rolled over and over. The things done, the wars fought. Murder, slaughter and deception.

'There was nothing to betray,' he said. 'They were not my brothers.'

'Because they made a different choice?'

'Because loyalty is everything,' and as he spoke the words, he heard the old truth that he had carried in him since he had been a boy standing in a cave looking at a knife that would kill his companions and make him a king. 'We were brothers and sons.'

'And that mattered more than oaths to an Imperium, more than duty, or truth?'

'You can't be loyal to an idea, priest, as your kind learned in the ashes of your first belief.'

A strange, dry rattle came from behind the teeth of Layak's mask. After a second, Abaddon realised that the priest was laughing.

'Belief is all that I have left, and loyalty to an idea is why I am here.'

'Chaos,' said Abaddon, his lips peeling back from his teeth.

'No...' said Layak with a shake of his head, 'the truth.'

Abaddon felt another question form in his mind, but cut it away and turned back to the bridge displays.

The ships of the Word Bearers and Thousand Sons within the fleet were already aligning, forming their own formation within the greater mass of Abaddon's armada, a subtle blade hidden amongst many. The vessels of this third force were few in number, a dozen only, but that was as it needed to be; their part in the greater plan required them to go unseen, while the eyes of the defenders of Sol were elsewhere. Within an hour, the bulk of Abaddon's armada would turn and begin the next stage of their descent towards the inner system. The Thousand Sons and the Word Bearers would carry on, though, cutting their engines so that they fell away silent and dark, down and down into the gulf between the turning planets. Only once they were closer to their goal would they relight their engines. Sorcery would wrap them, pulling eyes and minds away from them until their task was done.

'The sorcerers of Prospero and the warriors of my Legion will do what is ordained,' said Layak, as though following Abaddon's thoughts. 'But my path lies with you, Ezekyle Abaddon, and I will follow it. That is my choice and my place. Kill me if you must, but I will remain.'

Abaddon watched the dance of the void without replying, and when he looked around the priest was gone.

*Warship* Lance of Heaven, *Supra-Solar Gulf*

Jubal Khan listened to the last ghosts of voices fade into the crackle of the vox-link. He looked at the tech-adept linked to the signal unit.

'Send confirmation,' he said. The adept bowed its head with a whir of gears, and the constellations of lights on the unit began to blink. It would take over two hours for the reply to reach Terra, if it reached it at all. Distortion had been growing on the signal channels for days, squalling like a snagged storm wind. Sometimes it seemed as though there were voices, high and pained, drowning in the screech of interference, shouting from beyond the buzz of static.

*No*, thought Jubal. There *were* voices behind there, and he knew enough to know that the nightmares that wracked the astropaths were real, too. Both were echoes of the dead returning to the plane of the living, but whether they spoke warnings or lies he could not tell.

He turned slowly away from the vox-console. His body ached at the movement. It was as though every year of the life that he had lived was dragging on his bones. He would need to settle his spirit before they rode into the fire again. The storm... the storm was coming... He could hear it. He could feel it...

Changshi waited dutifully behind him, watching his khan with grey eyes that could not hide their worry. Changshi was a child of the storm. Like the rest of the token force on the *Lance of Heaven*, he was not of Chogoris, despite the name he bore. It, like the organs grafted into him, were a gift of his elevation from the forgotten ocean world he had been born on. There were many like him now: creations of necessity, made from and for these bitter times, warriors who had never known the joy that came from waging war for a reason other than survival. Both his nature and name had barely had time to settle into his being, and whether fate would give Changshi the time to become the warrior he could one day be, Jubal did not know.

'So we withdraw?' Changshi asked, frowning.

Jubal looked at him, holding the young warrior's gaze for a long moment, and then smiling.

'Yes. And no,' he said, pulling a strip of parchment from his belt and handing it to Changshi.

'Prepare signals to these of our ships, and see that these preparations are made throughout the *Lance*.'

The young warrior read the Chogorian script and his frown deepened.

'Master, I do not–'

'We have a duty to perform before we follow our orders. This spear-tip fleet is almost in the core of the system. We have tracked it, and we have bled it, but it will still strike like a bolt of thunder.' Jubal paused for a second, weighing his decision for a final time. 'We must take the heart of its strength before then.'

'Master, five thousand ships... We cannot destroy that many even if we harried them for ten thousand years...'

'I said we needed to take the heart of its strength, and that is not a ship. It is a man, a warrior like you and me. Great and terrible, and weak and vulnerable, as we all are...' And then he told the young warrior what would happen.

At the end, Changshi bowed his head, but his face was grim.

'What weighs on you?' asked Jubal.

'You said we had a duty, but how can we have a duty that drives against our orders?'

Jubal laughed and let the sound drain away slowly.

'Which matters more, to obey the word, or to obey the spirit?'

Changshi held his gaze still.

'When the words are the Great Khan's and Primarch Dorn's, is there a difference?'

'Always,' replied Jubal. 'Words are the weak children of the will and the soul. To see them truly, we must look through them, and ask what spirit moved to make those words.'

He reached down to his belt, drew his knife, tossed it up in the air, caught it by the blade and threw it to Changshi. The young warrior caught it. The blade was the length of a mortal human's forearm, curved like the moon, polished to a mirror sheen. Opals gleamed on its pommel.

'Put it in my heart,' Jubal said.

Changshi looked at him sharply.

Jubal grinned.

'Or at least try to,' he said.

Changshi was still for a second and then turned, his weight dropping, the curved blade vanishing behind his body. His

eyes had gone distant, fixed on nothing, but seeing everything. Jubal waited, relaxed, his hands at his sides, smile still
in place. Changshi nodded to himself as if deciding, then
paused and opened his mouth to ask a question.

He snapped forwards.

*Wind of truth, but the boy was fast,* thought Jubal. The
cover for the strike had been good too, combining timing
and subtle misdirection. But he was Jubal Khan, and he
had faced and bested many of the greatest weapon masters
of the age. He half turned his torso, let the blade go past,
brought his hand up, clamped Changshi's knife hand and
wrist, and threw him with a sharp twist. The young warrior
came to his feet in a blur. Jubal tapped the flat of the knife
on Changshi's head as he rose.

'Not quite,' he said.

Changshi closed his eyes, and Jubal could almost hear
the silent self-chastisement held behind the warrior's teeth.

'You know the truth of death?' Jubal asked.

Changshi let out a breath, and smiled.

'To embrace it like a brother, and laugh in its face.'

'Yes,' grinned Jubal, 'and the truth of the knife?'

'To be sharp.'

Jubal chuckled.

'Yes… but no.' He stepped away, turned, rolled his shoulders. 'To put a knife through someone's heart is the end. It
is not the means.' He could almost see the question forming on Changshi's lips, could hear the inhalation of breath
before the words.

Jubal spun and slashed with the knife. Changshi blocked
the first blow. Fast, very fast, but Jubal had already reversed
the knife, hooked the warrior's arm with it, and yanked
his guard aside. Changshi recovered, but Jubal flicked the
knife between his hands, slammed a palm into the young

warrior's breastplate to rock him back, cut, switched hands again before the first cut had been blocked, then pivoted back out of range of Changshi. The young warrior made to follow, but Jubal raised a hand.

'Look,' he said, pointing at Changshi's armour with the point of his knife. The young warrior looked. Long, straight cut marks scored the plate just above both of Changshi's wrists and elbows. 'And with the next clash, another cut...' said Jubal, stepping close to Changshi and tapping the tip of the blade against the young warrior's upper arm, against his fingers. 'And with each cut, a little more strength bleeds away, a little more rage is planted in the heart, a little more blindness in the eye, until...' He tapped the knife against Changshi's breastplate above the heart.

'Until the blow to the heart is not seen, and cannot be stopped,' said Changshi. Jubal nodded, and flicked the knife over and held it out to the young warrior pommel first.

'That is the truth of the knife, of life, of war... You kill with the last blow, but those cuts that come before allow that final blow to fall. Even Horus, master of the spear-thrust, knew that truth once. And now we will use it to kill which-ever of his sons he has sent at the head of this armada.'

Changshi took the knife, looking at it, the reflection of the crescent blade caught in his grey eyes. It was a beautiful weapon, made on Chogoris and fitted with a power field generator by the Legion smiths. It had been Jubal's father's, given to him when he left his family and his humanity behind. Now the young warrior, who bore a Chogorian name but had never seen its skies, looked at it and realisa-tion formed in his eyes.

'Master, I cannot accept this...'

'You can and you will. Just as you will go from my side and join the *Blade of the Endless Horizon* before the strike.'

'But–'

'You shall bear that knife and its truth, as this battle spirals down into the throat of the sun, and beyond.' He paused. 'Someone must ride beyond the horizon.'

The young warrior nodded, and Jubal began to turn away.

'You said that Horus knows the truth of knives in war...' began Changshi. Jubal turned back to look at the young warrior, feeling a frown form on his face. 'Then might we not be fighting the cuts, and not seeing the thrust to *our* heart?'

Jubal blinked, and then smiled.

'Yes,' he said. 'But we fight anyway.'

# TEN

Atonement
Small lives
Lords of war

*Strike Frigate* Persephone, *Outer Solar System*

The last defenders of Pluto fled towards the light of the sun. Ragged, scarred and with the blood of battle still marking their decks, they kept on. Where there had been hundreds, now there were barely enough to make a lone hundred. The *Ophelia* and *Persephone* circled their sisters and cousins, watching the fleet and the void around them. They could not see their pursuers, but they knew they were there. Aximand had suffered catastrophic losses, but new ships were still coming from the warp. There would be hunters at their backs, swift ships with cruel intent.

Some of the survivors fell even as they fled. Engines failed, wounded hulls broke apart under the stress of acceleration. The *Sword Sister*, which had endured battles since the first decades of the Great Crusade, became a silent hulk, ploughing on for hours on momentum. The *Sign of Truth* peeled away from the pack as its damaged reactors

began to overload. The light of its death chased its surviving kin.

On they ran, through the gulf of night, their hulls creaking with damage, their human crews feeling their world
shake, the Legion-born warriors pulling broken armour
from wounded muscles; past the wrecked ships of all the
invaders and usurpers who had fallen in the long millennia
since humanity had first left its cradle.

In the hold of the *Persephone*, Sigismund paused on the
threshold of the sanctuary. His armour hung from him in
torn shards, grinding as he moved. Blood caked his tabard
and had clotted inside the plates. He felt cold, the hot beat
of the pulse in his veins quieted after the roar of battle.

'It is what awaits us all in the end,' said Fafnir Rann
from beside him. 'By sword or bullet, it is coming for us
all.' Sigismund looked up at the captain of the Assault
Cadre. Blood and damage painted Rann's armour too,
and dried blood masked half of his face. 'He chose how
to meet it. There is nothing more any of us could ask.'
Rann paused, holding Sigismund's gaze with his own.
'And nothing more you can give him.'

Sigismund gave a small nod and keyed the door release.

The space beyond was small and the light low. Stone-clad
walls climbed to an arched roof. The names of every warrior who had ever called the ship home and died in battle
marched over every surface, incised in gilded letters. The
door sealed behind Sigismund. The low rasp-thump of
machinery beating a dual pulse filled the quiet.

The remains of a figure lay under a shaft of dim light.
They had tried to cut him from his armour, but armour
and flesh could not be separated without ending what the
Sons of Horus had begun. Tubes and pipes led from blocks
of machinery and jars of dark fluid. The rattling bubble of

breath drawn by a machine through fluid-filled lungs rose and fell in time with the pulse and thud of the tubes.

Sigismund stepped forwards. His armour growled. Something in the mass of sticky flesh and torn ceramite flickered and opened.

'L… o…' the sounds bubbled out. After a second, Sigismund realised it was a word, pulled out of the figure letter by letter as the machines gave it breath. 'L… o… r… d…'

He knelt then, servos grinding, his gaze fixed on Boreas' eye.

'No,' he said. 'I am no lord here, my brother.'

'Y…o…u…' began Boreas. 'You… li…ve…'

Sigismund nodded.

'The tech-priests–'

'I… know… I will… not… go to… the… iron sleep,' said Boreas. Sigismund shook his head. There would be no rebirth as a Dreadnought for Boreas, no half-life of metal and war until he died a second time.

Sigismund bowed his head.

'Why…' The word brought his head up. Boreas' eye was fixed on him, bright and unblinking. 'Why… did… you want… to die?'

He saw the flash in his mind of the blades and faces of the Sons of Horus.

So many… Too many.

'I…' began Sigismund and now it was his words that faltered. He closed his mouth. The hiss-thump and gurgle filled the moment. 'Atonement,' he said at last.

'For… what?'

'For an oath broken,' said Sigismund. The gaze of Boreas did not shift as he spoke, and the machines beat out the seconds. And Sigismund found himself speaking. He spoke of Euphrati Keeler, of the days after the first word of Horus' treachery had found Dorn. He spoke of a vision she had given him of the future, and the choice that went with that vision: to be here now, as the darkness came to swallow the sun, and raise his sword against it, or to follow his primarch's order and lead a fleet to strike at Horus in the earliest days of the war. He spoke of how he had chosen, and how he had returned with Dorn to Terra, and when the fleet that was his to command was lost, how he had told Dorn about his reason for returning and what he feared Keeler's vision meant. And last he spoke of Dorn's wrath at the reason.

*You are not my son.* The words echoed again in his mind, and he fell silent before they could come from his mouth.

'I failed,' he said, 'and I swore I would never fail him again.'

'You… were… right…'

'That is not for us to judge.'

'Death… is… not… atonement,' said Boreas. 'Not even… now… at the end…'

Sigismund felt something cold tighten within him. Boreas' gaze had gone distant; the rhythmic beat of the pumps rose, labouring. The tubes and flasks gurgled and sputtered. The fluid in the jars was dark.

'You… atone… by… living… until… until the last… blow… of the sword.' Something in the ruin of meat and twisted armour shifted. It might have been a hand reaching to grasp, or just the shudder of life fleeing the will holding it. 'Until… the last blow… of the sword… Swear it to me.'

'You have my oath,' said Sigismund.

The machines stopped. A high wail replaced the bubbling hiss and thump.

'And you… mine… my brother…' said Boreas. His eye flashed clear for a moment, his gaze steady as it held Sigismund's. 'Always.'

Beyond the stone walls of the room, beyond the hull of the ship lancing through the void, beyond the ships of the fleet that followed it, the Solar System turned on, silent and unceasing.

*Freighter ship* Antius, *Trans-Saturnian Gulf*

Vek paused outside the stateroom door, his hand on the release. Around him, the hum of the ship passing through the void vibrated gently through the air. The lights in all the compartments and companionways had dimmed to the night-cycle. Quiet shadows filled the edges of everything. Even on the bridge, the crew still on watch had talked little. Most had been stood down and gone to get some sleep. Vek hadn't, though. The thoughts that had followed him from the clamour and chaos of the flight from Uranus did not quiet in this time of silence.

He had gone to check on his children, and found them sleeping. Noon had been in his bunk, mouth wide, snoring, hands tucked under his head, and he had frowned and turned over as Vek had kissed him on the forehead. Mori was not in her bunk. She had taken her blankets and curled in the corner of the room. An auto-scribe book had slipped out of her hands onto the deck. Vek had picked it up. She had sucked a breath as if to call out, raised her head and looked as though she were about to open her eyes. Vek had frozen, and Mori's head had dropped back. After a moment her breathing had fallen back to the slow rhythm of sleep. She was frowning, he noticed, and for a blink of his mind's eye he saw the same expression cross his memory of her mother's face.

He had glanced at the words Mori had auto-scribed across the page of the book.

*I don't know where we are going,* it read. *No one is telling me.
Maybe they don't want to say. Maybe they don't know.*

He had looked at the words for a long while and then put
the auto-scribe book back beside his daughter. He bent and
kissed her lightly and went to the door. In the night-dimmed
corridor he rubbed the heels of his hands across his eyes.
When he took them away, there were worms of neon light
still clinging to his sight.

*I don't know where we are going…*

He should think, try to think about what they would do
when they reached Jupiter. Had the war reached there yet?
Did they have enough food to make it?

He swayed.

He was tired…

His feet started to move…

He should sleep…

But he would not, could not sleep. Not now…

He walked, and the ship shivered with a familiar rhythm
that once would have given him comfort. He walked and
the world and past and questions turned in his head, until
he found that he had stopped.

He blinked at the doors of the staterooms in front of
him. He began to wonder why he was here. But, of course,
he knew why…

He raised his hand, and knocked.

'Mistress Oliton,' he said.

The door opened from the inside before he could knock
again.

The lights were on in the stateroom. Mersadie Oliton
looked at him. There was an expression on her face that he
could not quite read. Sadness? Resignation?

'You have questions,' she said, and moved back to a chair
set beneath a glow lamp. The bed had not been used, he

noticed. She picked up a cup from a low table and put it to her lips. Steam and the smell of caffeine rose from it. He glanced at where the decorative samostill sat on a plinth at the other end of the room. An open tin of grounds sat beside it, some gritting the polished wood. There was a pop and a gurgle, and a curl of steam rose from a brass vent-tube.

'I think that samostill is meant to be decorative...' he said. 'I have certainly never used it.'

'Ah,' said Mersadie, 'that would explain why it took so long to get working.'

He looked at her and thought he saw the ghost of a smile on her face.

'There seemed to be no shortage of caffeine, though.'

'Part of the family business,' he said. 'We held the transit monopoly on Kaderine Caffeine through Uranus orbits for twelve decades...' He trailed off, realising that he was still standing by the open door.

'Do you want some?' asked Mersadie. 'I think I made too much.'

'No,' he said, turning and closing the door. 'No, I think I might want to try to sleep later, but thank you. Too much of that, and you won't sleep for days.'

'That's what I am hoping...' she said.

They lapsed into silence as he sat on one of the other chairs. She took another drink from her cup, and waited.

He opened his mouth, not sure what he was going to say, but she spoke instead.

'You want to know about her, don't you? About Keeler.'

He closed his mouth, then nodded.

'Yes,' he said.

'You believe, don't you? You are a follower of the *Lectitio Divinitatus*.'

'My wife...' he began, then paused, closing and opening his mouth. 'No, not really, but...'

'A dangerous thing to be part of a proscribed cult – even worse if your soul isn't in it.'

'I... Do you... Are you...'

'Do I believe?' she said. She smiled, took another sip from her cup, then gave a short laugh. 'I have seen things... When you know the truth, does that leave room for faith or does it become fact?'

'But Keeler,' he asked, and heard the hunger in the words as they came from his mouth. 'She is real then, you knew her?'

Mersadie looked at him for a long moment, and then put the cup down.

'I owe you thanks, Master Vek, thanks and apologies that you do not have to accept. But I can't offer you certainty. I can't even offer hope.'

'You said, though, that you needed to reach the Praetorian, that the saint... that Keeler–'

'Do you know what the Crusade and the Betrayal have taught me?' She was looking directly at him, now, and there was a hardness in her eyes. 'We are small things, we humans. We mean very little. Our lives are narrow and short, and our dreams, even if noble, will not shift the stars in the sky. We are not the movers of this age. Horus is, and the Emperor. The choices and the hope and the ruin belong to them.'

Vek breathed in sharply. His hands twitched. Mersadie did not move.

'I am sorry, Master Vek,' she said. 'You asked about Keeler, about what I am doing and why I am doing it. I thought you deserved an answer.'

'But you talk of...' He paused, the fear taking the sounds

of the name from his tongue. 'You talk of the Warmaster, not the saint.'

'Because if there are arch-traitors and saints, then hope is their realm, the realm of cosmic change and slaughter and sorrow. They are the ones who will decide tomorrow, and if there are any tomorrows after that. We are human, Master Vek. Our lives only matter in quantity. We can dream and despair and cling on to what we have, but those things live only in us. Our hope is our own, and if the universe cares, it does so by accident. That is why people pray to the Emperor and call my old friend a saint. Because deep down, they know that they cannot change the great course of events.'

'You have a very bleak view for someone claiming to be trying to help save the last fortress of humanity.'

'I have seen Horus,' she said. 'I have heard his voice. One day everyone who can say that will be gone, and no one will remember. But I remember, and for years I have tried to hold on to that memory.'

'What? Why?'

'Because it *matters*. What I saw *mattered*. Horus was greater and more noble and more terrible than any human could ever be. It was not just the armies, you see. It was not just his sons. It was that he was something beyond us, something that spoke like us and wore a face that was like ours, but was from another order of existence. He *existed* in a greater way. The smallest things he did, and choices he made could send cracks across the shell of life. He was a creature who turned, and half the galaxy turned with him…'

'And burned,' said Vek, and began to rise. He could feel a headache building at the edges of his eyes. This was not what he had come for, but it was his fault that he had come here at all.

'I can't lie to you,' she said. 'You have done too much for

me not to tell you what I believe before you can choose what *you* believe. I can tell you that I am carrying information from my old friend, who is now the saint of a rogue cult that worships the Emperor as a god, a friend who spoke to me in dreams. You can hear that and believe that I am carrying a message from the divine to a primarch, that I am chosen, that this is something only I can do, that I do the will of the Emperor and that He protects us. You can believe that you are doing good, that it will mean that everything is going to be all right...' She trailed off, shrugged. She looked very tired, he realised, drained in a way that he thought was deeper than a lack of sleep. She gave a half-smile. 'Or you can believe that I am insane and dangerous. That it was the worst mistake of your life to help us, that it is all going to end badly. You can believe that, instead.' She stood up and went to the samostill, and filled her cup again. 'And all of those things might be true at the same time.'

'But you believe...' he said.

'I *know* I need to do what I can. And yes, I believe... I believe that we are small, and that our dreams cannot change the stars. But sometimes our deeds can change the universe, even if it is only by accident. If you want to, you can find your hope in that.'

Vek found that he was smiling.

'And that is enough?'

'It is all we have,' she said.

Vek stood, poured a cup of caffeine and winced. 'I always hated this stuff.' He stood, and went to the door.

He had his hand on the release and the door open when she spoke again.

'Thank you, Master Vek.'

'For what?' he asked, half turning.

'For believing.'

He was still for a moment, not certain if he did believe, but knowing that he had made his choice.

'You should sleep,' he said, and pulled the door shut behind him.

*Battle-barge* War Oath, *Supra-Solar Gulf*

'They come,' whispered Abaddon to himself as he watched the enemy close.

The grey-white ships did not come as a single fleet, but in a wild, pattern-less rush. First came the *Blade of the Endless Horizon* and its caste of torpedo frigates, burning on a spiralling path, loosing torpedoes seemingly at random, closing so fast that it seemed they would fly straight into the guns of Abaddon's fleet. They did not. As the first salvoes from long-range batteries reached for them, they turned and scattered like droplets of water from forge-hot iron.

The twin strike cruisers *Truth of the Wind* and *Storm Soul* cut in. Running side by side, they dived towards the armada and then slammed out of their dives at the edge of the Sons of Horus' range. They cut laterally, spiralling and dancing as explosions chased them.

Watching them in his helm display Abaddon remembered a story told by Yoden Croweaver of the VI. When ships would meet on the seas of Fenris, warriors would run the oars of the boats in full armour with weapons drawn, bounding from oar-haft to oar-haft as the sea rose and fell and their enemies watched. Even if one boat met twenty in a storm, still a lone warrior would run the oars. Abaddon had understood why.

'To show their contempt of death,' he had said. 'To show that even if cut down by greater numbers they were still worthy of the life they led.'

*Yoden had shrugged, and nodded.*

*'Is there any other way to face death than by laughing?'*

The torpedoes loosed from the first attack wave struck their targets. Explosions blossomed across the armada's lead ships. Fire and plasma ripped wounds in armoured skin. In a dozen warships, thousands died in the pinprick flashes that sparkled in Abaddon's eyes.

'No sign of the *Lance of Heaven?*' he said into the vox.

*'None yet, brother,'* came the reply from Krushan. Abaddon had left helm command to the veteran line-captain.

'She will come,' replied Abaddon. 'Commit as soon as she does.'

*'As you will it, brother.'*

Abaddon cut the vox, but kept the sensor feed running in the corner of his right eye as he stalked into the teleportation chamber. A throng of black-armoured warriors greeted him with raised fists and weapons. These were his finest, the elite of the First Company: Justaerin, Reavers and Death Marked. All of them had fought at each other's side for years before the war, and had thrived in the battles that came after. There was Sycar, his lieutenant and commander of the components that would strike at their target's engines and power conduits, grinning at Ralkor with sharp, steel teeth; Tybar and his squad were fixing oath parchments to their bolters. Some wore talismans that showed they had founded alliances with one of the many faces of the powers of the warp.

Abaddon moved amongst them, returning their greetings with a nod, pausing to grip the hand and wrist of Gultaron, the young warrior still recovering from the wounds dealt to him in pursuit of the Wolves during Beta Garmon.

'My captain,' said Gultaron, bowing his head briefly. Abaddon moved on, feeling the pre-battle tension rising and spreading through the force like a thunderhead before the storm. He smiled inside his helm. This was his home. In these moments amongst these brothers and warriors he felt the universe align, become clear, become as it should be.

Urskar and Gedephron were standing together, serfs clustered around them as the last plates of their Cataphractii armour were slotted into place. The breeches of Urskar's reaper cannon cycled as boxes of heavy rounds locked into its loader. His crimson helm glinted with silver-filled scars, an echo of the face beneath. Gedephron was snapping the power field of his power mace on and off, flexing his grip and shoulders.

They did not bow their heads as Abaddon approached, or show any sign of acknowledgement. They did not need to. They had fought at his side for longer than any other. They had saved his life and he theirs. He was their captain but they needed no sign to mark the bonds of respect and blood that bound them.

Abaddon was about to speak when he felt stillness ripple through the chamber. Gedephron's head jerked up, the rest of his body motionless.

'The dogs of ashes…' he growled aloud. Abaddon turned, following his brother's gaze. Layak and his blade slaves walked across the deck. The chatter and bark of voices quieted. Eyes followed the three Word Bearers. Abaddon waited, feeling the fire rise to his tongue and pulling his lips back from his teeth.

'Why are you here?'

Layak paused, looked around slowly.

'To face the enemy at your side,' he said.

The room remained still. All it would take was the smallest gesture, not even a word, and the three Word Bearers would be dead on the deck. Again the question of why he had let

Layak remain with him surfaced in Abaddon's mind, and
found no clear answer.

He turned his back on them without reply, and blinked
the ship's sensor feed so that it filled his right eye. The flash
of explosions hundreds of kilometres in size replaced the
sight of his brothers.

The White Scars were coming again, wheeling in, formations changing, ships moving between squadrons like birds
spiralling on the wind. It was dazzling. Sixty-one ships in
the outer shell of the armada had taken serious damage. This
was the White Scars' purpose, not to kill unless they had a
chance, but to slice a thousand times so that the ships that
struck the inner Solar System would be already bleeding,
already weak. The privateers and vagabond ships that had
split from the armada had drawn off much of the White Scars'
void-strength, but not enough. The grey-and-white ships had
not taken the bait, but spun away, gathered and come back
at the main bulk of Abaddon's ships with fresh focus. That
took vision and control that even the best Legion void commanders would struggle to wield. Abaddon could ill afford
to let their strength bleed away before they reached their true
objective. So they would bring this dance to an end.

Abaddon's armada did not halt. If it deviated from its
path, it would lose the advantages bought by the blood and
sorcery that had let it emerge so far inside the sphere of the
Solar System. So, it fought as it ploughed on, a single vast
beast tormented by the bites of the falcons that now spun
across its path.

*'That's the problem with that Cthonian directness you so value –
it works too well.' Abaddon had let a spark of annoyance show
on his face. Jubal Khan had just laughed and put a hand on his
shoulder, as though they had known each other for decades. 'You
get so used to using it, you forget that it is not the only way to kill.'*

Amongst the Sons of Horus ships in the outer layers of the armada, one vessel started to list. It was named the *Aeolus*, a heavy cruiser, Mars-forged and spear blade-hulled. Multiple torpedoes had slid through its shields and burst through its armoured flanks. Fire had spread through its starboard decks and compartments. Plumes of air flashed as they streamed through its void shields. Now it began to veer off course, engines stuttering and flaring. Its fleet sisters plunged on, not slowing as it struggled for direction and speed. The White Scars ships circled as the wounded *Aeolus* fell away from its siblings. Its engines fired again, burning with star-bright desperation, like a wounded animal falling behind the safety of the herd, fighting against the inevitable as its killers watched and circled.

But it wasn't dying. It was bleeding, but its weakness was feigned.

The White Scars began to whirl inwards towards their kill. They drew together and now amongst them, like a ghost gathered from the dark, was a great vessel, its engines tracing a bright sickle in the stars.

'The *Lance of Heaven*…' breathed Abaddon, as he saw the battle-barge slide into sight. He thought of the Legion brothers that he had killed to see this sight, brothers slain on the *Aeolus* as fire roared through its decks and explosions tore its skin. He had killed those warriors, he knew. The enemy had held the knife but they had died because of him, for him, so that he could stand in this moment and see his opponent come from the ocean of night to meet him. There were wounds that could not be affected, prices that had to be paid in the only coin that mattered.

The *Lance of Heaven* held fire as it closed. The *Aeolus* rolled, its engines misfiring and sending it spinning like an arrow loosed from a broken bow.

The *Lance of Heaven* fired. Beams of plasma lashed across the night. The last of the *Aeolus'* void shields vanished. The wheeling ships hurled ordnance at it. Blisters of molten metal formed and burst on its hull. The *Lance of Heaven* kept closing. Shorter-ranged batteries opened up. The *Aeolus* spun on. Chunks of debris arced from its sides.

Watching the exchange, Abaddon could almost see the White Scars' need for the kill driving them on.

The *Lance of Heaven* curved close, burning hard to slice the fire of its broadside batteries across the *Aeolus'* engines: a final slice to leave it stricken in the void. It was a cut too far.

'Strike,' Abaddon ordered.

The *War Oath* speared forwards. The ships of the armada that had shielded it parted. Power had built in its reactors, and the adepts of the New Mechanicum had held the fury of its plasma exchanges in balance until they screamed. Released, that power roared from its engines and plunged it towards the *Lance of Heaven* like a thunderbolt from a night sky. Heat and radiation killed hundreds on the engine decks. Three escort ships came with the *War Oath*, soaring wide to bracket their prey.

Too late, the White Scars ship broke off its attack run, and turned to dive back into the night. But the *War Oath* was already close enough. In the teleportarium, the air pulsed with static and ball lighting.

'For the Warmaster,' said Abaddon into the vox, and the ranks of warriors gathered around him vanished in a flash of strobing light.

*Warship* Lance of Heaven, *Supra-Solar Gulf*

The warriors in black appeared out of a whirl of green lightning in the passages of the *Lance of Heaven*'s command castle. Abaddon felt sensation briefly drain from his limbs as reality slammed back into place around him. Gunfire met them as the teleport light vanished with a howl. Etheric blast waves ripped out, shrieking with the voices of human fear. The Sons of Horus fired back, blasting through defence turrets and bulkheads as they charged. There was no hesitation in their movements, no doubt. They read their surroundings and were moving and killing before the humans facing them had loosed more than a shot.

'Forwards,' called Abaddon, firing and moving with his brothers.

Squads clamped charges on to sealed bulkheads and spun aside as metal flashed to shrapnel and smoke. The men and women who opposed them were drilled and disciplined, recruited and bound to serve the White Scars with honour and skill at arms. But they were still mortal. Bodies exploded inside pressure suits as they were slammed into walls by explosions. Chain teeth carved through meat and bone. Blood slicked the decks. Bolt-rounds filled corridors with shrapnel and pulped bodies.

Within three minutes, strike forces had speared through the defences around critical locations across the *Lance of Heaven*'s command castle and engine decks. Abaddon reached the main doors to the bridge as Ralkor, his signal master, was attempting a violation of the machine-spirit governing its locks. Abaddon gave a single shake of his head and gestured with a digit of his power fist. Two Reaver squads ran forwards pulling charges from backpacks and belts. The charges locked in place as Abaddon took his next step. His mind was cold, the progress of the assault a breath of thoughts at the back of his awareness. Resistance had been low, far too low for a capital ship of this size.

The charges on the bridge doors detonated. Melta waves

bored white-hot holes through the armour slabs a second
before breaching charges cleaved through the warping metal.
A squad of Terminators went through first, ramming through
the cooling debris, firing as they advanced. Servitors and
serf crew became shreds of meat under the hail of rounds.
Abaddon followed in their wake, his helm display showing
a scattering of threat runes that vanished as bolt-rounds and
volkite beams found their marks. He reached the centre of
the bridge as silence fell.

'Where is he?' asked Layak, following Abaddon, ghost
and shade-light spiralling over him. His blade slaves
flanked him, their swords drawn, their bodies bloated,
shedding cinders and ashes with every step. 'Where are
any of them?'

Abaddon turned, his mind shifting between possibilities.
The bridge was silent, the few serf and servitor crew just
those needed to keep the *Lance of Heaven* on course... No:
to keep it on a trajectory that the *War Oath* could intercept.
Hung out before them like a lure on a snare...

'Brother!' shouted Ralkor. Abaddon had time to turn
and to see a spinning mote of light beyond the viewports
streaking towards them. The armourglass imploded in a
wave of fire as the assault rams hit the *Lance of Heaven*'s
bridge. There were two of them, chisel-shaped blocks of
armour and engines that carried five warriors in each tine of
their forked hulls. Each mounted melta weapons powerful
enough to punch a hole in the skin of a warship. Striking the unshielded bridge, those weapons reduced half the
chamber to glowing slag.

The blast wave struck Abaddon and staggered him. Shards
of wreckage and blobs of molten metal ricocheted from his
battleplate. Tybar and his squad took the force of the hit and
became fire and ash. The assault rams ripped through the

bridge, embedding their prows deep in the deck. Sheets of metal scattered into the air. The assault rams' front hatches blew open. Warriors in white leaped to the glowing deck. Bolter and plasma fire lashed out. Sons of Horus fell. Gunfire blazed back. Layak and his blade slaves stood amongst the ruin, the pale fire and shadow that wreathed them shredding bullets and debris to burning dust. Another assault ram ploughed through the hole left by the first two.

Abaddon rose. Gouges and pits marked his Terminator plate. The black lacquer of the Justaerin had burned away, replaced by the red of cooling ceramite and black of soot. Urskar and Gedephron stood with him. Air rushed past them into the void. Inside Abaddon's helm the noise of battle reached him as a vibration through his feet. He saw his enemy then, a warrior running amongst the white-armoured figures charging across the deck: plumed helm, Chogorian hunt marks running across the plates of his armour, guandao spinning in his hands like the flash of lightning, like a bark of laughter as the rain fell.

Jubal Khan, a warrior who had fought across the stars and left a reputation that few could hope to touch. Jubal, whom he had met on the spires of Nissek, just before the counter-attack by the Arch-Drake's horde. The Lord of Summer Lightning, the Death that Laughs. And here he was, a lord of war left to fight almost alone in this abyss. Left to fight and to die here.

Abaddon began to run to greet him.

'Sycar,' he growled as he took the first stride. 'Kill the power generators.'

He heard gunfire chop through the vox as his lieutenant answered.

'It won't be clean, brother.'

'Do it.'

'With pleasure and obedience,' said Sycar, and Abaddon heard his Legion brother smiling.

He was five strides across the deck. Jubal had seen him. The White Scar whirled his blade out, and another of the Sons of Horus was falling, helm split and blood burning on the guandao's power field.

'Brace for gravity loss!' shouted Urskar over the vox, firing a stream of heavy rounds into the White Scars still leaping from the assault rams.

A vibration rose through the deck. The few remaining lights cut out. Abaddon felt the lurch in his stomach as gravity vanished. His boots mag-locked to the deck an instant later. One of the battered assault rams, still moving under the momentum of its impact, spun from the deck. Debris showered upwards. Half of the White Scars rose into the air. Bolt-rounds punched into them as they tumbled through the vanishing atmosphere. The rest mag-locked their feet to the deck in time. Jubal kept moving, his strides slowed but his speed still dazzling. Abaddon surged to meet him. Rounds blurred past him. The war shouts of the living and the dead filled his ears. His sword was in his hand, wreathed in lightning, his armour and blood and muscle flowing as one.

Jubal's guandao flashed out, reaching across the space between them. It was so fast that it might have been the glint of light from a mirror. Abaddon brought his sword up to meet it.

But the weapons never met. Jubal flicked the guandao back as though the steel were a rope, and then slashed it out again. The blade edge kissed Abaddon's right gauntlet. The power field bit deep. A spike of pain flared up his arm. He spun his sword, and sheared the guandao away, and struck back, turning the parry into an overhead cut. Jubal stepped away. The deck vibrated as the mag-locks in their boots released and engaged once more.

Abaddon struck again and again, pouring the force of each blow into the next so that their strength grew like a storm-sea clashing against the land. Jubal went back, pivoting and parrying. They were fighting on the deck before the wreck of the assault ram. Light flashed from the meeting of blades. Abaddon did not slow or step back. The battle was becoming silent as the last air drained from the bridge. The sound of his hearts filled his world, became the surge and murmur of war.

Jubal went back again, fast. Abaddon saw an opening and thrust. But Jubal clamped his feet to the deck halfway through his step and slashed his blade back. It was not a cut that a savant of any blade school would recognise, but it struck Abaddon's sword arm, just above the elbow. Razor edge and power field sliced through the thinner armour of the joint. Pain flared, and a bright string of red pearls bubbled into the vacuum. It punched into his mind and stole the instant before he realised that Jubal was open. Mind and body shunted the pain aside, and he cut. Jubal somehow met the kill-stroke. The force of impact jolted through Abaddon. Jubal released the mag-locks holding him to the deck, and the impact of his strike sent him arcing over Abaddon's head.

Jubal's feet found the deck and his boots gripped him to the floor. He snapped the guandao out as he landed. The long haft slid through his right hand, the tip reaching out to Abaddon like a thunderbolt.

It was dazzling. From the first reversal of Abaddon's plan to kill the leader of the Falcon fleets to this dance of blood and edges, this was war and killing on a level that rose to something beyond even the post-human. Abaddon would

strike, and Jubal would slice, and bit by bit those cuts would
bleed Abaddon, slow him, pull him down into more mistakes. They would follow this pattern on and on, cut after
cut, and it would never cease, only flow into its next phase,
like wind and storm-rain split by the flash of lightning.

Except it wouldn't. It could not. He knew Jubal, had known
him before and knew him better for these last moments.

Abaddon raised his sword to meet the guandao spearing
towards him. To a human it would have been too fast to follow, but Jubal would have seen it, would have been waiting
for it. The guandao flicked aside. Power fields grazed each
other in a plume of sparks. Jubal's feet locked to the floor
as he turned his cut inside Abaddon's parry.

Abaddon slammed his sword forwards. All his strength
and all his skill focused in the blow. It struck the guandao. Sheets of sparks flashed out. Jubal flinched back, the
flow of his strikes shattered as force jolted through his
weapon and up his arms. Abaddon activated the field of
his power fist and slammed it forwards, palm open. The
lightning-wreathed fingers closed on the guandao with a
flash of light. Jubal whirled back but Abaddon had already
read the movement. His sword-thrust struck Jubal in the gut
and cut upwards, sawing through armour, flesh and bone.

Blood poured into the air, glistening, burning in the
sword's power field. Jubal's arms swung, still bearing his
broken weapon. Abaddon stepped back, pulling the sword
free and kicking the corpse off his blade. And the Lord of
Summer Lightning tumbled away, limbs suddenly slack,
blood venting in spheres into the all-but-vanished air.

Abaddon stood for a second, hearing his own breath
inside his helm, watching the warrior he had killed.

Then the sound rose up through the deck, vibrating
through his armour.

Abaddon's awareness snapped back, sharp and bright. Light was building in the front of one of the assault rams embedded in the deck. Abaddon had a stretching, momentary perception of the chamber before him, of the bolts and beams of energy reaching between the surviving White Scars and the Sons of Horus. The corpses already spinning through the air. The flicker of detonations out in the void beyond. And the light of the beam of heat building, ripping through the deck beneath his feet as the assault ram fired its magna-melta. For the narrowest sliver of an instant the deck plating seemed to contain it, glowing through red to white. Then the moment passed.

Heat and molten metal exploded outwards. The melta-beam sliced through the deck towards Abaddon. He felt the deck pitch as it began to crumple like parchment in a furnace. He was still moving, but these moments were slow, the last grains falling in an hourglass.

The molten beam struck an invisible wall. Frost exploded to steam as it spread across the torn deck. The sound of screaming voices filled Abaddon's ears, shrieking and pleading. Shadows spiralled around him. He could smell burning parchment and incense.

Zardu Layak stepped to Abaddon's side. His hand was raised. A device burned on his palm.

+Move…+ said Layak's voice in Abaddon's mind. Layak stood for another second, the hemisphere of shadow holding back the blast. Then Layak closed his hand. The shield of shadows and the melta-beam vanished. Stillness filled the second. Then Layak opened his hand and the fire leapt out, like light trapped in a shuttered lamp. The assault ram exploded. Half of the deck vanished in a flash of white heat.

A moment later the gunfire ceased.

Abaddon walked to Layak. Blood bubbled from under

the priest's mask, dark and thick. Voices rose from the vox in Abaddon's ears, but he did not listen. He was looking at the grey-armoured priest of the Word Bearers. He blinked his vox-channel to a direct link to Layak.

'Saving a life forms a bond, First Son of Horus,' said Layak looking up at him, the eyes of his horned and fanged mask glowing. 'Remember that, always.'

# ELEVEN

---

The bitter angels of our hearts
Limit of kindness
Here for you

*Freighter ship* Antius, *Jovian Gulf*

'Signal contact. Distance adjusting.'

The tech-priest's drone buzzed across the bridge.

The watch officer, who had been nodding off, jerked upright, blinking. Vek had been sitting in a vacant helm cradle, trying to stave off the alternating fatigue and nerves.

'What is it?' asked Vek.

'Uncertain,' said the tech-priest. She had come up from the engine decks and wired herself into the helm and sensor instruments after they had broken from Uranus' orbit. That had reassured Vek a little. The tech-priest, who he thought was called Chi-32-Beta, was cold and unfeeling, but she did not seem to sleep, nor to be as open to panic as the all-too-human bridge crew. 'It is a small void-craft, fast, and its signal signature is tenuous,' continued Chi-32-Beta. 'If I was extending analysis to informed speculation, I might venture that it was equipped with counter-auspex systems.'

'It's hiding,' said Vek.

'That analysis is not accurate. It is less that it is hiding, and rather that we do not have the eyes to see it.'

'Military?'

'Almost a certainty,' said the tech-priest.

'Has it seen us? Is it coming closer?' he asked.

'To the first question – I would theorise that if its sacred machine systems are enough to fog the fidelity of our own auspex, then it will be more than blessed with the ability to have been aware of us for some time.' The tech-priest paused. Vek saw cogs turn inside the sculpted lips of her brushed-steel mask. 'As to whether it is closing, passing or attenuating, I have no data.'

Vek bit his lip. He thought of calling for Koln, but the brevet captain of the *Antius* had withdrawn further and further over the days since they ran from Uranus. When she spoke it was often as though she were not fully aware or present, and when she was focused she seethed with barely suppressed rage. She was seen on the bridge less and less, and Vek was happy not to know where it was she was going. But he was no void officer...

'Go and find Sub-mistress Koln,' he called to one of the junior deck officers, who looked barely old enough to hold rank. 'Get her back to the bridge now.'

The officer nodded and left.

Vek closed his eyes and rubbed them with the heels of his hands. A headache had been growing in the space behind his eyes for hours now. The pain was becoming sharper as the adrenaline of the first days of their flight drained, and they had pushed further towards Jupiter and the system core beyond. Everyone was the same, though. He had heard the crew muttering to each other about their dreams after they returned from the few hours most of them had managed to sleep.

Everything was fraying. There had been incidents: shouted arguments between superiors and subordinates. This was a civilian ship, a short-range freighter. Its crew were not military and the habits of authority and command were barely surviving this new reality. And the refugees in the hold… He had gone down to see them every day until today. The last time he had stepped into the holds they had swarmed not to him but towards the door, and there had been a blank-eyed desperation to them.

*Refugees…* Isn't that what they all were now?

'Signal intensity altering!' said Chi-32-Beta. 'Secondary signal return detaching from the primary. Plotting location and vector.'

'What is happening?' he asked.

'A second return has separated from the first. It is smaller, and not sensor baffled. In more easily parsed terms, the ship that we detected has launched a shuttle- or lighter-sized void-craft. It is visible to our auspex. I am using it to extrapolate data on the primary return.' The tech-priest was silent for a second. Vek heard a metallic whir from inside her mask that made him think of a sharp inhalation. 'Recommend brace condition and immediate internal lockdown!'

The officers of the bridge woke from lethargy into panicked motion. Crimson lights began to blink and strobe.

Vek started towards the tech-priest, but she was already calling out.

'They are very close – they must have been gaining on us for hours, and the smaller craft that they have launched is approaching directly and swiftly.'

'What is it?'

'I would speculate that it is a class of assault craft.' The tech-priest rotated her head on her shoulders to look fully at Vek. Her eyes were two circles of crystal-brushed steel. 'They mean to board us.'

'How long?' Vek asked, and as though in reply a machine-voice boomed from vox-speakers across the bridge.

'Brace! Ten seconds to impact! Brace!'

Vek turned to look at the viewport in time to see a sleek shape fall on them like a fiery arrow shot from the night.

*All those people gone, just gone, and Vek did not even pause…*

*Pulled a gun, yes, he pulled a gun, and what choice did you have then?*

*You had to. He left the captain. He killed her. What choice did you have?*

*None.*

*And all for his brats. All to keep two rich little brats alive.*

*How many died?*

*He killed them. Yes, Vek killed them, not you. You gave the order to break from the dock, but he would have shot you.*

*You had no choice.*

Down in the quiet, Zadia Koln, once sub-mistress and now brevet captain of the system freighter *Antius* listened to the thoughts roll and roar through her head. The passage was dark. The pistol in her hands hung in her fingers, still smoking, the slide open on an empty breech. Fat brass shell cases littered the floor around where she crouched. Further off, half folded in shadow, lay the bodies. Five of them, or maybe more. She was not sure. For a second, she caught them out of the edge of her eye.

She'd had no choice.

She had been walking the decks. They had come out of nowhere as she was sealing the bulkhead, and she had pulled the gun and…

Koln glanced up at the sealed door across the passage.

She had come down to the decks to check that all of them were secure...

No that was a lie... She had just wanted to get away from the bridge, with its stink of fear, and Vek and his bodyguard watching everything like they didn't trust Koln.

The thought of them brought the rage again, spearing up through her, sucking in terror as fuel like a firestorm drawing in air.

She hadn't asked for this! How *dare* they doubt her. She was the one who had to give the orders, to keep the ship moving through the void...

She had spent most of her four decades on this ship or one of its sisters. Ore and supplies, back and forwards through the circles of Uranus' moons, again and again, predictable and certain. A mundane life filled with boredom, but there had been the temple, the quiet gatherings in the silence of the docks off Miranda. She had been flattered to be asked to join, then intrigued. The frisson of secrecy had spiced the thought that she was, for once in her life, doing something not permitted. Something special. It had been just as mundane after a while, though, men and woman in tattered hoods, and nonsense words spoken to recognise each other. Tokens and coins, and meetings which were half-ritual and half the kind of talk you could have in any dock drinking hole.

Her eye settled on one of the corpses; its hand was open... Clear stars but it looked still alive. What was it they had shouted before she shot? Food, something about food.

What had she done?

No, no, no... It was not her fault.

What was Vek thinking? Almost a thousand refugees on a ship with provisions for its crew alone. Vek should have known... They had nothing. Hunger had begun to bite after only days. Soon it would make the refugees in the holds go further than this passage. They had just come running out of the dark and she had…

She had…

They should not have been there…

*'It's not your fault.'*

The voice froze her. Her eyes fastened on the dead refugees. She heard the thump of her heart. Then she laughed, the sound echoing and then collapsing into tears. It was her voice, of course it was. Hers. The words had come from her thoughts into her mouth without her realising.

'It's not your fault, Zadia Koln.' She heard herself speak, and felt the words puff into the air, cold and glittering with frost.

*'It's not your fault…'*

She heard the footsteps then, slow and deliberate, walking towards her across the deck.

She tried to look up.

She could not look up.

She could not move.

The beat of her heart had stopped. The frost of her breath hung in the air, glittering dust hanging before her eyes.

*'You had no choice then, and you have none now…'*

There was a shape at the edge of her sight, a shape like the shadow of something that walked like a man. She wanted to close her eyes, she wanted to look away. Her eyes stayed open as the figure stopped just next to her.

*'But you did have one choice…'*

She could smell burnt meat, and something that brought to mind the incense they had burned in the temple on Miranda. A temple… a temple that was just a room with some candles, and marks scratched on the floor, and bowls set under a flow of water from a broken pipe.

'*You all have a choice of which angels to listen to…*'

Frost was creeping over her limbs and up her neck.

'*You can listen to those voices that you know are true, and which will keep you safe, even if it means that you must be just a small flame, rather than the light of eternity…*'

Blood… She could smell blood, and… and water…

'*Or you can listen to all the hate, and rage, and resentment that you carry like a parent does a child…*'

The thing shifted, and she could see it now.

'*And all of you humans always make the same choice…*'

Something sharp hooked under her chin and pulled it up. Two yellow eyes looked down at her.

'*You always choose to listen to the bitter angels of your hearts…*'

She could not draw breath to scream.

'*And we listen.*'

'You are from Terra?' asked the boy.

'Yes,' replied Mersadie. 'I was born there.' She moved the glass tile across a slot in the metal game board. The boy frowned at it. His sister sat curled on a chair, eyes sunk in a sullen face, listening. She was older than the boy by at least half a decade, maybe a little more. She was called Mori, and he was Noon. They were Vek's children. They had found their way into the room she was sleeping in two days ago, and seemed to have adopted her as a curiosity – a distraction from the situation they all found themselves in. She had told them a story, and the boy, at least, had come back for more. Vek had let them, and the bodyguard, Aksinya, had come with them, a cold-eyed shadow at the edge of the room.

Mersadie talked and told stories as the *Antius* plunged on through the dark of the gulf between Uranus and Jupiter. Apparently, the gas giants were at a stage in their orbital cycle that put Jupiter on a direct course between Uranus and the inner system. There were no explosions now, no rush and boom of sudden events, just the slow, grinding passing of moments as the pressure rose inside the thoughts of all those on board.

'What's it like, the Throneworld? What's it like?' asked Noon.

Mersadie shrugged, and smiled.

'I don't know what it is like now. I haven't been there for a long time. But do you want to know the truth?' She leaned across the board of coloured tiles, and lowered her voice to a stage whisper. 'I always thought it was ugly. There is this haze in the sky. There used to be seas once, longer ago than anyone can remember. Now there is just dust and stink. Lots of buildings grown too high. And there are people, more people than you can imagine.'

'Where did you go?' asked Mori from across the room. Mersadie looked around at the girl, who had barely moved but was looking at her with a sharp gaze. 'If you were away from Terra for a long time – where did you go?'

Mersadie held the girl's gaze, thinking about how to answer.

'I went to see the Imperium being made.'

'What does that mean?' asked the girl.

'Enough questions,' said Aksinya, from the corner.

Mersadie looked at the bodyguard, then back at the coloured tiles on the board, then up at Noon. 'I think you might have won,' said Mersadie to Noon.

Alarms screamed out all around them.

The assault pod struck the *Antius* on its spine. Claws snapped down from the pod's flanks, dug in and pulled its bulk close against the hull. Rings of drill teeth began to rotate. Melta-beams fired at point-blank range. The skin of the hull bubbled and oozed orange. Shaped charges in the pod's base fired. The blast punched into the blistering metal and turned it into a jet of white-hot liquid. The pod rocked, but its blade-legs dug deeper, pulling the spinning teeth of its maw down into the glowing wound.

The second set of charges fired and tore through the last inches of the ship's hull. A shock wave ripped down the passageways near the breach. Half-sealed hatches ripped off their hinges. A lone crewman close to the impact point was slammed into the wall and became a broken doll of crushed meat and shattered bone.

An iris hatch set between the pod's drill teeth snapped open. Figures dropped through. Crimson void armour bulked their forms. Pressure hoses snaked from the canisters on their backs to their domed helms.

In the staterooms towards the ship's stern, Mersadie came up off the floor to standing as the breaching blast sent a shiver down the hull.

Aksinya was already in motion, scooping up the two children and making for the door in a blur. The bodyguard had a long-barrelled pistol in one hand.

'Aksinya,' called Mersadie. There was something wrong, something blurring at the edges of awareness that Mersadie could not focus on. The skin on the back of her neck and arms was prickling. In her mind's eye she could see the dream image of the wolf, smiling at her with its sharp, bloody teeth. 'Don't go. There is something–'

The bodyguard turned, keying the door.

'I need to reach Master Vek.' The door opened, and she glanced back at Mersadie, the mask of control slipping for a second to show only contempt. 'You brought this down on us. They can have you.' She turned. Noon's eyes were wide as he looked back at her from beside Aksinya's grasp.

'No,' called Mersadie. She was shaking, the tremor running out from her core like a charge searching for a way out. In her mind the image of the symbols she had seen in the dream with Keeler rose, planets and signs, symbols and meanings. The marks had changed, had shifted; they were glowing with heat, weeping smoke. And as clearly as if it had been shouted in her ear, she knew that it was a warning. 'There is something else... something coming... Don't go!'

Aksinya looked like she would not even pause. Then she stopped, pulled a compact laspistol from inside her robes and threw it onto the floor at Mersadie's feet.

'Consider that the limit of my kindness.'

Then she was gone, pulling the children with her into the flashing lights of the corridor outside. Mersadie looked at the gun for a second, swaying as the sense of danger and threat poured through her. Then she hissed a curse, bent down, picked up the gun and ran after the bodyguard.

Vek was already running as the assault pod detonated its second charge. The jolt ran through the deck. Shouts swallowed the alarms. Some of the bridge crew were reaching for sidearms they had drawn from the *Antius*' weapon locker. Vek had a lasgun. His hands fumbled on the arming stud as he went for the door off the bridge. Sweat poured from him. Breath sawed from his lungs. His bulk shook beneath his clothes. Someone might have called after him, but he did not hear or stop. All he could think of was the children. The children he had left two decks down. Close to the breach.

*'The Emperor protects.'* That was what Sadia, his wife, had said when she had first introduced him to the Temple of the Saviour Emperor. *'He always has and He always will.'*

He went down the spiral of stairs from the helm platform. He saw a guard, but the man turned and fled as Vek shouted at him.

'*But how can that be true when billions die?*' he had asked. '*How can there be a war if He protects?*'

*His wife had shrugged.*

'*If there were not the dark, and the chance of loss, what need would there be for Him to protect us?*'

Another jolt shook the deck. The walls rang like a struck gong. He was panting, the sweat pouring into his eyes.

'He protects, He protects...' he panted, and echoed in his head. *Please let Him protect them.*

He reached the door of the bridge. There was shouting behind him, the machine burble of the tech-priest.

The doors blew apart in a spray of shrapnel. Vek was blasted backwards.

Something struck him in the gut. He tumbled. Air rushed from his lungs, and he was falling, dimly aware of his hands still clutching the lasgun. Another blow followed, to his ribs, as he collided with a support pillar and tumbled to the floor.

There were figures around him and above him. Armoured figures pouring through the opening. Red armour, domed helms with black slots for eyes, squat guns fuming static. Beams of light flashed out. Vek tried to rise, tried to move forwards, tried to bring the gun up...

'*You should trust more,*' Sadia had said.

None of his limbs would move. Nothing felt like anything. '*That is the root of faith – not just belief but trust...*'

The armoured figures moved up, firing with every step, swift but steady. Vek thought that the screaming was fading, but the world was soft and fuzzed and leaking red at the edge of his sight.

'*There is a plan, and He watches all of us...*'

'Cleared,' came a machine-distorted voice from somewhere out of sight.

*'All you need to do is trust...'*

Vek could see Noon and Mori's faces in his mind, more clear than the red shadows that moved close.

'This one is alive,' said a voice from close by. Vek suddenly realised how quiet everything had become. The lights still blinked, but there were no alarms, no shouts...

*'Just trust?' he had asked. 'That does not seem like much.'*

*'It is everything,' she had said. 'It is everything, my love.'*

He was looking up into a black eye-slot set into a crimson-lacquered helm.

'The Emperor...' he managed, hearing the gurgle and rasp in his own words. The barrel of the gun eclipsed the sight of the room. He could see the scorching inside its muzzle. 'The Emperor p–'

Mersadie saw the gunfire from around the corner. She slowed, crouching low against the wall. She gripped the gun tight. Rounds were whipping past, shot pellets sparking off pipes and grates. She was breathing hard. A bitter taste filled her mouth and nose. She looked back at the way she had come. Blast doors had sealed behind her. Could she open them? If she could, where would she go? What about Nilus? Where was the Navigator?

A child's cry jerked her head up. Another blast of shot. Another cry. The thought of going back vanished. Mersadie snatched a look around the corner.

The next door was only twenty paces away. It was a small, ovoid opening. The two children crouched behind a projecting pipe halfway between Mersadie and the door. Mori hugged her brother close as a shot sparked off the wall above their heads. Aksinya was beside the open door, pistols in hand, shooting through the hatch as guns barked from the dark beyond. She crouched back as a fresh squall of shot ripped up the corridor. Mersadie caught her eye, and thought she saw a curse form on the bodyguard's lips. There was a deeper boom from beyond the open hatch and a bolt-round ripped down the corridor and exploded on the wall opposite the corner. Mersadie saw the gleam of red armour in the muzzle flash just before she ducked back. There were figures advancing on the other side of the hatch from Aksinya. The bodyguard and the children were trapped.

'Mersadie!' shouted Aksinya.

'I hear you,' she shouted back. Another bolt burned down the corridor. Mersadie heard the chattering bark of Aksinya's pistols.

'Your shuttle,' shouted the bodyguard. 'It's two decks down. Key command override for the launch doors is "Juno".'

'I understand,' Mersadie shouted back. And she did.

'Get the children and then get to the shuttle.'

Mersadie nodded. All thoughts of Nilus, of greater purposes and of final ends had become very distant. A high ringing was rising in her head and ears. Her limbs were suddenly shaking. Aksinya held her gaze for a heartbeat more.

'Get ready!' she called. Mersadie nodded again, her mouth and throat dry. 'Now!' shouted Aksinya and half rose, pistols blazing through the hatch. Mersadie started up. She made it two strides. A trooper in heavy red armour was already at the hatch. Whether Aksinya had not realised how close they were, or if they had simply waded through her fire to reach the door, Mersadie would never know. She ducked to the side of the passage as the gun in the crimson trooper's hands boomed. A round tore a hole in the floor where she had been.

Aksinya did not pause. Her first shot hit the crimson-clad

trooper in the chest. The second hit the same mark a second later and punched through the red armour. The trooper
tumbled back. Blood flared bright. Aksinya twitched aside
as a beam of light stabbed through the doorway. Mersadie
heard the air hiss as the beam pulsed. Aksinya was turning,
spinning low with the momentum of her dodge to kick her
heel into the crotch of the next figure through the door.
Aksinya came up, a blade in hand. The crimson trooper
brought its hand up to block the thrust, but the point of the
blade slid up under the chin of its helm. Aksinya activated
the blade's power field, and the trooper's skull exploded in
its helm. The corpse began to fall. Aksinya let go of the dagger, yanked the pins from the grenades hanging from the
trooper's bandolier, and kicked the corpse back through
the doorway before it could hit the floor. She ducked to the
side, scooping up the knife as she moved. Beams of light
snapped through the door at her.

Mersadie met the bodyguard's gaze. There were scorch
marks on Aksinya's clothes and a spreading dark red stain on
her stomach. Rage burned in her eyes as they met Mersadie's.

'Get the children to the shuttle!' she shouted.

An orange blast wave punched through the open door.
Pieces of burning fabric and broken armour scattered across
the decking. Smoke clotted the air. Mersadie yelled in pain as
the pressure broke over her. Beams lit the smoke pall, strobing out of time with the red pulse of alert lumens. Aksinya
snapped a shot off through the hatch. For a second, in the red
flash of light, Mersadie saw pain contort the bodyguard's face.

'Go!' Aksinya shouted, and fired around the door again.

Mersadie pushed up from the wall and ran to the two
children huddled beside the pipe. Noon was weeping, wet
tears pouring down his cheeks. Mori was wide-eyed and
breathing hard as she looked up at Mersadie. The girl said

something, but the ringing was still filling Mersadie's ears, blurring into her skull. She felt like she was going to vomit.

'Come with me,' said Mersadie, reaching for Mori. The girl flinched back. 'We need to go, Mori.' The girl hesitated, then nodded and was up, grabbing hold of Mersadie's hand and pulling her brother up with the other. Aksinya fired through the door as Mersadie and the children ran for the turn in the passage, back the way Mersadie had come. They came round the corner. Behind them, energy beams snapped through the air. Mersadie could see the blast door at the end of the passage. Thirty paces. Thirty paces and then...

The lights on the distant door's lock blinked to green. Mersadie's stride faltered. The blast door began to open, pulling back into the passage walls. She heard a snarl of pain from back where Aksinya was crouched beside the other door out of the corridor. Energy beams were smacking the passage walls. Mori was still running forwards, her hand now pulling on Mersadie's. There were figures on the other side of the door ahead, their gloss armour red.

Mersadie yanked back on Mori's hand as the first crimson-armoured trooper stepped into sight, gun rising. Mori saw, her mouth opening wide to scream. The trooper fired as Mersadie pulled them down behind a wall bracing. Hard shot rang off the walls and floor. More troopers poured into the passage from the other end. From their only way out.

Mersadie could see back to where Aksinya now sat on the floor beside the hatch. The dark stains had spread across the bodyguard's torso and a wet chunk was missing from her right upper thigh. She was reloading her pistol, face set and hard. Mersadie felt the weight of the pistol in her own hand, and fired two shots off. The snap of recoil jerked the shots high. The world was roaring with gunfire, closing in, pressing closed like a vice. Mori was shaking, her brother howling.

And in her mind, all she could think of was the moon on water, of sharp teeth and a pair of yellow eyes. Words hissed in a dream blew into her thoughts.

*We are coming for you… We know… We are here for you…*

Panic punched through her, flooding her with adrenaline. She needed to run. She needed to get away.

She half rose. Mori yanked her back.

'What are you doing?' shouted the girl.

Mersadie tried to shake her off. She needed to run, the instinct so pure and raw that it left her other thoughts shouting in its wake.

*'They will try to stop you,'* said Keeler's face in the dream. *'Old friends and enemies alike. They will come for you.'*

She tried to rise from the cover of the support pillar again.

A pair of crimson troopers were four paces away, guns levelled, fingers on triggers. Time became an instant caught between drawn breaths. Mersadie could see it all.

The armoured soldiers advancing… The beams and shot-rounds threading the gloom… The blur of Aksinya as she tried to rise and face the figures coming through the other hatch…

And then she saw the shadow. It was standing in the open blast doors that the second squad of troopers had just poured through. It was still. Upright. A freeze-frame on a pict-stream.

The ringing in her head was building, and all she could think of was the message she carried in her memory, and the smell of wet fur and blood and frost.

The troopers were still advancing, their fingers squeezing back on triggers as the passing instants blinked in time with the alert lights.

Red, black…

Red, black…

Red, black...

*Red.*

The shadow was behind them.

*Black.*

And now the shadow was next to them, and Mersadie could hear the siren-scream in her head beating with the blink of seconds.

*Red.*

Blood sprayed out. The troopers were turning, and the shadow was amongst them, moving in jerks like a broken pict-feed.

*Black.*

Aksinya was still on the floor by the hatch, her pistol frozen in her hand. There was red frost climbing the walls. Bodies flying back, broken, pulped.

*Red.*

The shadow was standing still now, washed in gore, its head turning to Mersadie, and she could see the face within shadow, eyes stained red in the black-veined skull of Sub-mistress Koln.

'*We are here for you,*' said the thing and it reached out fingers that stretched into shadows through the air, and all Mersadie could think of was running in dreams through dark woods and the howls rising behind her. '*We are the–*'

The las-blast ripped the side of Koln's skull off. The shadow-wrapped body jerked back. Mersadie fired again, and again, stepping forwards as the thing staggered and the blasts ripped through it. It juddered, flesh and blood shuddering as it fell.

She stood over it, still, panting, the charge pack depletion light blinking red on the pistol in her hand. The only sound was the patter of blood falling to the deck from the ceiling above.

# THE WARP

∞

Snow boils from the black sky as the old man begins to climb the mountain. Ice-caked fur and black rags wrap his body. The wind strikes him, and he staggers, half falling. His hands plunge into the snow.

Cold.

Burning cold.

Beyond fire, beyond water.

He gasps, and for a moment the snow is not snow, but every moment of pain ever suffered: the wail of a mother beside a small bundle, the last thought of a man dying before his time, the touch of a knife. Cold, sharp, burning…

He pushes himself up.

At his back he hears the cry of wolves. He stops, turns. The light of the burning torch in his hand ripples out in the gusting wind. His eyes catch the light of the fire as he looks back down the slope at the forest. The trees have grown upwards, bare branches reaching to catch the wind. Eyes look back at him, red, green and fever-yellow. In the distance, still visible above and beyond the tops of the trees, he can see the lights of the tower he has left to make this journey. The wind gusts and the wolves come with it, forming from darkness and frost as they leap. He swings the torch. The wolves' jaws are wide, broken fangs in rotten gums. Molten brass scatters from iron teeth, blue fire from black glass claws. The torch strikes the first wolf–

Flash of lightning.

Shattered night.

Burning snow.

The wolves fall back, cries shaking gales of snow from the sky.

The old man runs up the side of the mountain, legs sinking into the drifts, hands grasping at ice-skinned rock. The howls rise again. The opening to the cave is so close, just there, between the stones. Another step, another push of will and he will reach its sanctuary. Claws reach for him. He can feel their breath at his back. He turns, and throws the burning torch high. A jagged pillar of lightning catches it and strikes down. White light drowns the mountainside. The shadows of wolves melt into the ground but more are already coming. He leaps for the stone doorway into the mountain, and...

Quiet. The smell of stone and earth. Stillness.

The cave stretches down in front of him. Rough steps have been hacked into the floor. Seams of crystal glitter in raw stone walls. The sound of water dripping onto rock touches his ears. A glow of fire seeps up the steps as he descends. A square door waits at the bottom. He pauses on the threshold, then steps through.

The cave is small but has been enlarged, first with stone axes, and then with tools of bronze and iron. The light comes from burning wicks set in a bowl of clear oil. Stone benches line the walls either side of the door. The seats are smooth, worn by time and those who have come here. Channels run down the floor from where a lump of raw crystal rises. Symbols crawl over the crystal: a half-man half-equine, water falling from a cup, a figure with the head of a bull.

The man in black rags and fur stops.

Another man, swathed in golden robes, sits on one of the benches. He holds a staff in his hand, and a folded plait of laurel leaves and silver thread sits on his head. He looks young.

The two look at each other for a long moment. Then the old man in the frost-covered fur shakes himself, and pulls the cloak from his back. The black tunic beneath is tattered and stained by sweat. The muscles on his arms are withered cords, his shoulders hunched by age, his scalp bare of hair and liver-spotted. Golden rings gleam on his fingers: a ram's head, a rayed sun, a grey opal.

'Hello, old friend,' says the young man in gold.

The old man in black rags nods, and comes forwards. For a second his step falters. His eyes shut with pain. The rock of the cave creaks. A spill of dust falls from the ceiling. The man in gold looks up, and then back at the man in black as he lowers himself onto the bench opposite.

'Here,' says the young man, holding out a wooden bowl. 'Bread and salt and meat.'

The old man takes the bowl with a nod and begins to eat. The man in gold lifts his own bowl, and takes small mouthfuls, never taking his eyes from his companion.

'I am sorry to call you here,' says the man in gold when there are only crumbs in the old man's bowl, 'but we need to speak.' The man in black wipes the back of his hand across his mouth. His eyes are black depths in the weathered skin of his face. 'Things are pressing in and in,' continues the young man. 'So far the attack has been as we would expect. But there is something else, something that is outside of that…'

The man in gold begins to lay cards down on the stone bench between the bowls. The cards are old and the images on them faded: a figure in a dark cloak, its face turned away, climbing towards a high tower; a wolf-headed man with a bundle of swords hidden beneath a cloak; a wheel of stars turning around a darkening moon… Card after card, the pattern growing with each one placed.

'You see,' says the man in gold. 'It changes, but the core of a pattern is always there, a growing resonance in the warp, like notes rising and harmonising, or pieces being placed on a board, or a weapon being assembled bit by bit… I can't see what it is, only its shadow, but it is there. Behind the night and the bloodshed, it is there.' The man in black is still looking down at the cards. 'There are other things, too. Factors that are out of place. The timing of the assault, for instance. It began at midwinter, in the pit of the cosmic nadir. And the order of things… The position of the planets is particular at this moment. It is a rare conjunction that has not occurred since… well, since before the last darkness. We have always presumed that the timing of the assault is driven by haste, but what if it is something else? What if it is something m–'

'Yes,' says the man in black. He stands. For a second the light of the oil flames cast his shadow on the wall, and for an eye-blink it is not the shadow of an old man, but of a figure on a throne, his hands gripping its arms, his head held straight. 'It is there, under the surface, beyond the edge of night. I can… feel it growing.'

'What is it?' asks the young man. 'What are they doing?'

The man in black is still for a second, his eyes distant. It has cost him much to send part of himself here, to this meeting of minds in one of the last sanctuaries that remain. Far off, and only a thought away, is the crushing dark, held back moment to moment, a flood tide halted on the shore's edge by will alone.

'I cannot see,' says the Emperor, furs shifting over His aged frame. 'Not within, nor beyond the edge of Night. The present is darkness and the future a horizon. There is only the struggle.'

Malcador, young and clad in gold, is still for a moment and then nods once, his face a mask that cannot hide his worry.

'The others know,' says Malcador at last. 'The Khan, the Angel, the commanders... Rogal, in particular. The actions of the enemy don't add up, and they see that there is a gap, a shadow in their understanding.'

'That is what they are there to do,' says the Emperor, picking up the furs from which the ice and frost has barely thawed. 'To be tooth and claw, to fight and not to yield. The rest is yours to mind – to shield them so that they can be what they need to be.'

The Emperors turns for the door.

'Can we still win this?' asks Malcador.

'That is not the question you are really asking,' says the Emperor, turning His head but still facing away.

Malcador gives a sad smile, and nods to concede the point.

'Farewell,' says the Emperor, pulling on His cloak of fur, and turning for the small door out into the night and winter.

Malcador stays where he is, looking at the black space beyond the crude arch of stone. After a moment that in reality lasts no more than the span of a thought, he looks back at the pattern of cards laid out on the stone bench beside him. Then he reaches down and picks up the image of the high tower shattering beneath a thunderbolt.

'Can we survive this? Can anything?' he asks, and closes his eyes.

The idea and the image of the cave folds out of being, and the howling dark rushes in to claim the place it left.

PART THREE

# OUR GATES
# AND OATHS BROKEN

# TWELVE

Solatarium
I am here
Battlefield of time

*Battle-barge* Ankhtowe, *Supra-Solar Gulf*

Ahzek Ahriman, Chief Librarian of the Thousand Sons Legion, watched as blood formed in the crystal sphere. Crimson puffed into being within its polished depths, swirled and then ran to the edge of the orb. Cold light gathered around it, and Ahriman heard the melody in his mind change as notes and harmonies shifted. He watched the orb for another second as it spun on through the space above him.

+Does that fall within the necessary conjunction?+ Ahriman spoke in thought.

+It does,+ croaked Menkaura's thought-reply. Ahriman could feel fatigue bleeding out of the sending. He understood why. To be in this chamber was to feel and hear the flow of the immaterium without break or moderation. It was a solatarium like those once used by long-dead scholars to predict the movements of the heavenly bodies across Terra's skies. In those devices, stone and glass spheres had turned around a crystal simulacrum of the sun. In this chamber the same basic principle applied, but there the similarity ended. Just as the telescopes of ancient astronomers concentrated the light of the heavens, so did this chamber draw the infinite resonance of the warp down to the point where its patterns were visible.

A constellation of spheres and discs turned in the space above him, its outer elements spinning wide enough to almost touch the curved walls. The whole chamber was a sphere itself, eighty-one cubits in diameter, cut by telekinesis from a single block of jade. No living hand had ever touched its surface, or polluted it with memory. The spheres and coins of the solatarium at its centre moved on psychic currents. Most represented the physical Solar System, but others, principles no less real but ultimately intangible, spun beside them: Strength Ascendant, the Justice of Winter, the Crow's Flight. The smaller spheres and discs were made of rock, metal and bone taken from the planets, moons and void bodies that lay within the light of Sol. Each planet was a sphere of crystal formed in the warp by will alone and brought into reality by sacrifice. When the final component had been set in place, the resonance had created a delicate shriek that had killed the last of the eighty-one psychic craftsmen who had made it. Since then, the sound of its turning had ached through Ahriman's mind even when he was not in the chamber. It had been a vile price to pay, but there would be worse yet. Of that he was certain.

Ahriman and Ignis floated through the arrangement on silver discs. Both of them would leave as soon as this reading was complete. Out beyond its curved walls, the *Ankhtowe* plunged on towards its goal, moved by the half-lost science of machines. But in here, as the Sea of Souls fled past, they were standing still, looking out upon a growing hurricane. Only Menkaura would remain in the solatarium throughout the ritual. The War-Augur sat on his own disc, which hung upside down, relative to Ahriman, next to the golden sphere of the sun. Tarnish had spread across the silver of the disc, and Menkaura looked ragged and half-dead. The lacquer had peeled from his armour, and rust scabbed its plates. His head was bare, and the empty sockets of his eyes glowed with ghost-light and wept pus.

The sound of a diamond quill tip scratching on glass broke the quiet. Ahriman looked over to where Ignis was marking a line of calculations on a sheet of obsidian. The Master of the Order of Ruin looked up, the geometric tattoos on his face sliding into a new pattern. Ahriman sent a whisper of query by thought. In the solatarium chamber every thought was a shout, every sending a scream.

+The progress overall is within the calculations supplied by the primarch of the Fourth and his warsmiths,+ replied Ignis. +There are errors in the specifics that will need to be compensated for in the numeration of the final formulation.+

+That is what happens when plans touch reality,+ sent Ahriman. +Things fall apart.+

Ignis blinked, the patterns reforming again on his face as he considered the statement.

+In some cases,+ he replied, and then went back to his calculations and the diamond quill's scratching whine. Ahriman watched Ignis for a second and then let his sight move back to the spheres. His eyes moved between them, noting the path and details of each. Emotions and visions from across the gulf of space yanked at his thoughts as he did so.

*The face of a human pressed into a crawlspace, trying to make themselves small as giants in midnight-blue armour stalked past, their vox-speakers screaming the cries of those who had already been found; a powerless ship drifting through the dark, those within clinging to their last, shallow breaths as the air ran out; a warship tumbling over and over, blazing like a torch as its death fires fed on the fuel within its drives–*

Ahriman cut the visions away with a pulse of will and steadied his mind in the thought patterns of the ninth enumeration. He felt a breath briefly frost the inside of his helm. To observe the solatarium was not just to see it with your eyes, but to be part of it – to feel it turning as it tried to pull you into its whirlpool embrace.

+You are discomforted,+ stated Ignis.

Ahriman did not answer, but looked at Menkaura and opened his thoughts to send them.

+It can still be undone,+ said Menkaura, sending the answer to the question Ahriman was about to ask. +The balance of resonances in the arrangement is such that... it is not certain. Everything is blindness and dust on the wind...+

Ahriman felt another question rise in his mind and then let it fall. Ever since Menkaura had taken on the penance of watching the Configuration, his thoughts and words had strayed into prophecy, as though his mind and will were kites dragged by storm winds into distant lands of perception. For all his skill of foresight and mastery of the occult, Ahriman found that he was disturbed by what was happening to his brother.

+Come,+ he sent to Ignis, and turned his silver disc with a flick of will. It floated down to the lone opening cut in the chamber wall. His eyes flashed across a blue-and-white-spun sphere as he turned, and he–

*Blue and white stones in his hand, rounded by water, their faces dancing with patterns of herons and serpents...*

*The fire and blood light of the sun setting through Terra's haze of pollution, the smell of the dust and the static tang of a building storm...*

*The clack as Ormuzd placed three stones into the recesses of the old, wooden board and smiled up at him...*

*'What is it, brother? Can't think what move to make?' asked his twin.*

Ahriman pulled his senses back and the vision drained from his sight. Menkaura was looking down at him from the other side of the turning orbs and discs. The eyeless seer had his head cocked to the side, and Ahriman could feel the mind behind the empty sockets regarding him.

+It is a cruel thing to return home and find it changed, but not as changed as we are.+ Menkaura's words lingered as an echo in Ahriman's skull as he let his disc sink through the opening in the chamber wall.

Ahriman pulled the helm from his head as soon as he was outside the solatarium. Around him, the *Ankhtowe* hummed with the familiar sounds of a ship under power: the buzz of power conduits, and the rumble of distant engines. It felt reassuringly real. He took a breath and reached out with his mind, skimming over the thoughts of his brothers and crew. All was well. Their small fleet was still on course and unseen. They had left the great flock of Abaddon's armada and the Mechanicum fleet far behind. Now they were few again, all but alone in the night, heading for a distant speck of light. He sent a brief thought to touch the psychic bonds between him and the Word Bearers that rode at their sides. He did not linger over the contact, and he came away with the taste of ashes on his tongue.

He shivered, and lowered his thoughts into the lesser enumerations.

'You do not... like this,' said Ignis from behind him.

Somehow his thoughts had been disturbed enough that he had not noticed his Legion brother at his shoulder.

'No,' replied Ahriman, still tasting ashes in his mouth as he spoke. 'No, I do not like it.'

'I know,' said Ignis, looking at him with an utterly unchanged expression. 'I have already made and stated that observation.'

Ahriman turned away.

'The question that attends the observation is why you perceive our circumstances as you do?' asked Ignis.

Ahriman let out a breath and looked back at the Master of the Order of Ruin.

'I do not like what we are doing for every reason,' he said. 'For *every* reason, brother.'

*Freighter ship* Antius, *Jovian Gulf*

*Door slamming open.*

There was a metallic taste in Mersadie's mouth.

*Heavy metal-on-metal footsteps.*

Vengeful Spirit…

*She was on the* Vengeful Spirit. *There were… there were bodies heaped on the deck. Limbs tangled. Flesh ripped. Blood pooling. Something rose from the gore. Slicked fur. Red muzzle. Dripping-fang grin.*

'Mersadie…'

*She knew it was a Space Marine even before the impossibly huge shadow fell over her.*

'Mersadie, wake up…'

*A moon high in the winter sky. Its face a curve of silver, now a dividing line of light and dark.*

'Mersadie, wake up! Wake up now!'

*She turned to see a shadow form behind her.*

*The Warmaster's equerry…*

*Maloghurst was known as 'the Twisted', as much for his laby-rinthine mind as the horrible injuries that had broken his body and left him grotesquely malformed.*

'Loken,' he said, 'these are civilians.'

'I can vouch for them,' said Loken.

*Maloghurst turned his eyes to her. A hand fell on her shoulder.*

'Wake up now!'

The hand on her shoulder shook her.

She opened her eyes.

The smell of blood and split organs filled her mouth and nose. Her head arched up and she vomited. Red light was flicking through the passage.

On. Off.

On. Off.

For a moment the walls and decking swam and warped.

*Vengeful Spirit...* She *was* on the...

She was on the *Antius*.

'Mersadie.' She looked up. Nilus was crouching beside her, his long fingers just withdrawing from where they had shaken her shoulder. The Navigator's skin was white, the shadows soaking up the red blinking light. His eyes were wide. He looked as though he was about to be sick himself. Or about to run.

'Where...' she began, but then she remembered Koln, saw the flicker-skip of movement, the bodies of the crimson troopers torn to shreds, and then the flare and kick of the pistol and Koln's head coming apart. No, that was the dream... the dream...

She twisted, eyes going to the gore on the walls and floor, the heaps of meat and cloth, the gun lying next to her on the deck. Fresh bile surged up her throat, and splattered the deck. Nilus flinched back.

'Where are the children?' she gasped, pushing herself up.

Nilus jerked his head to where two small shapes lay slumped against the wall. Further down the corridor Aksinya lay beside the open door hatch. Her weapons were still in her hands beside her. Blood had soaked her clothes black. A last additional gunshot wound had ripped a hole in her neck. Her eyes were open, but they would see nothing any more.

Mersadie lunged for the children, found warmth in their hands.

'Catatonic,' said Nilus. 'Whatever happened here...'

But Mersadie was shaking the girl and boy, not listening to the Navigator.

'Mori, Noon! Listen to me! You have to wake up!'

'We have to get to the shuttle,' said Nilus, his voice rising from cold to shrill. 'I didn't see anyone alive coming here and the engines are still on. I think all the crew are dead. We are rudderless...'

'We're not going to the shuttle.'

'If they killed the crew then this is a tomb.'

'No!' Mersadie snarled. Her head snapped up to look at the Navigator. He took a step back. 'There are hundreds of people on this ship, and I am not leaving them to die while I run.'

'That did not stop you before.'

'It does now.' She looked down at the children. 'And in all those people there might be some who might be able to get us to safety.'

'You are serious, aren't you?'

She nodded. 'Go if you want.'

Nilus swore, looked around, and then swore again.

'I'll go to the bridge,' he said. 'I know something about ships.'

Mersadie heard him move away down the corridor. She bent over the still girl.

'Mori…' she said, and shook her. The girl's head twitched.
'Mori!' The girl's eyes flickered and opened and her shriek
split the air. 'Mori, look at me! Look at me!' Mersadie held
tight to the girl's hands. Mori's eyes steadied. She was breathing hard, face flecked with drying red. 'Mori, I need you
to listen to me. We are going to be fine, but your brother
needs you. He needs you to help him stay safe. You can
help him, can't you.'

The girl nodded once and then again, faster, her eyes
twitching but not moving from Mersadie's.

'Noon,' she whispered. 'Noon… Is he?'

'He is asleep, just like you were. He will wake up, but we
need to get out of here.'

'Father…?'

Mersadie blinked. She thought of what Nilus had said about
the crew being dead, about the crimson troopers, about the
shadow creature that had been Sub-mistress Koln.

Daemon… an old word but one that was true nonetheless.

'Your father would want you safe,' said Mersadie, 'so I am
going to make sure you are.'

Mori nodded.

'All right,' said Mersadie. 'I need you to stand up and keep
hold of your brother's hand.'

Mersadie lifted the boy, his sister gripping his dangling
hand. He was heavy, and her muscles ached as she took the
first step towards the open door hatch. Mori's eyes found the
still shape of Aksinya, and she heard the girl draw breath to
cry. Thick fluid was still dripping from the ceiling.

'Look at your brother,' said Mersadie. 'That's it, look at
your brother. Keep walking.'

They reached the hatch.

*Down*, thought Mersadie. They needed to go down to the
cargo decks. She thought she could remember the route

from when Aksinya had taken her to see the refugees. The image of angry eyes in cold faces rose from out of memory. She paused halfway through the door hatch.

'Hold your brother,' she said to Mori. The girl took the boy, hugging him. Mersadie stepped back through the door, bent down and took the pistol from out of Aksinya's hand, and the fresh clips from the bandolier beneath the body-guard's cloak. She tried not to look at the woman's face.

'What are you doing?' asked Mori.

'Making sure I don't fail her,' said Mersadie. She tucked the pistol and ammo under her clothes, stepped back through the door and took the still unwaking boy from Mori. 'Remember, keep hold of his hand.'

*The* Phalanx, *Terran high orbit*

Brother Massak, former Librarian of the Imperial Fists Legion, knew he was dreaming. He had spent the last seven years in the same chamber he knelt in now. He and his three brothers had seen almost no one else in that time. Their armour, their weapons and the silence of their minds were their only concern. Time had become divisions of equipment maintenance, combat practice and meditation, repeated over and over again.

The clash of axe and sword, the circle of lapping powder over yellow-and-blue ceramite, the slow exchange of breath…

On and on.

This was their duty now: to wait for a day that might never come, and to keep their minds locked from the powers that had been their craft of war.

In other Legions, the Emperor's ban on the use of psykers had seen Librarians returned to other duties, trusted to abstain from using their powers. But that was in other Legions. The VII did not adhere to rules in spirit alone. So Massak and his brothers had remained in this chamber on the *Phalanx*, wrapped in silence within and without.

But still he dreamed.

They always came back, sliding into his moments of rest. And recently, the dream images had shaken his meditation even when he was awake.

*He walked through caves of stone and through the darkness of forests he had never seen. Stars wheeled and turned. He saw the faces of creatures that were neither human nor beast but both. He saw a woman walking through the passages of a ship he did not recognise. He saw a door open…*

His eyes opened. He was sweating, moisture beading his skin beneath his robe. His brothers' eyes opened a second later, looking at him from across the meditation circle. Cadus, the youngest and lowest in rank, was swaying where he knelt. His left pupil was grossly dilated, the right a pinprick.

'The tides of the warp… are… growing stronger…' said Cadus.

'Turn your minds inwards, my brothers,' said Massak. 'What passes beyond is not our concern. Our oaths are to endure and that is what we shall do.'

'Do you feel that?' said Sollon. The venerable Codicier moved his hand to the deck beside him. 'The *Phalanx* is moving.'

Massak closed his eyes.

'Return to the centre, brothers. Our eyes gaze inwards. Our thoughts are the foundations of our beings. Our duty the life we lead…'

Silence fell again, and Massak felt the patterns of meditative quieting spiral his awareness away, down and down to stillness. He would wait. But part of him – a part that had waited and listened while the storm rose in the spirit realm – knew that the dreams would come again.

*Battle-barge* Monarch of Fire, *Uranus high orbit*

The *Monarch of Fire* fired even as it burned. A fifty-metre-wide wound gleamed with the light of internal explosions from where a kinetic shot had punched through its skin. The shot had missed vital systems by a few metres, but left flames drawing through its decks.

Lines of plasma poured from its spine and port batteries. A scythe of light cut across the face of the closing Iron Warriors battleships. There were twelve of them, main force class all, skinned by metal and wrapped by dozens of void shields. Each of them could weather a point-blank broadside from a ship that was its equal. But the *Monarch of Fire* was not their equal. She was an empress of destruction and they mere lords.

The void shields on five of the Iron Warriors ships vanished, collapsing one after another, flashing as they overloaded. Plasma flooded across their hulls. Plasteel and stone flashed to gas, melted, scattered into the dark. White vapour fumed from the *Monarch of Fire* as coolant breathed through its guns and hull. Its remaining opponents did not hesitate. Beams of turbo laser fire raked its shields as they flickered.

On the *Monarch of Fire*'s bridge, Lord Castellan Halbract felt the ship judder as it drew breath to bellow again. Lights dimmed. The surge of vox-traffic chopped and quieted. Tactical displays faded to hololithic snow. A moment of quiet and stillness fell as the great vessel inhaled power from its systems to fire upon its foes.

They had pulled back to the volume around Oberon.

Ships and supplies still streamed from the last moon in loyalist hands. It would not remain that way for long. A cascade of explosions had stripped it of most of its defences, but even if they had still been in place, its fate was sealed. The Iron Warriors had moved through the orbits of Uranus bit by bit, taking what they could and destroying what they could not. Where they met resistance they applied more force, brought more ships from the Elysian Gate, and replaced the ships and soldiers that fell with more.

At the star fort *Phuran*, unable to break its void shields, and with troops prevented from advancing beyond their beachheads, they had deployed two vast ships to overwhelm the defences. The pair had lost their names and become codes in the data-looms of the IV Legion: I-D-I and I-V-II. Both ships had been grain haulers taken from the Imperial supply lines. Their cargo gone to feed the forges supplying the Warmaster's armies, their guts became city-sized barracks for tens of thousands of gang fighters harvested from the worlds around Ullanor. Kalma soporifics had been pumped through their holds to subdue the human cargo for transit. As they closed with the *Phuran*, the gas mix changed and frenzon and slaught fogged their holds. The tens of thousands of gangers began to wake, and kill each other.

Halbract's ships had tried to cripple the two behemoths before they reached the star fort, but Iron Warriors warships cut them off. By the time the pair had reached the *Phuran*, they had lost ten thousand of their human cargo. More than enough remained. I-D-I and I-V-II docked at the Iron Warriors' beachhead points, and opened their internal doors. Passages designed to drain billions of tonnes of grain now became exits for over a hundred thousand drug-fuelled killers. The troops defending the star fort held for six hours.

After it was done, the Iron Warriors opened the station to the void and let the vacuum deal with the gangers.

On and on, the brutal pragmatism of Perturabo had pushed the defenders back and back again. Now the remainder of the Second Sphere fleet was battered and wounded, circling the moon of Oberon. A hundred warships from three times that number, facing twenty times that strength – those were odds that made for stories to echo through the ages. But this would be no last stand, no final rest in death found in fire. The burning of Pluto's moons was a ploy that could only be used once. Halbract had seen the enemy forces alter their tactics. There were no hidden charges or annihilating data-jinns laid before the Elysian Gate, but Perturabo did not know that.

Machine adepts scoured the moons and stations the traitors had already taken. Already careful, the enemy became even more cautious. Large ship strengths were held back from recently taken ground. Anything that held no worth was destroyed by distant bombardment. It slowed them, and in that it proved as effective a weapon as a fresh battlefleet. In the buzzing half-silence as the *Monarch of Fire* passed through its power cycle, Halbract reflected that, measured on the axis of time, this battle had gone in their favour. It was just on every other count that it tasted bitter on his tongue.

'Begin to divert power to engines and shields,' he said softly. 'Give us one more cycle of the guns. Send the withdrawal signal to all other ships.'

The command crew answered with silent action. They all knew this moment was coming. They could not remain where they were. Ships closed on them from every plane of orbit, and soon the path out to the sunward gulf would close. But they would not fall back to the long night without claiming a final price from the traitors.

Power blinked back through the bridge. Holo-displays snapped into clarity. The red gleams of enemy craft lit across targeting consoles.

'Fire,' said Halbract, and the *Monarch of Fire* roared his word into the dark. Three warships died in a stuttering blink of destruction. Plasma bored through unshielded hulls. Reactors and munitions detonated in their bellies. They burst, showering brilliant light and gas out and out.

The lights on the *Monarch of Fire* dimmed, but deep in her hull, power had already been syphoned to her engines. She pushed loose of Oberon's orbit. The rest of her fleet was already falling into formation, ships breaking off and turning their prows towards the distant light of the sun. Signals reached after them from Oberon, pleading and railing and cursing, carrying the rage of people who knew that their fate was sealed. Halbract listened to them all, hearing the bitter words as the *Monarch of Fire* made for the cold depths. As predicted, the enemy did not chase them. They were cautious, and besides, they had won.

The signals from Oberon stopped as they reached the edge of deep sensor range. Halbract cut the link as the last whisper became static.

'Signal Terra,' he said, taking the helmet off his head. 'Uranus belongs to the enemy.'

The officers around him bowed their heads at the words.

'We are beyond the enemy's likely interception range,' said the senior tech-priest overseeing the ship's signal and auspex systems. 'Do you wish to send the rendezvous codes, lord castellan?'

Halbract nodded, his eyes on the damage and casualty reports from the rest of his fleet. It had taken Dorn's personal word to convince him of this part of the strategy. It went against almost every instinct. Faced with an enemy, no matter how strong or numerous, one advanced, or stood and trusted to the strength of shield and sword and bolter. You did not yield ground that the enemy desired.

But that was what they were doing now, and what they had planned to do since before the ships of the traitors had breached the gates.

'Now, in this moment, walls and strongholds are not our battle-field,' Rogal Dorn had said, his voice strong even through the distortion-laced signal from Terra. 'Our battlefield is time, and the battles we fight are to deny that to the enemy. They thirst for time, need it and cannot waste a second of it. And so we must deny it to them. Everything must be measured against that. We cannot stop them, my son, but we can make them bleed in time and strength before they reach the walls of the Palace. That is worth more than any fortress or line that is not on the soil of Terra.'

'I will do what is needed,' Halbract had replied and sent three hundred ships from the defence of Uranus into the night to wait.

He had bowed his head then, and he did so again now…

Over three hundred ships hanging in the lightless gulf between Uranus and the core of the system… Over three hundred guns that had not spoken to hold back the enemy from the *Phuran*, or Cordelia, or Oberon, or…

Would it have made a difference? Would it make a difference now? To an enemy not expecting a fresh and undamaged force waiting for it as it leaped deeper into the system… It might. It had to.

'Send the codes,' he said, raising his head. 'Bring us on course to meet the rest of the fleet.'

# THIRTEEN

Calculations and errors
Come with me
Dreams

*Bhab Bastion, The Imperial Palace, Terra*

'They have failed,' said Jaghatai Khan. 'Horus has failed.'

The annex of the Grand Borealis Strategium was quiet. Four humans, three primarchs and one near-human stood in silence, looking at the Praetorian of Terra through the veil of holo-light. A single tactical projection turned at the centre of the room, its surface flashing as the data cycled across its sphere. Malcador the Regent stood between Sanguinius and the Khan; beside them were Magos-Emissary Kazzim-Aleph-1 and High Primary Solar General Niborran. Su-Kassen stood to Dorn's right, and the ghost-like presence of Senior Astropath Armina Fel filled the space to his left.

None of them spoke after the Khan's pronouncement. It was undoubtedly correct, but...

Su-Kassen watched as Kazzim-Aleph-1 extended a chromed digit and stopped the projection, as though halting the spin of a child's top.

'The outer reaches are the enemy's,' said the magos-emissary. 'They advance into the inner system. Mars, sacred cradle of the machine, will be next. If disciples of the false Mechanicum rise from their pit, the Fourth Sphere fleet will be unable to drive them back. I estimate its primary strength will erode in main force effectiveness at a rate of three-point-six-one-two per cent per hour. That cannot be sustained. The Lost Forges will fall to the invaders.'

'But they will be left with almost no forces that can be brought to bear here on the Throneworld or in orbit,' said Niborran. The old general's silver augmetic eyes did not seem to flinch from the display. The death rubies bonded to his right socket gleamed against the darkness of his skin as he gave a single nod. 'Even if they do, it will not be in time. My lord Jaghatai is correct, the position is clear – they have failed. Their forces are too few, arriving too late and in parts. We can meet them, hold them and break them one after another. They will still be clawing at the walls when Lord Guilliman arrives.'

'But what of sacred Mars?' hissed Kazzim-Aleph-1. Su-Kassen thought he had never sounded so human. 'Liberation was promised. Promised and encoded with oaths. This…'

'Liberation requires victory,' snarled Niborran. 'And that requires a price to be paid now, by Mars too, just as it was by Pluto, by Uranus.'

Kazzim-Aleph-1 clicked and whirred, lenses rotating beneath his hood. Su-Kassen looked at Rogal Dorn. The primarch was still, his eyes steady on the magos-emissary and the general. Niborran was Dorn's man, she knew. Born in the rings of Saturn and raised in the disciplines of the Saturnine Ordos, he was a veteran sharpened by a century and a half of war, and time had not taken his edge. Of all the Imperial Army and Militia units on Terra, several hundreds of millions were now his to command, but here in this chamber and at this moment he was here to speak the words that Dorn could not.

'The Fabricator General shall learn of this and make objection,' said Kazzim-Aleph-1. 'There are forces available. They should be moved to Mars.'

'An enemy fleet the equal of that making for Mars is descending towards Luna,' said Malcador mildly. The Regent reached out and keyed a control that set the holo-display slowly rotating again. He still looked exhausted and drained, but there was a spark of strength in his eyes and words. 'Unless you would suggest leaving the orbits of Terra unguarded, honoured magos-emissary? If you are not suggesting stripping those defences, then you can only be referring to the *Phalanx* and its attendant ships.'

'The principal Seventh Legion craft is of a size and capability that would make a significant statistical difference to the outcome of these engagements.'

'The *Phalanx* is mine to command,' said Rogal Dorn, his words falling like an axe at the end of the magos' words. 'It goes where I will it.'

Kazzim-Aleph-1 recoiled with a click of turning cogs, and then dipped his head slightly in what might have been a nod.

'But you wait, brother,' said Sanguinius. 'Move it to either Mars or Luna and the enemy in those spheres will be banished and Horus' failure will be sealed.'

Dorn's eyes moved from the holo-display to his brother primarch. The two held each other's gaze, and in the moment of quiet Su-Kassen spoke the question that had been asked again and again in the past weeks.

'Where is Horus?' Eyes and faces turned towards her. 'If we believe our intelligence was flawed...' She saw Malcador give the smallest movement of his head. 'For all the enemies that we can see there must be more, and so where are they, and where is he?'

'Waiting for the primary attacks to strike home,' said Niborran. 'Any forces he still has to deploy will be moving through the Elysian and Khthonic Gates. Even at best speed those fresh forces will not arrive in time to reinforce the two inner system assaults.'

'But what do these two strikes at the inner system achieve?'

'They pin us in place,' said Niborran. 'They keep us from moving forces to counter-assault into the outer system. They are the claw-holds for a rapid assault. That was your assessment before, admiral. Are you disavowing it now?'

Su-Kassen shook her head.

'No, it still stands, but Horus has failed, according to our assessment – failed, and never even taken the field in person.'

Sanguinius gave a small shiver. The feathers of his furled wings shook.

'No,' he said. 'He is coming. I know. This ends with him here, on this ground.'

Malcador's eyes lingered on the Angel for a long moment.

Dorn stepped forwards and collapsed the projection with a hand.

'This has yet to end. Move now and we may just as likely seal defeat as seize victory.' He looked at the magos-emissary, his features unreadable. 'The *Phalanx* remains. And we wait.'

'For what?' asked the Khan.

'To see if our traitor brother has truly failed,' said Dorn. 'Or if we have.'

*Freighter ship* Antius, *Jovian Gulf*

Mersadie heard the shouting before she reached the cargo bays. Even through plasteel, the noise echoed down the corridor. She paused as she saw the hazard-striped door. Beside her Mori looked up. The girl was still clutching her brother's hand. He had not stirred. The deck had lurched beneath her feet as they reached this level.

Rudderless, Nilus had said, but what else had the assault done?

Mersadie took a step towards the door. Something crashed into the other side.

'I don't think that we should be here,' said Mori, taking a step back. 'I don't want to be here.'

Mersadie turned and lowered Noon into the girl's arms. 'It's all right. It will be all right. Just keep hold of your brother and make sure he is safe.'

'My father,' said the girl, 'we should find my father.'

'Nilus has gone to the bridge to look for him,' said Mersadie.

'Who…' began the girl, but another wave of impacts rang against the door into the cargo space. Mersadie took out Aksinya's pistol. It was surprisingly light, but she was not sure how its mechanisms worked.

Her mother had tried to teach her pistol shooting in the pinnacle-born fashion of her ancestors. Mersadie had not liked it. Like most other things her family valued, it had been a source of anger and disappointment.

Mersadie worked the cocking mechanism and checked the safety. There was still blood on the rapier-style grip, she noticed.

*Aksinya's dead eyes… The shadow… The red-black blink as the shadow tore towards her…*

'We are here for you…'

She could not move. Blood had seeped into the carved bone-and-silver design behind the trigger: a half-horse half-man, rearing and drawing a bow to shoot, a centaur… a *sagittar*. She wrenched her head up, and the past flooded into her eyes.

*The practice hall on the* Vengeful Spirit *looked back at her, unfolding out of memory in a waking fever-dream.*

*A dozen soldiers marched in. She recognised uniforms of the Imperial Army, but saw that their badges of unit and rank had been removed. And amongst them the icy, golden-eyed features of Petronella Vivar's bodyguard. She recalled that his name was Maggard.*

*'Take the iterator and the remembrancer back to their quarters,' said Maloghurst. 'Post guards and ensure that there are no more breaches.' Maggard nodded and stepped forwards. Mersadie tried to avoid him, but he was quick and strong. His hand grabbed her neck and he yanked her towards the door. Sindermann had not resisted.*

*Maloghurst stood between Loken and the door. If Loken wanted to stop Maggard and his men, he would have to go through Maloghurst.*

*Mersadie tried to look back. She could see Loken beyond Maloghurst's robed form, looking like a caged animal ready to attack. The door slammed shut.*

'No,' she shouted, and heard the word come out as a whisper as she made to try to run towards a closed door.

She stopped. She still had the gun in her hand, she realised, and the entryway in front of her was not a hatch on the *Vengeful Spirit*, but a yellow-and-black chevroned blast door closing off a hold on the *Antius*.

Mori was looking at her, eyes wide with fresh fear. For a second, Mersadie saw a reflection of her own terror in the girl's stare. With a breath she forced her hands to still, and then tucked the gun out of sight. She turned back to the door. There was a vox-horn next to the locking mechanism. She pushed the green intoning rune beside it. A snap of static spat from the speaker-grille. A wail of distortion rose over the shouting. The banging on the other side of the door stopped. Mersadie swallowed in a dry throat.

'If you can…' she began, then stopped as the sound of her own voice hummed through the speaker. 'If you can hear me,' she said, and felt the words gain strength as she spoke, 'then you are alive. A military force tried to board the ship. They are dead. As far as I know the crew are dead too. The ship is drifting.' She paused, hearing her words echo. She sounded calm, she realised. In control. 'We can all get out of this, but only if we all stay steady. I am going to open the door in a moment. If there are any of you who have crewed a ship before, or know about anything that will keep one going, then come forwards.' She stopped again and turned away from the vox-horn. Then she turned back and keyed it on again. 'My name is Mersadie Oliton,' she said.

She reached for the door lock release, paused, closed her eyes. She thought of the shuttle sitting in the hangar just a few hundred metres away. Nilus had thought they should run, leave this ship of the desperate and the dead. The world inside her skull was spinning, but her thoughts had found a clear centre. There was only one way she would let herself survive this.

Her hand found the release and punched in the code Aksinya had used. The piston locks released with a thump. Carefully she pushed the door inwards. The light inside was dim, stained orange by the red and yellow of slowly pulsing emergency lights. She stepped inside, hands open at her sides. Eyes looked back at her from a ring of faces. The gun, tucked out of sight, pressed sharp against her back. The lights pulsed in the lengthening seconds. In the distance something creaked and echoed through the hull.

A man stepped out of the crowd. Mersadie suppressed the instinct to flinch. The man was big, tall in the way that only the void-born were but bulked out with grafted muscle. He looked at her for a moment, and then nodded.

'I was a second on a belt trader,' he said. 'I know ships.'

She looked at him for a moment, and then nodded.

'Thank you,' she said. The man nodded back.

'I was a dock pilot,' said a woman with a lined face and a liver-spotted scalp. And the silence broke as they came forwards in a babble of hope.

*Hab Block 287, Worker Hab Plateau 67, Terra*

Mekcrol woke, the scream from his dream still on his lips. The dim light of the night-cycle light set in the ceiling still shone. Familiar shadows fell from where his robe and rebreather mask hung by the door. The ventilation fan turned behind its grating, thumping and scraping as it pushed the smells of smoke and oil into the room. Mekcrol turned his head slowly. He was shivering. Sweat slicked his skin.

It was not real… Just a dream… Just a dream…

Still he did not move.

*In the dream he had been standing in front of the door out of his hab-unit. He had been waiting for someone… Someone he knew… The white paint on the metal frame had the same pattern of grime and scratches beside the lock release as he saw every day as he left. Except there was something else there in the dream, something smudged and red… like the marks of fingers. Like the marks of bleeding fingers…*

*The door had opened. Air had gusted in. The smell. Could you smell in dreams? The air smelled of frost. It smelled clean, sharp. The space beyond the door was dark. He had stepped through. Lights had flickered on.*

*The corridor stretched away to either side. Closed doors led off every two metres. There was no one else there. That was not strange. Hab allocation was linked to shift rotations, so that people would not jam the corridors as they all left or returned at the same time. Mekcrol was lucky. His mother had secured an enhancement to their hereditary indenturing that had made her son a Twentieth Degree Supervisory Menial. That gave him a unit to himself, and an extra hour of rest.*

*The door had closed behind him. The sound echoed up the corridor. Air brushed past his cheek. Mekcrol had turned his head towards the breeze. It was cold. A flake of snow touched his face.*

*'Son.'*

*He turned. His mother was there, standing in an open door. Behind her, he could see white snow, and a black sky. Shapes like the stretched shadows of pylons grasped at the silver circle of a moon. Were those trees? Was that what a forest looked like?*

*'Son, please...'*

*He looked at his mother. She was thin, almost nothing between the folds of her skin and her bones. Vomit crusted her lips and the front of her smock. Her eyes were unfocused, half-closed. She had been like that the last time he had seen her. She had died while he was on shift. When he had come back, another resident had already been allocated to her hab-unit. It had been a decade ago.*

*But here she was...*

*'Son...' she said, voice rattling, 'why did you leave me alone?'*

*He took a step back, reached for the door back into his unit. His hand found the lock release. It opened... Night sky and a blast of ice wind. She was standing there. Frost rimed her, freezing air fogging like smoke around her, ice clogging her eyes.*

*'Son...'*

*He ran. Doors flew open as he passed. Night and snow poured in. His mother stood behind every door, calling to him, reaching for him, her cries following him.*

*'Son...*

*'...Son...*

*'...Son.*

*'Why…*
*'…did you…*
*'…leave me…*
*'…alone.'*
*He had shouted then.*
*'You are gone. You are gone… Who are you?'*
*And the wind and rattling branches had answered.*
*'We are the man beside you…'*
*And the doors were opening in front of him as he ran, and hands were reaching for him, grabbing at him, tearing his skin, and he was screaming, and the wind was laughing.*

Sitting up on his sweat-soaked bed, the slow beat of the fan pushing warm air through the room, it still seemed very real. He reached for the flask beside the bed, fingers shaking. He took a sip of water. It tasted of dust and metal. Water rations had been halved in the last few weeks. Like the constant drone of ready-sirens, it was another needle in the flesh of life. He looked up at the shift clock above the door. He had two hours left before his first rotation of the day.

He would not go back to sleep.

He did not want to go back to sleep.

He took another sip of his water, and stood up, rubbed his eyes. He would go out into the hab. There was a viewing cupola on Level 3490. He could get there and back in time to suit up for his shift. He wondered if the shift numbers would be lower. Lots of people were getting pulled into militia. He was not certain why, and the rumours… well, the rumours were laughable. It was an excuse to squeeze more out of the indents like him, he was sure, ship labour to some other complex and tell those left that they had to work twice as hard with half-rations because of some kind of crisis. It was all just a play.

But the sirens were sounding a general alert, and Nula

from work gang 67 had said that there were press gangs patrolling the west zones. They had shot people for resisting. That was what she had said, anyway. Mekcrol did not know what to believe. Just like bad dreams, there was nothing you could do about rumours except to try to get your head together and get on. He would go to the view cupola and look out down the street canyon towards the Iron Spire. It might be lit, but then again, the power had been rationed too, so more likely not.

He unlocked the door and opened it.

A blast of wind rocked him back. A figure was standing in the door, vomit and frost on her smock, bloody hands gripping the door frame, empty eyes looking at him. Skin folded, flesh stretched. Teeth grew.

'We... are... coming...' gasped the voice of his mother as she stepped across the threshold.

Mekcrol did not wake again. He died screaming, falling through his dreams. No one in his block noticed and by the time his absence from his work shift was logged, no one was wondering about where a low-level indent supervisor was.

The next night, half of the people across the northern hemisphere woke from dreams of things without eyes, or of creatures squatting on their chests in the dark, wearing the skinned faces of loved ones and crooning in the voices of past pain. People fell and fell forever through abysses of night lit with lambent eyes and bared teeth, the screams of their descent following them down and down. The sound of hooves and the howl of wolves rolled through the dark as night passed across the face of Terra.

After three nights of dreams the riots began. Fires lit the Arctic fringe hives and hab-warrens. Crowds poured through breached curfew zones. Arson flames blazed across hundreds of kilometres. Pacification cohorts were deployed. The death count rose, and the nightmares galloped on with the turning of the heavens.

# FOURTEEN

Edge of survival
Wolf of the new moon
Monsters

*Freighter ship* Antius, *Jovian Gulf*

Mersadie found Vek on the bridge. She had sent the children back to their cabin, and the mass of refugee volunteers seemed to follow her commands with the intensity of the desperate. They had held back when she told them she wanted to go to the bridge alone. They had not questioned why.

Part of her had known. There had been no sign of Vek in the rest of the ship and she could not believe he would not have tried to find Mori and Noon.

She had known. But knowing was different to seeing what was left of him lying on the deck of the bridge. There were others, scattered on each level and gantry. No one had been left alive. The boarding force had been efficient. She noticed that a lone figure in crimson armour lay amongst the dead. It looked as though he had been hacked in half. For a tiny, sickening instant she wondered what had done that. She looked back at Vek. Once, maybe, she would have felt the need to weep. Now she just felt cold, as though ice had poured into the space where grief could once have lived inside her.

'They didn't damage the systems,' Nilus called down from the helm platform. She looked up. The Navigator looked down over the brass rail. 'I presume they were just going to scuttle the ship once they were done.'

'It's still working, though?' she called.

'As far as I can tell.'

A tremor shook the deck. Lights blinked across the console.

'If the engines are still working then what is that?'

'I don't know,' said Nilus. 'Maybe from whatever they punched into the hull to get inside.'

Mersadie looked back down at Vek's remains. It felt as though she should stop, as though time should stand still and mark this moment. The deck shuddered again. Nilus said something she only half heard. She shook herself, lifted a fallen officer's cloak and draped it over Vek. Nilus shouted something that was lost under another rumble of metal.

'What is it?' she asked, turning away and mounting the stairs up to the helm platform.

Behind her, she could hear the sounds of people coming down the corridor to the open bridge doors. Nilus was bent over on the deck, looking at a slick of blood and oil on the brass-and-iron floor.

'I said that I hadn't seen any sign of the ship's enginseer amongst the dead.'

'Chi-32-Beta,' said Mersadie. The deck pitched for a moment.

'What?' said Nilus.

'That was her name, the ship's tech-priest. Her name was Chi-32-Beta.'

Nilus shrugged the irrelevance away.

'We need her. Even with a crew, we can't control the ship's systems without a tech-priest…' He moved forwards, eyes on the smeared liquid. Mersadie heard cries from the lower level of the bridge as the refugees saw the slaughter. Nilus reached a section of wall lined with thick seams and rivets. A crack ran from floor to ceiling between two plates, like a door left just ajar. The smear of oil and blood vanished into the wall.

Nilus was looking at it, his skin somehow even paler than normal. He had stopped and was staring at the crack running down the wall. The sound of voices and footsteps was coming up the stairs to the platform. Nilus was backing away now. The ship shook, and Mersadie noticed that a fresh dribble of black fluid seeped out from the crack onto the floor.

'Nilus,' said Mersadie. 'What is wrong?' But the Navigator was backing away still, glancing at the other set of stairs leading down to the prow section of the bridge. He began to move towards them.

'The shuttle is still there,' he hissed, as though to himself. 'I will make sure it's still there. Yes, just in case…'

He made for the forward stairs, loping down them just as the first of the refugees came up the aft stairs. Mersadie was about to call after him, but he was already out of sight.

'Everyone's dead,' said one of them. It was the big man who had come forwards first; Gade, he had said his name was. His eyes were wide, sweat sheening his skin. 'Everyone…'

Mersadie looked back at the crack running down the wall. She stepped forwards, put her hand into the opening and pulled a section of the wall wide.

A figure lay coiled in the tangle of wires in the niche behind the hidden door. Motes of light and worms of static were running up and down some of the cables. Blood and oil matted the red robes of the figure, and trickled down through the knots of wires. Its hooded head twitched up, and the ship trembled again. Static breathed out through a hiss of noise that might have been speech.

Mersadie moved forwards, but the figure raised a brass hand, and now she could see that the cables ran into the mass of its body beneath the robes.

'We…' wheezed Chi-32-Beta. 'We need to run. They are… Their ship… They are still out there.'

*The Imperial Palace, Terra*

The grey warrior came to the Regent on the fifth day of the dream riots. No guards or doors barred his passing. The lone sigil on his shoulder and the clearance codes transmitted by his armour let him move like a ghost through the Palace, unquestioned and unseen. Only when he reached the last door of the Regent's sanctuary did a lowered guardian spear halt his progress.

Su-Kassen watched the grey-armoured warrior turn his head to look at the Custodian. The image from the Custodian's helm-feed showed the set of his features in perfect clarity. It could have been a handsome face, but gene-craft had broadened and morphed it so that its humanity was lost beneath a hardness that made the hairs rise on Su-Kassen's neck. There were the eyes, too, still and unblinking, and as cold as distant stars. She knew his name. As a member of the War Council of Terra she was aware of the existence of the Regent's Knights Errant, although not the details of what they did or why. She also knew that the warrior looking directly up into the pict-capture had been a captain of the Luna Wolves Legion and a close confidant of Horus Lupercal himself. His name was Garviel Loken, and now he was a warrior whose grey armour marked him as a ghost trapped between loyalty and circumstance, fighting a war beyond the light of morality.

'Do you wish me to leave, Lord Regent?' she asked.

Malcador shook his head but did not look up from the screen set on his desk. The latest gathering of the council had broken up minutes before. It had been brief and grim.

Five days before, the horrors had begun to haunt the sleep of all those on the nightside of Terra. The dreams had no pattern or consistent element except one: terror. They were containing the unrest, but the dreams were fraying the already-thin threads of control. Only inside the Palace did the night pass without terrors. Renewed *Lectitio Divinitatus* cult activity had also been reported. It would have been difficult to deal with even under normal circumstances. With the outer spheres of the Solar System ablaze and the enemy closing with every hour, it was bordering on catastrophic.

'Fate,' Malcador said softly, looking at the face of the grey-armoured warrior and letting out a breath, 'always manifests in the small things.' Su-Kassen remained still, uncertain whether he had been talking to her. 'Let him pass,' he said. A second later the door to the tower chamber opened.

'Captain Loken,' said Malcador. Loken looked at the Regent and, despite the anger fuming from him, bowed his head for a second. 'Something vexes you.'

'You issued a kill order for the prisoners held on Titan,' said Loken.

Malcador held the Space Marine's gaze.

'The high-risk prisoners held in the facility above Titan were moved. Some of them were being moved through Uranus orbital transfer when the assault began. The ships holding them were hit. There were losses, and it appears that some of the prisoners were able to escape. The standing orders are for a hunt-and-kill protocol to be pursued without limit, and yes, those orders were mine.'

'That is–' began Loken.

'That is what is needed in this war, captain,' said Malcador, his voice suddenly hard. 'Even now, at this hour, and with all that we face. Innocence proves nothing and can even be a weapon.'

'You have no right,' growled Loken, leaning forwards, gauntlets resting on the polished wood of the desk. Aggression was boiling off him. Su-Kassen felt her hand twitch towards the holster of the shot-pistol that she had surrendered at the chamber door.

Malcador stood, eyes bright, face hard, and the frailty that had clung to him fell away. He seemed taller, his shadow lengthening as the lights around the chamber dimmed.

'I have a duty,' he said. 'A duty to see all that our enemy would destroy survive, and in holding to that duty I will do what others will not. We are all expendable. You, me, every adult and every child, every hope we held, every dream that we clung to. All of it. *All* of it, captain. *That* is my duty, and I will see it done, even if others do not like the price that they would not pay themselves.'

Loken had not moved, but the anger in his eyes seemed to have become something else, something colder.

'I would pay that price, but not with the coin you offer.'

'That is why I stand where I do. Because if we fail then there will be nothing left, not even the memory of what was lost. Would you rather that? Would you rather the future that your gene-sire Horus dreams for humanity? If you would, then honour your convictions and try to kill me now, because I will not stop, and I will not explain myself to you again.'

Loken rocked back. The shadow of Malcador drew upwards,

spreading across the ceiling. Su-Kassen felt her nerves screaming to run, to get away from the cold rage that was flooding
out as the light dimmed.

Then it was gone, and the old man standing with the help
of his staff looked old and exhausted. Loken's face was fixed,
but pale. Malcador closed his eyes for a second, and then
took an unsteady step forwards, and put a hand on Loken's
shoulder guard. Beneath the fingers, the emblem of an eye
etched into the grey ceramite gleamed coldly for an instant.

'I am sorry,' said Malcador. 'I understand, but these are
necessities, captain. If it helps, it was not a specific order
relating to Mistress Oliton. The hunt-and-termination protocols are general, a contingency put in place a long time ago.'

Loken shrugged free of the Regent's touch, face still stone-
like.

'There was a signal picked up on the military channels
around Uranus,' he said.

Malcador nodded.

'You knew?' asked Loken.

'Of course,' said Malcador. 'Although communications
being what they are, I only learned of it very recently.' He
paused. 'As did you.'

Loken nodded once, and then turned towards the door.

'I am taking a ship. If you know of the signal, then you
know that the last report from one of your hunter cadres
had the ship she was suspected to be aboard heading for
Jupiter. That is where I am going. Send a signal – call off
the hunters.'

'You know as well as I that may not be possible.'

'Then you will have forfeited their lives, too,' said Loken,
and turned for the door.

'If they have not found her, Loken, there is little hope
that you will.'

'Isn't that why you chose us, Lord Regent? To do what others could not?'

Malcador did not reply. Loken moved to the door. It opened and Su-Kassen could see the Custodians standing beyond it. Loken paused, his foot across the threshold and turned his stare back on Malcador.

'If you did know that she was being hunted, would you have countermanded the orders?'

Malcador held Loken's gaze for a long moment.

'No,' he said at last.

Loken gave a single nod, and then was gone. The door shut after him.

Malcador let out a breath and limped around his desk and lowered himself back into his chair.

'Thank you, admiral,' he said after a second.

'For what?' she asked.

'If you had not been here, I have a suspicion he would have done what time and the blades of our enemies have so far failed to accomplish.'

'I do not think so, lord, and if he had tried, I don't think he would have succeeded.'

Malcador gave a tired smile.

'Perhaps not...'

He picked up a data-slate from his desk and began to scan it.

'We could stop him,' said Su-Kassen after a moment. 'He needs your authority to move through the Palace. Even if he reaches a ship, it could be halted before it breaks orbit.'

Malcador shook his head.

'Let him go. Maybe he is right. In such times, perhaps the small acts of nobility matter more, not less.'

'He did not say that, lord...'

'Did he not?' said Malcador, and looked up at her, eyes

sharp. 'Then maybe I am just succumbing to weakness and sentimentality. Does that sound more believable to you, admiral?'

'No, lord. It does not.'

'No...' he said, nodding as though considering the point, before looking back to his work. 'Perhaps not.'

*Battleship* Iron Blood, *Uranus high orbit*

Forrix closed his eyes for three seconds and then opened them again to the light of stars and war. Fatigue, long banished by ascension to the Legion, had begun to creep into his being over the years of conflict and the demands of this phase of the operation. He had begun to find that moments like these, when his eyes touched the vastness of reality rather than the coldness of data, were like a rudder holding him true. Here, on a squat tower set high on the spine of the *Iron Blood*, was one of the few places you could look out at space with the naked eye, and so it had become his haunt.

A ragged fleet poured from the Elysian Gate before his eyes. Craft after craft slid into being, lit their engines and powered away into the dark. Some of them had once been proud ships of war, their old colours lost under battle scars and heraldry that marked them as without lord or mistress. These were the wild swarms of mercenaries, pirates and reavers that had flourished in the age of Horus' war, and now came hungry for the fruits of Sol. Most were human-led, their captains deserters from one cause or another. Others were fanatics, ships full of converts to the worship of old gods with new faces, come to make bloody pilgrimage on ancient ground. They came in converted haulers festooned with billions of scraps of parchment, others in sleek warships scorched black to remove the marks of their old allegiances.

There were Space Marines amongst the horde, too. Ships commanded by warriors that had taken new colours and new names: The Burnt Word, the Brotherhood of Set, the Twelfth Truth – oath breakers all. Forrix had felt a twinge of instinct tug at him as a battleship in the red and black colours of one of these mongrel bands turned across the *Iron Blood's* sensor screens. With a word the craft could have been reduced to broken metal and molten stone, a fate worthy of such creatures.

Beside them were ships that still wore the colours of their Legion, even if those colours were only a mask. Midnight-hulled vessels of the Night Lords, and ships of the III Legion painted like carnival masks, their vox-channels babbling noise. In Forrix's eyes, these were almost worse than the others, carrion-reavers, and self-appointed warlords, the mockery of their lineage painted with contempt.

They served a purpose though; they knew the art of mayhem as war. They had been held in the warp until Uranus was secured, wrapped in screams and nightmares, and now were loosed on the outer Solar System. They had no mission, only a direction. The rest was left to their nature. In days, they would fall on Neptune, and Jupiter. The slaughter and bloodshed would begin. Without a specific mission, the reaver forces would kill and die, and inflict pain. Blood and screams would follow fire. Confusion and fear would spread. Those mortals that could flee would do so, and their flight would carry the terror with them.

Behind him he heard the doors release, and felt the aching buzz of Perturabo's armour as the primarch entered the viewing cupola. He turned to kneel, but a twitch of Perturabo's hands held Forrix standing. The weapon pods and pistons of the primarch's armour hissed and breathed cold gas as they cycled. Forrix watched his lord out of the corner of his eye. Perturabo had suddenly become utterly still. That stillness had seized the primarch more and more in the time since they had gone to fetch Angron back to the war from the borders of Ultramar. It was unsettling in a way that Forrix did not want to think about. Perturabo watched the tide of monsters breach into being.

The *Daughter of Woe* hung above the murk of the Elysian Gate. Iron Warriors ships clustered around the space hulk, suckling from her scarred skin. A blackened cleft a kilometre long and two hundred metres deep had been carved into her face by the plasma fusillade of the *Monarch of Fire*. Forrix had thought, for a moment during the engagement, that the Imperial Fists ship was going to ram the *Daughter of Woe*, or try to board her in force. It would have been suicide, but the defiance of the Imperial Fists over the last days of the assault had seemed to drift to recklessness.

*The pride finally surfacing from beneath the stone,* Forrix had thought at the time. The sons of Dorn had pulled back from the assault, though.

'How long?' asked Perturabo, only his lips moving in the mask of his face. The ammo feeds linked to his arms cycled again. It reminded Forrix of a muscle twitching.

'Our ships are ready,' said Forrix.

Perturabo looked at him then and gave a single nod at the data projections.

'How much did we lose?'

Forrix licked his lips. The Lord of Iron knew the answer to the question already. No scrap or thread of data escaped him in the battle sphere.

'Thirty-six hours, lord,' replied Forrix.

'By such things are our deeds now weighed,' said Perturabo. 'By the slow slice of time, and not the blood that turns its wheel...'

Forrix shifted uncomfortably.

'It is likely that this is Dorn's strategy. If he knows that Guilliman is coming...'

'He knows,' said Perturabo, 'or suspects, and that is more than enough for him to make time a weapon against us. Bleed us. Slow us. Cut by cut, minute by minute. We come to the cradle of all war and find that its craft is what we always knew it to be. Not a flash of blades or the fire of heroism, but the slow grinding of bloody inches. It can't be escaped.'

Forrix thought of all they had given, of the legionaries that had died to slow the coming of the Ultramarines and those they had left to try to slow the inevitable.

Silence fell again.

'The losses in our core fleet strength have been compensated for,' said Forrix at last. 'The ships that are not battle ready will remain and oversee the consolidation. The rest...'

'Stand at ninety-eight-point-seven-five combat effectiveness,' said Perturabo softly, and moved to the viewports on the other side of the tower.

Forrix began to reply then stopped himself. Time passed in the slow, buzzing pulse of Perturabo's armour. Out beyond the armourglass hung the orb of Uranus, its face dark against the stars.

'The strategic timetable still holds, lord. If we launch now we will still be within your margin of error.'

Perturabo did not reply. From the edge of the disc of Uranus a light began to gleam. Thin rays reached out and slid past the drifts of debris and the schools of ships. The sun...

Forrix blinked.

'So many battlefields,' said Perturabo, staring directly at the distant dot of brilliance. 'So much blood and iron poured down into the earth to earn our place here...' The Lord of Iron's eyes seemed black in the pale glare, his armour slick with cold shadow. 'We are coming, my brother. We are coming, my father. We have returned...' He turned to Forrix. The coldness had gone from his eyes. Fire caught in their depths, and the edges of his exo-plates gleamed in the distant sunlight and made him seem skinned in blades and shadow. 'Give the order. Launch for Jupiter.'

# FIFTEEN

---

Shrine
Songs of fear, dreams of war
My father's side

*Comet shrine, Inner System Gulf*

The comet was not undefended. Eight gun platforms ringed it, tracking its flight through the heavens with batteries of turbo lasers and rockets. Their auspex and targeting systems had enough power to see far beyond the reach of their guns. Once they detected and locked on to a target, they could coordinate fire with enough precision to equal the kill output of a star fort. It was enough that anything less than multiple battleships would be ill-advised to approach uninvited.

The servitors wired into the weapon platform's auspex twitched in their cradles. Somewhere, out on the edge of their machine sight, something was moving, something large.

All weapon batteries cycled to ready. Vox signals flickered between each gun platform. The servitors looked deeper, focusing all their systems on the approaching ship. None of them noticed the frost forming on their skin and wiring.

Fingers of thought brushed their lobotomised minds, pulling them deeper into their focus, drawing their sight away from everything that was not that distant glimmer of a ship getting nearer. They did not see the gunships sliding towards them out of the dark. Unmarked by engine heat, the small craft had begun their flight beyond the limit of the platform's sight. Minds inside the gunships reached out, focusing down and down into the root meat of the servitors' minds.

The gunships' engines fired. The servitor-governed systems saw nothing. They were still seeing nothing as missiles blew holes in the skin of each platform. Now alarms did begin to sound. Weapon servitors jerked to life, but too late. Crimson-armoured warriors were already inside the corridors. Waves of telekinesis blew in bulkheads, and bolter fire shredded servitors and systems. The gun platforms were silent as the lone ship closing on the comet became twelve.

Ahriman did not watch any of the last stages of the assault play out. In the dark of his gunship, as it burned towards its target, he focused his mind on the growing pattern surrounding it in the ether. He had been preparing, body, mind and spirit, for days, locking patterns of thought and symbolism into his subconscious. The roots of the Colchisian symbol sets and the Word Bearers' pseudo-occult rites had required a great deal of refinement and integration into the Prosperine system. It was like trying to mix oil and water, or gold and iron slag. He had done it, though. Few others could have, he fancied.

+There is a failsafe in the comet shrine itself,+ came Ignis' thought voice, cutting into Ahriman's reflections. +A detection system slaved to a series of kill charges.+

+Disable it,+ replied Ahriman.

+That is in progress, but the detection system also has an

etheric monitor grafted to its core. Our remote viewing of the outer halls almost triggered it. I have sent in Credence to remove the detection system's core.+

Ahriman thought of the automaton that now followed the Master of Ruin like a looming shadow.

+It is a machine, brother. To give it a name is to try to call a soul into something that has neither the spirit nor the will to make choices.+

Silence fell between their minds.

Around Ahriman the minds of his brothers whirled on, patterning the ether with their thoughts. Each of them was looping a set of symbols and words through his subconscious. Those of greater power and ability spun more complex weaves of thought, all overlapping and meshing with one another. Together, their minds were like the cogs of a single colossal machine. At the pattern's core was Ahriman, subsections of his own thoughts meshing with those of his brothers. This feat alone was beyond the bounds of comprehension of even the most able of adepts, but it was only the beginning. One part of the key to turn a greater lock.

It had taken days for Ahriman to comprehend the details of what they were doing, and then he had shivered. Even Magnus had fallen silent when it had been laid before them. For this… thing that they were doing was not their design. It was something higher and darker and greater, the design of a creature who had never been human and now stood between mortality and godhood. It was Horus' act, and they were the tools that did his work.

+Why do we do this?+ he had asked Magnus the Red.

+You know why, my son…+ Magnus had replied. +Because everything we want, everything we need lies beyond the fall of my father.+ Ahriman had nodded, but not tried to hide the doubt *in his mind. The image of Magnus in the scrying mirror had given a sad smile. +Besides, Ahzek, do you not wish to see the Towers of Leth again, or to walk the Scribe Vaults? Do you not wish to go home?+*

*+They burned our home.+*

*The image had shimmered in the haze of cedar smoke.*

*+To all of humanity, Terra is home. That is why it must fall, my son.+*

+The detection and trigger device has been disabled on the comet,+ came Ignis' thought voice, cutting through the memory. +You may proceed.+

Ahriman's gunship shot on towards the comet. With it came flights of others, trailing out behind it like the wings of a great bird. The Word Bearers fell into place amongst them. The wings of their craft gleamed a deeper crimson in the sunlight. Lines of script covered them from nose to tail, each word an exultation of the powers of the warp. The minds of the warriors in each craft hissed and echoed with prayers. For them this was not just an act of occult war; it was a sacred devotion. Ahriman felt a wave of revulsion and pulled his senses away from them.

The surface of the comet loomed before them. Plugs of plasteel and raw iron covered old wounds from boarding torpedoes and weapons fire. These were the scars from when the Imperial Fists had purged the shrine in the early years of the war.

The whole comet had been hollowed out two centuries before and become a resting place for the bones of the greatest heroes from the War of Unification and the Great Crusade. The skull of Skand, first of the Thunder Lords to fall in battle, had been laid here beside that of Maxilla, Barkeria Vu and thousands more. It had been a shrine to unity and heroism, and the Word Bearers had guarded its halls since the time before they had borne that name. They were still there when their treachery had been revealed, and so Rogal Dorn had sent his sons to slay them. They had done that. But, with the limited insight typical of the VII Legion, they had not thought to ask a deeper question: why had the Word Bearers remained at all?

Rockets loosed from the wings of the gunships. Fire erupted across the sealed breaches in the comet's skin. Shreds of metal and stone erupted into the vacuum. The gunships slid through the reopened wounds into the comet's interior.

Ahriman was on his feet before the gunship settled. His brothers followed, turning in perfect time as they moved to match him. Air misted into the cold dark as the hatch released. The space beyond was silent and still. Sunlight shone in through the holes to the void. Soot and scorch marks covered the visible floor and walls. Dry, broken bones lay at the base of walls of skulls. Ahriman's eyes picked out names and deeds carved across the foreheads of each. Thousands of empty eye sockets returned his gaze. He let out a breath inside his helm. It tasted of dust.

He felt the ghosts of myriad wars whisper and rattle at the edge of his senses. Voices of ancient battles clung to the teeth of the skulls. The blood spilt by the Word Bearers before their purging filled his mouth with the taste of copper and iron. Around him the rest of the Thousand Sons spread out in rings, their eyes turned out, and their thoughts turning in harmony.

Beyond them, the hatches on three Word Bearers gunships opened. Bones and parchment covered the warriors that emerged. Half of them led thin humans in white robes. Unsuited, the mortals began to choke as they staggered down the ramp and knelt. The Word Bearers cut their throats before their hearts stopped. The prayers in each of the humans'

minds became a shriek as their death thrust the words deep
into the ether. Blood splashed the scorched floor.

A last figure walked from the gunship, arms raised in bless-
ing, black-and-red armour gleaming with the crude runes of
the greater aspects of the warp. A helm of brushed bronze
enclosed his head, eyeless and mouthless. Books hung from
his waist on chains, and his hand held a sceptre of black iron
topped by a rough stone star. A thin human in a skin-tight
black pressure suit walked one step behind its master. Its
eyes were lidless and pinned open behind fluid-filled gog-
gles. A vox-amplifier filled the space where its mouth would
have been. It was the voice-slave of its master, bound by
crude telepathy to the warrior that it followed like a shadow.
That master had no name. He was just the Apostle of the
Unspeaking. The lack of a name would have struck Ahriman as typically ridiculous if it had not been for the fact
that the Apostle's mind was both shadowed and elusive,
his thoughts and emotions dissolving from sight as soon as
Ahriman's senses turned towards them. That and the fact that
he had never heard of this warrior before made him wonder. Much had changed in the years of the Thousand Sons'
exile, and even before then there were millions of legionaries divided between Legions spread across the galaxy. But
there was something about the blankness of this Apostle
that made Ahriman wonder what soul moved beneath the
bronze mask.

The Apostle bent down, dipped his fingers in the blood of
one of the sacrifices and scattered it into the void. A single
jagged word echoed from the Apostle's mind. Around him,
all the Word Bearers knelt.

Ahriman felt the psychic resonance in the shrine alter,
unbalancing for a moment. He held his will steady, felt the
patterns in his thoughts compensate.

+Do not do that again,+ he sent, edging the sending with flat command. The Apostle turned his blank helm towards Ahriman.

'This is a sacred thing,' rasped the voice-slave's vox. 'It must be marked. The rites and offerings must be observed.'

+Do nothing that I do not command. I will not see your ignorance undo this work.+

'We do the work of the gods here, sorcerer. It was us that seeded the ground for this act long before you even saw your place in the universe. Do not think that this is a matter of knowledge and power. The gods laugh at such arrogance, but bless those who submit to them.'

Ahriman felt anger spark within him, and cut it away with a flick of will. He drew a breath and his humours balanced again.

He turned from the Word Bearers as Ignis approached from where his gunship had settled behind the rest. The Master of Ruin's Terminator armour was the orange of furnace flame, and threaded with lines that echoed the tattoos that marked his face. His remade automaton walked behind him, its weapon mounts tracking the Word Bearers as they moved through the chamber.

+Faith and ignorance are so often alloyed that they might as well be called one,+ sent Ignis.

+An observation we can agree on,+ replied Ahriman.

+It is not an observation. It is an objective truth.+

Ahriman watched as the Word Bearers moved across the chamber. Occasionally one of them would stop, and Ahriman would hear the thought-echo of a canticle spill into the ether.

+The artificial gravity is stable?+ he sent to Ignis, still watching the Apostle and the other Word Bearers.

+It is. The primary systems of this facility were maintained to an adequate level. Power, gravity, atmosphere – it is all functioning.+

Ahriman nodded. In the churn and swell of the ether he felt something shift, something that cast a shadow across his thoughts and tugged at their patterns. For a second, he felt as though he had just stepped off the edge of a hidden precipice. He steadied himself, turning his will and sight inwards until the sensation of falling passed.

+Breach the walls and bring them in.+

Ignis gave a small nod. Ahriman felt a pulse of thought pass out through the shrine walls to where the ships waited. A second later, a patch of the vaulted ceiling above began to glow with heat. Then it blew outwards. A new glowing hole over a hundred metres wide opened to reveal the sunlight and the hull of the *Ankhtowe*. Tugs and haulers swarmed forwards as more fresh holes appeared in the comet's skin. Black, slab-shaped containers the size of battle tanks slid through the openings. Spider-limbed servitors detached from the tugs and began to unfasten the containers. Ahriman could feel the growling ache of psychic noise from within as the first layers of sedation faded from their cargo. The tugs pulled back until the solatarium hung in the void between the ship and comet.

Silver and plasteel sheathed the solatarium sphere. Rune-stamped chains had been welded to the casing and five tugs had dragged it from the guts of the *Ankhtowe* and into the vacuum. Worms of light played up and down the chains. It creaked and shivered as it moved, its dimensions seeming to flick between being close and far off even as you looked at it. Ahriman held his mind in a state of perfect balance as the sealed sphere was lowered through the hole like an eye being set back in its socket. The chains holding the solatarium broke before they were unfastened, their substance dissolving to light and smoke. It hung a metre above the floor of the chamber. Sparks of multicoloured light earthed into the void. Two of the Word Bearers were on their knees, tongueless mouths filling with blood as they thanked their gods.

Ahriman felt the storm winds rising in the realm beyond. He gave a single nod.

+We begin.+

*Battle-barge* Monarch of Fire, *Jovian Gulf*

The *Iron Blood* gathered speed as it cut towards the glimmer of Jupiter. Beside it and around it, the main force of its daughters and cousins rode in formation. Together they formed a cylinder thousands of kilometres long, stretching behind the flagship like the shaft of an arrow. Its path was direct, a line cut through the Jovian Gulf to cross the space between Uranus and Jupiter in the shortest time. It would pass through the orbit of Saturn, but the ringed planet was on the other side of the Solar disc. It was predictable to the defenders, but it was also swift, and Perturabo and his Legion had greater need of speed than they did subtlety. The timetable of war would bear nothing else.

Watching from above the path of the Iron Warriors fleet, Halbract found little comfort in what he saw. In the cold light of tactical displays there was one question that he found his mind returning to again and again. This force was behaving as Dorn and his senior commanders had predicted. The traitors were bloodied and had suffered great losses in taking Uranus. They had lost days and they would lose more strength and time as they made this passage. Even now the mines and dead-fall munitions strung along their route would be activating. The first ultra-long-range nova

cannon shots from Halbract's fleet were zeroed and ready for
his command. They would accelerate down to intersect with
the Iron Warriors' predicted path. Once they had accelerated to maximum velocity, they would cut loose their rocket
boosters and fall down towards their detonation points.
Almost undetectable, they would strike amongst the enemy
like arrows shot by an unseen archer.

Then Halbract's ships would follow their path and engage
the Iron Warriors as they advanced, forcing them to turn
and fight or press on and die. But that would not stop the
IV Legion. That bitter fact lingered in Halbract's thoughts.

'Loose,' he said, without looking up from the displays. The
nova cannons began to fire. He waited, feeling the silence
ache under the dome of the *Monarch of Fire*'s bridge. He
waited and watched. The fleet with him would have been
enough to break a star kingdom. Hundreds of warships
from the remains of the Imperial Fists fleet augmented by
ships of the Blood Angels, and more from the fleets of Saturn and Jupiter. Most had been held back from the battle
around Uranus, floating silently in the interplanetary gulf,
waiting for this battle. But it still would only be enough to
wound, not to kill. Not to make an end.

Halbract looked up. The eyes of his command crew gazed
down at him from the stacked tiers of platforms circling the
command dais.

'Forwards,' he said.

And the Second Sphere fleet lit its engines and plunged
down towards the traitors.

The Iron Warriors saw them when they were still distant.
They began to run calculations estimating strength and risk.
They did not slow or break formation. They could not. They
did not have time to spare.

The first of the nova shells reached its detonation zone

and exploded. The blast wave stripped void shields from five warships. Another struck, and another and another, until the Iron Warriors fleet was strobing with fire.

The *Monarch of Fire* was the first ship to engage as it entered range. Plasma poured from it. Three ships vanished in curtains of light. The fleet behind it split, lancing into the Iron Warriors. Macro shells flew from batteries to meet them, and the night vanished in the flash of explosions.

### Outer Solar System

Terror grew at the edge of the light of the sun.

On Neptune's moon Laomedia, the quiet followers of a sect called the Paths of Revelation pumped kalma gas into the habitats sunk into the satellite's skin.

The Paths of Revelation had grown from old seeds planted in Old Night. Laomedia was not a kind home. Fuel reservoirs and processing plants ate its people. The wars between xenos, pirates and empire builders had seen it change hands many times. Its population had been slaves and citizens and the meat fed into the machine of its industries. The Unity of the Imperium had changed some of that, but not all. And in the uncertainty of that life, the Paths of Revelation had found generations of followers. They were patient, waiting for their time to come, knowing that one day the spirits of truth would come, and both they and all those that had preceded them would ascend as one to a realm without want, or hunger, or limit of delight.

And now that time had come. They had heard the call crooned into their ears as they slept. So after they sent the habitats to sleep, they overrode the mag-locks of every fourth hab-unit. They went between the unlocked doors, clothed in tattered rags bleached white or stained red. They took something from those who slept inside each door they opened. A trinket, a hand, a face. And when Laomedia woke again, it woke screaming.

In the warp, the tides of delight and spite heard the screams and sang in chorus.

On Saturn, the dead came as terror's heralds.

Night Lords had taken civilian ships fleeing Uranus. There were bulk haulers and shuttle transports, packed with people fleeing towards the hoped-for safety of Saturn or the interplanetary gulfs. They found no safety or mercy. Their holds bearing the dead and dying, their helms and engines locked on course, the ships drove at Saturn. The first warnings and hails from the planet's defences triggered vox-recordings in each ship. Wails, screams and pleas filled the ears of the defenders as they fired, and tore the first slaughter ship from the void. More and more ships of the dead came to burn on the edge of the great planet's rings. Blood poured into the void and froze; screams vanished into the vacuum. And just out of weapons range, the ships of the VIII Legion circled, watched and laughed.

In the light of the guns and in the sound of last pleas for mercy, thirsting things drank.

On the Grylor city-station death came from within.

The size of a hive city, the station had grown from old ships moored next to each other that had been bound by bridges and growths of welded metal. Tethered to an asteroid on a slow orbit of the sun, it was a layover for ships plying the outer system trade routes. But no ships had come for weeks. No signals from the Throneworld, no news or warnings – just the flashes of distant lights, and the dreams of red rivers flowing between forests of pale trees without leaves. On and on the quiet went.

The blight began with food. Starch paste grew green-and-yellow blooms. Tanks of nutrient base soured to black sludge. Bit by bit, Grylor's food stores went bad. Some ate it anyway. They died screaming, voiding fluids, blood clogging their eyes. The water was next. Salts formed in reservoir tanks and pipes. Those that drank it wasted to nothing, unable to weep from thirst. After four days the whole of the city-station was deserted. Its atmosphere systems circulated air through corridors and rooms peopled only by corpses covered in forests of mould and pale fungus.

In the light of fizzing lumens, rotting things pupated and swelled as they breathed in the silence.

*Strike Frigate* Persephone, *Inner System Gulf*

Sigismund saw the dead ship fall back. Silence hung over the *Persephone* as the image of the vessel receded until it was marked only by the blink of a rune on the tactical display.

'More names to mark on the walls of the fallen,' said Rann, a growl edging his low voice. 'The traitors will pay, my brother. We will ensure it.'

Sigismund did not reply, but watched the marker rune until the sensors lost hold of the dead ship's signal. It had been the *Sun Child* – a young ship, set to the void in the year before the war had begun. Now it would drift as a tomb. Maybe one day its hull would be reclaimed by the victor of this last battle, but if not it would drift on the solar tides, cold and dark, until the sun claimed it or its iron corpse became a cloud of debris.

They had been losing ships day by day and hour by hour. It was as though the Solar System were claiming a blood price for every step they took towards Terra. Battle damage had claimed some early on, others had succumbed to their wounds over time. They had scuttled some, taking what crew and supplies they could and sending the ships to death pyres that lit the gulf of night. Others, like the *Sun Child*, they had simply had to let fall back as their damaged reactors failed. There was no choice, and all of the surviving fleet knew it. They could see the battle-light glimmer around Mars, and hear the broken signals from Uranus and Saturn. The jaws of the enemy were biting deep.

There were enemies loose in the gulf between the worlds too, wild fleets and carrion feeder ships looking for easy prey. Some had tried to slow Sigismund's force. All who had tried had died.

'We are entering the inner system,' came the voice of one of the command crew. Sigismund could hear the exhaustion and the control in the officer's voice. 'My lords, what is our course?'

Sigismund did not need to look at the display to know the position. There were fleets down around Mars and swarming from the outer system to the inner. A large force was bearing down on Terra and Luna from above the orbital disc. It was not a choice of where they could make a difference. He had brought fewer than a hundred ships to this point – all were damaged and under-strength in contingent and crew. The battles they were riding towards would be the clash of thousands of forces as great as or greater than those they had faced at Pluto. The choice was simply where they would stand in this next passage of war and where their blood would fall.

'On the ground of the world that bore me. At the heart of the Imperium that made me,' said Sigismund, hearing the words come to his lips in answer to the thoughts turning in his head. He looked at Rann, and the scarred warrior, who smiled through victory and death just the same, gave a grim nod. 'I will stand there, at my father's side.'

'And I will stand there with you,' said Rann.

'Terra,' said Sigismund, feeling the tug of old prophecy at the edge of his thoughts. 'Hold course for Terra.'

# SIXTEEN

Caul's edge
The birthplace of wolves
Mars crowned by fire

*Freighter ship* Antius, *Jovian Caul*

The *Antius* sped on through the night towards the growing orb of Jupiter. Behind it, in the dark gulf it had crossed from Uranus, the pinprick flares of battle glittered like mica dust cast into a ray of sunlight. Before it lay the Jovian Caul, glimmering like a reflection of the distant battle-light.

Since days long past, Jupiter had been the seat of the Jovian Void Clans and home to shipyards that made spacecraft unlike any other in the light of Sol or beyond. Ancient mysteries went into the design of those ships, some unknown even to the priests of Mars. The blood-bound clans had been allowed to keep much of their power and many of their secrets in exchange for their fealty to Terra. The xenos breed that had dominated their moons had been destroyed in the early months of the Great Crusade. In spite of that liberation, some amongst the Consanguinities left unspoken the belief that they had exchanged inhuman tyrants for a single human one. That strain of doubt had not stopped Jupiter's shipyards becoming a nursery from which many of the fleets of the Great Crusade were born, first into a war of conquest and then a war for survival.

The Caul was the sphere of micro debris that surrounded Jupiter's shipyards and manufactoria. It extended deep into space in every direction. There, new ships were born, refitted or torn apart in the mazes of the equatorial breakers yards. On the edge of the great planet's gravity lived the low-caste reclaimers, who pulled scrap from the dark of the inner system gulf. In the polar Shoal city-stations, the high clans ruled populations bound to them by blood, marriage and oath. The void was in them all, it was said – a coldness in their blood that the illumination of the Imperial Truth could not banish. Now, as the enemies of that Imperium came, the void-born of Jupiter swarmed into the dark to defend their home.

Amongst the gun-sloops and brigantines of the Jovian clans moved the ships of the Third Sphere fleet. These were warships of the Imperial Army, and the VII and IX Legions. All stood ready for battle. Signals had arrived from Uranus and from Terra. They knew that coming for them was the power that had broken the Elysian Gate. They knew that, this side of Luna, Jupiter and its sphere of dominance was the greatest force that the invaders would have to overcome. No commander hoping to take Terra could leave the void might of Jupiter uncontested.

On the bridge of the *Antius*, hurtling towards Jupiter, Mersadie Oliton could see neither what waited, nor what lay behind them.

Red lights blinked on consoles. The light reflected from the blood and oil running from the tech-priest that lay at her feet. Chi-32-Beta was dying.

'What ship is still out there?' she asked. 'The ship that the assault was launched from?'

Chi-32-Beta nodded. A fresh wash of dark liquid oozed from beneath the enginseer's robes. Behind Mersadie, a growing crowd of refugees from the ship's holds were filling the helm platform.

'They… they have been attempting to establish vox contact with their assault party, but…' Chi-32-Beta's voice became a burble of static and the lights on the consoles across the bridge flickered. 'But there has been no… no reply…'

'They are dead,' said Mersadie.

'H-How…'

'It does not matter. Can you get the ship under control?'

Chi-32-Beta trembled, and a second later the motion spread through the lights.

'No… not control. It is wounded, but it will run true. Crew…'

'We have crew,' said Mersadie, looking around at the ragged figures on the platform. A few were moving between the consoles. There were still spatters of blood on some of the equipment, though the bodies of the dead had been removed and unsuccessful attempts made to clean the stains and scorches from deck and helm. Most of the refugee crew were looking at her and the tech-priest. Terror and uncertainty blended in their eyes. She looked at Gade. The former dock pilot was glancing at the screens and levers next to the main helm control banks.

'Gade,' she called, using the man's name and putting every scrap of the confidence she was not feeling into her words. He looked around at her. 'Get someone on every position. Do it now.'

Gade nodded and turned. She heard him begin to shout.

'Mil…' began Chi-32-Beta. 'It is a military ship… I have

been trying to make... interference... so that... so that our enemy won't realise...' The enginseer coughed a mouthful of half-binary.

'The engines,' asked Mersadie. 'Are they working?'

'Yes, but if we change course they will see, they will real-ise... Weapons, they will have weapons...'

The words sank cold into Mersadie. They could have blown the *Antius* to dust. They still could now. But they had come to make sure that she was dead. That was what was holding them back now: the need to be certain that she was no more. Somewhere out there, eyes were watch-ing auspex and signal screens, kill orders held on tongues.

'Can you see it?' she asked. 'Can the ship's sensors see this enemy?'

'A ghost on the edge of sight...' Chi-32-Beta hissed. 'And there are... other things, too... further away and getting closer... I... I don't know what... who they are...'

'How close are we to Jupiter?'

'We are approaching the Caul. I can... feel sensors look-ing deep into the void. They may offer no sanctuary. They may end us.'

Mersadie paused. Around her she could hear the calls of the people crowding the command deck.

'We have to reach Jupiter. Can we outrun them?'

'This is a tertiary-grade system freighter. They... they are likely to outclass us in both speed and power output.'

'Is there an alternative?' she asked.

Chi-32-Beta paused.

'No.'

'Then we try to run hard and hope,' she said. 'Hold on, and get ready.'

The enginseer coughed what might have been an assent.

'I... doubt we will survive, but... there is a probability

that we might,' Chi-32-Beta began. 'You are... the prisoner, are you not?'

She nodded.

'Yes, I am.'

The enginseer was silent for a moment.

'Thank you.'

She blinked for a second, not certain how to reply. She stood.

'Thank me if we live.'

### Luna

The torpedo wave hit the edge of the assault fleet. Defence turrets opened fire. Las-beams and shells punched through warheads. Explosions bubbled out as the torpedoes detonated. Multicoloured spheres formed and burst in a foam of fire. Ordnance had loosed from launch platforms and the Luna picket fleets in a coordinated barrage lasting twenty-one minutes. It struck the hulls of Abaddon's vanguard ships.

The armada had no advantage of surprise. Word had come from the White Scars Falcon fleets that had harried it all the way down the path of its descent. The Lunar defences were ready and primed. The old face of grey-silver, which had looked down on autumn harvest and winter snow, hid beneath the scars and growths of tens of thousands of years of human occupation. Girding Luna was the Ring, a great hoop of stone and metal spiked with docks and gun bastions. Ancient field generators and gravitic stabilisers held it steady and true. In its shadow lay the Circuit, a trench cut into the surface of the moon as though gouged by a god's chisel. Towers and domes dotted its surface. These were the fortresses of the Silent Sisters, and the Naval dynasties founded after the Pacification of Luna.

The moon had once been the birthplace of the Legions. The gene-looms of the Selenar had taken the genius born in the Emperor's laboratories and brought forth the armies of the Great Crusade. Millions of youths had entered its Halls of Making. Hundreds of thousands had emerged as the warriors of the new age. Space Marines. That time, though, had passed as the Crusade had progressed far beyond the bounds of Sol's light.

The gene-looms and their keepers had decayed and fallen from use and power. Luna had taken up a new role as base for the fleet and forces that watched over Terra. Here the Silent Sisterhood had made its fortress, the Assassin clades their training temples, and the Knights Errant and Chosen of the Sigillite their unnamed base of operations. But the true strength of Luna lay in the defences that spiralled out from the Ring in overlapping arcs. Its guns could target anything that moved into Terra's orbit. Before the war, it had the firepower to deal with any invasion that might reach the Throneworld. Five years of Rogal Dorn's care had added to that strength many times over. Here, moving amongst the defences, were ships of the Jovian fleets, the Imperial Fists, the Blood Angels, the Saturnine flotillas and the steelclads of Neptune.

On the other side of Terra lay the *Phalanx*, holding orbit above the world like a golden shadow to Luna's silver. A school of lesser ships clustered around the great fortress, glimmering like coins cast into a sunbeam.

Abaddon had known what was waiting for him. The data supplied to Horus by the XX Legion had told him much, and distant optical analysis had supplied the rest. His was an armada of the finest ships under Horus' control, crewed and filled by the greatest of the XVI Legion, but still it would not be enough to break through Luna and take the skies of Terra.

Not enough by far. That would take a force many times greater than that which now rode down into the guns of Luna.

This strike, deep within the circle of the Solar System, was a spear thrust against a cliff. If it struck home, it would shatter. It was a death mission, a task that could bring glory only to fanatics like Layak who craved martyrdom. Yet here he stood, listening to the *War Oath* shiver as it plunged down into the fire.

*'Do you trust me, my son?' Horus had said when he had given Abaddon command of the attack.*

*'Of course, sire,' he had replied and bowed his head. It had been difficult even for him to stand in his father's presence. Light folded into shadow around the Warmaster, and voices whispered in the silence.*

*'You are my truest son, Abaddon, more like me than perhaps any other. I have never failed, and I will not now.' Horus' hand touched Abaddon's shoulder. 'You understand how to strike this blow, I know. You know what is needed and why. This alone I trust to you. And you will not fail me, my son.'*

Fire swallowed the tip of the armada. A ship died, and then another, and another. Torpedoes punched through armour and exploded. Metal skin became shrapnel. Black vacuum became bright flame. Abaddon watched and heard the oaths of his Legion brothers fill his ears, their last signals arriving seconds after the light of their deaths.

'Martyrdom...' said Layak from his position on the bridge's command dais. Abaddon kept his eyes on the sea of fire and Luna waiting beyond. He blinked.

*He was gasping, amnion-fluid pouring from his mouth as he struggled for air. The world around him was black. He vomited and tasted iron on his tongue.*

*'Do you wish this to be the end?' came a voice. It rolled and echoed, bouncing off bare stone.*

*Abaddon became still. The voice was not one of the gene-witches. It was strong in a way that made ice run down his spine. He had been in the black caverns for weeks, maybe months. He had tried to hold on to time but it had fled from him as he bled, and grew, and felt the scalpel arms and needle saws do their work. And between the flesh work, he floated in a sea of images and voices as the hypno-units deluged his mind with learning. When he slept, it was in a lightless pool, drowning in oxygen-infused amnion while his body healed and accepted what it was becoming. Every time he had woken, it had been to the grey and silver presences of the Selenar dragging him up from the water. This was the first time he had woken to pitch-dark.*

*'Who are you?' he managed as a shiver rolled through him. The warm fluid was cold rather than warm, its sheen like ice on his skin.*

*'You killed your father,' said the voice, 'or that is what I have been told.'*

*Abaddon went still, trying to feel what direction it was coming from.*

*'I did,' he said, and heard the words echo and re-echo in the blackness.*

*'Are you ashamed of that?'*

*'No,' said Abaddon. 'He was less than a man.'*

*'He was a king.'*

*'A crown means nothing.'*

*Laughter, warm and rich in the dark.*

*'And what does have meaning, son of Cthonia?' asked the voice.*

*'Truth.'*

*'Quite right,' said the voice.*

*A pause in which he had just heard his breath slowing and the soft ripple of the pool around him.*

*'Who are you?' asked Abaddon again.*

*'I am the one who has come to bring you illumination.'*

A clatter of gears, a hiss of pistons and then light. Brilliant light, pouring down on him, swallowing his sight. He made to shut his eyes, but they were already diluting the glare, dragging it down to brilliance that illuminated but did not blind. He turned his head. The amniotic pool was circular and set into a floor of perfectly smooth black stone. The ceiling above was a dome of the same material. An iris had opened at its centre and a beam of light shone from above.

Primary starlight, said a whisper of new hypno-implanted knowledge at the back of his mind. This was the light of the sun shining down through a shaft through the surface of the moon. He felt radiation fizz across his skin.

There was only one other figure standing beside the pool, a huge figure in a black tunic. His head was bare, his features broad and strong. But it was his eyes that held Abaddon: dark, unblinking.

'You are Lord Horus Lupercal,' said Abaddon.

Horus nodded, not shifting his stare.

'And you are the son of Cthonia of whom I have heard much…'

'There are thousands of us, thousands and thousands. I am just one.'

Horus gave a snort of laughter, then shrugged.

'You will be amongst the last to be reborn here. The forging of our warriors will happen out there now, amongst the stars we conquer. For decades we have stepped from these pools into our new lives. Soon that will not be the case. We will take the name and the memory. Luna Wolves… that is our brotherhood. Wolves made by the moon, and raised from night to illumination…' The primarch reached out with an open hand to Abaddon. A mirror-coin glinted on the open palm.

'My sons are not given to exaggeration, and Sejanus says that, of all this last generation, I should be here to welcome you into our brotherhood.'

Abaddon looked at the hand of the being whose strength now flowed in his own veins.

'My lord,' he said, and felt the truth of it in the space left by all that he had burned and left behind.

'Rise, Abaddon,' said Horus.

'Why does this feel like dying?'

'Because it is. Because when you take my hand you will not be a son of Cthonia, or the heir of a dead king…'

'I will be a Luna Wolf.'

'Yes,' said Horus. 'You shall.'

And then, from a place that he had forgotten, came another word, one that felt like an oath.

'Father,' said Abaddon.

Horus nodded once.

'Will you serve me, Abaddon?' Horus asked.

'I will,' he had replied, and taken the coin from Horus' proffered hand.

Abaddon's eyelids blinked open.

The *War Oath* ran on into the fire. The ruin of the vanguard spun past, chewed pieces of metal tumbling, stray impacts exploding against shields. Behind it, the bulk of the armada followed it down.

Martyrdom. Another word for suicide, for slaughter in the name of empty ideals.

'Sub-spears, begin your assault runs,' Abaddon said.

Hundred-ship-strong formations cleaved from the armada's bulk in blade-shaped configurations. They curved out and began to unleash their own payloads of torpedoes and bomber wings.

The defence batteries of the Luna Ring and defence shoal fired in a coordinated volley. The first of the attackers' munitions exploded in the void.

The sub-spear fleets were moving to try to stab through the edge of the defending fleet. They fired their second volley. Boarding torpedoes flew free of tubes. Clouds of escort wings formed around them. The defenders assessed the manoeuvre and opened fire with macro-cannons. The volumes in the path of the boarding torpedo waves boiled with explosions.

Alarms filled the inside of the torpedoes and bombers as they plunged into the blaze. Shrapnel ripped into armour panels. Torpedoes tore in two. Figures in sea-green armour tumbled into the fire and night.

The bulk of the armada was still holding around the *War Oath*, a column formation of a thousand ships. The ships of the defenders spread before it in a convex disc. Fire cut into the armada's flanks. Shields flared, and the flash of cannons shone around the waning sickle of the moon in the night skies of Terra.

*Battle-barge* Fortress of Eternity, *Mars high orbit*

The Guardians of Mars had watched the light of the attackers grow in the sky for days. First had come word from the Falcon fleets, winding their paths above and below the disc of the Solar System. The eyes of the Fourth Sphere fleet had turned to the abyss above them. Ocular and sensor arrays peered into the dark, sifting starlight and the dance of asteroids for the signs of the enemy. The first light of engines glimmered in the dark, fresh stars igniting beside those that had formed the patterns of heroes and monsters in ages long past.

On the surface of the planet beneath, silence had fallen, and stillness settled across the red plains. For over half a decade, rocket launches and beams of energy had criss-crossed the thin atmosphere as the disciples of Kelbor-Hal's New Mechanicum threw fire at the blockade fleet. Mars had blistered with explosions and swum with the dust of fallout as the factions on the surface tore at each other. Now, silence and stillness spread across its surface, as though the planet of war was holding an inhaled breath.

In Mars' orbit, the Fourth Sphere fleet reformed. It was the largest of the four defence fleets in the Solar System. Monitor craft from the Solar Auxilia and the Jovian Void Clans bulked its numbers, and with them were the great orbital assault and bombardment craft of the Imperial Fists. The gun-studded bulk of the *Blade of Inwit* lay beside the *Blade Absolute*, *Fist of Judgement*, *Truth's Warden* and *Tyrant Bane*. Sub-fleets of gunboats, destroyers and lance cruisers orbited the largest vessels. For years they had fought and held the enemy to the surface of the Red Planet; now they broke that cordon.

On the battle-barge *Fortress of Eternity*, Lord Castellan Camba Diaz waited. He had recalled all his forces from the surface of Mars. Raiding expeditions had been pulled back. Reconnaissance companies had shed their wargear and taken up the weapons of void war. Lexmechanics and magos-ordinators zeroed in guns. Minelayers swept the volumes of space that the enemy would have to move through. Faint and broken signals reached out to the Falcon fleets of the White Scars that were tracking the enemy as they closed on the planet.

Camba Diaz listened to the scratched, crackling words alone in his arming chamber. Other than the sounds of the signals, he waited in silence. That was his way, the way of the planet that bore him, the people that had raised him and the Legion that had been his life. Inwit, by turns burning and dark, had been a remorseless teacher and cold parent to men of stone who bore the burdens and pains that others would not. He thought of all those who could have faced this moment. Pollux, thought dead at Phall, now half a galaxy away; Sigismund, sent to watch the edge of night with a sword in his hand; Halbract; Rann – all of them brothers, all of them warriors that another age would have made masters of war.

Rogal Dorn had told him why the Fourth Sphere command was his, though.

'Temperament,' the Praetorian had said, and Camba Diaz had thought that he had understood his lord's meaning. In the years of conflict around and on the Red Planet – sapping endless war, thousands of cuts drawing blood bit by bit – he had felt his stillness and patience become the foundation of his command. His temperament allowed him to bear those trials and rise to conflict each day afresh. He had thought that was what Dorn had meant. He thought he had understood his lord. He had not.

Temperament... the stone-soul of Inwit, and the will to look up at the stars falling from the sky and not blink. This was a moment that tested temperament, the moment when the heavens were falling.

The lights of the descending fleet grew. Auspex readings and reports from the Falcon fleets began to build a picture of what each growing mote of light was, of what was coming for them – seven thousand ships counted at an estimate...

They were not Legion ships either. These were ships of the Mechanicum, each one a relic and expression of their master's power and knowledge. All of them were disciples of the new path of the Machine Cult. Somehow, this new creed had spread far beyond Mars, beyond the Solar System. It had infected forge worlds and tech-fanes and remade those that embraced it into something new and terrible. The things that they made were not mysteries or wonders; they were abominations. Machines that broke reality, and creatures that were neither flesh nor machine yet lived – all

these things came from their craft. Time and simple senti-
ment had given them a name that followed them across the
stars and clung to the shadow of their passing. The Dark
Mechanicum they were named, and now they had returned
to claim the seat of their empire.

The first shot was theirs. Fired from beyond the range of
Camba Diaz's weapons. A beam of cold light a hundred
metres wide bored down through the dark. The ships in
its path tried to move, but the beam twitched and coiled
through the void like a snake. It struck the cruiser *First Truth*.
The energy flowed over its void shields and hull like water
around a stone. On board, its crew had seconds to watch as
their system readouts spiked. Then the flow of energy sank
through the void shields and into the ship's hull. Every system and machine cut out. Light vanished. Engines died.

There was a moment of silence filled with the breaths of
the crew. Then every machine on the *First Truth* screamed.
Cogitators melted. Power governors exploded. Vox-processors
howled static. The ship came apart, components scattering
out as gravitic generators reversed. Layers of metal and stone
peeled back until its reactors spun free, arcing with power,
an exposed heart still beating in an opened chest. Then the
reactors overloaded and a wave of burning light tore through
the broken hull.

The beam snapped across the void, seeking another victim even as ships burned thrusters to move out of its way.

The Fourth Sphere fleet began to loose torpedoes and
maximum-range shots at the oncoming Dark Mechanicum.
The guns of all their ships spoke and the space between the
two fleets became a blaze.

Rockets and beams of energy rose from Mars towards
the ships in close orbit. Its thin atmosphere flashed and
shivered. Craft built in the forges of the fallen magi rose

from caverns hidden under the Red Planet's crust. They were things from the fever dreams of tortured machines. Wings of brass feathers spread from under cases of steel and black glass. Tails and necks uncoiled from fuselages, and multi-coloured flame roared from engines.

The ships of the Fourth Sphere fleet watching the planet opened fire with torrents of shells that exploded in low orbit. Waves of haywire energy and shrapnel ripped swarms of machines apart and sent them tumbling back down to the red dust below. Some remade themselves as they fell, flame-wreathed metal knitting together, wreckage gathering into new shapes that clawed back up into the sky.

Long gone was the silence that had wrapped Camba Diaz as he waited for this battle. Every ship and every channel echoed with the shaking roar of war. He heard it all, a deluge of sound: shouts echoing over breaking vox-channels, orders given with last breaths, the metallic howl of beast-machines rising through the air. Shells and munitions were exploding amongst the ships now. Scrap code bored into communications signals and spilled over into sensor units.

Camba Diaz listened, then cut the links and spoke to the warriors that had followed him through half a decade of war.

'Break them,' he said, his voice not loud, but weighted, a promise as much as a command.

Chaos spread through the defenders' battle line. A wave of torpedoes, launched from a quartet of monitor ships, detonated as they exited their tubes, ripping the ships apart. The macro-carrier *Daedalus* vented atmosphere from two-thirds of its decks as scrap code flooded its cogitator systems. Squadrons vanished in spheres of cold light.

But Camba Diaz's ships had faced and fought the forces of the false tech-priests many times. They heard the word of their commander and rose to meet their enemies without pause.

# SEVENTEEN

Within sight of safety
Occult resonance
Old friends

*Freighter ship* Antius, *Jovian Caul*

Mersadie held her breath for a moment, eyes closed, letting sound recede. The reek of blood and ash was thick on her tongue.

*Blood on matted fur…*

*Teeth…*

Vengeful Spirit…

*Maloghurst's eyes looking at her…*

*'Loken, these are civilians.'*

She released the breath and opened her eyes. Frightened faces turned towards her. Lights blinked on consoles. Hands trembled where they rested on levers and dials. In her niche, Chi-32-Beta was shivering in her cocoon of cables. The blood had clotted but the enginseer had curled her body into a tight ball. The rest of the crew stood, waiting. There were dock officers, a shuttle pilot, a bonded maintenance adept and landing guides. She had no idea if they knew enough to control a ship in the void for even a brief time. She had no idea whether or not they would fall apart when the next slice of the future fell. She had no idea if she would fall along with them. She thought of the hundreds of people still in the rest of the ship, of Noon and Mori huddled together in their stateroom.

'Go,' she said. At the helm, the big pilot called Gade nodded and tensed to pull down a brass lever. His skin was ice-pale.

'Reactor output reaching peak,' said Chi-32-Beta. Gade pulled the lever on the helm console. Lights flared across the bridge. The deck lurched as the reactor dumped its bloated heart into the void, and the ship burned forwards.

Behind it, the hunter ship that had been watching the *Antius* fired without hesitation. Las-beams stitched the dark. The *Antius* began to corkscrew, as the hands on its helm fought to control it. Shouts and confusion filled the bridge. Machines were screaming. Some of those at consoles froze with terror while others screamed, their eyes wide as fresh banks of red warnings lit. Gade was staring at the helm console, his mouth open like a fish drowning in air. Shouts roared louder than the machines. That chaos saved the ship. As the hunter's guns fired again, the freighter's wild course pulled it away from the shots that would have torn its hull apart.

But the hunter was accelerating. It was a small ship, smaller even than the *Antius*. A tapered block of metal a little over two hundred metres long, half of it was engines; it was fast. The *Antius* tumbled on. Before it, the glittering sea of the Jovian Caul beckoned. The hunter fired again, and this time its shots struck the keel of the freighter's hull. Metal and ceramite plating burned away. Gas and bilge fluid sprayed out. The clamour of panic on the *Antius'* bridge warred with the shriek of sirens. In her tangle of cables, Chi-32-Beta flinched as bulkheads locked off the damaged portion of the ship. The hunter cut its fire and burned closer, eating up the distance.

'We… The ship…' gasped Chi-32-Beta. Sparks were flowing over the enginseer. The smell of burning wire and cooking flesh rose. 'It can't go on. Its heart and spirit are burning…'

'We must go on or die,' said Mersadie.

The tech-priest spasmed, limbs thrashing. Arcs of charge whipped out from consoles. Gade juddered in place at the helm, hands locked to the controls.

Out in the void, the hunter closed. It was close enough now that its targeters could hold a lock no matter what its prey did. It charged its guns. Power built in turbo laser reservoirs.

The *Antius* rolled over. Micro-debris rattled off its hull. A piece of rock hit the hunter and gouged a crater in its armour. Jupiter's outer cloud of orbital detritus began to ring off both ships like rain.

The hunter held course. Targeting systems locked firing solutions. Gun turrets swung. It had been following this prey since the first hours after the destruction of the prison ship off Uranus. It had tracked it through the fires of battle and across the dark gulfs between the outer planets. For all those days it had been silent, almost every system cycled down so that it ran cold and dark, without heed to anything besides its prey. As it closed for the final kill, it reached out across the dark to the ships and stations of Jupiter. It knew that the first of the enemy was not far behind and that Jupiter's defenders could not risk waiting to see if ships coming from the void were friend or foe. Clearance codes flew out to silence the guns that would be turning to greet them. It would make its kill and then burn on past Jupiter, its duty done.

It closed the final few thousand kilometres, its course spiralling to match the *Antius'*. Larger pieces of drift-debris rattled from them. Chunks of rock and old shards of dead ships puffed to dust on the hunter's shields. On the *Antius'* bridge, the hull was singing with the plink-ring of impacts. People were weeping. Gade had slumped over the controls. His hands were charred black by electro-discharge, but somehow he was still breathing, still holding course.

'Hold,' she heard a voice call, clear and strong. It took her a second to realise that it was hers. 'Have faith…'

The hunter slid into its final firing position. The lights of the Jovian Caul were brighter than the stars now. It locked its guns to firing solutions.

The *Antius'* engines sputtered.

The hunter loosed its execution shot.

A destroyer came out of the dark and tore the hunter from the night in a volley of macro-cannon fire. Rings of plasma erupted from its hull, sending the pieces of its corpse shooting out as they melted.

The destroyer slammed through the debris of its kill. Screams and cacophonous sounds rolled out from it on every vox- and signal-channel. It had once been a ship of war and conquest, but the years of its betrayal had stripped it of that divinity. It had come to the Solar System in answer to the carrion promise of war and had soared ahead of the ships of the Iron Warriors as they broke the orbits of Uranus. Hunger, caprice and the will of the power that had created it had pulled it on and on towards Jupiter.

Blossom-pink, acidic-green, turquoise, orange, purple and tox-yellow swirled and clashed across its hull. Symbols etched by the claws of things that lived in nightmares swam across its length. Oily dust shook from it like pollen from a summer flower. Its crew were gone, flesh and bone melded into the fabric of the ship. Their voices lived on, though, singing and screaming into the night as the ship hunted. It shivered as the fire of its kill touched its hull. Its howls became shrieks of delight.

On the bridge of the *Antius*, screams and wails burst from every vox-speaker. The hull vibrated through high notes like a struck glass. In the holds and on the bridge, people fell to the ground, blood running from their ears as the taste of roses, honey and ash filled their mouths. On and on the sounds echoed. Mersadie felt it slice through her, felt it touch the edge of things she had tried to remember but wanted to forget.

*'What is this?' she had asked.*

*'Nothing,' said a deep voice from behind her, and she had turned from Maloghurst to see another set of eyes looking down at her from above and a smile that held no kindness. 'Nothing at all…'*

Then the voice from her dream of Keeler, strong and undoubtable.

*'You must reach him. You must tell him before it is too late. Remember! Remember what you have seen!'*

*And the circles of symbols rose before Mersadie, no longer stone and metal but burning in the air.*

And the howl of the multicoloured destroyer as it broke from the flames and turned towards the *Antius* was the roar of guns in her memory and the shriek of the oncoming storm in a dream that she could not wake from.

And then it was gone.

The many-coloured ship turned, swooped past the *Antius*, and dived back into the dark.

The howls died in the throats of the vox-horns and left those on the bridge of the *Antius* shaking and weeping, but alive.

'What…' breathed Gade. The man was on his hands and knees, trembling like a whipped dog. 'What just happened?'

Mersadie looked back at Gade, at the console lights blinking in time to alarms that seemed soft in the shadow of the sounds that had just passed.

'I don't know,' she said. 'Just get us to a dock around Jupiter.'

Chi-32-Beta's head rose suddenly.

'We are being targeted…' gasped the enginseer.

'By what?' she asked.

'Defence platforms, ships, other vessels. I can't identify them…'

Mersadie felt cold realisation sink through the space left by the brief flutter of hope that they would make it to a place of safety. They would not; they would die on the edge of survival.

'We are being hailed…' buzzed the tech-priest.

The vox-speakers gave a bark of distortion and then a voice came from them, speaking through the static.

'*Freighter vessel* Antius, *confirm you are carrying the remembrancer Mersadie Oliton. I repeat, confirm you are carrying the remembrancer Mersadie Oliton.*'

Faces turned towards her. The frame of the ship was still humming with the power that pushed it through the debris cloud towards the waiting guns of the Jovian defences.

Mersadie was still, frozen in place. Her limbs were numb.

'Reply…' she said at last.

'Vox-channel open,' stuttered Chi-32-Beta. The speakers buzzed again.

Mersadie swallowed.

'This is…' she began, and then the words stopped on her tongue. *After all this time…*

'I am here,' she said at last. 'This is Mersadie Oliton.'

'*Cut your engines,*' said the voice that had spoken before. '*We will bring you in.*'

Mersadie closed her eyes for a second and nodded. Inside her head, she thought she could see the image of Keeler smiling at her.

'Thank you…' she said. 'Thank you, old friend.'

The vox clicked, as though the speaker on the other end had paused for a second before speaking again.

'*You are safe now,*' said the voice of Garviel Loken.

### Comet shrine, Inner System Gulf

The ghosts of Unification led Ahriman through the places where they had died. The transitions from one memory to another were abrupt, as sharp as the slice of a final second from a thread of life.

He walked a maze of ice beneath the Antarctic domes, watching a woman fire her last bullets into an oncoming wall of chimeric flesh and fur… He was striding in an exo-rig across the burning seas of Hattusa-B… He was looking down the side of the Truscan Hive. Fires burned at the mountain's foot and wound up its sides, shining bright in the shadow cast by its bulk. The wind was strong and held the scent of the inferno that had flooded the mountain's lower levels. It was not a mountain, of course. It was a city. Down at its root, far beneath the level of the land, were structures made so far back in the past that their makers had known Terra when it was green and blue and still dreamed of serenity under the gaze of its sun. The cities that had been its seeds had names that resonated in the consciousness even though their histories were forgotten: Azinc, Opolis, Riance. Now its fate would be to be torn apart and have its bones folded into a structure that would be called a palace, but was larger than the empires of mankind's youth.

'You died here,' said Ahriman, 'in the taking of the Truscan hive…'

Beside him, the mute image of a bond-warrior in the Balgran tek-tribes looked at him. The man was covered with the blood of the wounds that had killed him. He nodded to Ahriman.

'I am sorry,' said Ahriman. 'I cannot remain, but I will remember.' The bloodied man nodded again, then turned away.

Ahriman looked out for a second more, hearing the distant thump of rockets pounding the strongpoints on the hive's north face. It had taken the Thunder Legions and the armies of Unity a month to break Anak, but when the end came it had been swift and seen hundreds of thousands dead in the turning of a single day.

+There is no time for this.+ Ignis' sending cut through the psychometric vision, smearing its clarity. The smoke-hazed sky above froze, and the image of the hive blurred.

+There is time enough,+ replied Ahriman.

+There are approximately one million, seven hundred and forty sets of individual remains within this… facility. To extract psychometric impressions from them all will take–+

+I am aware of the factors involved,+ sent Ahriman.

+Then you know that it is not possible.+

+I do,+ replied Ahriman.

+Then why–+

+Because it matters.+ Ahriman straightened and looked up again at the image that he had pulled from the psy-resonance of one of the skulls lining the walls of the comet shrine. +In the end, everything is dust – but what we do before we become dust matters. What things *were* matters.+

+If you say so.+

Ahriman turned and the image collapsed into dust, and then folded into the reality of a room of bone. The central chamber of the comet shrine had already been stained by blood and battle. Bolt shells had ripped skulls from walls and torn carved femurs and vertebrae from the supports of the high, domed roof. The Imperial Fists had cleared away the debris when they had finished their purge.

Ahriman could feel the disgust of the sons of Dorn at what the Word Bearers had done to this place. Their anger lingered in the marks left by their bolters and blades. Those thoughts and emotions sang in the churn of the shrine's past, present and future. It was created to remember the dead and the sacrifices they had made in life, but it had been remade into something else by the Word Bearers, something more terrible and profound than a place for dry bones and memories to rest.

In the decades of their stewardship, the Word Bearers had spilled blood in the comet shrine to honour their new-found gods. They had cut subtle sigils into its substance and saturated its shadows with malignancy. Threads of the warp had wormed into the bones, feeding on the memories of the dead. Whispered prayers had rooted in the gloom, locked inside the comet as it turned around the sun.

Even when Sigismund and the Imperial Fists had come and killed those Word Bearers left here, their actions had only fed the pool of occult potential lying just under the skin of reality. The Word Bearers' deaths had been an act of martyrdom in service to the powers of the warp, and, whether Ahriman thought that belief naive or not, the act had power. The comet shrine resonated with ritual significance. Whispers and vortices of emotion trailed behind it as it pulled across the heavens.

Whether what the Word Bearers had done was driven by chance or foresight did not matter. They had created a tool that could be used by more able hands.

Ahriman turned to the centre of the chamber. The stone sphere of the solatarium floated above the floor. Arcs of ghost-light whipped from its surface and earthed in the floor and ceiling. The dimensions of the room swam as he looked at it, and he had to force his mind to stay balanced. Power was building in the immaterium, taking shape and form second by second. Around the chamber, at the eight points of the compass, the pitiful cargo brought in the black containers knelt on the floor. Three thousand and twenty-four mortals. Each of them had a spark of connection to the warp. All of them had been selected from the holds of Black Ships hunted and taken by Horus' forces. There were scions of planetary rulers, beggars, men, women, the kind, the corrupt and the desperate. Iron, brass and silver chains held them to the deck while silent Word Bearers moved amongst them, painting their scalps and faces with ash ink. Some began to drool blood as the sigils marked their skin. Ahriman's fellow Thousand Sons stood between the lines of mortals, breathing calm and passivity into their minds. Light and shadow was beginning to fume off them, hazing reality overhead.

He thought of the sacrifices he had made in pursuit of the truth, of salvation for his father, things that weighed true only when balanced against the greatest of needs. Was this need enough for the atrocity they would commit? He was not sure, but he was sure that it was too late to make another choice.

Ahriman breathed out. A ghost-image of his thought puffed into being in the air, spread feathered wings, and then dissolved before it could take flight. He reached his mind out to Menkaura, at the centre of the solatarium. It was like calling through a rising gale.

+How long until conjunction?+

+It is approaching.+ Ahriman could feel the effort in Menkaura's reply. +Each house aligns. The orbs of the heavens sing, but not all… Blood still remains to be shed. The Queen of Heaven wears a crown of growing fire. The Water Bearer pours his bloody cup into the night. But the Wolf Coin still shines clear. The wheel turns. The sands run…+

Images flowed over the connection with Menkaura's mind. Ahriman saw Pluto, its face and moons sliding from cold reality to silver coins set in the sockets of a skull. Sigils in tongues never spoken by men ran through the dark, leading the inner eye on a spiral. He saw the symbols of the old zodiac, of apocalyptic calendars from the dawn of history: the twinned faces, the serpent that circles the fire, the keys of sleep, all dancing with the substance of smoke against the stars that were their eyes. All of the grand mechanism was moving, its parts aligning, resonating with each other, pulling tighter and tighter.

The fires of battle fed it. Fear and the blood of the dead drove it on. Even the desperate hopes and defiance of the defenders added to its momentum in the warp. It existed nowhere but linked to everything – to every moment of the past, every thought of the future and every deed unborn. It was the most breathtaking and terrible thing Ahriman had ever comprehended. He saw beyond it, to the ships swarming in the warp, holding still in currents that would normally have torn them apart. Thousands of them. Tens of thousands of them, great and small. Daemonic creatures circled them, colour and form shifting and changing.

He drew his mind back, felt himself sway slightly as reality washed the vision away.

He was standing on the shrine again. The Apostle was standing on the other side of the chamber, his blank helm turned so that Ahriman was certain that eyes were fixed upon him behind the smooth bronze.

'The moment of alignment is close,' he said into the vox. The Apostle nodded once.

'As was written.'

'As long as the final elements come together, that is,' replied Ahriman, hearing the coldness in his voice.

'Have faith, sorcerer. Not all is art and design. The gods ordain that all be done. Have faith…'

Ahriman did not answer but turned away.

+Bring the ships in. Begin pulling our brothers out. We must not be here when the end of this begins.+

+And the Word Bearers?+ asked Ignis.

Ahriman looked at the crimson-clad warriors moving amongst the chained psykers.

+Something tells me that they do not intend on becoming martyrs.+

+Unlike Menkaura,+ stated Ignis. Ahriman felt his thoughts twitch back to his eyeless brother, now locked in the stone sphere of the solatarium. +But of course that is different. He will have the comfort that his memory matters to you.+

+Make the ships ready,+ sent Ahriman again, after a long pause.

+As you will it,+ replied Ignis and then withdrew his thoughts, leaving Ahriman to the voices of the shrine's ghosts.

# EIGHTEEN

On grey wings
Spear thrust
Alignment

*Unnamed Warship, Inner System Gulf*

The grey ship flew. It left the Caul of Jupiter. None of the guns it passed turned to follow it; none of the ships holding station moved to mark its passing. Auspexes that looked at it found their augurs turning away, their questions answered by cipher codes that removed even the beginning of the question. On it flew, grey in the night, a shadow at the edge of sight, into the dark, towards the glimmer that was the sun.

Mersadie looked back at Jupiter as the gas giant shrank. An enhanced pane of vision had opened in front of the circular viewport. She could see the lights of void engagements. The ships of the invaders were coming from the outer system in growing force now.

'The vanguard,' said Loken softly, coming to stand beside her. She had not heard him enter. No hiss of door pistons or thump of locks, and his armour followed his movements without a sound.

The chamber that they waited in was small, but with a high ceiling and a lone viewport set into its wall. It was a small and quiet space, a refuge of solitude on a ship of whispers. The servitors that she had seen had been hooded in grey, and moved with fluidity and in silence. The ship itself did not growl or tremble with power but slid through the night seemingly without effort, gathering speed in silence.

Mersadie looked around at Loken, who nodded at the image of the orb of Jupiter.

'The enemy have loosed jackals to harry our lines. The true force is still crossing the gulf from Uranus. It will be in battle range in hours.' He let out a breath. 'And then those lights will seem just the sparks falling before the inferno comes.' She twitched and he looked around to meet her gaze. 'The humans you brought from Uranus will be free of the planet's sphere by then. They have been put on ships, and those ships sent out amongst the asteroid colonies.'

'Thank you,' she said, quietly.

'It may not save them,' said Loken. 'There are no safe places any more. But you brought them as far as you could.'

Mersadie did not answer but looked around. Mori and Noon lay curled together beneath a blanket under the light of a glow-globe. They had refused to leave her, and so had come with her onto the grey ship. They had slept most of the time since then; perhaps they had succumbed to exhaustion and shock, or perhaps the sense that they had finally reached a place of safety had given them the gift of rest. That gift had not been given to Mersadie.

Things like the shadows of wolves had been waiting for her during the few moments in which she had closed her eyes.

Perhaps it was the presence of Loken, or the quiet of the ship, but she found memories coming to her, sharp and unasked for. Maloghurst the Twisted looking down at her, his eyes hard, the corridors of the *Vengeful Spirit*, a smell of blood and smoke.

She shivered, and blinked. Loken was still looking at her, eyes steady, face unmoving. For a second, in the reflected light of Jupiter, he looked almost human.

'How long?' she asked, trying to suppress the tremor running through her nerves.

'There are no ships swifter than the one we stand on,' he said. 'It will not take us long, but we may arrive to find that the enemy has made that journey, too. There are traitor forces moving into the inner system from above the orbital disc.'

Mersadie glanced back at the sleeping children.

'It's not too late,' she said. 'We still have time. Not much, but some.'

'How do you know?' he asked.

'I can feel it,' she replied. 'It is like the cogs of a device turning just on the edge of hearing. It is still turning…'

Loken opened his mouth to say something…

'*Captain Loken,*' said Maloghurst. *The image of the Warmaster's equerry turned its gaze on her.* '*He trusts you.*'

'*I am a remembrancer. I am recording his experiences for posterity.*'

'*Remembrance… A strange idea to take to the stars, I have always thought.*'

'*I don't understand.*' *She thought of looking around but that cold gaze held her.* '*I thought I was to be returned to my quarters,*' *she said.*

*She had been taken from the training decks on the* Vengeful Spirit *by the bodyguard Maggard and a squad of soldiers. Sindermann and the others had been peeled away under their own guard, but Maggard had stayed with her, leading her through passages and corridors that she had not seen before. After a while he had stopped, and he had gestured at a door leading off the corridor.*

*Mersadie, the blood roaring in her ears, had not moved until Maggard shoved her forwards.*

*'Tell me,' said Maloghurst, his power armour buzzing as he shifted. 'Does he trust you?'*

*'What?'*

*'Does Captain Loken trust you?'*

*'I... I don't–'*

*'He favours you, talks to you, shares his remembrances with you. I think that he does trust you a great deal, Mersadie Oliton.'*

*The equerry to the Warmaster had smiled, and unwilled she began to turn to run. A hand on her shoulder stopped her dead. Heavy fingers squeezed with the smallest amount of pressure and the promise of bone-breaking force.*

*'You see, Mistress Oliton,' said Maloghurst, 'we do not trust him, at all.'*

'Is there something wrong?' asked Loken.

Mersadie found herself leaning against the armourglass of the viewport. Distant explosions flashed like tiny stars under her fingers. She shook her head, swallowing a breath that tasted cold in her throat.

'Memories,' she said, blinking. 'Just memories...'

But that memory of Maloghurst had not happened, said a voice in the back of her mind. What she had just remembered had never happened. She had been taken from the training chambers and returned to her quarters at Maloghurst's orders. It had not happened...

'Memories of what?' he asked.

'You, Sindermann, the *Vengeful Spirit*, how this all began.'

He looked like he was going to ask a question, when a light blinked in the collar of his armour. She heard a low chime, and the clatter of a vox-link connecting and decrypting. Loken turned his head to listen to words only he could hear.

'So ordered,' he said after a second, and began to move towards the door. 'A major engagement is in progress around Luna. We will have to chart a course to skirt it.'

Mersadie nodded, still trying to grasp the strand of the memory that had risen in her mind. It was fading though, sinking back beneath the surface of the immediate, slipping through her grasp... There was something she had forgotten...

'Loken,' she said as he moved away. He stopped and looked over his shoulder. 'There was a Navigator on the prison ship who escaped with me. I have not seen him since we reached the Caul – was he amongst the refugees that got off the ship?'

Loken gave a small shake of his head.

'I do not know. I saw no Navigator, but it is possible.'

A laugh came to her lips as a thought struck her.

'You might have known him, before I mean, during the crusade. He was a Navigator on the *Thunder Break*, part of the Sixty-Third Expeditionary Fleet – Nilus Yeshar.'

'I never met a Navigator of that name,' he said, and shrugged.

'The universe is smaller than it seems sometimes, isn't it.'

Loken frowned. 'Is there a reason he would try to hide from you, and then flee without telling you?'

She thought of Nilus, of how the Imperium had tried to imprison and kill him ever since he had returned to it.

'Every reason,' she said.

*The* Phalanx, *Terran orbit*

The *Phalanx* moved by the will of Rogal Dorn. Greater than any ship of the Imperium, it was a moon of gilded armour

and stone. Gun-fortresses rose in mountain ranges on its
spine, and launch bays dotted its surface. A skin of atmosphere and ash from its engines surrounded it. Sunlight
gleamed from the glass set in the cities borne on its back.
It was not a ship; that was too small a title for it. It was war
and empire given form and set amongst the stars.

Kilometre-long cones of fire stretched in its wake as its
engines began to pull it up the incline of Terra's gravity well.
Its court of ships came with it: the *Regis Astra*, the *Eagle of
Inwit* and the *Noon Star*, warships all, and around them the
attendant destroyers and strike cruisers that held the honour of being heralds to the empress of war.

Su-Kassen fancied she could feel a tremble as the great
ship began to move. She and half of the command staff had
relocated with Rogal Dorn to the *Phalanx*'s command bastion. It was a fortress grown from a greater fortress; a third of
a kilometre long, the command bastion rose in two towers
of black stone linked by bridges of plasteel and marble. The
bridge, command-seat of the ship was the aftward tower; the
forward and broader of the two was the strategium. From
the bridge, the chosen captain of the vessel commanded
the *Phalanx*'s movement. From the strategium, the master
of a Legion commanded crusades and conquests. At this
moment, Rogal Dorn stood in the strategium, linked by vox
and hololith with Shipmaster Sora on the bridge.

The strategium itself hung in tiers from a domed roof
above a plane of crystal, over a hololithic pit thirty metres
deep at its midpoint. Blue light flooded the space, rising
and rippling from the tactical projections emanating from
the pit. Command staff, tech-priests and Legion warriors
looked down into the bowl of light, focusing on portions
of the displays through lenses and screens. Dorn, Su-Kassen,
Archamus and a clutch of senior command staff stood on

a platform directly above the holo-pit's centre. Huscarls in Indominatus Terminator plate stood amongst the tiered galleries, immobile and watchful. Most of the staff in the strategium had been here when Dorn and his retinue arrived. A mirror of those in the Bhab Bastion's Grand Borealis Strategium, they had assumed their duties seamlessly.

'Signal the fleet elements in Terran orbit,' said Dorn as data-lenses rose around the platform edge. 'All forces to integrate to our command. All are to stand by for engagement order.'

He had given the order to move his command to the *Phalanx* two hours before, and the transports had been in the air and reaching for the heavens minutes later. He had not given his reasons, but Su-Kassen had seen half of the catalyst and guessed the rest in his words.

She had wondered if it was now, after the weeks of feeling the darkness and the threat of fire rolling closer, that he needed to take up the sword, not in principle but in fact. The fires of war could be seen as Luna rose in the night sky above the Palace. And so now, Rogal Dorn would throw the traitors back into the dark with his own hand.

The pit of holo-light began to flare and boil. Su-Kassen began to syphon off information from the wider battle sphere, stretching her awareness out to the engagements around Mars, folding in the intelligence from Uranus, Neptune, Saturn and Jupiter.

The Solar System was ablaze. Battle data spiralled and multiplied as she watched. In places where there was need, she issued orders that would commit ships to battle; in others she pulled back what she could and watched the loss increments rise and rise. This was a war now measured in casualty estimates, lives spent by the thousand – because if they were not then what life would remain for anyone? This was her role, her duty, while Dorn turned his will to where it was needed, to the point where it could tip the scales of battle.

An alert light blinked at the edge of her sight from where the personal signal channel controls rose in a pillar of brushed bronze.

'Admiral,' said the officer a second later, 'my lord Praetorian.' She turned. 'There is a ship closing at speed. It bears the clearance of the Lord Regent.' Dorn was turning to look now, too. 'It says that it brings someone you must see.'

'Who?' asked Dorn.

### Battle-barge War Oath, *Luna*

The defenders knew the weapons of their attackers. The protectors of Luna, the veteran regiments, the ships of Su-Kassen's fleets and the warriors of the VII and IX Legions knew that every thrust and manoeuvre of the assault had one aim: to allow the Sons of Horus to bring their legionary forces to bear on the surface and in the sub-surface warrens of the moon. Centuries ago, when the same Legion had spearheaded the conquest of Luna for the Emperor, the same had been true. The difference now was that Luna was not defended by the weapons of a gene-cult of Old Night, but by the arms and might of the Imperium. And those defences held the assault to the vacuum above.

Fire circled the moon. Rolling impacts struck void shields and peeled them back in flashes of light. Chains of plasma annihilators mounted on the Luna Ring spoke in sequence, one gun cooling while another poured sun-bright energy into the enemy ships. Swarms of bombers and interceptors spun amongst the fields of fire, thousands of tiny battles squeezed between exchanges that burned the dark like the fury of ancient gods.

Thirty Solar Auxilia bombers dodged through the grids of fire surrounding the Sons of Horus bombardment vessel *Chieftain of the Red Blade*. They were about to unleash their payloads just as a broadside struck the ship's void shields. Arcs of discharge from the collapsing shields overloaded the bombers' systems. They slewed off course, ploughing into the gun ports of the ship. Their payloads detonated. Fire punched into the *Chieftain of the Red Blade*'s gunnery decks and cooked off a macro shell being hauled towards a breech. Explosions ripped through the ship from the inside.

The Blood Angels ships *Red Tear* and *Lamentation of War* cut wide of the close formations of the main fleets and came about to unleash boarding torpedoes into the flanks of ships vying for the gulf between Luna and Terra. Each torpedo carried ten sons of Sanguinius. All had painted a portion of their armour with the black saltire of a death oath. Each knew that he would fall in this fight, and that his oath of moment would be his last. The twin ships fired as their torpedoes ran on to their targets. Plasma and macro-shells struck the attacking ships just as they were trying to find range on the closing ordnance. The torpedoes struck home and stabbed deep. Melta charges in their nose cones detonated. Walls and bulkheads became vapour. The Blood Angels squads charged out of the torpedoes. Orange light caught wings of gold and silver worked into their red armour.

They had chosen their targets well – ships carrying Sons of Horus from the 21st, 345th and 71st Companies. The Blood Angels met their traitor brothers. Blades lit with lightning. Bolters poured fire into armoured bodies. Broken ceramite, shell casings and blood fell to the deck.

And on the fight went, spread in a shifting crescent around Luna.

Abaddon felt the charge in the air around him as the *War*

*Oath*'s teleporters built with power. He could taste metal and ash on his teeth. Layak stood at his shoulder, the two blade slaves seeming to shiver in the warp-charged air. His brothers were around him. They were all there: Thonas, Gedephron, Tybar, Ralkor, Sycar, Justaerin, Reavers, warriors clad in black and marked with red and gold. And behind them, he could feel the presence of all the rest, dead in all but memory: Sejanus, Syrakul, Torgaddon, Gul, Kars, Dask, Graidon – silent ghosts watching him as he took his sword from the hand of a serf.

'We shall become death,' said Layak. Incense smoke was fuming from his staff. 'Our knives shall become the spears of angels, our hands the thunderbolts of the gods.' Abaddon turned his gaze on the priest, who looked back at him with eye-lenses like burning coals. 'I am glad, Abaddon, that I stand with you now at this sacred moment.'

Abaddon turned and gave the first order.

'Full speed.'

The *War Oath*'s engines burned brighter. The ship had been prepared for this moment in its long fall from above the solar disc. Disciples of Kelbor-Hal had worked in its engine spaces and generatoria decks. They had modified and mutilated, changed the nature of the ship from the inside. Only the shell of the one-time Imperial Fists ship existed, the bones symbol enough for its purpose. As it leapt forwards, it screamed. Bulkheads began to vibrate. Plasma poured into reactor chambers and mixed with exotic energies. Speed built. The ships surrounding the *War Oath* peeled aside as it bore down towards Luna. They had protected and followed it as their flagship, but it was that no longer. The attacking fleet parted before it.

The defenders saw it come, its speed building second by second. Auspex screens fogged and stuttered as sensors tried to lock on to its passage. In its hull, the crew that still lived spoke their prayers to the gods that had claimed their souls.

Ships moved to block the *War Oath*'s path and its fleet moved to protect it in turn. Fire tore into their shields and armour.

In the teleportation chamber, Abaddon felt his skin tighten inside his armour. Arcs of lightning split the air.

The ships closest to the Luna Ring moved aside as the great ship plunged down. The Ring's guns fired, half-blind. Explosions tore the *War Oath*'s shields and raked its flanks. Inside its engine spaces, tech-priests in black robes intoned their last commands to its reactors and folded themselves out of reality. The ship accelerated in a last jet of flame. Sections of plasteel ripped free. The fire pouring from the defences broke its shields. Balls of lightning burst across its hull. A hundred-metre-long section tore from its prow and ploughed back across its spine, striking the bridge castle.

The *War Oath* shrieked as it began to break apart. It was almost at the Ring.

Abaddon closed his eyes.

'Activate,' he said.

The teleportation generators convulsed and threw them into the void beyond.

A second later, the wounded ship struck the Luna Ring. Shock waves rippled through the vast hoop. The *War Oath* ploughed on for an instant. The Ring twisted like rope. The plasma reactors and munitions in the *War Oath*'s hull detonated. A sphere of energy exploded. Stone flashed to light. Metal became dust.

The tremors spilled into the warp as the destruction rolled out through the materium. Then the occult energies laced into the ship's reactors flooded out. Paradox overtook reality. Fire unravelled substance. Light passed through stone and flesh. A twenty-kilometre-long section of the Ring vanished into a cloud of shadow.

An aching instant of time unfurled. On Terra, the image of a black moon rose in the nightmares of those few who slept.

Then the energies and the moment collapsed. Matter and light rushed back into the point where the *War Oath* had vanished. For a second there was just an empty volume of space. Then glowing cracks lashed out, flowing through the void, threading through the space where ships still moved and poured fire at each other.

The broken circle of the Ring trembled, then began to fall, sliding back down into the weak grasp of the moon it had protected. Vast sections of docks and defences met the grey Lunar surface. Clouds of rock and dust fountained up and up in the faint gravity.

Abaddon opened his eyes. Around him the whirlwind of darkness became the smooth stone of Luna's caverns. There were figures moving beyond the settling shadows, clad in amber-yellow, guns firing, bolts and beams converging on him and the circle of warriors around him.

Reality asserted itself like a hammer blow.

'Fire,' he said, and around him the first of Horus' warriors to set foot on the moon that made them obeyed.

*Comet shrine, Inner System Gulf*

+Go,+ willed Ahriman. The gunship kicked free of the comet shrine. Around it dozens of others flew free, engines bright as they raced for the ships already moving to make distance from the comet.

Ahriman felt the universe turn under the surface of reality. Images bled into his mind's eye. The spin of the Solar System above the night sky of Terra. The sages and sorcerers of ancient times, looking up and imagining the truth of the universe in the movement of stars. They were wrong, of course, but within their ignorance they were also right. They had thought that existence revolved around that Old Earth. It did not, not in the way they thought. The planets and stars and the arcing swirl of the galaxy turned without thought or care for the ball of rock that had spawned humanity. But another universe, one that lived in ideas and dreams, followed different rules. In that realm, the importance and power of objects and people did not follow the dry rules of atoms and gravity. Things made themselves important by the place they held in hopes and fears and in the stories that people told themselves. And now, at this moment, this small sun and its circle of moons and planets truly was the axis of all existence.

Ahriman saw Menkaura, his blind brother, floating in the centre of the solatarium. Cords of light held him aloft as bloody and burning spheres turned through the air. Ahriman felt perception and time and space flatten and bend, felt his inner eye fill with a view that held everything from the sun's core to night's edge.

Blood and pain and terror spilled into the warp and flowed inwards, cascading down through the patterns of old rituals and beliefs like the waters of a broken dam. It was all Ahriman could do to hold his thoughts steady in the enumerations. He felt the *War Oath* strike the Ring of Luna, saw the fire billow across the moon's surface. He tasted blood. Across his connection with Menkaura he saw the symbols of the Solar System slow in their orbits. Blood was filling the crystal sphere marked with the Lunar sigil. The other spheres were glowing with flame and shadow.

Everything had been for this. The assaults planned by Perturabo, the strike of the fleets deep in-system – all had taken ground, killed, weakened defences. But more than that, they had formed this alignment, this moment of ritual power written in the planets and stars.

+Now,+ he sent. And in the caverns of the comet shrine, the Word Bearers who remained put their knives to the throats of the psykers chained to the floor. And as the mortals' death screams poured into the warp, the torrent they formed met the flood-tide already surging in.

Ahriman withdrew his mind, and had a second to feel his breath gasp ice from his lungs as the gunship accelerated away.

The comet vanished.

Time blinked.

Night fell to blinding light.

Sound.

Voices.

Night.

Across the Solar System, every being felt a tremor in their soul, like something stood behind them but inhaling through their mouths.

Then the sun went dark.

# NINETEEN

Trust the messenger
The man beside you
Fane of rebirth

*The* Phalanx, *Inner System Gulf*

The grey ship docked with the *Phalanx* as it broke Terran orbit. Huscarls surrounded Mersadie and Loken as they crossed the docking limb. All around them the *Phalanx* trembled as it pushed into open space and towards its enemy.

Mersadie recognised some of the sights they passed, statues of heroes, images inlaid in stone, floors of black-and-white marble. She had been here before, years ago, after they had fled Isstvan on the *Eisenstein*. She remembered walking through the…

*Vengeful Spirit, Maggard and the soldiers all around her. The sound of the ship, the silence that followed them as they went further. Something was wrong. She was…*

…walking through the *Phalanx*, Loken at her side, a wall of Imperial Fists around her.

'Dorn…' she said, feeling the word rise from within. She felt disconnected. Something deep in her mind was screaming that it was almost too late, that she was almost out of time. There were things moving in the root of her memory and mind, vast unseen gears turning. 'I must reach Dorn...' Her feet were still moving. A buzzing had started in her head that might have been static or water falling down onto rock or wind blowing through a dry valley filled with skulls...

'We are almost there,' replied Loken.

'Why?' asked Su-Kassen. She was almost running to keep up with Dorn as he strode into his sanctum. Glow-globes lit as he crossed the black marble floor. 'What can a remembrancer have to tell us?'

Archamus and a squad of Huscarls spread through the room, feet ringing on the floor. Dorn stopped, and turned to look at her. His gaze almost made her stumble. His eyes were dark mirrors in a face of carved stone.

'Because once before messengers came to me in the ship. They told me the truth that we all now live – that the Warmaster was a betrayer. I did not believe them then, I did not want to hear...'

Su-Kassen thought she saw something then, something in the deep distance of his eyes, something she could not place in a being like Rogal Dorn.

'It is not often that we get to learn from the mistakes of the past,' said Dorn. 'Mersadie Oliton showed me the truth. Here, in this room...' He turned his head to look at a point in open space, as though something moved in the still air. 'She showed me what she had seen... and that changed everything.' He looked back at Su-Kassen.

She could feel herself frowning, a doubt forming on her lips.

A shrill alarm rang out.

Su-Kassen gasped.

Blackness, a feeling of nausea, a sound of screaming.

She blinked and put a holo-monocle to her eye. Light flooded her vision as alert information poured onto the display.

Cold flooded her.

'Lord Praetorian,' she said, staring at the tactical data as the sound of alarms rose to a clamour. 'Something is happening in the inner system...'

Static was suddenly washing through the vox-link. The holo-monocle shorted out. She stumbled back.

A sound bubbled up in her earpiece, rustling, laughing, saying something that sounded like words.

'...*is all around you... the only name you will hear...*'

'Lord...' she began.

'Bring the ship to full alert,' said Dorn, and began striding for the doors.

Mersadie stumbled. The floor of the passage met her hand as she caught herself. Lights popped and bubbled in her eyes. Voices and memories tumbled over each other in her skull.

'*Take the iterator and the remembrancer back to their quarters,*' said Maloghurst...

*Maggard shoving her through a door...*

'*Euphrati, what is wrong? You never talked like–*'

'*You need to understand, Mersadie.*'

'*I understand you have a story,*' she said. The wolf stood before her, the white fur of its back silver beneath the moonlight. '*A particularly entertaining one. I'd like to remember it, for posterity.*'

*The wolf turned, its teeth a smile of sorrow.*

'*Which story?*'

'*Horus killing the Emperor.*'

'Where...' she managed, pushing herself up as Loken reached to help her. 'Where are we?'

'The *Phalanx*,' he said. His eyes were dark, human, not the eyes of a wolf.

'The *Phalanx*…' she repeated, blinking, feeling the world turn around her.

The eyes of five Imperial Fists held on her, red in black-and-yellow helms.

'The *Phalanx*, yes, of course. Rogal Dorn… There is not much time.'

'Mersadie, it is all right…'

'No… There is something else… I need… to see him.'

She forced her legs to move. Something was happening, something that she could feel but not understand.

There were doors opening in front of them…

*On, on further through the night, through the passages of the* Vengeful Spirit *to a door…*

'What was that?' she heard herself say, as the glow-globes flickered in their settings.

'Something is happening,' said Loken, but his voice seemed further away now, 'system-wide anomalies. There is something wrong with the vox…'

*She had been here before, in these corridors before, carrying memories… images spooled in her head… blood and betrayal and the truth… What had she forgotten?*

The lights spluttered again. She could see a set of doors in front of her. She had been here before, with Keeler, with Garro.

'What is that?' growled one of the Imperial Fists. There was a noise, a hissing, like static, like the whisper of wind blowing through dry valleys. Like a voice…

Dorn's sanctuary… the *Phalanx*… She had been here before…

The lights blinked red.

'What is happening?' asked Loken.

'Full alert,' replied one of the Huscarls. 'Something is happening in the Inner System Gulf…'

The doors were opening in front of them…

'We need to get you secured,' said one of the Imperial Fists.

'I need to see Lord Dorn…' she mumbled. 'I need to…'

'There is someone speaking on the vox…' said another of the Huscarls.

*The shove of Maggard's hand on her back, pushing her through the door.*

*'Greetings, Mersadie Oliton,' said Maloghurst, looking up at her. His eyes were the eyes of a wolf…*

Loken had stopped moving suddenly. She looked at him blinking.

'It sounds like a voice,' he said, 'trying to break through the interference.'

The sound was hissing in her ears… rising and falling…

*'S… here…'*

'Dorn…' she gasped, 'I need to see Rogal Dorn now!'

*'Sam… is…'*

'That sound, that voice,' he said. 'I have heard that voice before…'

*'Sa… mu… is…'*

Loken's gun was in his hand. The Huscarls were moving, turning; shadows were spreading up the wall.

Everything was distant, like something happening on a pict screen hung just in front of her face. There was someone behind her. Just behind her. A shadow…

'He is here.'

Loken snapped around to look at her.

'What did you say?'

She shrugged, feeling more words coming to her tongue. Her muscles were moving but she was not moving them.

'Samus is here,' she said, and backhanded Loken into the wall. He struck it with a sound of shearing ceramite.

Mersadie looked at her hand. It was red.

Guns roared around her. Red fire. Blinking. Red on her hand.

She tried to take a step, put her hand out and fell...

A thin hand caught her arm, steadied her.

*'That's it. You are all right. I have you.'*

She blinked. Nilus was standing next to her, holding her arm and shoulder, looking at her with black eyes in a pale, pale face. The face of a friend. The rest of the world had become blurred, a tableau through which something was moving faster than sight, clawed and furred and toothed. Slowly – oh so slowly – the yellow-armoured warriors were coming apart.

Red... The world was bright and dark and red.

'But you were not here...' she said, looking at the face of the Navigator standing just next to her. There was blood on his face she noticed, splattered right across him, bright and dripping.

Nilus shrugged, smiled, and now he looked nothing like a human, and nothing like a friend.

*'I am always here,'* he said. *'I am the man beside you.'*

## Inner System Gulf

The comet shrine blazed back into being. Light poured out of the point where it had vanished. Lightning leaped across the gulfs of space, brighter than the vanished sunlight. Every soul asleep under the light of the sun woke with a cry. Every person awake, from Space Marine to child, felt the touch of knives on their skin.

A vortex of energy poured into the hole punched through reality by the comet. Circling daemons were caught by the hurricane force and were unmade. The storm narrowed, became a point, became a blade. It dragged through the skin of reality, ripping back along the arc that the comet shrine had passed in the last decades. The lips of the wound peeled back. The light of paradox spilled out, bubbling, flowing, curdling the dark across tens of millions of kilometres. The warp breach gaped, drooling half-formed matter, a bloody smile opening in the dark.

For an instant, it was the only thing that moved. Stars and planets were still in the face of this violation. The black sun hung in a bleached sky, a mute and cold disc.

Then the slit tore wide. Matter vomited into being. Half-formed ideas of teeth and limbs, of beasts and mouths tumbled over each other, writhing as they dissolved and coagulated.

The sun blazed back to light, screaming.

Across Terra, every person looking at the sky could see it: a burning wound across the night, or a scar of midnight in the daylight.

Through it came ships from the realm beyond, dragging cloaks of insects and shadow. Winged creatures circled them, flying like birds in the gale of etheric energy. Bolts of lightning leapt from the wound, strobing across space. And here were the vessels that had been absent from the weeks of war already waged. Here was the *Conqueror*, its white hull red with smoking gore. Here were the ships of the World Eaters, their murder cries echoing from the vox, and the voice of every legionary. Angron stood on the hull of his capital ship, a vast and ragged shadow axe raised to the sunlight, roaring his fury at the circle of Terra. There were the ships of the Emperor's Children, fuming musk and grey dust from jewel-crusted hulls. In the guts of the *Pride of the Emperor*, Fulgrim coiled and looked out through the eyes of every soul in his fleet, and laughed with delight.

And there – following the rest, like the chariot of a king

come in triumph – came the *Vengeful Spirit*. Warships flanked it. Daemons flew as its heralds. High on its hull, on the fortress that it bore upon its back, Horus, Warmaster, First Son of the Emperor, Chosen Champion of the Dark Gods, looked out at Terra. The seat of his father's empire glimmered beyond the prow of his ship. Shadow bled from him, and the daemons that held to the shadows of his court hissed and bowed their heads as the light of the sun touched his face.

The ships poured from the rift, spreading out in a swarm of glinting lights. A hundred, a thousand, ten times a thousand, more and more that had been waiting in the warp for the way to open to the heart of the Solar System. Even if Horus' forces had used both the Elysian and Khthonic Gates, it would have taken such a force days to translate back into reality. Now they swam from the warp into the gulfs of the inner system, not an army or a fleet, but a host sent by the will of gods and the art of mortals.

The ships clustered and divided as their engines caught on the cold vacuum and turned them towards Mars and Luna and the small orb of Terra all alone in the dark.

Horus watched, and then gave a single nod.

'Begin,' he said.

### The Warp

'I am a remembrancer. I am recording his experiences for posterity.'

'Remembrance... A strange idea to take to the stars, I have always thought.'

'I don't understand.' She thought of looking around but Maloghurst's gaze held her. 'I thought I was to be returned to my quarters.'

'Tell me,' said Maloghurst, his power armour buzzing as he shifted. 'Does he trust you?'

'What?'

'Does Captain Loken trust you?'

'I… I don't–'

'He favours you, talks to you, shares his remembrances with you. I think that he trusts you a great deal, Mersadie Oliton.'

The equerry to the Warmaster had smiled, and unwilled she began to turn to run. A hand on her shoulder stopped her dead. Heavy fingers squeezed with the promise of bone-breaking force.

'You see, Mistress Oliton,' said Maloghurst. 'We do not trust him, at all… And we need to be sure. We need to know what he hides from us. We need to know which way he will choose. I have my suspicions as to that, but the Warmaster wants to be certain.' He nodded, smiled. 'Loken was a favoured son after all. You can forgive a father wishing to give his son every chance, and so you are going to help us see Captain Loken clearly.'

Mersadie could not move. There was something behind her.

A shadow, breath on the back of her neck.

'You remembrancers wanted to see the Great Crusade…' continued Maloghurst. He turned aside and she could see a low stone table, just behind him. Candles burned above it. The smell of scorched human hair filled her nose. There were objects on the table: a silver knife, a brass bowl filled with water, a pile of finger bones, a silver coin and a human eye, still leaking fluid onto the cold stone, looking up at her with a grey-flecked gaze.

'You wanted to know the truth, to look into all the places where your curiosity took you…' said Maloghurst. His fingers traced a sign in the air.

She tried to move but could not. The shape Maloghurst had drawn burned red, bleeding in her sight.

'Well now you will do just that, Mistress Oliton. You will see, and we will look through your eyes…'

He reached down, picked up the knife. The rune burning in the air glowed. Everything was going black, rushing past like *the embers of a fire pulled apart by a gale. Hot breath prickled on the back of her head. A hand touched her shoulder. She felt the tips of claws.*

*Maloghurst was very close now, looming above her, the buzz of his armour aching in her teeth, a rank incense smell coiling from him. And now he was stepping towards her, knife rising to her face, to her left eye…*

*He slowed, his movements blurring like a pict capture run at one-tenth speed.*

*'You see…' growled a voice from behind her. 'The eyes… windows to the soul… and what were you but a set of eyes watching the world.' The tip and edge of the silver knife filled her sight. It was all she could see. 'You never know what use things will be…' Mersadie tried to draw breath. The scream in her throat burned but did not sound. 'All they wanted was to see what you saw, to know what you knew, to use your insight…' A chuckle through sharp teeth. 'So limited, but the seed was planted, the bridge and link made. And the warp remembers…'*

*'I…' began Mersadie. 'I was used…'*

*A laugh now, a full, high laugh that might have been Nilus, or Keeler, or Loken, or the howl of wolves in a winter-shrouded forest.*

And the image of Maloghurst, the knife and the stone table vanished.

A view across the mountains of Terra blinked into being behind high windows. A breeze was sliding through a half-opened door to the enclosed garden beyond. The thin curtains stirred. The polished wood floor was warm beneath Mersadie's feet.

*'Nothing like being back home,'* said a voice behind her. She turned, half expecting not to be able to move.

The face of Euphrati Keeler looked up at her. Coloured

tiles and beads lay on the floor around her, some broken, some ground to dust. There was blood on Keeler's grey robe, a wet, bright splatter from forehead to fingers. She was picking her teeth with a piece of broken glass.

'You were never Keeler,' said Mersadie.

'*No,*' said the bloody face of Keeler. '*But you wanted to believe so much that it made it an easy choice of what face to wear.*'

'Where is she?'

The bloody woman on the floor laughed.

'*Really? At this point, you are still worried about your friend?*'

Mersadie began to take a step forwards, anger rising. She froze, locking in place.

'*My, my, there is still some strength in you,*' said the image of Keeler, standing, the shard of glass still in her hand, held loose, dripping blood. '*Euphrati Keeler, the real Euphrati Keeler still lives, still follows her lies about the false God-Emperor, but it was never her speaking to you.*' Mersadie felt a hollowness open in her. '*Oh, you are wondering about before – about the dream and message about Loken... about "saying goodbye". Did you like that touch?*'

Mersadie tried to force her jaw to open. The mouth in Keeler's face twitched and she shrugged. Mersadie gasped.

'When...'

'*On the* Vengeful Spirit, *of course, in one of those slivers of time that you don't even realise you don't remember. That is the strange thing about being so sure of your memory – it makes hiding things easy. You never doubted because you believed in yourself.*'

'Maloghurst...'

'*A little bit of sorcery used for a simple task. They really did just want to know where Garviel Loken stood – as though it weren't obvious.'* The image of Keeler snorted. *'They wanted an eye on him, watching from where he would not expect.'* The thing raised the shard of glass and pointed it at Mersadie's left eye. *'So they put that eye in you. It didn't turn out to be much use in the end. But it was there...'*

'But now... Maloghurst could not have known that I would be here.'

The thing was shivering slightly. Its grin was wide, too wide, and leaking red at the corners. The wind was moaning as it rose outside of the windows.

*'Of course not, but the connection was there, the door made. This path you have walked, this end that you serve is a later improvisation by Horus, a use of available assets.'*

'The message... the design in the warp... None of it was real.'

*'No, all of it was real,'* said the thing. It was looking at its arm like a child at a toy that it did not understand. It placed the tip of the glass against the skin. Black ran from the point. *'The best lies are truth. There is a great design in the warp that is undoing the barrier between worlds and delivering the Warmaster to the heart of the Solar System. You are a part of it – a small part, but a part. Dorn could see the edges of it and he is disposed to trust messengers. Especially messengers bearing the truth, especially messengers he has trusted before.'* It looked up at her. Its eyes were red, blood-red, and smoking. *'Especially you.'*

The wind exploded through the windows around them. Shards of glass spun through the air, struck the thing that looked like Keeler, ripped through flesh and bone. And it was stepping forwards, skin and blood falling off it in the razor gale. The image of Nilus was underneath, tall and spindle-limbed.

And Mersadie saw herself again on the prison ship, alone

at the controls of the shuttle, arriving on the *Antius* alone; talking to herself in her cabin; following the blood trail to find the enginseer hiding on the ship's bridge.

She had been alone all the time, part of her mind locked from noticing that Nilus was never mentioned by anyone else, and never there when she wasn't by herself.

'It was all me...' she said, feeling the shock roll through her as the creature got closer. Nilus was gone now too. It was a juddering shadow now.

'*We are here for you...*' said a voice, a voice that sounded like it was stitched together from a chorus of howls. She saw the red light blinking through the corridor of the *Antius*, the troopers who had come to kill her becoming red splatter and shreds as the shadow tore them apart.

'It was not trying to kill me,' she said. 'It was–'

'*No, we are the end and the death, but not yours... Not yet...*'

The flashes of red memory vanished.

Somewhere far off someone was shouting. She could hear the rattle of gunfire, and the boom of explosions.

It was dark, the night air frosted. A red, sickle moon curved just beyond the reach of bare branches. A pool of black water lay before her. Ice ran around its edge. A figure that looked like a wolf crossed with a skinned man rose from the water. Freezing water scattered from matted fur as it grew.

'*We are here,*' it said.

### Seventh Fane of the Selenar, Luna

The gunfire ripped through the servitor. Abaddon rammed through the wreckage of its torso. Pieces of armour and flesh splattered across the ground. Another half-machine clanked forwards on tracks. It fired. A stream of rounds struck Abaddon. His helm lit with damage. Chunks of armour tore from his chest. He ran into the gunfire. Behind him, his Justaerin were firing down into the side corridors.

They were deep under the surface of Luna, in the warren of smooth black stone divided by circular doors and twisted into spirals like the inside of a seashell. The air was still and cold. Mica and crystal flecks gleamed in the walls as gunfire shattered the dark. Even echoing with the sounds of battle the warren seemed quiet, as if the weight of its silence dragged the sound from the air. Abaddon felt it pull memories into the moments between the muzzle flashes, old memories held deep but not forgotten: sharp silver and flesh, water and blood, darkness and blinding pain. This was the domain of the Selenar, the seat of the Luna gene-cults, the place of his rebirth.

Before him lay a circular door set in the curve of the passage wall. Low relief images moved across its surface in silver, figures with crescent headdresses and burning torches. Spiralling haloes of symbols wreathed them: tau-aleph, gamma-kaf. Beyond lay one of the last fanes of the gene-cult, a sanctuary against time and decline. They had come this far, hacking and killing without pause. Most of the resistance came from servitors following blunt battle programs. But those half-machines still had weapons that could kill a legionary.

A figure of piston limbs and armour plates unfolded from a niche in the wall and launched itself at Abaddon. The human flesh that guided it was lost beneath a frame of tarnished silver and black carbon. Stretched out it would have stood taller than Abaddon, but its power had been bunched and folded into the shape of a monstrous feline, six-limbed and blade-clawed. Its head was a fanged mask, with a mane of chromed hair. It was a sacred sentinel, one of the guardian beasts of the Selenar's inner sanctums. Lightning wreathed its jaws as it leapt.

Abaddon jerked backwards. The guardian beast landed in the space where he had been. He raised his power fist. The beast sprang at him, fore and mid-limbs wide, jaws open. It was quick – very, very quick. But he had killed quicker prey. He punched his fist into its mouth. The fist's power field activated as it made contact. Its head exploded. Shards of silver and brain matter struck the tunnel walls. Its movement did not stop. Nerve clusters and brain segments drove it on. Damage runes lit in Abaddon's helm as the beast's limbs fastened on his arm and shoulder. He snarled and lifted the creature from the ground. It was twisting, its hind limbs reversing to arc up over its back like scorpion stings. Abaddon pivoted, battering it into the tunnel wall. Armour splintered. He could see the lightning wreathing the thing's claw blades.

Heavy rounds tore through the thing's body. Pulped meat and twisted metal showered in every direction. It lashed out. Abaddon brought up his bolter and fired a stream of rounds into it. Chrome and carbon splinters rang against his faceplate. He hurled the remains against the wall and dumped another burst of bolter fire into it before what was left of it could move.

'Hard kills,' growled Urskar, closing with Abaddon, reaper cannon still smoking from the fire he had poured into the beast. 'But you didn't need all that much help.'

Abaddon looked at the chosen warrior's red helm. The silver-filled scars glinted across its snout, like teeth behind a grin. Abaddon laughed, the sound blending with the sound of gunfire. For a second he felt the weight of the moment lift; he had come back to the place that had made him, that had made the Legion that was everything; unlike that moment of birth he was not alone.

'Will you ever be anything but a jackal, brother?' he said over a direct vox.

'I doubt it,' growled Urskar. Then his head twitched as he looked beyond Abaddon. 'I smell the dung of gods and priests.' Abaddon turned to see Layak advancing down the passage. Shapes made of shadow and cold light spiralled around him. The blade slaves walked behind their master, swords drawn, bodies bloated with power as the daemons within the blades rode their flesh.

'A last temple to old lies,' said Layak, looking up at the doors.

Abaddon felt his lip curl but did not answer.

'Breach it,' he said. Reavers in black power armour ran forwards to clamp clusters of melta charges in place. Abaddon's chosen formed around him, guns braced, weapons lit and sweating lightning.

'Detonating!' came the call, and the silver door vanished. A blast wave of super-heated, molten metal broke over Abaddon and his warriors. They did not flinch – they went forwards. Guardian servitors bounded through the glowing cloud. Bolt- and autocannon rounds tore through silvered armour. Abaddon saw the head of Gedephron's power mace crash through the chest of a beast shaped like a bear of black iron. He saw another one fasten its gaze on him and begin to pounce. He fired, pounding its body to shards as it reached for him.

He was out of the other side of the debris cloud. Actinic light filled the chamber beyond. It was spherical, its walls curving up and up to a circular opening set at its apex. Staircases and platforms spiralled up the walls. Pods frosted with crystal hung from spun carbon cable in the central void.

Abaddon could see clusters of vials and silver coolant tubes nested inside the pods. At the far end of the chamber was a lone figure, hovering just above the ground. Grey gauze billowed around her on the currents of false gravity. A crest of silver tubes rose from her back to halo her head. A silver mask moulded into an expression of false serenity hid her face. She twisted in the air as the Justaerin burst from the debris cloud. Abaddon could see a spiralled arrangement of crystal pipes rising from the floor in front of her. Her hands were moving between vials of liquid, combining fluids in a spinning device. For an instant the blank eyes of the woman's mask met Abaddon's gaze.

Buzzing curtains of energy unfurled across the room as Abaddon and his brothers advanced. Figures in segmented black armour with sprung legs bounded forwards. Energy beams snapped out. Bolt-rounds exploded on walls of glowing force. Abaddon was charging forwards, his strides cracking the black stone floor.

The curtains of energy were changing, flicking out and then snapping back into place in different positions. He saw Ekaron from the second Reavers squad split by a sheet of glowing light as it appeared. The halves of his body fell to the floor, burning.

Black lightning reached from behind him and exploded a guardian servitor as it sprang at Abaddon. He twisted to see Layak keeping pace with him, one of his blade slaves at his side.

'You won't reach her in time,' called Layak. 'This is a void maze. If they have power to keep it active it will protect her until it is too late.'

'There is a way through,' snarled Abaddon. Part of his mind had already read the shifting pattern of the energy fields as they activated – read them and seen that there was a flaw.

'Too slow,' was all Layak said. Abaddon felt something shift in the air. The taste of burnt sugar formed on his tongue. A high note, like the sound of breaking glass, drawn out to the point of pain. The world stuttered. Layak was moving past Abaddon, his blade slave charging with raised sword. Abaddon saw a fresh curtain of energy unfold into being across their path in the stopped-clock moment. Shadows were spilling from Layak. The blade slave struck the energy field. Light and dark flashed out. Every scrap of shadow became a pool of blinding light, every light a hole into night. The sword screamed as its edge cut. A hole – no, a wound – opened in the energy field, haloed by cold light and sparks. Layak raised his staff as the sword cut, and spoke a word.

Silence screamed in Abaddon's ears. He tasted jagged iron on his tongue and in his throat. The cut in the energy curtain ripped wider, and beyond it the layers of fields parted. Layak had gone still now. His hand was smoking where it gripped his staff. Blood was running from the bottom edge of his mask.

Abaddon was moving forwards through the opening, gun rising, eyes fixed on the woman at the centre of the room. The devices and vials in her hand were spinning, the fluids inside fusing into dark red. He did not understand the ways of the Selenar, but he did not need to understand their mysteries to know what she was doing. She was Heliosa-78, sole surviving matriarch of the Selenar, and in her hands she was mixing death with which to poison the last remains of all her kind held sacred.

In these halls the gene-seed of the Legions had been multiplied and implanted, and here the means to do that again remained. It was a prize great enough that Horus had sent his most favoured son to secure it – a victory beyond breaking the defences of Luna. Luna would become a birthplace for warriors again, but now their war would not be in distant stars but on the surface of the world that hung in the sky above. But not if he failed.

He saw her half turn to look at him as the curtains of energy split.

Layak was beside him, holding out his staff.

The guardian beast rose from a hole in the floor. Its shape was that of a lion crossed with a scorpion skinned in graphite and oxidised bronze. It bounded into Layak. The priest spun, but the beast was faster. It struck Layak and cannoned him back off his feet. Armour tore, blood scattered across black stone.

# TWENTY

Samus
Librarius
Will of stone and fire

*The* Phalanx, *Inner System Gulf*

Shadows flowed through the *Phalanx*. The darkness gathered at the edge of flame-light billowed out and up, spreading across walls, swallowing shape, dissolving brightness. The shadows roared as they spread and their voice was the sound of wind blowing through the teeth of skulls.

*'The end and the death...'*

*'We are here...'*

*'We are beside you...'*

*'Death is beside you...'*

*'The end is here...'*

It flowed on, boiling with coalescing shapes. It passed through bulkheads and through the cracks around closed doors. Strange forms clawed across ceilings, and blizzards of shadows boiled down corridors. It was not one creature but many, a tide of murderous power poured into cold reality like ink into clear water.

Gunfire met the tide. There were over three thousand
Imperial Fists on the ship. Ten thousand Jovian and Solar
Auxilia elite, and every oath-bound crew member was a
warrior.

In the decks beneath the *Phalanx*'s strategium fortress,
twenty Huscarls in Indominatus Terminator plate met the
daemon tide. Assault cannons spun up. Target displays
flashed red with threat markers as the shadows became
vast hounds and hunched figures dragging swords.

The Huscarls opened fire. Bolt-rounds and volkite beams
punched into the wall of darkness. Brass cases rang on the
granite floor. Bodies formed as shadow broke into muscle
and sinew. One of the Huscarls brought his cannon around
as a hound made of smoke and blood leapt for him, jaws
wide. The deluge of shells shredded the creature. A second
later, a figure of spindle limbs and bloody skin rammed a
sword clean through the Huscarl's flesh and armour.

In the primary signal-processing chamber, the darkness
came as silence. Millions of cables and noospheric links
all converged at this point. Men and woman sat wired into
consoles, listening, filtering and diverting the flow of messages from across different regions of the *Phalanx*. Their
mouths moved constantly, hissing echoes of the words and
codes passing through them. Auto-scribes clattered. Data
conduits beeped. It was never quiet and more than a day
in the chamber would leave an unprotected human deaf.

One of the signal governor servitors began to twitch. The
words coming from her mouth speaker stopped. She shook
her head as though trying to clear it.

'Samus…?' she said, unsure, as though part of her lobotomised brain had heard the word once before but could
not remember where.

'Samus..?' she said again. The servitors to either side of her twitched and went still. The lights on their consoles flashed amber. 'Samus... Samus... Samus...' More insistent now. One of the supervising tech-priests was moving towards her. Alarms were sounding, lights flashing.

'Samus.'

A ten-metre bank of vox-consoles went silent. The servitors at their stations froze and then exploded.

'Samus! Samus! Samus!'

The tech-priest dropped to the floor. Smoke poured from his ears as his remaining flesh cooked. Silence spread. The babble of voices and the hum of signals vanished. In her cradle the lone servitor remained, twitching in place, shouting the only thing her slowly melting brain could hear.

'Samus! Samus is here! Samus is the man beside you!'

Darkness bubbled up out of the hull along the *Phalanx*'s spine. Swarms of creatures pulled their wings from the dark and launched into the vacuum. Close-defence turrets opened up. Las-bolts blasted ghost flesh to slime. One of the *Phalanx*'s escorts became a scream of detonating void shields and splintering armour.

Su-Kassen was shouting as the darkness poured into the chamber she and Dorn had been waiting in. Coiling strands of night flowed through the open doors. Beyond, she had a glimpse of a dark shape, like the shadow of a vast wolf cast against a wall by an inferno. It was growing, stretching. The Huscarls around her and Dorn were firing. She could smell ozone and blood, spun sugar and sulphur. The shadow of the wolf beyond the door turned its head as she looked at it. Red eyes met hers. She raised her shot-pistol and pulled the trigger. A cloud of metal fragments tore into the space between her and the shadows and became flares of light.

A shape detached from the spreading dark. It grew as it moved, sheathing itself in bloody meat and bone as it ran.

Su-Kassen fired again, and again, punching the dog-like thing backwards.

Dorn moved past her, a golden blur against the shadow. She had never seen him in battle. They had conducted war together for over half a decade, but it had always been remote, his genius and nature expressed in insight, in cold logic and plans that unfolded at a distance. She had never seen him fight in front of her. Not so close that she felt the rush of his passing. He did not have *Storm's Teeth*. The great chainsword that he bore in battle was in his chambers. But he was still a primarch, a weapon that needed no other.

His first blow hit the daemon hound and exploded its skull and body down to his hind legs. The wall of shadow drew back, rising like a cresting wave as it touched the ceiling. Dorn had his bolter in his hands. Shots punched into the oily matter. It rushed forwards.

'No!' Su-Kassen went forwards, firing her pistol. Dorn stood his ground, a lone figure, face set, lit by muzzle flash. The tide coiled above them.

Dorn fired another burst and turned to one of the still-open exits from the chamber.

'Move!' he shouted. Su-Kassen dived after him as he went through the doorway. He turned as he crossed the threshold, grabbed the doors and pushed, his face pale and taut. The doors were three-metre-high slabs of plasteel inlaid with silver images of lightning bolts. The piston systems that shut them normally were capable of crushing an armoured Space Marine. Dorn rammed the doors shut with his hands. They shook as something struck the other side.

'Seal them!' he called, but Su-Kassen was already at the manual locking handle, yanking it down with all of her strength. Bolts shot into place with a drum roll of cogs.

The doors began to glow red with heat. Dorn turned as warriors in yellow armour and black cloaks ran to circle them.

'Lord,' called Archamus, as the Huscarls formed a triangle around their primarch, guns facing outwards.

The silver on the doors was beginning to melt.

'Go to the silent vault. Unshackle my forgotten sons. They join the battle by my will,' said Dorn, his voice clear. 'Now.'

Archamus paused and looked at Dorn.

'And you, my lord?'

'We need to reach the bridge.'

Archamus nodded and was already moving; half of the Huscarls broke away and formed up on him.

Dorn was moving towards one of the other doors that led to the arterial connection to the bridge.

'With me, admiral,' he called. Behind them, the doors began to flake chunks of molten metal.

*Strike Frigate* Persephone, *Inner System Gulf*

'Auspex failure!'

'Long-range vox failure!'

'Fleet target integration lost!'

Alarms and voices cut across the *Persephone*'s bridge. Sigismund felt heat prickle his skin and the deck pitch as the *Persephone* rolled. An arc of lightning sliced across the void where she had been. Blood mist boiled out into the vacuum. Smoke was pouring from the helm machinery. Shouts and screams were echoing through his skull. The gravity on the bridge failed and for a second he was floating. Then it reasserted itself with crushing force. A human serf officer slammed into the deck nearby, skull and spine shattered.

'Reality is coming apart,' called the sensor officer. Blood

was running down her face. 'We cannot see the rest of the fleet. We cannot see anything.'

'We are losing navigational data,' intoned a lexmechanic from his cradle of brass-bound lenses.

Sigismund felt another jolt thump through the frigate.

'Get us a bearing now!' shouted Rann. The Assault commander was bareheaded, a fresh wound from falling debris seeping blood across his scars.

'It's gone…' said one of the officers. 'Every system is in seizure. We can't–'

'Open the blast shutters,' said Sigismund. Rann looked around at him, mouth opening in question. 'Open them now,' called Sigismund.

A second later the plates covering the viewports folded back with a rolling boom of metal slamming into metal. Horror poured in. Light boiled and spun through every colour; depth and distance flexed and reversed. Spheres of distant planets loomed large, swallowing the view of the stars before shrinking to pinpricks of light. And across it, vast and billowing like a shot-slashed sail, was a rift between worlds. Ships swarmed from it, glittering, cloaked in ectoplasm and warp-skinned creatures.

A part of Sigismund's mind saw and understood. The enemy had found a way to bring their host to the seat of the Solar System. The fight would not be in the void now. It would be decided where it was always going to end: on the soil of Terra, beneath a sky of fire and iron.

Human crew across the bridge moaned and screamed, and some of them vomited. Sigismund felt his jaw clamp shut and muscles bunch across his body, as though he were trying to stand still in the face of a hurricane.

'What–' began Rann.

'The sun,' said Sigismund, raising his hand to point through the roiling chaos surrounding them. 'We can see the sun still.' And there it was, its light shredded and stained, but shining yet. 'Set our course by that. Reach every ship we can – close formation, steer by the sun. Full speed.'

### Seventh Fane of the Selenar, Luna

Abaddon twisted aside as the guardian beast reared up, dragging Layak into the air like a broken doll. The blade slave whirled from where it was cutting through the wall of light. The opening in the fields began to shut in front of Abaddon.

Fire burst from Layak as he struggled in the beast's grasp. Its armour plates charred and distorted with heat, but it did not let go.

Around them, the troops and guardian creatures of the temple were falling as the Justaerin advanced through the maze of energy fields. At the edge of his sight Abaddon saw Urskar brace and fire a line of heavy rounds into four troopers as a field snapped from one position to another. The resistance would not last much longer, minutes at most, but minutes was all Matriarch Heliosa would need to empty her vials into the font of tubes in front of her. From there their contents would flow into the fane and beyond, poisoning, destroying, salting this sacred ground for those who would take it.

Abaddon saw Layak's blade slave swing at the guardian beast holding his master. Its sword was trailing smoke and blood. The beast's tail lashed out, extending like a whip, a metre-long blade at its tip. The blade slave took the impact on its chest. The sting punched through its armour and flesh. Black fluid and ash poured from the wound. The beast whipped its tail and the blade slave flew through the air into one of the energy fields. Flesh and armour flashed, burning and crumbling as it fell.

Layak twisted in the beast's grip. It opened a mouth filled with lightning-lit teeth.

Abaddon fired as he charged. Bolt-rounds struck the beast's mouth and exploded between its fangs. Its head jerked back. Abaddon felt his first blow uncoil through him. His power fist tore into the beast's flank. Bronze and black graphite shattered. The beast shuddered, back arching. Abaddon struck again and again, pounding through metal and ceramic to the human flesh within. Blood and shredded meat fountained out. The beast spasmed, toppling, the power fields around its claws flaring. Layak fell from its grasp. Abaddon punched up into the thing's inner guts, gripped and pushed upwards with all the strength of body and armour. The dying beast twisted in his grasp as he lifted it and threw it at the energy fields.

Blinding light filled the chamber as false thunder shrieked. The fields vanished. The remains of the great beast struck the floor, mangled, charred and half-melted.

Abaddon turned, the beast's blood lending the black plates of his armour a slick gloss. Layak was trying to rise. His armour was cracked, and half of the horned mask covering his face was torn. Abaddon had a moment to see a dark eye in a face of red, scarred flesh before the substance of the mask flowed over the features and solidified. Bolters roared behind Abaddon as the Justaerin and Reavers fired into the remaining guards and guardians. He stepped towards Layak and reached down to the sorcerer.

'What are you doing?' rasped Layak, not taking the offered hand.

'I remember and repay my bonds and oaths,' said Abaddon. 'You came to my side, now I come to yours.'

'But the mission… The way is open. The matriarch will destroy what you have come here for.'

'No,' said Abaddon. 'She will not.'

'What?' began Layak.

'Weakness,' said Abaddon. 'We do not need to be mighty when we are faced with weakness.'

Layak hesitated and then clasped Abaddon's hand and pulled himself to his feet. Blood fell from the sorcerer as he straightened, but shadows were already pooling in the breaks in his armour and pulling flesh and ceramite back together. Abaddon turned from him and strode towards where Matriarch Heliosa-78 was frantically locking vials of red liquid into the column of tubes and machinery in front of her. The gunfire began to fade from the chamber as the last of the guards crumpled to bloody debris. Abaddon's steps were unhurried as he approached the Selenar. Casually, he reached up and released his helm. His brothers did not move; they could read the balance of the moment and follow his lead without a direct command.

'Matriarch Heliosa,' he called, and his voice rang clear. He saw her half turn as she slotted another vial of the red liquid she had been concocting into the mass of tubes. 'You hold death in your hand, matriarch, but not mine.' Another vial slotted in place. Her hands were moving over fine silver levers, releasing, priming. 'I have no doubt that what you are about to do will destroy the value of this place to us. That is the gene font that links to all the gene-looms, stores and seed reservoirs in this complex. What is it you are going to unleash into it – a gene-scrambling toxin, a viral pollutant that will touch everything within your domain with imperfection?'

Heliosa did not stop in her movements.

'You should have destroyed this place already, matriarch,' he said, still advancing slowly. 'You must have known we would return, that we would want the cradle of our creation back. If you wanted to stop that you should have purged every mystery and person here.'

He was within five strides of her now, close enough to see that her limbs were shaking. He stopped.

'But you have not done that. We knew you wouldn't. We know you. After all, in a sense, are we not your sons?'

Her hands had stopped moving on the crystal tubes and vials.

'I am not here to kill you, matriarch. I am here to make you an offer. You could never let go of the hope of survival. This fane should be a ruin, but part of you can't do that – you cling on, hoping that a moment like this will come to save you. That is why you bent the knee to the false Emperor, why you sold your purity and made us for Him. So now I make you another offer, matriarch, the same bargain that you made with our creator – live and serve, or die and see all you believe and love become ashes.'

Heliosa looked at him, blank eyes in a silver helm.

Then, she bowed her head.

'The Selenar will serve,' she said. 'What is the will of the Warmaster?'

Abaddon looked at her for a long moment, then turned and began to walk back to his brothers and Layak. The smoke coiled from the torn remains covering the floor. The rest of Luna would fall within hours and there would be more killing until that was done, but they had accomplished what their father asked; they had the treasure of Luna in their grasp.

'Build us warriors, matriarch,' he said without looking at her. 'Build us Legions.'

*The* Phalanx, *Inner System Gulf*

Blood. There was blood all around Massak. Snow boiled out of the night sky. He was running, but the world was pulling away even as he tried to hold on to it.

*'Come, my son...'* cackled the voices of crows and insects. *'Come, you know what you must do. Come to us... Be free...'*

'No!' he shouted, forcing his will against the image in his head. Somewhere, far off, he could feel his hand clenched around the haft of an axe. Heat was pouring off it, charring his palm as he gripped harder and harder.

'No!' he shouted again, and pulled himself down into the well of pain. He opened his eyes, biting back the agony that had been his tether to reality. He was kneeling on the floor of the chamber. His hands were locked around the haft of his force axe. Heat glowed yellow from his gauntlets. Ice covered his armour and the floor around him. Beside him knelt his brothers. Light and heat and cold fumed off them. All were fighting within themselves now. The warp was clawing at them, ripping at their will, trying to pull them into the storm tide. Something vast and terrible was happening, something that he could feel as though it were as real as the floor beneath him and the armour covering his skin. It would kill him soon. He could feel it shredding his psyche, and he could not fight it. He had the weapons to defend himself, to bite back at the things that clawed at him, to raise the voice of his spirit and escape the sea that drowned him...

But he could not. He had given his oath. There was only his will, his mortal will standing against the hungering ocean. He would die here, in this cell that had held him and his brother Librarians for the last seven years. And facing that death would be his last duty.

Beside him he heard Kordal gasp as the pain escaped his mouth. Blood-jewelled frost covered the former Lexicanium, branching into sharp spikes over Kordal's skull.

'Hold, brother!' called Massak. 'We are our oaths. They are our strength. Pain is the anvil of our honour.'

Kordal was juddering in place, blood flowing from his eyes, mouth and ears and freezing on his face.

The boom of releasing bolts shook the walls. The blast doors at the far end of the chamber pulled wide. A Huscarl with the black cloak and white fur of the Praetorian's master bodyguard strode into sight, bolter and sword in hand.

'Rise, brothers,' said the figure. 'Rise. Your lord calls you to war.'

*'Cerberus…'* laughed a voice in the warrior's skull. *'You are amongst the dead and betrayed again, returned to the hell you fled…'*

He saw it all again: the Whisperheads, Xavyer Jubal rising from the floor, red light pouring from his eyes.

*'Samus is the man beside you…'*

Abaddon's blade cutting at him.

*'There was nothing to betray.'*

Mersadie Oliton looking up at him, eyes wide but not afraid.

*'I understand you have a story…'*

Mersadie… Mersadie…

Loken opened his eyes. There was blood across his sight, and blood dripping from the passage walls. He pulled himself up, feeling sharp edges grating against each other in his chest. Pieces of yellow armour and ragged meat lay in the congealing pool of blood covering the deck. Shadows writhed at the edge of sight.

*'Samus is here…'* the whisper distant, half-real, calling.

Something in the shape of a skinned dog was biting into the open ribcage of one of the Imperial Fists. It turned as Loken stood. Its mouth was a cave of needle teeth. It leaped. Loken met it with the edge of his chainsword. The spinning teeth chewed through the thing's head and back into its body. It writhed, scrabbling at the air as black ichor sprayed out, but Loken was already surging forwards. He burst through its remains and began to run. In his head the call was rising, the scent in the air, shivering through his senses. He was Cerberus again now, forsaken and betrayed, loyal and inexorable, last hunter of the Luna Wolves, and he would have vengeance.

'Samus is here…'

'It's coming!' shouted Su-Kassen. Rogal Dorn did not turn. One of the trio of Huscarls spun to fire back down the passage behind them. Su-Kassen kept running.

*The end and the death, the end and the death, the end and the death…'* sounded across the vox and growled from the ship's alarm and speaker-horns.

Bolter fire sawed through the dark. The double-layered doors to the bridge slammed back into the walls in front of them. Su-Kassen looked behind her. Half-visible things with starved bodies and wings of rotting feathers tugged a Huscarl from the ground. Claws bit through armour. They lifted him, blood scattering as they peeled armour from flesh. A tide of black mist was pouring down the walls, strobing with red lightning. She could see the shadows of shapes inside the murk, bounding and rolling towards them on legs and tentacles.

She felt her mind flood with images of plains of dust and bone, her throat with the sting of bile.

Dorn was through the doors in front of her. She wrenched her eyes around and ran the last few strides.

A deluge of noise washed over them as she entered the bridge. It was a circular space a hundred metres in diameter, its command systems rising in tiered islands of stone from the black-and-white marble floor. Tactical displays ten metres high covered the walls, flashing with static and blurred images. Smoke was pouring from banks of machines. Crew lay on the floor, broken by the fluctuating gravity. The rest were moving under the called commands of Imperial Fists overseers as they tried to control the vast ship as it writhed in their grasp.

*'The end and the death, the end and the death, the end and the death...'* The hissing roar rose from every speaker and vox-system.

The doors they had come through began to swing shut. The daemon tide struck them. Gears and pistons jammed. Metal creaked and began to melt. The Huscarls in the chamber were running to Dorn's side as the primarch pivoted and fired back through the gap in between the closing doors.

Su-Kassen was already moving across the floor towards the tiered mass of the command dais.

'Shipmaster Sora,' she called, vaulting up the spirals of stairs. Sora turned to look at her, his blue augmetic eye shining as it zoomed. His yellow armour blinked between black and crimson in the flash of alert lights and the flare of burning machines. 'Full power to the engines – we need to push as far away from Terra as we can.'

'Helm control is intermittent and deteriorating,' he replied, his voice raised. 'If we push her further out, we won't be able to bring her back into the battle sphere of Luna.'

'That does not matter now,' she said, and saw the glimmer of understanding flash in his living eye. 'Begin contingency for reactor self-destruction.'

'Admiral, this is the *Phalanx!* She–'

'Would you rather she became a weapon for the enemy?'

'Lord Dorn–'

'This is his will, shipmaster.'

She looked around as a boom of shearing metal echoed

through the chamber. Doors and sections of walls blistered with heat began to buckle. Darkness poured in, coiling like soot blown on the wind. Shapes formed in it as it billowed inwards. Wings and legs and arms unfolded. Gunfire streaked the air. The Imperial Fists scattered through the chamber were forming gun lines. Bolt shells ripped half-real creatures apart even as more came.

Servitors rose into the air from their cradles and chairs, cables and pipes snapping free, blood and waste drooling to the floor. The creatures forming at the edge of the wave of shadow surged forwards. Su-Kassen had her pistol out. Shipmaster Sora was shouting orders. Swarms of winged daemons rose high above them. Su-Kassen put two rounds into a creature with a body and wings of grey skin and sinew. The deck was trembling under her feet. Something dropped onto the top of a console next to her, and leaped at her with open mouth and splayed claws. Her shot-blast punched it back in a spray of black foam.

Down on the deck, the wave of darkness broke over the Imperial Fists. Claws tore at helms. Armour split.

'The *Phalanx* is moving away from Terra,' called Sora from beside her, but she only half heard. She was looking down the slope of the command dais.

Rogal Dorn stood amongst his sons. He had a sword in his hand. The weapon was forged for a Space Marine, long-hafted with a blade as tall as a mortal human. The warrior that he had taken it from would have borne it to battle with both hands. Dorn wielded it with one, carving it through congealed flesh and bone without cease, flowing from cut to cut. He was advancing against the tide, cutting a path into it, his Huscarls following with blades and bolters. No step took him backwards.

And in that moment she understood something of what

the Khan had said of his brother. It was not just Dorn's choices that were charged by duty, but his nature – his will a chain holding back a storm that could pour out and break the world.

*'Samus is the only name you will hear...'* the voice growled amongst the static and the sound of battle. The billowing darkness was rising, reaching up and out like a thunder-head. Su-Kassen could smell offal and blood. The substance of the walls and floor was distorting, stone burning, metal cracking with frost. A shape moved within the cloud, pull-ing its tendrils of vapour into an image stitched together from the oldest of fears. Fur and flayed muscles and eyes that glowed like burning homes on a moonless night. This was not just a prince of the Ruinous Pantheon now; it was an arch-herald of destruction.

The head of a mortal crewman five paces from Su-Kassen exploded. She felt her mind shrink, felt herself fighting not to collapse as her thoughts fled back into a place where the world was simple and small.

The daemon of the storm stepped forwards. Ash cascaded from its tread. The tide of daemons at its feet pulled back before it.

*'Samus... Samus is all... Samus will be your end... Samus is the end...'*

The Huscarls began to fire up at it. Bolts burst in the congealing shadow of its torso. Casually, with speed that somehow blurred like an image drawn in a flick-book, it lashed out with a clawed hand. Bodies flew back, split open, blood showering from them. It picked one of the warri-ors up, cradling him as the legionary fired into its face. It closed its hand. Red sludge and shards of armour fell from its fingers.

Rogal Dorn looked up at the daemon. He paused for an

instant and then ran to meet it, sword in hand and face set in rage.

The daemon laughed in a voice stitched together from static and gunfire.

Dorn leaped. Claws blurred towards him, but he was already past the blow, already slicing – once, twice, a dozen times. Black fluid and ash fell to the floor and the daemon seemed to recoil. Then it snapped forwards and its claws were tearing sparks from Dorn's sword blade.

Across the bridge, corpses lifted into the air. Red fire lit in their dead eyes. Sora had drawn his serpenta pistol and was firing down at the dead as they rose. Su-Kassen found herself reloading and firing without thought. The daemons were clawing up the command dais.

Rogal Dorn was a figure of gold half-submerged in a sea of darkness. There was blood on his armour, but he was still striking, lightning flaring from where his sword met the daemon's claws.

*'Can you see?'* asked the voice just next to her. Mersadie tried to turn her head but could not. *'No, out there,'* said the voice that sounded like Nilus and Loken and Keeler and Horus, and like the wind sawing through the teeth of dry skulls. *'Do you see?'*

She looked. It was all she could do. She was still there, but separated from everything around her, a shadow out of sync with the reality it watched. It was like staring out through a window at a fog-filled street. And her senses stretched beyond. There was the great slice across the night, stretching wide, breathing out swarms of ships and spills of energy. There was the *Phalanx*, engines burning to push it wide of Luna and Terra even as it tumbled. Beside it, clouds of winged and clawed things scrabbled through the wreckage of its escorts. Across the dark, the barbed shapes of ships that had just come through the rift came closer, racing each other to be the first to cut the last threads of hope from the flagship of the VII Legion.

And down and down through the layers of stone and metal that were the ship, she saw the black tide boiling through cracks and walls. It was a flood, a mass of daemonic energy that would swallow the *Phalanx* and all in it. Then it would seep into its bones and make the mighty fortress its own. And she was the gateway.

'I did not do this,' she said.

'*No,*' said the voice behind her, '*perhaps not, but you have been very helpful…*'

She saw herself then. She was walking down one of the corridors of the ship. She was still there, still whole, but darkness unfolded from her shadow. The walls were blackening as she passed, tapestries and banners burning, stone cracking as ash danced in the air. Daemons were all around her, floating, spinning and gliding, a court following its queen. She looked old, her skin cracked parchment over a skull, her right eye boiled away, her left eye a pit of red fire. A ragged shadow walked at her side, its hands hanging low, its smile an arc of bloodied teeth.

'*You have made this last moment possible,*' said the voice. '*As the storm reaches into reality, you are a lightning rod and we are the thundercloud. All you needed to do was be here and we could find a path. You are our tether, our door, our messenger. Your thoughts are our way in…*'

'They will turn you back.'

'*Do you mean Rogal Dorn?*' chuckled the voice, and she felt warm, rank breath on the back of her neck. '*This is not a matter of arms and might, or did you think that a hero shouting on the seashore can truly turn the ocean back?*' She felt the laugh shiver through her. '*Watch…*' said the voice.

* * *

Massak formed his mind into fire. The thought flooded him.
He held it still for a second, tasted smoke in his mouth,
felt the flames roar through his sight, consuming it, blinding him. The sound of Archamus and his Huscarls firing,
of the warp creatures howling, all of it faded. The fire was
everything. He held its image, and felt its power grow millisecond by millisecond.

'Massak, we can't get through!' The voice was Archamus',
close but distant, dimmed by the voice of the fire.

He let go.

A white-hot inferno rushed from his outstretched hand.
His view through his helm dimmed. Warp creatures in the
fire's path boiled to slime. He strode forwards, panning the
flames across the space before him. Daemon flesh unravelled
to smoke and embers. Archamus and his Huscarls followed,
with his two brother Librarians. Lightning arced from their
swords as they cut daemons from the air.

Massak felt his will fight to control the power flowing
through him. He could see the inner blast door to the bridge
just ten strides away. It was no more than a gaping hole of
torn and fused metal.

As he ran forwards, bubbles of colour formed and burst at
the edge of his sight. The ether was burrowing through his
mind. Cold sweat poured from his skin inside his armour.

'It is… everywhere,' called one of his brothers. Massak
could feel the same truth. The warp was pouring through
the ship, twisting through its substance, grasping it like a
claw.

They were at the broken door. Archamus was at Massak's
side, firing and reloading without cease. Massak knew what
waited for them, seeing with his mind before he saw it with
his eyes. A wave of heat broke over him. Images drowned
in his thoughts: a wolf; a range of mountains, their canyons

piled with skulls; the hiss of water falling into a shrine-pool, down, down – skulls looking up, grinning with promise...

'Brother!' shouted a voice close by.

He snapped back to full awareness. In front of and above him, a figure of burnt flesh and blood-smoke clashed with a golden giant. Red lightning spat from where claw and blade met.

'Father...' breathed Massak. In his mortal sight, Dorn and the daemon were a blur, a giant of shadow and ghostly flesh and a demigod of war, gleaming against the darkness. Cold control poured from Dorn, cracking the flow of the warp, splintering the folding dark as it spiralled around him.

'Brothers,' he said, and the word echoed in the warp. +*Brothers.*+ Cold light was kindling on the edge of his force axe. He heard and felt the other Librarians answer, and fold their thoughts and minds to his.

Pain enfolded him. He saw the pasts of his brothers as though they were his own; saw the scraps of human lives left behind when they became warriors in a crusade among the stars; felt the pain of remaking over and over again, the trials of mind, terrors faced and overcome, purpose found and then taken away, long years in the dark, dreaming, waiting...

He was moving forwards, his brothers falling into step around him, force blades rising to mirror his own axe. Behind them, Archamus and the Huscarls were firing back into the throat of the door they had come from.

Massak felt the creature fighting Dorn become aware of them, felt its gaze turn as the Librarians advanced. Massak formed a thought and gripped it with all his will. The thought lit in the minds of his brothers. They began to glow, light and flame radiating off them in reality and the warp.

It had been a long time since they had united in this way, and even before the Edict of Nikaea they had been few amongst their Legion. But it had bound them, and now they were as they always had been, as they were always meant to be: a single weapon of many parts, unyielding alone, unbreakable as one.

A crowd of lesser daemons rushed towards them. Massak shifted his will, and the fire of his soul and the ice and lightning of his brothers' minds blazed forth. Daemon flesh flashed to smoke; howls and cries spun into the air. He saw the great daemon swell, felt it suck strength into its being from the realm beyond. It lashed forwards. Massak saw the movement as a smear of smoke, and felt the promise of death that it carried. Dorn's sword dragged lightning as it rose to meet the blow.

Massak's will and thought leaped out. He felt his brothers' pain as he yanked their minds with him. The air shrieked.

Feathers of burning gold unfolded out of nothing. Rubies of fire fell from etheric claws as the shape of their thoughts flew at the beast. It whipped around to meet it, and shadow claw met beak and talons. Blinding light flared. Daemons burst into showers of ash. Massak fell to his knees, his mind ringing. He could feel wounds opening across his body. The beast was still there, embers falling from its shredded limbs. Then Dorn struck.

In his dimming sight, the primarch's sword was a line drawn through the storm of the warp.

Liquid fire and black blood sprayed out. The beast howled. Dorn struck again, and the daemon's cry flung Massak down amongst his brothers. His sight was draining from him. He saw Dorn's sword rise again, saw the great beast coming apart even before it fell. Muscle became bloody slime, bone crumbled, claws dissolved like salt in rain.

'*Samus...*' hissed a voice carried on the wind that unravelled the last of its body. '*Samus is... coming...*'

And then it was not there. And the bridge was a charnel pit of dripping blood and settling ash. Dorn alone stood on the deck. Above them, other figures were pulling themselves to their feet on the command dais. Archamus and two remaining Huscarls were hurrying to Dorn's side as the primarch strode to where Massak was struggling to rise.

'My son,' began Dorn, but Massak was shaking his head. His mind was a storm of pain and echoes of thoughts that were not his own.

'Lord…' he began. 'There is something wrong… The creature…'

A cry rose from high on the command dais as failed systems sparked back to life.

'Lord Dorn, enemy ships are closing!'

Dorn was half turning.

'No…' said Massak, forcing the words from his lips, panting, blood running over tongue and teeth. 'It is not gone… That was just…'

*'Samus…'*

The corpse of one of the Huscarls raised its head from the deck behind Dorn. Its helm was torn. Its eyes were pits of red fire. And the dead rose into the air once more, fire bursting from within, as laughter echoed around them.

*'Samus will be your end…'*

Loken paced through the dark. The lights had failed and he had discarded his ruined helm. The world was grey now, its colours drained into shadows. He had heard the sound of gunfire in the distance several times, and had killed things that had taken the flesh of the dying.

*'In such visage, they turned upon their kin and gnawed then upon their bloody bones.'* The old words of *The Chronicles of Ursh* rose from a long-forgotten crack in his memory.

He had failed, just as he had failed before. He had not seen. He had failed his new oaths just as he had failed the old. He had failed her.

*Cerberus*… The old name, the old pull of instincts, which had followed him from madness, drew him on through the dark. He was close. It was close. He could feel it. It was right; Samus was right. It had always been there, the man beside him. The shadow that never left him. But now he would end it. The end and the death for shadow and man alike…

On he went, on through the dark to an end he could not see.

*Strike Frigate* Persephone, *Inner System Gulf*

Traitor ships poured from the warp rift towards the *Phalanx*. Thrusters fired across its vast hull, shaking the vessel as it fell out into the void beyond Terra's gravity. Her sisters and escorts were gone, burned from being, or left behind. Daemons gnawed her skin, peeling away bites, threading her hide like parasites in diseased meat.

Torpedoes began to strike her. First one, then a dozen. Then more, and more. Titan-sized warheads struck home, and ripped stone and metal away. Swarms of daemons spun and laughed as they tumbled into the void with the debris. The great ship trembled, its shields misfiring. The traitor ships came on, accelerating towards their prey with hunger. There were ships of all of Horus' greatest vassal Legions amongst them: the *Deathchain* of the World Eaters, *Sovereign Blade* of the Emperor's Children, and *Olympian* of the Iron Warriors, and dozens more.

Sigismund watched them close on the stricken *Phalanx*.

'They have not seen us,' growled Rann.

'Attack speed,' said Sigismund. 'All guns and all blades ready. Forwards.'

# TWENTY-ONE

Now you see
When swords will not cut
A story to tell

*The* Phalanx, *Inner System Gulf*

*'Now you see,'* said the voice behind Mersadie. *'There is no way out.'*

And she did see. She saw the frozen moment as Rogal Dorn swung his blade to meet the claws of the daemon for a second time. She saw the traitors closing on the *Phalanx* and the few wounded ships of Sigismund's fleet plunge into them firing, lashing out with desperate ferocity. She saw daemons stalking the *Phalanx*'s deep holds and machine spaces as Imperial Fists cut them down with bolter and blade.

And she saw that none of it mattered. This was the end. Dorn could win a battle and Samus would still be there, all around them, a shadow that could not be shed. The warp was pouring into it, sustaining it and remaking it endlessly. The daemons would keep coming no matter how many fell, and the Imperial Fists would die one by one in a fight with an enemy that could not be defeated.

*'That is the truth…'* said the voice behind her. *'Humanity can never be anything but slaves to us. We are made by you, and while you live we walk beside you. Mortals cannot win a war with what is eternal. What you have helped bring into being here, Mersadie Oliton, is just an example of that truth.'*

'What…' she began, hearing her voice echo flat in this realm of thoughts. 'What do you want of me? Why do you show me… this?'

A dry chuckle.

*'You are our gate, but a gate is just an idea – your mind our way into being. Your memories, remembrancer, are our shape and power. Is it not fair for you to see what you bring into being?'*

She saw again the cascade of vision, and the mockery of Ignace Karkasy's face in the grin of a creature as it plunged a rusted sword into a crewman's neck; saw shreds of Keeler's burning picts spin in the fire-wind as a fuel line ignited on a machine deck.

'All mine…' she said.

*'Yes, all yours…'* said the voice. *'And now… another relic of the past comes to show you his true face.'*

The visions vanished, and Mersadie saw where she truly was.

Massak felt the warp pour into the chamber, furnace-hot and ink-black. Cracks formed in the air as a thing that flickered between forms stepped out of the edge of sight. The corpses hanging in the air burst into a blaze. Molten fat and burning blood spun from them, falling up and congealing into arms, tentacles, eyes, chitin, fur and quills. Massak drew on his will but he could feel the currents of the warp coiling around him, squeezing, suffocating even as he tried to reshape it with his thoughts.

He saw Dorn raise his sword, bloodied but unbowed.

Samus looked at the primarch with eyes that held clusters of dying stars. And it lashed forwards, the world hissing its name as it reached for the Praetorian.

'No...' Massak cried. 'No, lord!' And he was stumbling forwards, his axe in his hand. 'Lord Dorn!

Archamus was at his shoulder, firing without pause. Warp-formed shapes exploded.

'He cannot win this,' gasped Massak at the Huscarl. Archamus flicked a glance at him. The front and side of his helm was a ruin of shredded ceramite.

'We cannot–'

'This is only a part of it,' Massak shouted back. 'A single hand of many. It is all around us!'

A sheet of lightning flashed out. Massak blinked away blindness in time to see the primarch ramming the blade of his sword into the beast's chest. It withered and shrank as Dorn sawed the lightning-wreathed edge upwards. Massak felt a surge of power in the realm beyond. Red spots of blood blistered his sight. The daemon was straightening, growing even as Rogal Dorn cut it. It grabbed the Praetorian's shoulder, claws burning as they touched gold. It pulled closer, the blade vanishing into its flesh, its other claw rising.

Loken slowed. His skin was prickling, his breath ice in his throat. Nothing stirred in the reactor chambers. Soot lay across the towers of machinery. White teeth grinned from charred heaps of flesh. There was no sign of living crew. The chamber hummed with the outpouring of reactors into conduits to feed the *Phalanx*'s flight. There should have been a company of warriors barring his path into this chamber, and a swarm of tech-priests and servitors tending the systems. He had seen none, just drifts of ashes. He was not alone, though. It was here. He could feel it now, gliding over his senses.

He blinked. There was light. Distant flickering around a corner, the blue of plasma.

He moved forwards, so that he could look around the cliff of machinery blocking his view.

A figure stood on a gantry that projected out before a pit of brilliant illumination. Beneath it shone a sphere of blue-hot plasma held in buzzing fields. Arcs of power flicked out of the sphere and burrowed down conduits lined with magnetic coils. Loken knew what it was, though not the mysteries of its working. It was a plasma junction, where the raw power of the reactor was pooled and then drawn off into hungering systems. The woman before it was looking down into it, light playing across her face. Blood dripped slowly from her fingers.

'Who are you?' he asked, taking a step forwards. A sound like wind whining through rock fissures slid into the silence. He had his sword in one hand, his bolter in the other.

He could feel the cold breath of the madness in his thoughts. He was Cerberus, the hound of the underworld, vengeance and death.

'Captain Loken,' said the figure. 'Do you have a story to tell?'

He did not hear but took another step forwards, finger ready by the trigger, thumb resting on his blade's power stud.

'I can see it. I can see it all. There it is, you see, in the falling water...' she said, raising her hand, and as she traced an arc up in the air, the world changed.

Loken froze. The reactor chamber was gone, the vast machines replaced by a slanting cavern of natural rock overlooking a deep fault. A spit of stone projected out over the blackness beneath. Water fell from above, spattering off the faces of the rocks. He knew this place. Even through the mist of madness, he would always know this place. This is where it had begun, where he had seen the first sign of what was to come: The Whisper-heads. Sixty-Three Nineteen. The beginning of the end. All again, here and now.

'Mersadie?' he asked. The kill instinct faded. He was not Cerberus. He was Loken, captain of the Luna Wolves.

Mersadie pointed at the cascade. 'Do you see your story? It's there. Just look.'

He felt himself begin to look… He stopped. His mind flashed clear.

Samus. It was Samus. He snapped forwards, sword lighting, arm rising, Cerberus snarling rage and vengeance with his mouth.

Mersadie turned. Blood had run from her eyes and clotted on her cheeks.

'Loken!' she cried, eyes wide with terror. 'Loken!'

His blow faltered.

'Mersadie?'

She took a step towards him. Hands rising, fingers shaking. *'Oh, you poor fool…'* she said. *'No.'* And she smiled as her hands closed on his wrists with a sound of shattering ceramite and snapping bone.

*Frigate* Persephone, *Inner System Gulf*

*'Lord Sigismund, we are approaching boarding range with the* Phalanx. *The* Ophelia *and* Son of Stars *are locking formation with us. Coming alongside now.'*

'For our oaths, my brothers,' Sigismund called, raising his voice over the roar of the ship as he brought his sword up and rested his head against the flat of the blade.

'Stand ready!' roared Rann, slamming his fist onto his shield.

The doors of the boarding gantry stood before him. Behind him and spread through the staging chambers was every warrior of his command who could yet wield a blade. They had taken a single oath of moment – find Rogal Dorn. The primarch was still alive, Sigismund was certain of it. Inside his helm, he watched the distance runes cycle down to nothing.

Too slow... much too slow...

The whole of the *Persephone* was shaking as it poured the last of its ammunition into the ships converging on the *Phalanx*. Sigismund's force had left its slower ships scattered in a thin arc between them and the oncoming enemy vessels.

The deck around them was quaking as vast gantries extended from the flank of the *Persephone*. Chains rattled through tank-sized spindles. Amber lights flashed from red back to amber. A metallic roll of thunder boomed through the chamber.

'Alongside now,' said the voice of the bridge officer in Sigismund's helm. 'Boarding gantries in hull contact.'

Sigismund closed his eyes, felt his will pull the beat of his hearts down into a low drumbeat of calm.

'Lord!' The shout filled his ears. The deck and walls shook and shook again. 'Lord there is a... *distortion around the* Phalanx, *lord. There are things in the void–*'

Something struck the ship, flipping it over like a toy thrown from a child's hand. Alarms blared as the world rolled over and over.

The metal of the doors before them bloomed with rust as creatures burst through in a wave of wide mouths and reaching claws.

*The* Phalanx, *Inner System Gulf*

'**Look at him,**' said the voice behind Mersadie. Around her, the image of the *Phalanx*'s reactor chamber blurred and blinked into the image of a family house on Terra, then it became the cell she had lived in for the last seven years, then it was a dark cave filled with the sound of falling water. In all of them, Loken stood before her, frozen as he staggered backwards, sword falling from his hand. But his eyes were alive, and alight with pain. *'Weakness is a habit, you know,'* said the voice behind her. *'You return to it like a dog to its vomit...'*

She felt her body move forwards and pluck Loken's sword from the air as it fell. She kicked him. The force and impact would have broken her leg but the strength that moved in her was not her own. Loken's frozen form tumbled back. The scene around them was still the cave. A black abyss opened beneath the spit of rock they stood on. Loken lay on its edge.

She felt her neck move, so that she was looking down at him. The sword in her grip felt light, its weight and bulk a feather.

*'Our dreams cannot change the stars. But sometimes, our deeds can change the universe even if it is only by accident.'* She heard the memory of her own words, and waited for the voice behind her to comment or laugh, but it was silent, focused on Loken lying on the floor next to the abyss.

*'You did the same thing with Jubal,'* said a voice that came from her mouth, but was not hers. *'And then with the lodges, and then with Horus... Even after all you have seen and all you have done, Loken, you just can't quite believe the worst is happening. And so you have hope, and pity, and so you suffer for your weakness.'* The sword in her hand rose, the point resting on Loken's throat just above the collar of his armour.

*'And that is enough?'* the memory of Vek's voice said.

Still there was no reaction.

*'We could let him choke,'* said the voice behind Mersadie. *'Stop the muscles in his lungs. Crush him bit by bit...'*

'It is all we have…'

'But I think this is better. Everything has meaning, and what does it say that this last lost son of wolves dies by his own sword.'

'No,' said Mersadie. She heard the word in her mind and felt it come from her mouth. The presence behind her, the shadow in her mind, recoiled. 'I think that his story ends somewhere else.'

And, slowly, with all the will and rage that gathered to her, and the voices of the dead shouting from memories, she turned around and looked behind her.

Blackness…

Stars…

Moon rising above bare trees…

Cold light caught in the water of a black pool. A shape like a man, fur and flayed skin, shadow and blood. The man in her shadow.

'The end,' she said. The thing snarled, its ragged shape looming to the sky. 'And the death.'

The sword struck the daemon in its throat and punched out of its back. Yellow eyes went wide. Shadows collapsed.

She jerked back, dragging the blade free, turning. And the vision of cave and moonlit night blurred. Substance became translucent, and for a second her sphere of sight was not narrow, but broad and infinite, and she could see along all the paths to the fragments of Samus' presence. She saw Rogal Dorn, blade locked with a thing of claws and flame; she saw the ships trying to dock with the *Phalanx* while coils of darkness gripped them.

Then the vision went and she was looking at Loken trying to rise from the floor. The chamber around them was whining as energy poured from reactors out into the ship. The ground they stood on was not a spit of rock but a gantry, the abyss the glowing light of the plasma junction.

There was a dead weight pulling her arm towards the deck. She looked down and saw that she still held Loken's sword. She let go of it. The blade struck the deck with a clang. Loken's eyes opened.

'Loken,' she said. He looked at her and there was suspicion and rage in his eyes. He was already halfway to his feet. Fresh blood scattered from tears in his armour. 'It's all right,' she said. She could feel a burning presence building in the distance of her thoughts, rushing towards the present like a thunderstorm racing across a still plain.

'It is you now,' he said, his voice hovering on the edge of a question. She looked just as she always had, bloodied but still the same. But that, of course, did not mean anything.

She nodded.

'It is me. The… the daemon is not here now, but it will be coming back. And this needs to be over before it does. If it cannot overwhelm the ship it will breach the reactors and burn it to nothing. It wants to make it a nest but if it cannot, it will make it a pyre.'

Loken was rising, his armour grinding, blood seeping from breaks and joints.

She stepped back, shaking her head. The skin across her back prickled with static.

Black spheres were forming in her sight, and she could hear a voice calling to her out of the depths of her mind, coming closer like the sound of pistons onrushing through a tunnel.

'It's going to be all right,' she said. 'The… the thing I brought here, it needs me, you see. It needs a door and for that door to be open. And while the door is open, it cannot be defeated. It's like a memory, or a story – it carries on for as long as it is told. But it's going to be all right.'

She saw the shadow fall across his face, then. Saw the flash in the night depths of his eyes.

'I am sorry,' she said, before he could speak. 'I am sorry, but I doubt anyone will ever know your story.' She laughed. 'Maybe for the best – it's a good tale, but I have always thought that I would struggle to do it justice. Ignace would have been better. It would have looked fine in verse. The making and undoing of a dream by beings greater than men, but weaker than gods.'

She saw him twitch. Blood coughed from his mouth. He spat, shook his head.

'I have always struggled with poetry,' he said. He looked at the sword lying on the deck between them.

A heartbeat of time passed. He did not move. The sword lay still on the metal of the gantry.

Mersadie smiled one last time.

'Thank you, old friend,' she said.

And let herself fall back into the glow of the plasma conduit.

A howl of rage tore into her mind as a presence like night poured back into her soul.

She fell, and the voices of her past spoke one last time.

*'I understand you have a story... I'd like to remember it, for posterity.'*

'Which story?'

Oblivion swallowed her, and the past fell silent.

# TWENTY-TWO

So fall the walls of heaven
Thirteenth of Secundus

*The* Phalanx, *Inner System Gulf*

Su-Kassen felt the world expand around her. Shrill pain stitched her skin. The fire and shadow filling the *Phalanx*'s bridge became a flat sheet stretched taut over the world. She breathed in. Sulphur and the reek of burnt metal filled her lungs. She felt bile rise to her tongue. Her head was spinning, echoing with the hiss of voices that sounded as though they were draining into the distance. She retched. Shipmaster Sora lay in a heap of many parts across the command dais. Lights pulsed red on consoles. Some of the human crew around her were sobbing; some were not moving. Some would never move again.

But the daemons were gone. Vanished away like nightmares after waking.

She focused on her breathing, and then on standing. The blare of sirens still echoed across the bridge, but there was no gunfire, no scream of blades. She still had her gun in her hand. She snapped its magazine open. It was empty and her fingers found the reloads gone from her belt. She looked at her hand. Blood caked her palm.

'Admiral.' The voice brought her head around.

Rogal Dorn was climbing the stairs of the dais.

There was shouting coming from the other side of the torn bulkhead doors, the clang of armoured feet, the whine as guns in the hands of the surviving Huscarls built charge. There were more Imperial Fists moving onto the bridge now. Some of the warriors bore the twin axe emblem of the elite Assault Cadre, others the black-and-white heraldry of the Templars. Holo-projections were blinking to life again, painting the sulphur-spiced air with a story of blood and disaster out in the void.

'Admiral,' said Dorn again. She focused on him. His face was streaked in soot and blood. The gold of his armour was scorched almost to black. But something in his presence held still the rush of her thoughts.

'What happened to–'

'The walls of heaven have fallen, admiral.' She looked at him. 'And so I must send you from my side.'

Loken limped onto the deck of the grey ship. It seemed untouched, as though the tide of neverborn had passed over it without realising it was there.

His broken hand rested on the pommel of his sheathed sword. His armour growled with every step.

'Cast off,' he said to the robed crew who glided forwards to meet him. 'Full speed to Terra.' The crew bowed assent but did not speak. He limped on step by step. Light shifted in the corridors he passed through. The hull rang as docking cradles unlocked and engines woke to full life. He walked on, silent, hollow.

He reached the sanctuary at last.

Wide eyes looked up at him as he keyed the door release.

Noon shifted from where he had been curled on Mori's lap. The girl just looked at him, fear in her eyes. The boy took a step towards Loken, and looked up.

'Where is Mersadie?' the boy asked.

Loken found that he could not reply.

Sigismund looked up as the image of the *Phalanx* became a golden speck in the darkness of the *Persephone*'s viewport. Before them, Terra shone. Shells burst in the night around them. The view hazed. It would be a short race to the Throneworld, a last journey to a final war.

He turned and saw Rogal Dorn standing a pace beside him. The Praetorian had sent his flagship out into the battles that still burned amongst the planets, but returned to Terra in person, the master of the citadel returning to its walls. The *Persephone* would carry him there, outrunning the tide as it rolled in.

Sigismund moved aside, bowing his head, waiting for his father to speak. The primarch did not look at him, and did not speak, but kept his eyes on the light of Terra.

Su-Kassen looked about her at the ruin of the command deck. Imperial Fists, servitors and tech-priests moved around her, securing the damaged bridge and repairing it as best they could. The dead had gone, but their blood remained.

'Transmit the signals as soon as we are clear of the primary battle sphere,' she said, to salutes and words of acknowledgement.

She looked around as one of the sets of holo-projectors activated and cast a sheet of blue light across the air. It was an enhanced image from visual sensors, a view of Terra alone against a field of stars.

'Go,' Rogal Dorn had said to her. 'It is as we talked of, admiral. The battle will blood the earth now, not the void, but there is still a war to fight, out there to the edge of the sun's circle. And the burden of that fight I must place on you.'

'Lord Dorn, this is the ship of your Legion,' she had said.

'And the flagship of your command now, admiral.' And he had nodded once, his eyes unblinking. 'It was always going to be like this. No matter what else we planned, or designed.' He had placed a hand on her shoulder. The golden digits felt heavy. 'You know what is needed, and when to return.'

'Yes, Lord Praetorian.'

'Admiral,' said a signal officer, 'we are picking up a signal in reply to our broadcast.'

'It is authentic?'

'The code ciphers match those agreed by the contingency protocols,' said the officer. 'It is a ship of the Fifth Legion.'

She nodded to herself. It was a beginning.


Darkness rolled through the light of the sun. Ships came from the rift cut into the skin of space without cease: ships touched by the warp and the hands of the Dark Gods, vessels of war and exploration now become cathedrals of iron weeping cries into the night.

In his throne room, Horus stood before the grand viewport set behind his throne and looked out at the void. He saw as the last survivors of Camba Diaz's fleet pulled away from Mars. He saw as the great slab-ships descended to the surface of the Red Planet, Hal's nine prime disciples, Nul to Oct, kneeling in the dust before the Fabricator General.

He saw the defences of Luna fall silent, bit by bit, and Abaddon – faithful and true Abaddon, first and best of his sons – pause beside a pool of water in a deep chamber as the echo of distant gunfire touched his ears. He saw Abaddon turn his head to look up through the shaft in the ceiling, and see not the sun but Terra looking back with reflected light. He saw Layak, the last of his soul dwindling, watching Abaddon, and listening to the distant song of a prophecy that Horus had not heard.

And the Warmaster's gaze went on.

He saw the *Phalanx* roll to come about, its golden hull bleeding from its wounds. Ships detached from its flanks, and fired their engines, boosting back across the gulf towards Terra.

The *Phalanx*'s engines flared as it arced away from Terra into the depths of the void above the system's orbital disc. Ships waited there: the scattered vessels of the V Legion, and the remains of the ships that had slowed Perturabo's passage from Uranus to Jupiter. The *Phalanx* would find its daughters and cousins, and spill more blood before all was done.

A detail, like the survival of Rogal Dorn, now running to Terra's walls – a detail that mattered little in the turning of this moment.

'All ends are mine,' he said to the light beyond. And in the void his host bore down on the Throneworld of the Imperium.

*Terra*

It was the thirteenth of Secundus, but day was still to break over the eastern battlements of the Palace. In the night sky above, the grey ship and the *Persephone* and *Ophelia* plunged down through the cordons of atmospheric defences as enemies chased after them. The guns of Terra started firing. The thickening atmosphere shook and screamed.

Surface batteries opened up. Across the face of Terra, rockets punched into the sky from buried silos.

One of the traitor vanguard struck a drift of mines on the edge of the high orbital defences. Plasma ripped through its hull. More mines detonated. Behind it, more and more ships swarmed into orbit.

The ships that had come from the *Phalanx*, and across the system from Pluto's fall, fired their retros as they burned through Terra's atmosphere. Drop-ships scattered from their flanks and plunged down towards the Palace, fire feathering their wings. Escort fighters fell into formation with them.

The light of the new day falling on the eastern Palace walls shredded to shadows as vast ships crowded across the sun. Across the face of the planet, from the hives still soaked in night to the southern polar fortresses, the guns fired. And far below the pillars of energy pouring up into the sky, people clung to each other in the dark, or cradled weapons that they barely knew how to use.

Gunships touched down amongst the towers of the Palace. Doors pistoned open. Warriors in yellow and black poured out. With them walked Rogal Dorn. He paused on the landing platform as, high above, a chain of orbital mines detonated in a rippling explosion. Debris fell as shooting stars. Fire spread across a sky growing dark with the ships. Aircraft swarmed and spun in high orbit, spreading and chasing flames through the burning air.

It was the thirteenth of Secundus, and the warning sirens, which had sounded for six weeks, rose in voice as the first shells fell from the sky.

# THE WARP

∞

'Here we are… Here we are at last…'

The man does not look up from the fire. It has almost died to embers. The glow held in each splintered branch is fading from yellow to red as he watches it. The stranger who stands on the other side of the fire is tall and broad, with a face distilled from the images of kings and conquerors through the ages. He wears black, just like the man sat beside the fire, but his garments are heavy and regal where the seated man's cloak and clothes are ragged and worn. The pelt across the standing man's shoulders is thick, and the head of a beast hangs over his shoulder. Rings glint on his gloved fingers, the gems set into each catching the dim light of the burning wood: amethyst, ruby, emerald, sapphire.

'Will you not talk now, father?' says Horus. 'Will you not tell me the truth?' He squats down, eyes catching the ember-glow just as the rings on his fingers do. 'I am here. I am alone.'

The man beside the fire raises His head slowly. He looks

old, His skin lined and folded with time, His hair white, but His eyes are black from edge to edge, like the holes left for eyes in the bronze statues of dead ages.

'You are never alone now,' He says, and turns His gaze to the shadows of the trees. 'I see you,' He says to the dark. For an instant the fire flares bright. Sparks fountain up, and the light is not dim but blinding. Brilliance pours into the spaces between the bare trunks and branches. Things of feather and fur and scale and bone shrink and snarl. But they do not retreat, and after the light fades, the shadows flow back to press close around the ember-glow.

'Hypocrisy and hubris, father,' says Horus. 'I don't know why it never struck me before it was revealed to me. You are a despot, no better than those whom you cast down to make your realm… A king with a false crown who built His throne on lies and slaughter and maintains it by force. Higher purpose, greater ends to justify any deed, all are just the painted skin on a rotting skull… I know, father. I have seen.'

The man beside the fire does not move, and the void of His gaze holds unblinking.

'Illumination…' says Horus. 'That is what you used to call our goal. Truth and light… Well, I have seen it, father. I am illuminated. All is revealed to my sight and there is no veil between me and the flame of truth.'

Horus shifts, and for a second he does not seem a man, but a shadow of something vast and hunched and furred caught in the light of a blaze much brighter than the fading embers before them.

'You still have some strength,' says Horus and raises his ringed hand. Slowly, he reaches down into the fire and grips a glowing shard of wood. He lifts it, smoke fuming from where his skin chars. Horus holds the ember up, and the red fire glow lights his face. The heat in the fire fades, becomes cold black, then powdered ash. Horus looks at the Emperor for a long second and then stands, his presence stretching up into the bare branches and night sky. 'But you are not strong enough. You never were.'

The Emperor looks back to the dead ash of the fire before Him. Then He closes His eyes, and the image of the forest and fire and the face of His false son flee away into the distance, and there is only the voice of Horus, cold and laughing as it echoes after.

'Run,' it calls. 'Run, father, and know that I am coming. Run!'

# SPECIAL THANKS

There are too many people to thank, but in particular thanks to Liz French for her love and understanding, to Ead Brown, for his friendship and steady presence, to Laurie Goulding, for those early chats, to Alan Bligh, for all the ideas left in memory, to Aaron Dembski-Bowden, for insight and clarity delivered at the perfect time, to Lindsey Priestley, for notes and thoughts, to Rachel Harrison, for amazing art direction, to Karen Miksza and Abigail Harvey, for making my mistakes appear as though they never were, to Neil Roberts, for that cover.

And lastly, but most importantly in my eyes, thank you to Nick Kyme, for the chance, for his faith in me, and for helping me cross the finish line. Thank you, my friend.

## ABOUT THE AUTHOR

**John French** is the author of several Horus
Heresy stories including the novels *The Solar War,*
*Mortis, Praetorian of Dorn, Tallarn* and *Slaves to*
*Darkness,* the novella *The Crimson Fist,* and the
audio dramas *Dark Compliance, Templar* and
*Warmaster.* For Warhammer 40,000 he has written
*Resurrection, Incarnation* and *Divination* for The
Horusian Wars and three tie-in audio dramas –
the Scribe Award-winning *Agent of the Throne:*
*Blood and Lies,* as well as *Agent of the Throne: Truth*
*and Dreams* and *Agent of the Throne: Ashes and*
*Oaths.* John has also written the Ahriman series
and many short stories.

# YOUR
# NEXT READ

**THE LOST AND THE DAMNED**
**by Guy Haley**

The Solar War is over. The Siege of Terra has begun. As the Traitors
unleash their deadliest weapons, the defenders of the Throneworld
face nightmare and plague – but Terra must stand.

For these stories and more, go to **blacklibrary.com**, **games-workshop.com**,
Games Workshop and Warhammer stores, all good book stores or visit one
of the thousands of independent retailers worldwide, which can be found at
**games-workshop.com/storefinder**